TERRY BROOKS

AUTHOR OF THE SCIONS OF SHANNARA

MAGIC KINGDOM
FOR SALE

A Magic Kingdom of Landover Novel

Ballantine / Del Rey/
Fawcett / Ivy /
Presidio Press

ISBN 0-345-31758-0

US $7.99 / Canada $11.99

9 780345 317582

50799

EAN

The catalogue item was listed in Rosen's Christmas Wishbook:

MAGIC KINGDOM FOR SALE

Landover—island of enchantment and adventure rescued from the mists of time, home of knights and knaves, of dragons and damsels, of wizards and warlocks. Magic mixes with iron, and chivalry is the code of life for the true hero. All of your fantasies become real in this kingdom from another world. Only one thread to this whole cloth is lacking—you, to rule over all as King and High Lord. Escape into your dreams and be born again.

Price: $1,000,000.

Personal interview and financial disclosure.

Inquire of Meeks, home office.

"This is nuts!" Ben Holiday muttered. And yet . . . Rosen's had a reputation for integrity. Even on these special Wishbook items, it delivered what was promised . . .

By Terry Brooks
Published by Ballantine Books.

FIRST KING OF SHANNARA
THE SWORD OF SHANNARA
THE ELFSTONES OF SHANNARA
THE WISHSONG OF SHANNARA

The Voyage of the Jerle Shannara:
THE VOYAGE OF THE JERLE SHANNARA: ISLE WITCH
THE VOYAGE OF THE JERLE SHANNARA: ANTRAX
THE VOYAGE OF THE JERLE SHANNARA: MORGAWR

The Heritage of Shannara:
THE SCIONS OF SHANNARA
THE DRUID OF SHANNARA
THE ELF QUEEN OF SHANNARA
THE TALISMANS OF SHANNARA

The Magic Kingdom of Landover:
MAGIC KINGDOM FOR SALE—SOLD!
THE BLACK UNICORN
WIZARD AT LARGE
THE TANGLE BOX
WITCHES' BREW

THE WORD AND THE VOID
RUNNING WITH THE DEMON
A KNIGHT OF THE WORD
ANGEL FIRE EAST
STAR WARS: EPISODE I—THE PHANTOM MENACE

TERRY BROOKS

MAGIC KINGDOM FOR SALE

**Book One:
The Magic Kingdom
of Landover**

DEL REY

A Del Rey® Book
BALLANTINE BOOKS • NEW YORK

A Dell Rey® Book
Published by The Ballantine Publishing Group
Copyright © 1986 by Terry Brooks

www.delreydigital.com

Library of Congress Catalog Card Number: 95-92546

ISBN 0-345-31758-0

Manufactured in the United States of America

Cover art by Darrell K. Sweet

Map by Shelly Shapiro

First Hardcover Edition: April 1986
First Mass Market Edition: April 1987

OPM   42   41   40   39   38   37   36   35   34

For Kennard, Vernon, Bill, John and Mike

It happened something like this . . .

The Witch of the North seemed to think for a time, with her head bowed and her eyes upon the ground. Then she looked up and said, "I do not know where Kansas is, for I have never heard that country mentioned before. But tell me, is it a civilized country?"

"Oh, yes," replied Dorothy.

"Then that accounts for it. In the civilized countries I believe there are no witches left, nor wizards, nor sorceresses, nor magicians. But, you see, the Land of Oz has never been civilized, for we are cut off from all the rest of the world. There we still have witches and wizards amongst us."

L. Frank Baum, *The Wizard of Oz*

Contents

Ben

The catalogue was from Rosen's, Ltd. It was the department store's annual Christmas Wishbook.

It was addressed to Annie.

Ben Holiday stood frozen before the open cubicle of his mailbox, eyes slipping across the gaily decorated cover of the catalogue to the white address label and the name of his dead wife. The lobby of the Chicago high rise seemed oddly still in the graying dusk of the late afternoon rush hour, empty of everyone but the security guard and himself. Outside, past the line of floor-to-ceiling windows that fronted the building entry, the autumn wind blew in chill gusts down the canyon of Michigan Avenue and whispered of winter's coming.

He ran his thumb over the smooth surface of the Wishbook. Annie had loved to shop, even when the shopping had only been through the mail-order catalogues. Rosen's had been one of her favorite stores.

Sudden tears filled his eyes. He hadn't gotten over losing her, even after two years. Sometimes it seemed to him that losing her was nothing more than a trick of his imagination— that when he came home she would still be there waiting for him.

He took a deep breath, fighting back against the emotions that were aroused in him simply by seeing her name on that catalogue cover. It was silly to feel like this. Nothing could bring her back to him. Nothing could change what had happened.

His eyes lifted to stare into the dark square of the now-empty mailbox. He remembered what it has been like when he had first learned that she had been killed. He had just returned from court, a pre-trial on the Microlab case with old Wilson Frink and his sons. Ben was in his office, thinking of ways to persuade his opposition, a lawyer named Bates, that his latest offer of settlement would serve everyone's best interests, when the call had come in. Annie had been in an accident on the Kennedy. She was at St. Jude's in critical condition. Could he come right over . . . ?

He shook his head. He could still hear the voice of the doctor telling him what had happened. The voice had sounded so calm and rational. He had known at once that Annie was dying. He had known instantly. By the time he had gotten to the hospital, she was dead. The baby was dead, too. Annie had been only three months pregnant.

"Mr. Holiday?"

He looked about sharply, startled by the voice. George, the security guard, was looking over at him from behind the lobby desk.

"Everything all right, sir?"

He nodded and forced a quick smile. "Yes—just thinking about something."

He closed the mailbox door, shoved everything he had taken from it save the catalogue into one coat pocket and, still gripping the Wishbook in both hands, moved to the ground-floor elevators. He didn't care for being caught off balance like that. Maybe it was the lawyer in him.

"Cold day out there," George offered, glancing out into the gray. "Going to be a tough winter. Lot of snow, they say. Like it was a couple of years ago."

"Looks that way." Ben barely heard him as he glanced

down again at the catalogue. Annie always enjoyed the Christmas Wishbook. She used to read him promos from some of its more bizarre items. She used to make up stories about the kind of people who might purchase such things.

He pushed the elevator call button and the doors opened immediately.

"Have a nice evening, sir," George called after him.

He rode the elevator to his penthouse suite, shucked off his topcoat, and walked into the front room, still clutching the catalogue. Shadows draped the furnishings and dappled the carpeting and walls, but he left the lights off and stood motionless before the bank of windows that looked out over the sunroof and the buildings of the city beyond. Lights glimmered through the evening gray, distant and solitary, each a source of life separate and apart from the thousands of others.

We are so much of the time alone, he thought. Wasn't it strange?

He looked down again at the catalogue. Why do you suppose they had sent it to Annie? Why were companies always sending mailers and flyers and free samples and God-knew-what-all to people long after they were dead and buried? It was an intrusion on their privacy. It was an affront. Didn't these companies update their mailing lists? Or was it simply that they refused ever to give up on a customer?

He checked his anger and, instead, smiled, bitter, ironic. Maybe he should phone it all in to Andy Rooney. Let him write about it.

He turned on the lights then and walked over to the wall bar to make himself a scotch, Glenlivet on the rocks with a splash of water; he measured it out and sipped at it experimentally. There was a bar meeting in a little less than two hours, and he had promised Miles that he would make this one. Miles Bennett was not only his partner, but he was probably his only real friend since Annie's death. All of the others had drifted away somehow, lost in the shufflings and rearrangings of life's social order. Couples and singles made a poor mix, and most of their friends had been couples. He hadn't done much to foster continuing friendships in any case, spending most of his time involved with his work and with his private, inviolate grief. He was not such good company anymore, and only Miles had had the patience and the perseverance to stay with him.

He drank some more of the scotch and wandered back again to the open windows. The lights of the city winked back at him. Being alone wasn't so bad, he reasoned. That was just the way of things. He frowned. Well, that was his way, in any case. It was his choice to be alone. He could have found companionship again from any one of a number of sources; he could have reintegrated himself into almost any of the city's myriad social circles. He had the necessary attributes. He was young still and successful; he was even wealthy, if money counted for anything—and in this world it almost always did. No, he didn't have to be alone.

And yet he did, because the problem was that he really didn't belong anyway.

He thought about that for a moment—forced himself to think about it. It wasn't simply his choosing to be alone that kept him that way; it was almost a condition of his existence. The feeling that he was an outsider had always been there. Becoming a lawyer had helped him deal with that feeling, giving him a place in life, giving him a ground upon which he might firmly stand. But the sense of not belonging had persisted, however diminished its intensity—a nagging certainty. Losing Annie had simply given it new life, emphasizing the transiency of any ties that bound him to whom and what he had let himself become. He often wondered if others felt as he did. He supposed they must; he supposed that to some extent everyone felt something of the same displacement. But not as strongly as he, he suspected. Never that strongly.

He knew Miles understood something of it—or at least something of Ben's sense of it. Miles didn't feel about it as Ben did, of course. Miles was the quintessential people person, always at home with others, always comfortable with his surroundings. He wanted Ben to be that way; he wanted to bring him out of that self-imposed shell and back into the mainstream of life. He viewed his friend as some sort of challenge in that regard. That was why Miles was so persistent about these damn bar meetings. That was why he kept after Ben to forget about Annie and get on with his life.

He finished the scotch and made himself another. He was drinking a lot lately, he knew—maybe more than was good for him. He glanced down at his watch. Forty-five minutes had gone by. Another forty-five and Miles would be there, his chaperone for the evening. He shook his head distastefully. Miles didn't understand nearly as much as he thought he did about some things.

Carrying his drink, he walked back across the room to the windows, stared out a moment, and turned away, closing the drapes against the night. He moved back to the couch, debating on whether to check the answer-phone, and saw the catalogue again. He must have put it down without realizing it. It was lying with the other mail on the coffee table in front of the sectional sofa, its glossy cover reflecting sharply in the lamplight.

Rosen's, Ltd.—Christmas Wishbook.

He sat down slowly in front of it and picked it up. A Christmas catalogue of wishes and dreams—he had seen the kind before. An annual release from a department store that ostensibly offered something for everyone, this particular catalogue was for the select few only—the wealthy few.

Annie had always liked it, though.

Slowly, he began to page through it. The offerings jumped out at him, a collection of gifts for the hard-to-please, an assortment of oddities that were essentially one-of-a-kind and could be found nowhere but in the Wishbook. Dinner for two in the private California home of a famous movie star, transportation included. A ten-day cruise for sixty on a yacht, fully crewed and catered to order. A week on a privately owned Caribbean island, including the use of wine cellar and fully stocked larder. A bottle of one-hundred-and-fifty-year-old wine. Hand-blown glass and diamond creations, designed per request. A gold toothpick. Sable coats for little girls' dolls. A collector's chess set of science fiction film characters carved from ebony. A hand-woven tapestry of the signing of the Declaration of Independence.

The list of offerings went on, item after item, each more exotic and strange than the one before. Ben took a strong pull on his scotch, almost repulsed by the extravagance of it all, but fascinated nevertheless. Then he thumbed ahead into the center of the catalogue. There was a transparent bathtub with live goldfish encased in the framework. There was a silver shaving kit with your initials inlaid in gold. Why in God's name would anyone . . . ?

He caught himself midway through the thought, his eyes drawn instantly to an artist's rendering of the item being offered on the pages that lay open before him.

The promo of the item read as follows:

MAGIC KINGDOM FOR SALE

> Landover—island of enchantment and adventure rescued from the mists of time, home of knights and knaves, of dragons and damsels, of wizards and warlocks. Magic mixes with iron, and chivalry is the code of life for the true hero. All of your fantasies become real in this kingdom from another world. Only one thread to this whole cloth is lacking—you, to rule over all as King and High Lord. Escape into your dreams, and be born again.
>
> Price: $1,000,000.
> Personal interview and financial disclosure.
> Inquire of Meeks, home office.

That was all it read. The artist's colorful rendering depicted a knight on horseback engaged in battle with a fire-breathing dragon, a beautiful and rather thinly clad damsel shrinking from the conflict before a tower wall, and a dark-robed wizard lifting his hands as if to cast an awesome and life-stealing spell. Some creatures that might have been Elves or Gnomes or some such scampered about in the background, and the towers and parapets of great castles loomed against a gathering of hills and mists.

It had the look of something out of King Arthur and the Knights of the Round Table.

"This is nuts!" he muttered almost without thinking.

He stared at the item in disbelief, certain that he must be mistaken. Then he read it again. He read it a third time. It read the same. He finished his scotch in a single gulp and chewed on the ice, irritated with the nonsensicality of the offering. A million dollars for a fairy-tale kingdom? It was ridiculous. It had to be some kind of joke.

He threw down the catalogue, jumped to his feet, and crossed to the bar to mix himself a fresh drink. He stared momentarily at his reflection in the mirrored cabinet—a man of medium height, lean, trim, and athletic-looking, his face rather drawn, with high cheekbones and forehead, slightly receding hairline, hawk nose and piercing blue eyes. He was a man of thirty-nine going on fifty, a man on the verge of passing into middle age too young.

Escape into your dreams . . .

He crossed back to the couch, placed the drink on the coffee table and picked up the Wishbook once more. Again he read the item on Landover. He shook his head. No such place could possibly exist. The promo was a tease, a hype—what the car business called puffing. The truth was masked in the rhetoric. He chewed gingerly at the inside of his lip. Still, there wasn't all that much rhetoric being used to promote the item. And Rosen's was a highly respected department store; they were not likely to offer anything that they could not deliver, should a buyer appear.

He grinned. What was he thinking? What buyer? Who in his right mind would even consider . . . ? But of course he was questioning himself now. He was the one considering. He had been standing there, drinking his drink and thinking about how he didn't belong; and when he had picked up the Wishbook, the item on Landover had caught his attention right away. He was the one who felt himself the outsider in his own world, who had always felt himself the outsider, who was seeking always a way to escape what he was.

And now here was his chance.

His grin broadened. This was crazy! He was actually contemplating doing something that no sane man would even think twice about!

The scotch was working its way to his head now, and he got up again to walk it off. He looked at his watch, thinking of Miles, and suddenly he didn't want to go to that bar meeting. He didn't want to go anywhere.

He walked to the phone and dialed his friend.

"Bennett," the familiar voice answered.

"Miles, I've decided not to go tonight. Hope you don't mind."

There was a pause. "Doc, is that you?"

"Yeah, it's me." Miles loved to call him Doc, ever since the early days when they went up against Wells-Fargo on that corporate buy-out. Doc Holiday, courtroom gunfighter. It drove Ben nuts. "Look, you go on without me."

"You're going." Miles was unflappable. "You said you were going and you're going. You promised."

"So I take it back. Lawyers do it all the time—you read the papers."

"Ben, you need to get out. You need to see something of the world besides your office and your apartment—however lavish the two may be. You need to let your colleagues in the profession know that you're still alive!"

"You tell them I'm alive. Tell them I'll make the next meeting for sure. Tell them anything. But forget about me for tonight."

There was another pause, this one longer. "Are you all right?"

"Fine. But I'm in the midst of something. I want to stay with it."

"You work too hard, Ben."

"Don't we all? See you tomorrow."

He placed the receiver back on the cradle before Miles could say anything further. He stood staring down at the phone. At least he hadn't lied. He was in the midst of something, and he did want to stay with it—however crazy it might be. He took a drink of the scotch. If Annie were there, she would understand. She had always understood his fascination with puzzles and with challenges that others might simply step around. She had shared so much of that with him.

He shook his head. Of course, if Annie were there, none of this would be happening. He wouldn't be thinking about escaping into a dream that couldn't possibly be.

He paused, struck by the implications of that thought. Then holding his drink in his hand, he crossed back to the sofa, picked up the catalogue, and began reading once more.

Ben was late getting to the offices of Holiday and Bennett, Ltd. the next morning, and by the time he arrived his disposition was less than agreeable. He had scheduled an early appearance on a merger contest and gone straight to the Courts Building from home, only to discover that somehow his setting had been removed from the docket. The clerks had no idea how this had happened, opposing counsel was nowhere to be found, and the judge presiding simply advised him that a resetting would be the best solution to the dilemma. Since time was of the essence in the case in question, he requested an early setting—only to be told that the earliest setting possible was in thirty days. Things were always busiest with the approach of the holiday season, the motions clerk announced unsympathetically. Unimpressed with an explanation that he had heard at least twenty times already that November, he requested a setting for a preliminary injunction—only to be told that the judge hearing stays and pleas for temporary relief was vacationing for the next thirty days at some ski resort in Colorado, and it hadn't been decided yet who would bear his docket load while he was gone. A decision on that would probably be made by the end of the week and he should check back then.

The looks directed at him by clerks and judge alike suggested that this was the way of things in the practice of law and that he, of all people, ought to realize it by now. He ought, in fact, simply to accept it.

He did not choose to accept it however, did not care in the least to accept it, and was, by God, sick and tired of the whole business. On the other hand, there was not very much he could do about it. So, frustrated and angered, he went on to work, greeted the girls in the reception area with a mumbled good morning, picked up his phone messages, and retired to the confines of his office to fume. He had enjoyed less than five minutes of that when Miles appeared through the doorway.

"Well, well, just a little ray of sunshine this morning, aren't we?" his friend needled cheerfully.

"Yeah, that's me," he agreed rocking back in his desk chair. "Joy to the world."

"Hearing didn't go so well, I gather?"

"Hearing didn't go at all. Some incompetent took it off the call. Now I'm told it can't be put back on until hell freezes over and cows fly." He shook his head. "What a life."

"Hey, it's a living. Besides, that's the way it all works—hurry up and wait, time is all we've got."

"Well, I'm fed up to the teeth with it!"

Miles moved over to occupy one of the client chairs that fronted the long oak desk. He was a big man, heavy through the middle, thick dark hair and mustache lending maturity to an almost cherubic face.

His eyes, perpetually lidded at half-mast, blinked slowly. "Know what your problem is, Ben?"

"I ought to. You've told me often enough."

"Then why don't you listen? Quit spending all of your time trying to change the things you can't!"

"Miles. . ."

"Annie's death and the way the legal system works—you can't change those kinds of things, Ben. Not now, not ever. You're like Don Quixote tilting with windmills! You're ruining your life, do you know that?"

Ben brushed Miles aside with a wave of his hand. "I do not know that, as a matter of fact. Besides, your equation doesn't balance. I know that nothing will bring Annie back—I've accepted that. But maybe it's not too late for the legal system—the system of justice that we used to know, the one we both went into the practice of law to uphold."

"You ought to listen to yourself sometime," Miles sighed. "There's nothing wrong with my equation, chief. My equation is painfully accurate. You have never accepted Annie's death. You live your life in a goddamned shell, because you won't accept what's happened—as if living like that is somehow going to change things! I'm your friend, Ben—maybe the only one you've got left. That's why I can talk to you like this—because you can't afford to lose me!"

The big man leaned forward. "And all of this crap about the way things used to be in the practice of law sounds like my father telling me how he used to walk five miles through the snow to get to school. What am I supposed to do—sell my car and walk to work from Barrington? You can't turn back the clock, no matter how much you might like to. You have to accept things as you find them."

Ben let Miles finish without interruption. Miles was right about one thing—only he could talk to him like this, and it was because he was his best friend. But Miles had always approached life differently than he, always preferring to blend in with his surroundings rather than to shape them, always preferring to make do. He just didn't understand that there were some things in life a man simply should not accept.

"Forget about Annie for the moment." Ben paused meaningfully before continuing. "Let me suggest that change is a fact of life, that it is a process brought about by the efforts of men and women dissatisfied with the status quo, and that it is essentially a good thing. Let me also suggest that change is frequently the result of what we have learned, not simply what we have envisioned. History plays a part in change. Therefore, what once was and was good ought not to be cast aside as being simply wishful reminiscence."

Miles brought up one hand. "Look, I'm not saying . . ."

"Can you honestly sit there, Miles, and tell me that you are satisfied with the direction that the practice of law in this country is taking? Can you even tell me that it is as good and true as it was fifteen years ago when we entered the profession? Look at what's happened, for Christ's sake! We are bogged down in a morass of legislation and regulation that reaches from here to China, and even the judges and lawyers don't understand half of it. We used to be able to call ourselves general practitioners—now we are lucky to be competent in one or two fields, simply because of the updating we must constantly do in order to keep ourselves current. The courts are slow and overburdened. The judges are all too often mediocre lawyers put on the bench through politics. The lawyers coming out of law school view their occupation as a way to make big bucks and get their names in the paper—forget the part about helping people. The whole profession has the worst press this side of Nazi Germany. We have advertising—advertising! Like used-car salesmen, or furniture-store dealers! We don't adequately educate ourselves. We don't adequately police ourselves. We just go through the motions and try to get by!"

Miles stared at him, his head cocked appraisingly. "Are you about finished?"

He nodded, slightly flushed. "Yeah, I suppose so. Did I leave anything out?"

Miles shook his head. "I think you covered the whole nine yards. Feel any better?"

"Much, thanks."

"Good. One final comment, then. I heard everything you said, I duly recorded every word, and I happen to agree with most of it. And I say to you nevertheless, so what? There have been thousands of speeches given, thousands of committee meetings held, thousands of articles written addressing the very problems you so eloquently outline in your tirade—and how much difference has any of it made?"

Ben sighed. "Not much."

"That is understating it. Since this is so, what difference do you think you are going to make?"

"I don't know. But that's not the point."

"No, I don't suppose it is for you. So, what the hell? If you want to enter into a one-man war with the system in an effort to change it, fine and dandy. But a little moderation in your commitment wouldn't hurt. A day off now and then for some of life's less pressing matters might give you some perspective and keep you from burning out completely. Okay?"

Ben nodded. "Okay. Yeah, okay. But I'm not good at moderation."

Miles grinned. "Tell me about it. Now let's talk about something else. Let's talk about last night. Believe it or not, a few people asked about you at the bar meeting—said they missed seeing you."

"They must be desperate for companionship, then."

Miles shrugged. "Maybe. What was so important that you had to cancel out? New case?"

Ben thought about it a moment, then shook his head. "No, nothing new. Just something I wanted to follow up on." He hesitated. Then impulsively he reached down into his briefcase and pulled out the Wishbook. "Miles, want to see something really odd? Take a look at this."

He thumbed the catalogue open to the item about Landover and passed it across the desk. His friend shifted forward to take it from him and then settled back again in the chair.

"Magic kingdom for sale . . . Landover—island of enchantment and adventure . . . Hey, what is this?'' Miles fumbled to find the cover.

"It's a Christmas catalogue," Ben explained to the big man quickly. "From Rosen's, Ltd. out of New York. A Wishbook. You've seen the type—full of one of a kind gifts."

Miles started reading again, finished, and looked up. "Only a million dollars, huh? What a bargain! Let's fly right to New York and apply—beat the rush."

"What do you make of it?"

Miles stared at him. "Same as you, I hope. Someone is nuts!"

He nodded slowly. "That's what I thought, too. But Rosen's wouldn't put an advertisement in a catalogue like this if they couldn't produce."

"Then it must be staged. The dragons must be overgrown lizards or something. The magic must be sleight of hand." Miles laughed. "Knights and damsels courtesy of Central Casting, dragons courtesy of the San Diego Zoo! Johnny Carson will have the whole menagerie on sometime next week!"

Ben waited for the big man's laughter to die away. "Think so?"

"Of course, I think so! Don't you?"

"I'm not sure."

Miles frowned, then read the advertisement one time more. When he was done, he passed the catalogue back across the desk. "Is this what kept you home last night?"

"In part, yes."

There was a long silence. Miles cleared his throat. "Ben, don't tell me that you're thinking of . . ."

The phone rang. Ben picked it up, listened for a moment and looked across the desk at his friend. "Mrs. Lang is here."

Miles glanced at his watch and rose. "Needs a new will drafted, I think." He hesitated, looked for a moment as if he might say something more, then jammed his hands in his pants pockets and turned for the door. "Well, enough of this. I've got to gĕt some work done. Catch you later."

He left the room frowning. Ben let him go.

Ben left work early that afternoon and went to the health club to work out. He spent an hour in the weight room, then spent another hour on the light and heavy fighter's bags he had persuaded them to install several years back. He had been a boxer in his teens—fought out of Northside for the better part of five years. He had been a silver glover and could have been a gold, but other interests had taken him away and then he had gone east to school. But he still kept his hand in—even sparring a couple of rounds now and then back at Northside when he found the time. For the most part, he simply worked out, staying fit, keeping himself sharp. He had done so religiously since Annie died. It had helped him to release some of the frustration and anger. It had helped him to fill the time.

It was true that he had not been able to accept her death, he thought as his cab worked its way through the rush hour traffic from the health club to the high rise. He could admit it to himself if not to Miles. The truth was that he didn't know how to accept it. He had loved her with an intensity that was frightening, and she him. They never spoke of it; they never had to. But it was always there. When she died, he had thought of killing himself. He had not done so only because he had known deep inside that he should not, that he should never give in to anything so obviously wrong, that Annie would not want him to. So he had gone on with his life in the best way that he could, but he had never found a way to accept that she was really gone. Perhaps he never would.

Frankly, he wasn't sure that it mattered all that much whether he did.

He paid the cabdriver at the curb, walked into the lobby of the high rise, greeted George, and boarded the elevator for his penthouse suite.

Miles saw him as a grief-stricken recluse, hiding from the world while he mourned his dead wife. Maybe that was the way everyone saw him. But Annie's death had not created the condition; it had merely emphasized it. He had been slipping back into himself more and more in recent years, dissatisfied with what he viewed as the continuing deterioration of his profession, frustrated with the way in which it seemed to sink down upon itself until it no longer served the purposes for which it had been created. Miles would think it odd that he should feel that way—Doc Holiday, the corporate trial lawyer who had slain more Goliaths than any David had ever dreamed of facing. What did he have to feel frustrated about when the system had worked so effectively for him? But of course one's personal successes sometimes only served to point up the inequities worked on others. It was that way with him.

He mixed a Glenlivet and water in his apartment and retired to the front room, seating himself on the sofa and staring out the window into the lights of the city. After a time, he pulled the Christmas Wishbook from Rosen's from his briefcase and opened it to the item on Landover. He had been thinking about it all day; he had been thinking of nothing else since he had first laid eyes on it last night.

What if it were real?

He sat there for a long time, the glass in his hand, the catalogue open before him, thinking about the possibility.

His present life, he felt, was at a standstill. Annie was dead. The profession of law—for him, at least—was just as dead. There were more cases to be taken, more courtroom battles to be won, more Goliaths for David to slay. But the excesses and deficiencies of the legal system would still be there. In the end, he would simply be going through the same ritual with its frustrations and disappointments, and it would all be meaningless. There had to be more for him in this life.

There had to be.

He looked at the colorful rendering of the knight in battle with the dragon, the damsel in the castle keep, the wizard casting his spell, the fairy folk looking on. Landover. A dream out of a Wishbook.

Escape into your dreams . . .

For one million dollars, of course. But he had the money. He had money enough to buy it three times over. His father and mother had both been wealthy and he had enjoyed a lucrative practice. The million dollars was there—if that was the way he chose to spend it.

And there was the interview with this fellow Meeks. That puzzled him. What was the purpose of the interview—to screen applicants? Did they anticipate there would be that many and was there some reason to choose among them? Perhaps, where a King was to be selected, there was.

He took a deep breath. What sort of King would he make? He had the price of the kingship—but so would others have it. He was physically and mentally fit—but others would be, too. He was experienced in dealing with people and with laws—others might not be. He was compassionate. He was honorable. He was farsighted.

He was crazy.

He finished off the drink, closed the Wishbook, and went into the kitchen to make dinner. He took his time about it, preparing a rather extravagant beef and vegetable dish, and served it to himself with wine. When the meal was finished, he moved back to the front room again and reseated himself on the sofa before the Wishbook.

He already knew what he was going to do. Perhaps he had known all along. He needed something to believe in again. He needed to recapture the magic that had first drawn him to the practice of law—the sense of wonder and excitement it had brought to his life. Most of all, he needed a challenge—because that was what gave life meaning.

Landover *could* offer him that.

He was not yet certain that it would, of course. Perhaps it was all an elaborate charade of the sort envisioned by Miles, where the dragons were large iguanas and the knights and wizards were all supplied by Central Casting. Perhaps the dream was a sham, an imitation of what the imagination would have it truly be. Even if it were all real—if it were all as described, all as the artist had rendered it to be—still it might be less than the dream. It might be as ordinary in truth as his present life.

Yet the gamble was worth it, because he had seen the parameters of his present life and there were no unknowns left in it. And somehow, in some unexplainable way, he knew that whatever choices he might make now, with Annie gone the only wrong choice he might make was to make no choice at all.

He crossed back to the bar and made himself an Irish Mist. He toasted himself solemnly in the mirror and drank.

He felt exhilarated.

The following morning, Ben went down to the office only long enough to cancel his appointments for the remainder of that week and the next and to wrap up a few small matters that needed immediate attention. He was taking a short vacation, he told the girls and the law student who clerked for them part-time, doing research. Everything could wait until he returned. Miles was in court in Crystal Lake, so there were no questions asked. It was just as well.

He called O'Hare then and booked a flight.

By noon, he was on his way to New York.

Meeks

New York City was cold, gray, and alien, the jagged edges of its bones cutting into a sky masked in clouds and mist, the flat planes of its skin glistening through a steady downpour. Ben watched it materialize beneath him as if by magic as the 727 slipped over the waters of the East River and settled down toward the empty runway. Traffic jammed the distant freeways, lifeblood flowing through arteries and veins, but the city had the feel of a corpse.

He took a cab from LaGuardia to the Waldorf, settled back in silence as the driver played reggae, and ignored him. He booked a single at the Waldorf, resisting the temptation of requesting a suite. There would be no such modern suites in Landover. It was a meaningless concession perhaps, but he had to start somewhere, and this was as good a place as any. One step at a time, as the saying went.

In his room, he took five minutes to unpack, then picked up the Manhattan phone directory and looked up the number to Rosen's. He found it in bold print, dialed and waited. When the department store switchboard answered, he asked for Customer Service and was transferred. He indicated to the new voice that he was interested in an item in the Christmas Wishbook and needed to make an appointment with Mr.

Meeks. There was a pause, a request for the item number, and again he was transferred.

This time he was kept waiting for several minutes. Then a third voice came on the line, a woman's also, this one soft and graveled. Could he give her his name, address and the number of a major credit card? He could. When did he wish to see Mr. Meeks? Tomorrow morning, if possible. He was visiting from Chicago for a few days only. Would tomorrow morning at ten o'clock be satisfactory? That would be fine. Ten o'clock sharp, then? Fine.

The line went dead. He stared at it for a moment, then hung up.

He went down to the lobby, bought a *Times*, drank several scotches—Glenlivet and water over ice, as usual—and went in to dinner. He ate with the paper before him, scanning its sections without interest, his mind elsewhere. He was back in his room by seven. He watched a news special on El Salvador, and wondered how after so many years people could continue to kill each other so casually. A variety hour special followed, but he let it play without watching, distracted by a sudden need to analyze the particulars of what he was about. He had thought it through at least a dozen times already that day, but there was always the same nagging uncertainty.

Did he really know what he was doing? Did he really appreciate what he was getting into?

The answers this time were the same as they had been each time before. Yes, he knew what he was doing. Yes, he appreciated what he was getting into. At least, as far as he was able to, he did. One step at a time, remember. He knew he would be leaving a lot behind him if he went and if this Kingdom of Landover proved to be real, but most of it would be in the nature of material possessions and creature comforts, and those really didn't matter to him anymore. Cars and trains and airplanes, refrigerators and stoves and dishwashers, indoor toilets and electric shavers—all the modern things that were left behind to go fishing in Canada. Except that on a fishing trip, such things were left behind for only a few weeks. That wouldn't be the case here. This would be for much longer than a few weeks, and it wouldn't be like any camping trip he had ever heard about—or at least he didn't think it would.

What would it be like, he wondered suddenly? What would it be like in this fairy-tale kingdom called Landover—this kingdom that had somehow come to be offered for sale in a department store catalogue? Would it be like the land of Oz with Munchkins and witches and a tin man who talked? Would there be a yellow brick road to follow?

He resisted a sudden urge to pack up his suitcase and get the hell out of New York before going any further with the whole business. When you got right down to it, what mattered was not the sanity of his inquiry or the future into which he might choose to step. What mattered was the conscious decision to make some change in his life and in making that change to find something that would offer him the purpose of being that he had lost. When you held your ground, the old saying went, you stopped moving. When you stopped moving, everything about you would eventually pass you by.

He sighed. Trouble was, those old bromides always sounded truer than they were.

The variety show gave way to the late news, weather, and sports. Ben undressed and put on pajamas (did people wear pajamas in Landover?), brushed his teeth (did people brush their teeth in Landover?), shut off the television, and went to bed.

He was awake early the next morning, having slept poorly as he always did the first night away from home on a trip. He showered, shaved, dressed in a dark blue business suit, caught the elevator to the lobby where he purchased an early edition of the *Times*, and went into Oscar's for breakfast.

By nine o'clock, he was on his way to Rosen's.

He chose to walk. The decision was a perverse mix of stubbornness and wariness. The store was only half a dozen blocks from the hotel on Lexington, and anything that close

ought to be walked. The day was iron gray and chill, but the
rains had moved northeast into New England. A cab was a
waste of money. Furthermore, by walking he could approach
the store at his own pace and on his own terms—kind of
work up to what he was going to do. The trial lawyer in him
always appreciated the advantage of being able to orches-
trate one's own entrance.

He took his time, letting the feel of the autumn morning
bring him fully awake, but he was there by nine-forty anyway. Rosen's was a fifteen-storey chrome-and-glass corner-
stone to two thirty-plus-storey skyscrapers that ran half a
block on Lexington and the better part of a short block on
the cross street west. An old establishment, the store had
obviously been remodeled when the skyscrapers had gone
in, the aged stone facade giving way to a more modern look.
Plate-glass display windows lined the walkway along Lexington, filled with fashions displayed on mannequins with
frozen smiles and empty stares. The late morning rush hour
traffic passed them by unsmiling, unseeing. Ben followed the
line of windows south to a recessed entry and passed through
two sets of double-doors sandwiching a weather foyer to the
store within.

The ground floor of Rosen's opened out before him, cavernous, polished, sterile. Rows of metal-and-glass display
cases filled with jewelry, cosmetics, and silver filled the hall,
gleaming and shining beneath a flood of fluorescent light. A
handful of shoppers browsed the aisles that ran between the
display cases while store personnel looked on. No one
seemed much interested in generating sales. It all had the
appearance of some arcane ritual. He glanced about. To his
right, an escalator climbed through the ceiling to the floor
above. To his left, a bank of elevators lined a distant wall.
Straight ahead, where even the most bewildered shopper
could not fail to see it, a glass-encased directory announced
the departments and the floors on which they could be found.

He took a moment to read the directory. There was no
listing for Meeks. He hadn't really expected that there would

be. The departments were listed alphabetically. Under the letter C he found the heading, Customer Service, special ordering—eleventh floor. Fair enough, he thought—he would try that. He angled his way through the maze of cases to the elevators, caught one standing open and took it to the eleventh floor.

He stepped from the elevator into a reception area comfortably furnished with overstuffed chairs and couches and fronted by a broad, wraparound desk and typing station. An attractive, thirtyish woman sat behind the desk, absorbed in a phone conversation. Rows of lighted buttons blinked on and off on her console.

She finished her conversation, hung up the phone and smiled pleasantly. "Good morning. May I help you?"

He nodded. "My name is Holiday. I have an appointment at ten with Mr. Meeks."

He might have imagined it, but he thought her smile faded slightly. "Yes, sir. Mr. Meeks does not use offices on this floor. Mr. Meeks uses offices on the penthouse level."

"The penthouse level?"

"Yes, sir." She pointed to another elevator in an alcove to Ben's right. "Simply press the button labeled PL. That will take you to Mr. Meeks. I will telephone to let his receptionist know that you are coming."

"Thank you." He hesitated. "This is the Mr. Meeks who is in charge of special ordering, isn't it?"

"Yes, sir. Mr. Meeks."

"The reason I ask is that your directory lists Customer Service, special ordering, on this floor."

The receptionist brushed nervously at her hair. "Sir, we post no listing for Mr. Meeks. He prefers that his clients come through us." She tried a quick smile. "Mr. Meeks handles only our specialty items—a very select collection of merchandise."

"The items in the Christmas Wishbook?"

"Oh, no. Most of those are handled by regular personnel. Mr. Meeks is not in the employ of Rosen's. Mr. Meeks is a privately employed sales specialist who acts as our agent in certain sales transactions. Mr. Meeks handles only the most exotic and unusual of the items offered in the Wishbook, Mr. Holiday." She leaned forward slightly. "He designates his own line of sales items, I understand."

Ben lifted his eyebrows in response. "Quite talented at his work, then, is he?"

She looked away again suddenly. "Yes, very." She reached for the phone. "I will call up for you, Mr. Holiday." She pointed to the second elevator. "They will be expecting you when you arrive. Good-bye."

He said good-bye in response, walked into the designated elevator and punched PL. The doors closed with the receptionist glancing covertly after him as she held the phone receiver to her ear.

He rode the elevator in silence, listening to the sound of the machinery. There were only four buttons on the panels above and next to the doors, numbered 1, 2, 3, and PL. They stayed dark for a time as the elevator rose, then began to light in sequence. The elevator did not stop for anyone else along the way. Ben almost wished that it had done so. He was beginning to feel as if he had stepped into the Twilight Zone.

The elevator stopped, the doors opened and he found himself back in a reception area almost identical to the one he had just left. This time the receptionist was an older woman, in her fifties perhaps, diligently engaged in sorting through a raft of papers stacked in piles on her desk while a harried-looking man of like age stood before her, his back to the elevator, his voice high-pitched and angry.

". . . don't have to do everything that old bastard tells us, and someday he's going to hear about it! Thinks every last one of us is at his beck and call! If he doesn't quit treating us like lackeys, then, damn it, I'll take this to . . ."

He cut himself short as the receptionist caught sight of Ben. Hesitating, he turned and stalked quickly into the open elevator. A moment later, the doors slid shut.

"Mr. Holiday?" the receptionist inquired, her voice soft and graveled. It was the woman he had spoken to on the phone the previous afternoon.

"Yes," he acknowledged. "I have an appointment with Mr. Meeks."

She picked up the phone and waited. "Mr. Holiday, sir. Yes. Yes, I will."

She placed the receiver back in its cradle and looked up. "It will only be a few moments, Mr. Holiday. Would you have a seat, please."

He glanced about, then took a seat at one end of a sofa. There were magazines and newspapers on a table beside him, but he ignored them. His gaze wandered idly about the reception area, a well-lighted, cheerful center with solid wood desks and cabinets and cool colors on the walls and floors.

A few minutes passed and the phone on the receptionist's desk rang. She picked up the receiver, listened momentarily, and hung up.

"Mr. Holiday?" She rose and beckoned. "This way, please."

She led him into a corridor that opened up behind her work area. The corridor ran past a series of closed doors and branched left and right. That was all the further Ben could see.

"Follow the hallway back, left up the stairs to the door at its end. Mr. Meeks will be expecting you."

She turned and walked back to her desk. Ben Holiday stood where he was for a moment, glancing first at the empty corridor, then at the retreating figure of the receptionist, then back again at the corridor.

So what are you waiting for? he asked himself admonishingly.

He went along the corridor to where it branched and turned left. The doors he passed were closed and bore no title designation or number. Fluorescent ceiling lights seemed pale against the pastel greens and blues of the corridor walls. Thick pile carpet absorbed the sound of his shoes as he walked. It was very still.

He hummed the theme from *The Twilight Zone* under his breath as he reached the staircase and began to climb.

The staircase ended at a heavy oak door with raised panels and the name "Meeks" stamped on a brass back plate screwed into the wood. He stopped before the door, knocked, turned the sculpted metal handle and stepped inside.

Meeks was standing directly in front of him.

He was very tall, well over six feet, old and bent, his face craggy, his hair white and grizzled. He wore a black leather glove on his left hand. His right hand and arm were missing completely, the empty sleeve of his corduroy jacket tucked into a lower pocket. Pale blue eyes that were hard and steady met Ben's. Meeks looked as if he had fought and survived more than a few battles.

"Mr. Holiday?" he asked, his voice almost a whisper. He sounded a good deal like his receptionist. Ben nodded. "I'm Meeks." The head dipped slightly. He didn't offer his hand and neither did Ben. "Please come in and have a chair."

He turned and shuffled away, hunching as he went as if his legs no longer worked properly. Ben followed him wordlessly, glancing about as he went. The office was elegant, a richly appointed room furnished with a massive old desk of scrolled oak, matching chairs with stuffed leather seats and backs, and workbenches and endtables covered with charts and magazines and what appeared to be work files. Floor-to-ceiling bookcases lined three walls, filled with ancient tomes and artifacts of all kinds. A bank of windows comprised the fourth wall, but the curtains were drawn tight across them and there were only the ceiling lamps to give the room its oddly muted light. Deep pile carpet of earthen brown sprouted from the floor like dried saw grass. The room smelled faintly of furniture polish and old leather.

"Sit down, Mr. Holiday." Meeks beckoned to a chair drawn up before the desk, then shuffled his way around to the overstuffed swivel chair on the other side, easing himself down into the worn leather gingerly. "Can't move like I used to. Weather tightens the bones. Age and weather. How old are you, Mr. Holiday?"

Ben glanced up, midway through the process of seating himself. The sharp, old eyes were fixed on him. "Forty, come January," he answered.

"A good age." Meeks smiled faintly, but without humor. "A man's still got his strength at forty. He knows most of what he's going to learn, and he's got the strength to put it to good use. Is that so with you, Mr. Holiday?"

Ben hesitated. "I guess so."

"That's what your eyes say. Eyes tell more about a man than anything he says. Eyes reflect a man's soul. They reflect a man's heart. Sometimes they even tell the truths a man wants to keep hidden." He paused. "Can I offer you something to drink? Coffee, a cocktail, perhaps?"

"No, nothing, thank you." Ben shifted in his chair impatiently.

"You don't believe that it's possible, do you?" Meeks' brows furrowed deeply, his voice soft. "Landover. You don't believe it exists."

Ben studied the other man thoughtfully. "I'm not sure."

"You appreciate the possibilities, but you question them, too. You seek the challenges that are promised, but you fear they may be only paper windmills. Think of it—a world like nothing anyone on this earth has ever seen! But it sounds impossible. If I might invoke a time-honored cliché, it sounds too good to be true."

"It does."

"Like a man walking on the moon?"

Ben thought a moment. "More like truth in lending. Or full faith and credit between sister states. Or perhaps consumer protection against false advertising."

Meeks stared at him. "You are a lawyer, Mr. Holiday?"

"I am."

"And you believe in our system of justice, then?"

"I do."

"You do, but you know as well that it doesn't always work, don't you? You want to believe in it, but it disappoints you much too often."

He waited. "That's a fair statement, I suppose," Ben admitted.

"And you think it might be that way with Landover as well." Meeks made it a statement of fact, not a question. He leaned forward, his craggy face intense. "Well, it isn't. Landover is exactly what the advertisement promises. It has everything that the advertisement says that it has and much more—things that are only myth in this world, things only barely imagined. But real in Landover, Mr. Holiday. Real!"

"Dragons, Mr. Meeks?"

"All of the mythical fairy creatures, Mr. Holiday—exactly as promised."

Ben folded his hands before him. "I'd like to believe you, Mr. Meeks. I came to New York to inquire about this . . . catalogue item because I want to believe it exists. Can you show me anything that would help prove what you say?"

"You mean flyers, color brochures, pictures of the land, references?" His face tightened. "They don't exist, Mr. Holiday. This item is a carefully protected treasure. The specifics of where it lies, what it looks like, what it offers—that is all privileged information which can be released only to the buyer whom I, as the seller's designated agent, ultimately select. As a lawyer, I am sure that you can appreciate the limitations imposed upon me by the word 'privileged,' Mr. Holiday."

"Is the identity of the seller privileged as well, Mr. Meeks?"

"It is."

"And the reason that this item is being offered for sale in the first place?"

"Privileged, Mr. Holiday."

"Why would anyone sell something as marvelous as this fantasy kingdom, Mr. Meeks? I keep asking myself that question. I keep asking myself if I'm not somehow buying a piece of the Brooklyn Bridge. How do I know that your seller even has the authority to sell Landover?"

Meeks smiled, an attempt at reassurance. "That was all checked carefully prior to listing. I supervised the inquiry myself."

Ben nodded. "So it all comes down to your word, doesn't it?"

Meeks sat back again. "No, Mr. Holiday. It comes down to the worldwide reputation of Rosen's as a department store that always delivers what it offers exactly as promised in its catalogues and advertisements. It comes down to the terms of the contract the store offers to the buyer on specialty items such as this one—a contract that permits recovery of the entire purchase price less a small handling fee should the item fail to prove satisfactory. It comes down to the way we do business."

"Could I see a copy of this contract?"

Meeks bridged the fingers of his gloved hand against his chin and stroked the ridges and lines of his face. "Mr. Holiday, I wonder if we might first back this conversation up a bit to permit me to fulfill the terms of my consignment of this specialty item. You are here to decide whether or not you wish to purchase Landover. But you are also here so that I might decide whether or not you qualify as a purchaser. Would a few questions to that end be an imposition?"

Ben shook his head. "I wouldn't think so. But I'll tell you if they are."

Meeks smiled like the Cheshire Cat and nodded his understanding.

For the next thirty minutes or so, he asked his questions. He asked them very much the way a skilled attorney would ask them of a witness at an oral deposition in pre-trial discovery—with tact, with brevity, and with purpose. Meeks knew what he was looking for, and he probed for it with the experienced touch of a surgeon. Ben Holiday had seen a good many trial lawyers in his years of practice, some of them more accomplished than he. But he had never seen anyone as good as Meeks.

In the end, a lot of ground was covered. Ben had graduated fifteen years earlier from Chicago University's School of Law, Order of the Coif, *summa cum laude*. He had gone into practice immediately with one of the larger firms, then left after five years to form his own firm with Miles, specializing in litigation. He had won a number of nationally reported corporate law cases as a plaintiff's attorney and settled dozens more. He was respected by his fellow attorneys as one of the best in his field. He had served as president of the Chicago Bar Association and as chairman of a number of committees on the Illinois State Bar. There was talk of running him for president of the American Trial Lawyers Association.

He came from a very wealthy family. His mother had been born into money; his father had made his in futures. Both were dead. He had no brothers or sisters. With Annie's death, he had been left essentially alone. There were some distaff cousins on the West Coast and an uncle in Virginia, but he hadn't see any of them for better than five years. He had few close friends—in truth, he had only Miles. His colleagues respected him, but he kept them at a distance. His life in the past few years revolved almost exclusively around his work.

"Have you any administrative experience, Mr. Holiday?" Meeks asked him at one point, a rather veiled look to the hard, old eyes that suggested the question asked something more.

"No."

"Any hobbies?"

"None," he answered, thinking as he did that it was true, that he in fact had no hobbies nor personal pastimes save for the time he spent in training at Northside. He almost amended his answer, then decided it did not matter.

He gave to Meeks the financial statement he had prepared in response to the catalogue advertisement, detailing his net worth. Meeks examined it wordlessly, nodded in satisfaction and set it on the desk before him.

"You are an ideal candidate, Mr. Holiday," he said softly, the whisper quality of his voice becoming almost a hiss. "You are a man whose roots can be easily severed—a man who will not have to worry about leaving family or friends who will enquire too closely of his whereabouts. Because, you see, you will not be able to communicate with anyone but myself during your first year away. That is one of the conditions of acceptance. This should pose no problem for you. You are also a man with sufficient assets to make the purchase—hard assets, not paper assets. You can appreciate the difference. But most importantly, perhaps, you are a man who has something to offer as King of Landover. I don't suppose you've thought much of that, but it is something that matters a great deal to those for whom we act as agent. You have something very special to offer."

He paused. "Which is?" Ben asked.

"Your professional background, Mr. Holiday. You are a lawyer. Think of the good that you can do as not simply one who interprets the law but as one who makes it. A king needs a sense of justice to reign. Your intelligence and your education should serve you well."

"You mean that I shall have need of them in Landover, Mr. Meeks?"

"Certainly." The other's face was expressionless. "A king always has need of intelligence and education."

For an instant Ben thought he detected something in the other's voice that made the statement almost a private joke. "You have personal knowledge of what a king needs, Mr. Meeks?"

Meeks smiled, hard and quick. "If you mean, do I have personal knowledge of what a King of Landover needs, the answer is yes. Background is required of our clients in a listing such as this, and the background provided me suggests that Landover's ruler will have need of the qualities that you possess."

Ben nodded slowly. "Does this mean that my application has been accepted?"

The old man leaned back again in his chair. "What of your own questions, Mr. Holiday? Hadn't we better address those first?"

Ben shrugged. "I'll want them addressed sometime. It might as well be now. Why don't we begin with the contract—the one that's guaranteed to protect me from making what most people would consider a foolish investment."

"You are not most people, Mr. Holiday." The craggy face dropped a shade, changing the configuration of lines and hollows like a twisted rubber mask. "The agreement is this. You will have ten days to examine your purchase with no obligation. If at the end of that time you find it not to be as advertised or to be otherwise unsatisfactory, you may return here for a full refund of your purchase price less a handling fee of five percent. A reasonable charge, I'm sure you'll agree."

"That's it? That's the whole contract?" Ben was incredulous. "All it takes is my decision to back out?"

"That's all it takes." Meeks smiled. "Of course, the decision must be made in the first ten days, you understand."

Ben stared at him. "And everything that's been advertised in the catalogue will be there as promised? All of it? The dragons and knights and witches and warlocks and fairy creatures?"

"And you will be their King, Mr. Holiday. You will be the man to whom all must answer. A great deal of power— but also a great deal of responsibility. Do you think that you are equal to the challenge?"

The room went still as Ben sat before old Meeks and thought of the roads in his life that had led down to this moment. Except for Annie, he had lost little on his journey. He had taken the opportunities that mattered and made the most of them. Now he was presented with an opportunity greater than any previously offered and in taking it he would be leaving nothing of consequence behind. With Annie gone, everything that mattered lay ahead.

Nevertheless, he hesitated. "Could I see a copy of that contract now, Mr. Meeks?"

The old man reached into his center desk drawer and withdrew a single sheet of paper backed in triplicate. He passed it across the desk to Ben. Ben picked up the contract and read it through carefully. It was exactly as the old man had promised. The Kingship of Landover was to be sold to him for a price of one million dollars. The language of the catalogue promo was repeated with appropriate warranties. The closing paragraphs provided for a full refund of the purchase price less the handling charge if within ten days of arrival in Landover the purchaser chose to return the specialty item and withdraw from the Kingdom. A key for such withdrawal would be provided at time of purchase.

Ben paused on reading the final lines. The purchaser agreed on forfeiture of the full purchase price if he or she returned the item anytime after the first ten days *or* if he or she chose to abandon Landover for any reason during the first year of Kingship.

"What is the point of this final covenant?" he asked, glancing back again at Meeks. "Why can't I leave for a visit back?"

Meeks smiled—a rather poor attempt. "My client is concerned that the purchaser of Landover appreciate the responsibilities that Kingship entail. A man not willing to—what is the saying?—'stick it out' for at least a year is not a worthy candidate for the job. The agreement assures that you will not wander off and leave the duties of the throne unattended—at least for that first year."

Ben frowned. "I guess I can understand your client's concern." He placed the contract back on the desk, one hand resting on it lightly. "But I'm still a bit skeptical about the offer in general, Mr. Meeks. I think I should be candid. It all seems a bit too easy. A mythical kingdom with fairy creatures that no one has ever seen or heard about before? A place no one has ever been to, that no one has ever come across? And all I have to do is to give Rosen's one million dollars and I own it?''

Meeks said nothing. His aged, craggy face was expressionless.

"Is this kingdom in North America?" Ben pressed.

Meeks said nothing.

"Do I need a passport to reach it? Or medical protection from its diseases?''

Meeks shook his head slowly. "You need no passport or immunization. You need only courage, Mr. Holiday."

Ben flushed slightly. "I think some common sense might be called for as well, Mr. Meeks."

"A purchase such as the one you propose to make, Mr. Holiday, requires least of all common sense. If common sense were the basis of the sale, neither one of us would be having this conversation, would we?" The old man's smile was cold. "Let us be candid, as you suggest. You are a man seeking something that is not available to you in the world you know. You are a man who is tired of his life and all of its trappings. If you were not, you would not be here. I am a man who specializes in selling specialty items—items that are bizarre, that appeal to a limited market, that are invariably difficult to merchandise. I am a man who cannot afford to jeopardize his reputation by selling something that is in any way counterfeit. If I did so, I would not have lasted long in this business. I play no games with you, and I sense that you play none with me.

"Nevertheless, there are certain things that both of us must accept on faith. I must accept you as a potential ruler of Landover basically on faith, knowing little of your real character, but only so much as I have surmised from our short interview. And you must accept much of what I tell you of Landover on faith as well, because there is no meaningful way to show it to you. You must experience it, Mr. Holiday. You must go there and learn of it for yourself."

"In ten days, Mr. Meeks?"

"Time enough, believe me, Mr. Holiday. If you find otherwise, simply use the key provided you to return."

There was a long silence. "Does this mean that you have decided to offer me the purchase?" Ben asked.

Meeks nodded. "I have. I think you are eminently qualified. What do you say to that, Mr. Holiday?"

Ben looked down at the contract. "I'd like to think about it a bit."

Meeks chuckled dryly. "The caution of a lawyer—well and good. I can give you twenty-four hours before the item becomes available to the open market once more, Mr. Holiday. My next appointment is scheduled at one o'clock tomorrow. Take longer if you wish, but I can promise nothing after one day's time."

Ben nodded. "Twenty-four hours should be enough."

He reached for the contract, but Meeks slipped it quickly back. "My policy—and the store's—is not to allow copies of our contracts out of the office prior to signing. You may, of course, examine it again tomorrow at your convenience if you decide to buy."

Ben climbed to his feet and Meeks rose with him, tall and stooped. "You should make the purchase, Mr. Holiday," the old man's whispered voice encouraged. "You are the man for the job, I think."

Ben pursed his lips. "Maybe."

"If you decide to make the purchase, the contract will be waiting for you at the receptionist's desk. Thirty days will be allowed to complete arrangements for payment of the list price. Upon receiving payment in full, I will make available to you instructions for undertaking the journey to Landover and assuming the throne."

He walked Ben to the office door and opened it. "Do yourself a favor. Make the purchase, Mr. Holiday."

The door swung closed again, and Ben stood alone.

He walked back to the Waldorf through the noonday rush, had a leisurely lunch and retired to the lounge just off the lobby. With a yellow pad and pen in hand, he began to make notes about his interview with Meeks.

A number of things still troubled him. One of them was Meeks himself. There was something odd about that old man—something that went beyond his rough appearance. He had the instincts of a seasoned trial lawyer—hard-nosed and predatory. He was pleasant enough, but beneath the surface was a shell of armor two inches thick. The bits and pieces of conversation Ben had overheard in the reception areas and the looks he had seen in the receptionists' faces suggested that Meeks was not the easiest man to work with.

Yet it was more than that. Ben just couldn't seem to put his finger on what it was.

There was the problem, too, of still not having learned much of anything about Landover. No pictures, no flyers, no brochures—nothing. Too difficult to describe, Meeks had hedged. You have to see it. You have to accept the sale on faith. Ben grimaced. If their roles were switched and Meeks were the purchaser, he didn't think for one minute that that old man would settle for what he had been told!

He hadn't really learned anything about Landover in the interview that he hadn't known going into it. He didn't know where it was or what it looked like. He didn't know anything other than what had been described in the brochure.

Escape into your dreams . . .

Maybe.

And maybe he would be escaping into his nightmares.

All he had to fall back on was the clause in the contract that let him out of the purchase if he chose to rescind within ten days. That was fair enough. More than fair, really. He would lose only the fifty-thousand-dollar handling fee—an expensive, but not unbearable loss. He could journey to this magical kingdom with its fairy folk, with its dragons and damsel and all, and if he found it to be any sort of ripoff, he could journey back again and reclaim his money.

Guaranteed.

He scribbled notes hastily on the pad for a moment, and

then looked up suddenly and stared out across the empty lounge.

The truth was that none of that mattered a whit. The truth was that he was prepared to make the purchase just as things stood.

And that was the real problem. That was the thing that bothered him the most. He was prepared to spend a million dollars on a dream because his life had reached a point where nothing that he was or had mattered to him anymore. Anything was preferable to that—even something as wild as what he was considering, a fantasy like Landover with iguanas and Hollywood make-believe. Miles would say he needed help if he were even considering this ridiculous purchase—serious, professional help. Miles would be right, too.

So why was it that none of that made any difference to him? Why was it that he was probably going to make the purchase nevertheless?

His lean frame stretched in the cushioned easy chair. Because, he answered himself. Because I want to try something that other men just dream about. Because I don't know if I can do it, and I want to find out. Because this is the first real challenge that I have come across since losing Annie, and without that challenge, without something to pull me from the mire of my present existence . . .

He took a deep breath, the sentence left unfinished in his mind. Because life is a series of chances, he thought instead, and the bigger the chance, the greater the satisfaction if he were to succeed.

And he would succeed. He knew he would.

He tore the notes from his yellow pad and shredded them.

He slept on the matter as he had promised himself that he would, but his mind was already made up. At ten o'clock the next morning he was back at Rosen's, back in the penthouse at the receptionist's desk fronting the corridor that led to Meeks' secluded office. The receptionist did not seem at all surprised to see him. She handed him the contract with its triplicate carbons together with a statement of Rosen's payment policy allowing thirty days same as cash on all specialty items purchased. He read the contract once again, saw that it was the same, and signed it. With a carbon copy tucked into his suit pocket, he departed the building and caught a cab to LaGuardia.

By noon, he was on his way back to Chicago. He felt better than he had felt in a very long time.

Landover

The good feeling lasted until the next morning when he began to discover that no one else was quite as keen as he was on this proposed change in his life.

He called his accountant first. He had known Ed Samuelson for better than ten years; while they were not close friends, they were nevertheless close business associates who respected each other's advice. Ben had served as attorney for the accountancy firm of Haines, Samuelson and Roper, Inc. for almost the whole of that time. Ed Samuelson had been his accountant from the beginning. Ed was probably the only man alive who knew the full extent of his holdings. Ed had worked with him when his parents had passed away. He had suggested most of the investments that Ben had bought into. He knew Ben to be a shrewd and astute businessman.

But when Ben called him that morning and told him—*told* him, not asked him—to sell bonds and securities valued at almost one million dollars and to do so within the next ten days, it was clear to him that Ben had lost his mind. He exploded through the phone receiver. A sale such as that was unadulterated madness! Bonds and CDs could be liquidated only at a loss, because the penalty for early withdrawal was severe. Stocks would have to be sold at market value and in many cases the market was down. Ben would lose money all the way around. Even the tax deductions available from such a rash act couldn't begin to compensate him for the losses he would suffer! Why, in God's name, was it necessary to do this? Why did he suddenly need a million dollars in cash?

Patiently, if somewhat evasively, Ben explained that he had decided to complete purchase of an item that required cash up front and no delay. The tone of his voice made it clear that he was not prepared to reveal the nature of the item. Ed hesitated. Was Ben in some kind of trouble? Ben assured him that he was not. This was simply a decision that he had come to after some extended thought and he would appreciate Ed's help in securing the capital needed.

There wasn't much more to discuss. Reluctantly, Ed Samuelson agreed to do as he was asked. Ben hung up.

Things were even worse at the law office. He called Miles in first; when his friend had seated himself, coffee in hand, Ben told him that he had decided to take a leave of absence from the firm. Miles almost dropped the coffee.

"A leave of absence? What in the hell are you talking about, Doc? This law firm's your whole life! Practicing law is your whole life—has been since Annie died!"

"Maybe that's some of the problem, Miles. Maybe I need to get away from everything for a time—get a fresh perspective on things." Ben shrugged. "You're the one who's been telling me how I need to get out more, see something of the world besides this office and my apartment."

"Yeah, sure, but I don't see . . . Wait a minute, what kind of a leave of absence are you talking about? How long are you planning to be gone? A couple of weeks? A month?"

"A year."

Miles stared at him.

"At least," Ben added. "Maybe more."

"A year? A whole goddamn year? At least?" Miles was flushed with anger. "That's not a leave of absence, Doc—

that's retirement! What are we supposed to do with the practice while you're gone? What about your clients? They're not going to sit around a whole year waiting for you to come back! They'll pack it in and find another firm! And what about the trials you've scheduled? What about the cases you've got pending? For Christ's sake, you can't just . . ."

"Calm down a minute, will you?" Ben interrupted quickly. "I'm not bailing out and leaving the ship to sink. I've thought it all through. I'll notify all of my clients personally. Cases pending will be disposed of or reassigned. If anyone's unhappy, I'll refer them to another firm. I think most will stay with you."

Miles shifted his bulky frame forward against the desk. "Doc, let's be honest here. Maybe what you say is true—for the most part, at least. Maybe you can satisfy most of your clients. Maybe they'll accept your taking a leave of absence from the firm. But for a year? Or longer? They'll drift, Doc. And what about the trial work you do? No one can just step in and handle that. We'll lose those clients for sure."

"We can stand to lose a few if that's the way it has to be."

"But that's the point. That's not the way it has to be."

"What if I died, Miles? Tonight, just like that. Dead and buried. What would you do then? You'd have the same problem, basically. How would you solve it?"

"It's not the same thing, damn it, and you know it! The analogy stinks!" Miles came to his feet and leaned forward abruptly, arms braced on the desk. "I don't understand what in the hell has gotten into you, Doc. I don't understand at all. You've always been so damn dependable! A bit unorthodox in the courtroom, sure—but always level-headed, always under control. And a really brilliant trial lawyer. Hell, if I had half of your talent . . ."

"Miles, will you give me a break . . . ?"

The big man brushed the comment aside with a shake of his head. "A whole goddamn year you want to go trooping about? Just like that? First you fly off to New York without a word of explanation, chasing after God knows what, leaving the same day you decide to go, not even talking with me about it, not a word since we sat here and talked about that crazy item in that catalogue, whatever the name of it was, Ross, or Rosenberg's or whatever the hell, and now off again, just like . . .''

He stopped suddenly, the words dying away in his throat. His face froze in stunned recognition. "Oh, my God!" he whispered softly. His head shook slowly from side to side. "Oh, my God! It's that damn catalogue fantasyland, isn't it?"

Ben didn't answer him for a moment, undecided as to whether he should. He had intended to keep Landover a secret. He had intended to say nothing of it to anyone.

"Miles, sit back down, will you?" he said finally.

"Sit down? How in God's name do you expect me to sit down after . . . ?

"Just sit the hell down, Miles!" Ben cut his friend short.

Miles went still, held his position a moment longer, then sank slowly back into his chair. The stunned look stayed on his florid face.

Now it was Ben who leaned forward. His face was hard. "We've been together a long time, Miles—as friends and partners both. We know a lot about each other. Most of it we've learned from experiences shared. But we don't know everything about each other because that's not possible. No two human beings can know everything about each other, even under the best of circumstances. That's why certain things we do always remain a mystery to everyone else."

He cocked his head. "Remember the times you've warned me about backing away from a case because there was something not quite right about it? Remember, Miles? Drop that case, you'd tell me. It's bad news. It's a loser. Drop it. Sometimes I'd do it. I'd agree with you and I'd drop it. But sometimes I wouldn't. Sometimes I'd take the case anyway, and I'd tell you I was taking it because it felt right to me. You'd

go along with that decision—even though you didn't agree
with it and you really didn't understand it. But you trusted
me to take the chance, didn't you?''

He paused. "Well, that's what I'm asking you to do now.
You can't understand and you won't agree. So just put all
that aside and trust me."

Miles' eyes shifted to the desk top and up again. "Doc,
you're talking a million dollars here!''

Ben shook his head slowly. "No, I'm not. I'm talking
about saving myself, Miles. I'm talking about something that
doesn't have a price tag."

"But this is . . . crazy!" Miles' hands gripped the edge of
the desk top until the knuckles were white. "This is irre-
sponsible! It's just plain stupid, damn it!''

"I don't see it that way."

"You don't? Shucking off your professional responsibilities, your life's work? Going off to live in a castle and fight
dragons—assuming there are any and you're not simply getting fleeced? No TV, no Bears games, no Wrigley Field, no
cold beer, no goddamn electricity or showers with hot water
or indoor toilets or anything? Leaving behind your home and
your friends and . . . Jesus Christ, Doc!''

"Just think of it as an extended camping trip—the kind
where you get away from it all."

"Great! A million-dollar camping trip!"

"My mind is made up on this, Miles."

"Off to some godforsaken . . ."

"My mind is made up!"

The hard edge to his voice left them both shaken. They
stared at each other in silence for a moment, feeling the distance between them widening as if a chasm had opened. Then
Ben rose and came quickly around the desk. Miles rose as
well. Ben put a hand on his shoulder and gripped it.

"If I don't do something, Miles, I'm going to lose myself,"
he whispered. "It may take a few months or even a year,
but in the end I'm going to slip into the cracks and be gone.
I can't let that happen."

His friend looked at him wordlessly, sighed and nodded. "It's your life, Doc. I can't tell you how to live it. I never could." He squared himself. "Will you at least take a few days to think about this some more? That's not asking too much, is it?"

Ben smiled wearily. "I've already thought it through a hundred different ways. That's enough. I'm all done thinking."

Miles shook his head. "Guess a blind man could tell that, couldn't he?"

"I'm going to tell the others now. I'd appreciate it if you'd keep what you know to yourself."

"Sure. Why not? Why let anybody else know that the leading light of the firm is deranged?" He gave Ben a final glance, shrugged and turned toward the office door. "You're nuts, Doc."

Ben followed him out. "Yeah, I'll miss you, too, Miles."

He called the staff together then and told them of his plans for a leave of absence from the firm. He told them of his need to get away from his present life, the city, the practice, everything familiar; he told them that he would be leaving in the next few weeks and that he might be gone for better than a year. There was stunned silence and then a flurry of questions. He answered them all patiently. Then he left and went home.

He never mentioned Landover to any of them. Neither did Miles.

It took him the better part of three weeks to put his affairs in order. Most of that time was spent in tying up the loose ends of his law practice—communicating with clients, clearing his court calendar, and reassigning his case load. The transition was difficult. The staff had accepted his decision with stoic resolve, but there was an undercurrent of dissatisfaction in their looks and conversation that he could not mistake. They felt that he was deserting them, bailing out. And truth be told, he was feeling a bit ambivalent about that possibility himself. On the one hand, the loosening of ties with the firm and his profession gave him a newfound sense of freedom and relief. He felt as if he were escaping a trap—as if he were beginning his life all over again with a chance to discover things he had missed the first time around. On the other hand, there were undeniable twinges of uncertainty and regret at letting go of what he had spent the better part of his adult life building for himself. There was that sense of abandoning the familiar for the unknown that characterizes all journeys made for the first time.

Still, he could come back whenever he chose, he reminded himself. There was really nothing permanent in any of this—at least, not yet.

So he went about the business at hand and tried not to think about the ambivalent feelings, but the more he tried not to think about them, the more he did, and in the end he gave up on it altogether and accepted that it was inevitable. He let the feelings buffet and rage within him, let the doubts and the uncertainties gnaw, and found that he gained a certain measure of strength by being able to withstand them. He had made his decision; he found now that he could live with it.

The three weeks came to an end and he had completed the transition at the firm. He was free of his professional obligations, free to pursue whatever other paths he might choose to follow. In this instance, the path he had chosen led to a mythical kingdom called Landover. Only Miles knew the truth, and Miles wasn't talking. Not to him, not to anyone. Miles was in a determined funk. Miles was convinced he was crazy.

"There will come a time, Doc—a time in the not-too-distant future, unless I miss my guess—when a lightbulb will click on inside your muddled head and you will realize in a flash of belated wisdom that you made a huge mistake. When that happens, you'll come slinking back to the firm, feeling a bit sheepish and a lot poorer, and I will take enormous pleasure in saying 'I told you so' at least half a dozen times.

But that hasn't anything to do with anyone but you and me. So we'll just keep this bit of middle-aged foolishness between ourselves. No point in embarrassing the entire firm.''

That was the last comment Miles had made with regard to his decision to purchase Landover. He had made it the day after Ben had announced his decision to take a leave of absence to the partners and staff. Since then, he had kept his conversations with Ben confined strictly to business matters. Three weeks later, he had not said another word to his friend about Landover. He had contented himself instead with meaningful glances and a condescending manner suggestive of a shrink trying to glean some insight into the mind of his prize lunatic.

Ben tried to ignore this behavior, but his patience wore thin. The days dragged past, and he grew anxious to end the waiting. Ed Samuelson called to announce that the stocks and bonds had been liquidated and the money was available for the investment—if Ben was still certain that this was something that he wanted to do without further consultation. It was, Ben assured him as if missing the pointed suggestion, and wired the purchase price of Landover to Rosen's in New York, attention Meeks. He made arrangements with Samuelson to manage his financial affairs for an indefinite period of time, preparing suitable powers-of-attorney and supplemental authorizations. The accountant accepted them with a look that was suspiciously similar to the one recently adopted by Miles. Ben's patience ebbed some more. He paid his rent at the Towers for twelve months in advance and arranged for cleaning and security checks. He told George to keep an eye on things, and George seemed genuinely anxious that he have a good trip and a pleasant stay at wherever it was that he was going. George was probably the only one who felt that way, he decided. He prepared an update of his last will and testament, cancelled magazine and newspaper subscriptions, called the health club to advise them he would not be coming in for a time, but to keep the boxing facilities intact, put a hold on his mail at the post office effective the

first of next month and deposited the key to his bank lockbox
with Ed Samuelson.

Then he sat back to wait some more.

The waiting ended in the fourth week, three days before
the end of the month. Snow flurries spit and swirled in the
graying afternoon, the post-Thanksgiving pre-Christmas holiday weekend flooding the city with eager shoppers dying to
celebrate Christ's birth with an exchange of cash for goods.
His discontent with the waiting was breeding a rather nasty
cynicism. He was watching the madness from the confines
of his ivory tower when George called up to announce that
a special delivery envelope had arrived from New York.

It was from Meeks. There was a letter, airline tickets, a
roadmap of the state of Virginia and an odd-looking receipt.
The letter read as follows:

> Dear Mr. Holiday,
>
> I write to confirm your acquisition of the specialty
> item known as Landover, as listed in our most re-
> cent holiday catalogue. Your payment in full of the
> requisite purchase price has been received and es-
> crowed, pending the passage of ten days per our
> contractual agreement.
>
> I enclose airline tickets which will convey you
> from Chicago to Charlottesville, Virginia. The tick-
> ets will be honored on presentation to representa-
> tives of the appropriate carriers at any time during
> the next seven days.
>
> Upon arrival at the Charlottesville Allegheny ter-
> minal, please present the enclosed receipt at the
> courtesy desk. An automobile has been reserved in
> your name and will be made available upon your
> arrival. A package and written instructions will be
> waiting for you as well. Read the instructions care-
> fully and keep safe the contents of the package.
>
> The roadmap of the state of Virginia is marked in
> detail to enable you successfully to complete the

final leg of your journey to Landover. At its end, you will be met.

On behalf of Rosen's, Ltd., I wish you a pleasant journey.

Meeks

He read the letter through several times, glanced at the airline tickets and the receipt, then examined the roadmap. A red pen line traced a passage on the roadways leading west of the city of Charlottesville to a small "x" in the midst of the Blue Ridge Mountains just south of Waynesboro. There were cursory instructions printed in the margins of the map, numbered in consecutive paragraphs. He read them through, read the letter once more, then folded the entire packet up again and slipped it back into the envelope.

He sat there for a time on the sofa, staring out at the gray day with its flurry of white snowflakes and the distant sounds of the holiday rush. Then he walked into the bedroom, packed a small overnight bag and called down to George for a taxi.

He was at O'Hare by five o'clock.

It was beginning to snow harder.

It was not snowing in Virginia. It was cool and clear, the sky filled with sunlight that streaked a backdrop of forested mountains glimmering crystalline with morning dew. Ben eased the steel-blue New Yorker into the right lane of Interstate 64 traveling west out of Charlottesville toward Waynesboro.

It was midmorning of the following day. He had flown to Washington National, stayed overnight at the Marriott across from the airport, then caught Allegheny's 7:00 A.M. flight to Charlottesville. Once there, he had presented the odd-looking receipt at the terminal courtesy desk and received in exchange the keys to the New Yorker and a small box wrapped in plain brown paper addressed to him. In the box was a brief letter from Meeks and a medallion. The letter read:

> The medallion is your key into and out of Landover. Wear it, and you will be recognized as the rightful heir to the throne. Remove it, and you will be returned to the place marked "x" on the map. Only you can remove it. No one can take it from you. Lose it at your own peril.
>
> Meeks

The medallion was an aged, tarnished piece of metal, its face engraved with a mounted knight in battle harness advancing out of a morning sun that rose over a castle encircled by a lake. A double-link chain was fastened at its apex. It was an exquisite piece of workmanship, but badly worn. The tarnish would not come clean, even with rubbing. He had slipped it around his neck, picked up the car reserved in his name and turned south out of Charlottesville onto Interstate 64.

So far, so good, he thought to himself as he drove west toward the Blue Ridge. Everything had gone according to script.

The map supplied by Meeks lay open on the seat beside him. He had memorized the instructions written on it. He was to follow 64 west almost to Waynesboro and exit the Skyline Drive on the road south toward Lynchburg. Twenty miles in, he would come upon a wayside turn-around on a promontory overlooking a stretch of mountains and valleys within the George Washington National Forest. It would be marked with a small green sign with the number 13 in black. There would be a courtesy phone and a weather shelter. He was to pull over, park, and lock the car with the keys inside, and cross the roadway to the nature path on the opposite side. He was to follow the path into the mountains for approximately two miles. At that point, he would be met.

The map didn't say by whom. Neither did the letter.

The map did say that someone would come later to pick up the car. The phone could be used to arrange for transportation back again, should he decide later to return. A telephone number was provided.

A twinge of doubt tugged suddenly at him. He was a long way out in the middle of nowhere, and no one but Meeks knew exactly where he was. If he were simply to drop from sight, Meeks might suddenly be a million dollars richer— supposing for the sake of argument that this was all an elaborate hoax. Stranger things had happened and for much less.

He thought about it for a moment and then shook his head. It didn't make sense. Meeks was an agent for Rosen's, and a man in his position would have been thoroughly checked. Besides, there were too many ways that Meeks could be caught in such a thing. Miles knew of Ben's contact with the store and the reason for that contact. The funds he had cabled could be traced. Copies of the confirmation letter from Meeks were with his safe papers. And the ad for Landover's sale was public knowledge.

He forced the doubts from his mind and concentrated on the drive ahead. His anticipation of what lay ahead had been working on him for weeks. He was so keyed up that he could barely contain himself. He had slept poorly last night. He had been awake before sunrise. He was susceptible to all sorts of half-baked ideas.

He reached the entrance to Skyline Drive in a little more than thirty minutes and turned south onto it. The two lane highway wound steadily upward into the Blue Ridge, weaving through the tangle of forest and mountain rock, rising into the late November sunlight. Panoramic views spread away to either side, the sweep of the national forestlands and parkways slipping past in breathtaking still life. Traffic was light. He encountered three cars traveling in the opposite direction, families with camping gear and luggage, one pulling a fold-up trailer. He came across no one driving south.

Twenty minutes later, he caught sight of the turn-around

with its green sign stenciled with the number 13 in black. Easing off the gas pedal, he pulled the New Yorker off the parkway onto the gravel wayside and came to a stop before the courtesy phone and weather shelter. He climbed out of the car and looked about. To his right, the wayside ran several dozen feet to a chain and post guard rail and a promontory that overlooked miles of forestland and mountain ridges comprising a small part of the national park. To his left, across the deserted roadway, the mountainside lifted into the morning sunlight, a maze of trees and rocks wrapped in thin trailers of mist. He stared upward toward the mountain's summit, watching the mist swirl and stir like ribbons drawn through the air. The day was still and empty, and even the passing of the wind made no sound.

He turned, reached into the car and took out his overnight case. It was really little more than a glorified duffel bag filled with a few odd possessions he had thought to bring—a bottle of his beloved Glenlivet to be saved for a special occasion, toiletries, paper and pens, several books, a couple sets of boxing gloves, recent copies of magazines he was still reading, tape, antiseptic, an old sweatsuit, and running shoes. He hadn't bothered with much in the way of clothing. He knew that he would probably be better off wearing whatever they wore in Landover.

He closed the car and locked it, the keys inside. He slipped his billfold into his duffel, glanced about once again, and crossed the roadway. He was dressed in a light sweatsuit of navy blue with red and white piping and navy blue Nikes. He had brought the Nikes and the running shoes because he couldn't decide what better to wear on a journey such as this and because he doubted that there would be anything more comfortable in shoes once he got where he was going. It was odd, he reflected, that Meeks hadn't bothered with any instructions about clothing or personals.

He stopped at the far side of the roadway and scanned the forested slope before him. A small stream ran down off the rocks through a series of rapids that flashed silver in the dappled sunlight. A pathway crisscrossed the stream's banks and disappeared into the trees. Ben hitched the duffel over one shoulder and started up.

The pathway wound in a series of twists and turns along the stream, leveling off at intervals in small clearings where wooden benches provided a resting place for the weary hiker. The stream gurgled and lapped against the earthen banks and over rock falls, the only sound in the late November morning. The parkway and the car disappeared behind him as he climbed, and soon there was only the forest to be seen. The climb grew less steep, but the forest closed about on either side, and the pathway became more difficult to discern. Eventually, the stream branched away into a cliff side that dropped from a great height, and the pathway ran on alone.

Slowly a mist began to settle in about him.

He stopped then and again looked about. There was nothing to see. He listened. There was nothing to hear. Nevertheless, he had the unpleasant sensation of being followed. Momentary doubt tugged at his resolve; perhaps this whole business was one big, fat mistake. But he shoved the doubt aside quickly and started again along the trail. He had made the commitment weeks ago. He was determined to see it through.

The forest deepened and the mist grew thicker. Trees loomed tightly all about him, dark, skeletal sentries with their dying leaves and evergreen boughs, their trailers of vine and scrub and swatches of saw grass. He was having to push his way past the pine and spruce to keep on the trail, and the mist lent a hazy cast to a morning that had begun with sunshine. Pine needles and fallen leaves crunched underfoot; from beyond where he could see, small animals darted through the carpet.

At least he wasn't entirely alone, he thought.

He was growing extremely thirsty, but he hadn't thought to pack a water container. He could go back and try the stream water, but he was reluctant to lose time doing so. He turned his thoughts momentarily to Miles to take his mind off his thirst. He tried to picture Miles out here in the woods with him, trudging through the forest and the mist, huffing and grunting. He smiled. Miles hated all forms of exercise that did not involve beer cans and tableware. He thought Ben was crazy for continuing his boxing workouts so many years after he had ceased to box competitively. He thought athletes were basically little boys who had never grown up.

Ben shook his head. Miles thought a lot of things that didn't make much sense.

He slowed as the pathway ahead petered out into tall grass. A deep cluster of pine barred his passage forward. He pushed his way through and stopped.

"Uh-oh," he whispered.

A wall of towering, rugged oak rose before him, shrouded in layers of shadow. A tunnel had been cut through its center, hollowed out as if by giant's hands. The tunnel was dark and empty, a black hole with no end, a burrow that ran on into trailers of mist, stirred by invisible hands. Sounds drifted from out of the black, distant and unidentifiable.

Ben stood at the tunnel's entrance and stared into the mist and the dark. The tunnel was two dozen feet across and twice as high. He had never seen anything like it. He knew at once that nothing in his world had made it. He knew as well exactly where it led. Nevertheless, he hesitated. There was something about the tunnel that made him uneasy—something beyond the fact that it was an unnatural creation. There was a look and feel to it that bothered him.

He peered about warily. There was nothing to be seen. He might have been the only living thing in the forest— except that he could hear the sounds from somewhere ahead, like voices, only . . .

He experienced a sudden, violent urge to turn about and go straight back the way he had come. It was so powerful that he actually took a step backward before he could catch himself. The air from the tunnel seemed to reach out to him in a velvet touch that trailed moisture against his skin. He tightened his arm about the duffel and straightened, bracing himself against what he was feeling. He took a deep breath and exhaled slowly. Did he go on or did he turn back? Which choice for intrepid adventurer, Doc Holiday?

"Well," he said softly.

He started forward. The tunnel seemed to open before him, the darkness drawing back at precisely the rate at which he advanced. The mist caressed him, a lover's hands tender and eager in their touch. He walked steadily, purposefully, letting his eyes sweep briefly right and left, seeing nothing. The sounds continued to stray from out of the invisible distance, still unrecognizable. The forest earth had a soft, spongey feel to it, giving with the weight of his body as he trod upon it. Dark trunks and limbs wrapped about, walls and ceiling that locked away all but the faintest light, a web of damp bark and drying leaves.

Ben risked a quick glance back. The forest from which he had come was gone. The tunnel entrance was gone. It was the same distance back as forward, the same look either way.

"Special effects are pretty good." He forced a quick smile, thinking of Miles, thinking of how ridiculous it was to feel what he was feeling, thinking that he was liking this whole business less and less . . .

Then he heard the scream.

It lifted from out of the dark and the mist from somewhere behind him. He glanced back once more, still walking. There was movement in the tunnel dark. Figures darted from the trees—human in appearance, but so slight and willowy as to be almost ethereal. Faces appeared, thin and angular with sharp eyes that peered from beneath thatches of moss-hair and corn-silk brows.

The scream sounded again. He blinked. A monstrous, black apparition hung upon the misted air, a thing of scales and leathered wings, of claws and spines. The scream had come from it.

Ben quit walking altogether and stared. The special effects were getting better and better. This one looked almost real.

He dropped his duffel on the trail, put his hands on his hips and watched it assume three-dimensional proportions. It was an ugly thing, as big as a house and as frightening as the worst of his dreams. Still, he could tell illusion from reality. Meeks would have to do better than this if he expected Ben to . . .

He terminated the thought abruptly. The apparition was coming directly for him—and it didn't look quite so fake any longer. It was beginning to look decidedly real. He picked up the duffel and backed away. The thing screamed. Even the scream sounded real now.

Ben swallowed hard. Maybe that was because the thing *was* real.

He quit being rational and started to run. The apparition came on, the scream sounding once more. It was close to him now, a nightmare that could not be shaken out of sleep. It settled down upon the tunnel floor and ran upon four legs, the wings pulled back against it, the body compacted and steaming as if heated by an inner fire. And there was something on its back—a figure as dark as it, armored and misshapen, clawed hands grasping reins to guide the thing it rode.

Ben ran faster, his breathing labored and sounding of fear. He was in good condition, but the fear was eroding his strength quickly, and he could make no headway on the creature trailing. All about him he watched the strange faces materialize and then vanish, spirits wandered from the mists, lost in the trees—spectators to the chase taking place within the tunnel. He thought momentarily to break from the pathway and force his way into the forest with the gathering of faces. Perhaps the thing chasing him could not follow. It was so big that, even if he tried, the trees would at least slow its pursuit. But then he would be lost in the dark and the mist and might never find his way back. He stayed on the trail.

The apparition chasing him screamed again, and he could feel the tunnel floor shake with its approach.

"Meeks, damn you!" he cried desperately.

He could feel the medallion rub against his chest within the confines of his running suit. He clutched at it instinctively, the talisman he had been given to bring him safely into and—if need be—safely out of Landover. Maybe the medallion could dispell this thing . . .

Then a rider appeared suddenly at the edge of the darkness ahead, a ragged, hazy form. It was a knight, his armor battered and chipped, lance lowered until it almost rested upon the ground before it. Both rider and horse were soiled and unkempt, apparitions as unfriendly in their appearance as the thing that thundered toward Ben from behind. The rider's head lifted at his approach, and the lance came up. Behind it, there was a sudden trace of daylight.

Ben ran faster still. The tunnel was ending. He had to get clear of it; he had to escape.

The monster that pursued screamed, the sound dying into a frightening hiss. "Stay away from me, damn you!" Ben cried frantically.

Then the horse and rider loomed suddenly before him, grown huge and strangely awesome beneath their covering of dirt. An exclamation of surprise broke from Ben's lips. He had seen this knight before. He had seen his image engraved upon the medallion that he wore!

The breath of the black thing burned against the back of his neck, fetid and raw. Terror streaked through him, and there was the cold touch of something inhuman in his chest. The knight spurred his horse from the blaze of sunlight that marked the tunnel's end, and the faces in the forest whirled as if disembodied ghosts. Ben screamed. Black thing and knight closed at him from either direction, bearing down on him as if he were not there.

The knight reached him first, racing past at a full gallop, the flanks of the charging horse knocking him sprawling from the pathway. He tumbled headlong into the shadows, and his eyes closed tightly against a sudden explosion of light.

Blackness engulfed him, and everything spun wildly. The breath had been knocked from his body, and he was having trouble catching it again. He lay face downward against the earth, the feel of grass and leaves damp against his cheek. He kept his eyes tightly shut and waited for the spinning sensation to cease.

When at last it did, he opened his eyes cautiously. He was in a clearing. The forest rose up all about him, misted and dark, but he could still glimpse traces of daylight beyond its screen. He started to his feet.

It was then that he saw the dragon.

He froze in disbelief. The dragon lay sleeping several dozen yards to his left, curled in a ball against a row of dark trunks. It was a monstrous thing, all scales, spikes, claws, and spines, its wings folded against its body, its snout tucked down into its forelegs. Steam puffed in ragged geysers from its nostrils as it snored contentedly. The raw, white bones of something recently eaten were scattered all about.

Ben sucked in his breath slowly, certain for an instant that this was the black thing that had chased him through the tunnel. But, no, the black thing had been something different altogether . . .

He quit worrying about what it was and started worrying about how to get away from it. He wished he knew if any of this was real, but there was no time to debate the matter now.

Cautiously, he began to slip through the trees, edging his way past the sleeping dragon in the direction of the light. He had his duffel looped over one shoulder and clamped tightly against his side. The dragon appeared to be sleeping soundly. It would only take a few moments to get clear of it. Ben held his breath and continued to place one foot silently in front of the other. He was almost clear of the beast when one lidded eye suddenly slipped open.

Ben froze a second time. The dragon regarded him balefully, the single eye fixed on him as he stood there amid the trees. Ben held his ground a moment longer, then slowly began to back away.

The dragon's horn-crusted head swung quickly about, lowering against the forest earth. Ben back-pedalled faster, seeing the forest trees thin about him, sensing the light grow brighter behind. The dragon's lip curled back almost disdainfully to reveal row upon row of blackened teeth.

Then the dragon blew at him as a sleeping man might blow at a bothersome fly. The odorous breath picked Ben up and flung him like a rag doll through the forest mist. He closed his eyes, tucked into a ball, and braced himself. He struck the earth roughly, bounced a few times, and rolled to a stop.

When he opened his eyes again, he sat alone in a clover meadow.

Questor Thews

Sunshine seeped down through rifts in a clouded sky, bathing the meadow with bits and pieces of its warmth. Ben blinked and squinted through its brightness. The misted forest with its shadowed tunnel was gone. The apparitions were gone as well—that black thing, the battered knight, even the dragon.

Ben straightened. What in the hell had happened to them? He brushed at the sheen of sweat on his forehead. Hadn't they been real after all?

He swallowed hard. No, of course they weren't real! they couldn't have been! They were just some sort of mirage!

He glanced about quickly. The meadow in which he sat spread away before him in a carpet of muted greens, blues and pinks, a mix of colors he had never seen in grasses. The clover was white, but touched with crimson spots. The meadow dropped downward into a sprawling valley which rose again miles distant in a wall of mountains that formed a dark barrier against the skyline. Behind him, the trees of a forest loomed blackly against a mountain slope. Trailers of mist hung over everything.

The apparitions had been somewhere in the trees behind him, he thought suddenly. Where had they disappeared to?

And where was he?

He took a moment to collect his thoughts. He was still shaken from his ordeal in the forest tunnel, frightened by the dark things that had come at him, bewildered that he was sitting here in this meadow. He took several deep breaths to steady himself. Whatever it was that had seemed to threaten him in that forest, he was all right now. He was back in the Blue Ridge. He was in Virginia, some twenty miles or so below Waynesboro, a few miles in from the parkway that ran through the George Washington National Forest.

Except that . . .

He glanced about once again, more carefully this time. Something wasn't quite right. The weather was wrong, for one thing. It was too warm for late November in the Virginia mountains. He was sweating beneath his running suit and he shouldn't have been doing that, even with the scare he had just experienced. The air had been cooler than this by at least thirty degrees before he had entered that tunnel in the forest.

The clover was wrong, too. There shouldn't be clover blooming in November—especially clover that looked like this, white with crimson spots, like a polka-dot flower. He looked back at the forest. Why were there still leaves as green as summer's new growth on the trees? The leaves should be colored with autumn's touch. The only green should be on the pines and spruce.

He shoved himself hurriedly to one knee. A mix of panic and excitement crept through him. The sun was directly overhead, exactly where it ought to be. But in the distant skies two spheres hung low against the horizon—one faintly peach, the other a sort of washed-out mauve. Ben started. Moons? Two of them? No, they had to be planets. But when had the planets of his solar system ever been so clearly visible to the naked eye?

What in the hell was going on?

He sat back slowly, forcing himself to remain calm. There

was a logical explanation for all of this, he reasoned, fighting back against a mix of panic and excitement. The explanation was simple. This was what he had been promised. This was Landover. He glanced about at the green meadow with its spotted clover, at the summer trees of the forest, at the odd-looking spheres hanging above the horizon, and he nodded sagely. There was nothing to worry about. This was just more of the special effects he had experienced in the forest tunnel. This was only a broader projection of such effects within a pocket of land hidden away in the Blue Ridge Mountains of Virginia. He wasn't sure how it had been managed—especially in the middle of a national forest—but he was sure of what it was. He had to admit that it was pretty amazing. The valley with its summer temperatures could have been a lucky discovery, but the odd flowers, the spheres that looked like planets or moons, and the apparitions in the forest tunnel must have taken some effort and scientific know-how to create.

He came to his feet, slowly rebuilding his confidence. His experience in the forest had unnerved him badly. That black thing and the knight had seemed almost real. The knight's horse had felt very real when it galloped past, knocking him from the trail into the shadows. And he could still feel the breath of the dragon on his face. He might almost have believed . . .

He stopped short. His gaze, wandering across the floor of the valley below as he puzzled matters through, had caught sight of something.

It was a castle.

Ben stared. A huge swatch of green dominated the central portion of the valley, a checkerboard of meadows and fields dissected by meandering rivers. The castle stood at the near end of that checkerboard. An odd haze that hung over the whole of the valley had obscured his vision at first. But now he was beginning to pick things out, to see things clearly.

One of those things was the castle.

The castle was some miles distant from where he stood,

swathed in mist and shadows beyond a deep forest. It sat upon an island in the middle of a lake, forest and hills all about, patches of mist floating past like clouds dropped down to earth. It was a dark and forbidding citadel, appearing almost ghostlike within the swirling haze.

He squinted against the muted light of the sun to see more clearly. But the mist closed suddenly, and the castle was gone.

"Damn!" he muttered softly.

Had that been an apparition as well—another of Landover's special effects? A faint suspicion was beginning to gnaw at him. Was it possible that all of these special effects were not special effects at all? He felt a twinge of the panic and excitement return. What if everything he was seeing was real?

A voice boomed out behind him, and he jumped a foot.

"Well, then, here you are, wandering about in this meadow—not at all where you were supposed to be. Did you stray from the pathway? You look a bit fatigued, if you don't mind my saying so. Are you all right?"

Ben turned at once. The speaker stood about ten feet behind him—a bizarre caricature of some pop artist's gypsy. He was a tall man, well over six feet, but so lean as to be almost sticklike. A mop of curling white hair hung down over large ears, wisps of it mingling with beard and brows of the same color and kind. Gray robes cloaked the scarecrow form, but they were decorated with an array of brilliant sashes, cloth pouches, and jewelry that left the wearer looking something like a fragmented rainbow pinned against a departing thunderstorm. Soft leather boots too big for the feet curled up slightly at the toes and a hawklike nose dominated a pinched and owlish face. A gnarled walking stick guided the way as he came a step closer.

"You are Ben Holiday, aren't you?" the fellow asked, a sudden glint of suspicion in his eyes. A massive crystal dangled from a chain about his throat, and he stuffed it rather self-consciously into the recesses of his robes. "You do have the medallion?"

Ben didn't care for the look. "Who are you?" he replied trying to put the other man on the defensive.

"Ah, I asked you first." The other smiled amiably. "Courtesy dictates that you answer first."

Ben stiffened, a touch of impatience in his voice at being forced to play this cat-and-mouse game. "Okay. I'm Ben Holiday. Now who are you?"

"Yes, well, I will have to see the medallion." The smile broadened slightly. "You could be anyone, after all. Saying that you are Ben Holiday doesn't necessarily make it so."

"You could be anyone, too, couldn't you?" Ben asked in reply. "What gives you the right to ask me anything without first telling me who you are?"

"I am the one sent to meet you, as it happens—assuming, of course, that you are who you claim. Could I see the medallion?"

Ben hesitated, then pulled the medallion from beneath his clothing and, without removing it, held it out for examination. The tall man leaned forward, peered momentarily at the medallion and nodded.

"You are indeed who you claim. I apologize for questioning you, but caution is always well advised in these matters. And now for my own introduction." He bowed deeply from the waist. "Questor Thews, wizard of the court, chief advisor to the throne of Landover, your obedient servant."

"Wizard of the . . ." Ben glanced sharply about one time more. "Then this *is* Landover!"

"Landover and nowhere else. Welcome, High Lord Ben Holiday."

"So this is it," Ben murmured, his mind racing suddenly. He looked again at the other. "Where are we exactly?"

Questor Thews seemed puzzled. "Landover, High Lord."

"Yes, but where is Landover? I mean, where is Landover in the Blue Ridge? It must be close to Waynesboro, am I right?"

The wizard smiled. "Oh, well, you are no longer in your world. I thought you understood that. Landover bridges any number of worlds—a kind of gateway, you might say. The mists of the fairy realm connect her to your world and the others. Some bridge closer, of course, and some don't even have the barrier of the mists. But you will learn all that soon enough."

Ben stared. "I'm not in my world? This isn't Virginia?"

Questor Thews shook his head.

"Or the United States or North America or Earth? None of it?"

"No, High Lord. Did you think that the fairy-tale kingdom you bought would be in your world?"

Ben didn't hear him, a desperate obstinacy seizing hold. "I suppose that those planets in the sky over there aren't fake, either? I suppose that they're real?"

Questor turned. "Those are moons, not planets. Landover has eight of them. Only two are visible in the daylight hours, but the other six can be seen as well after dusk during most of the year."

Ben stared. Then he shook his head slowly. "I don't believe any of this. I don't believe one word of it."

Questor Thews looked at him curiously. "Why do you not believe, High Lord?"

"Because a place like this can't exist, damn it!"

"But you chose to come here, didn't you? Why would you come to Landover in the first place, if you did not believe that it could exist?"

Ben had no idea. He was no longer certain why it was that he had come. He was certain of only one thing—that he could not bring himself to accept what the other man was saying. Panic flooded through him at the very thought that Landover could be somewhere other than on Earth. He had never dreamed that it would be anywhere else. It meant that all of his ties with his old life were truly severed, that everything he had once known was really gone. It meant that he was alone in an alien world . . .

"High Lord, would you mind if we walked while we carry on this conversation?" the wizard interrupted his thoughts. "We have a good distance to cover before nightfall."

"We do? Where are we going?"

"To your castle, High Lord."

"My castle? Wait a minute—do you mean that castle that I saw just before you appeared, the one in the middle of the lake on an island?"

The other nodded. "The very place, High Lord. Shall we be on our way?"

Ben shook his head stubbornly. "Not a chance. I'm not going anywhere until I find out exactly what's going on. What about what happened to me in the forest! Are you telling me all that was real? Are you telling me there actually was a dragon sleeping back there in the trees?"

Questor shrugged nonchalantly. "There could have been. There is a dragon in the valley—and he often naps at the fringes of the mists. The mists were his home once."

Ben frowned. "His home, huh? Well, what about that black, winged thing and its rider?"

The wizard's shaggy brows lifted slightly. "A black, winged thing, you say? A thing that seemed a nightmare, perhaps?"

Ben nodded his head anxiously. "Yes—that was what it seemed."

"That was the Iron Mark." The other pursed his lips. "The Mark is a demon lord. I am surprised he would come after you there in the mists. I would have thought . . ." He stopped, smiled a quick smile of reassurance and shrugged. "A demon strays into Landover now and again. You happened to come across one of the worst."

"Come across it, my aunt Agatha!" Ben flared. "It was hunting me! It chased me down that forest tunnel and would have had me if not for that knight!"

This time Questor Thews' brows lifted a good deal further. "Knight? What knight?" he demanded quickly.

"The knight—the one on the medallion!"

"You saw the knight on the medallion, Ben Holiday?"

Ben hesitated, surprised at the other's sharp interest. "I saw him in the forest, after the black thing came at me. He appeared in front of me and rode at the black thing. I was caught between them, but the knight's horse side swiped me and knocked me from the trail. The next thing I knew I was sitting here in this meadow."

Questor Thews frowned thoughtfully. "Yes, the horse knocking you from the pathway would account for your appearance here rather than at your appointed destination . . ." He trailed off, then came slowly forward, bending close to look into Ben's eyes. "You might have imagined the knight, High Lord. You might have only thought to see him. Were you to think back on it, you might see something entirely different."

Ben flushed. "Were I to think back on it, I would see exactly the same thing exactly." He kept his gaze steady. "I would see the knight on the medallion."

There was a long moment of silence. Then Questor Thews stepped back again, one hand rubbing at his ear thoughtfully. "Well," he said. "Well, indeed." He looked surprised. More than that, he looked pleased. He pursed his lips once again, shifted his weight from one foot to the other and hunched his shoulders. "Well," he said a third time.

Then the look was gone as quickly as it had come. "We really do have to start walking now, High Lord," he said quickly. "The day is getting on and it would be best if we were to reach the castle before nightfall. Come along, please. It is a good distance off."

He shambled down through the meadow, a tall, ragtag, slightly stooped figure, his robes dragging through the grasses. Ben watched dumbly for a moment, glanced hastily about, then hitched up the duffel over one shoulder and followed reluctantly after.

They passed from the high meadow and began their descent toward the distant bowl of the valley. The valley stretched away below them, a patchwork quilt of farmlands, meadows, forests, lakes and rivers, and swatches of marsh and desert. Mountains ringed the valley tightly, forested and dark, awash in a sea of deep mist that strung its trailers down into the valley and cast its shadow over everything.

Ben Holiday's mind raced. He kept trying to fit what he was seeing into his mental picture of the Blue Ridge. But none of it worked. His eyes wandered across the slopes they were descending, seeing orchard groves, seeking out familiar fruit trees, finding apple, cherry, peach, and plum, but a dozen other fruits as well, many of a color and size completely unfamiliar to him. Grasses were varied shades of green, but also crimson, lavender and turquoise. Scattered through the whole of the strange collection of vegetation were large clumps of trees that vaguely resembled half-grown pin oaks except that they were colored trunk to leaf a brilliant blue.

None of it looked anything at all like the Blue Ridge Mountains of Virginia or the mountains of any other part of the United States that he had ever heard about.

Even the cast of the day was strange. The mist lent a shadowed look to the whole of the valley, and it reflected in the color tones of the earth. Everything seemed to have developed a somewhat wintry look—though the air was warm like a midsummer's day and the sun shone down through the clouds in the sky.

Ben savored cautiously the look, smell, and feel of the land, and he discovered in doing so that he could almost believe that Landover was exactly what Questor Thews had said that it was—another world completely.

He mulled this prospect over in his mind as he kept pace with his guide. This was no small concession that he was being asked to make. Every shred of logic and every bit of common sense that he could muster in his lawyer's mind argued that Landover was some sort of trick, that fairy worlds were writer's dreams and that what he was seeing was a pocket of merry old England tucked away in the Blue

Ridge, castles and knights-in-armor included. Logic and common sense said that the existence of a world such as this, a world outside but somehow linked to his own, a world that no one had ever seen, was so farfetched as to be one step short of impossible: Twilight Zone; Outer Limits. And one step short only because it could be argued that anything after all was *theoretically* possible.

Yet here he was, and there it was, and what was the explanation for it, if it wasn't what Questor Thews said it was? It looked, smelled, and felt real. It had the look of something real—but at the same time it had the look of something completely foreign to his world, something beyond anything he had ever known or even heard about this side of King Arthur. This land *was* a fantasy, a mix of color and shape and being that surprised and bewildered him at every turn—and frightened him, as well.

But already his initial skepticism had begun to erode. What if Landover truly was another world? What if it was exactly what Meeks had promised?

The thought exhilarated him. It left him stunned.

He glanced surreptitiously at Questor. The tall, stooped figure marched dutifully next to him, gray robes dragging through the grasses, patched with the scarfs and sashes and pouches of gaily colored silk, his whitish hair and beard fringing the owlish face. Questor certainly seemed to feel at home.

His gaze wandered back over the sweep of the valley, and he consciously opened a few heretofore padlocked doors in the deep recesses of his mind. Perhaps logic and common sense ought to take a backseat to instinct for a while, he decided.

Still, a few discreet questions wouldn't hurt.

"How is it that you and I happen to speak the same language?" he asked his guide suddenly. "Where did you learn to speak English?"

"Hmmmmm?" The wizard glanced over, preoccupied with something else.

"If Landover is in another world, how does it happen that you speak English so well?"

Questor shook his head. "I don't speak English at all. I speak the language of my country—at least, I speak the language used by humans."

Ben frowned. "But you're speaking English right now, damn it! How else could we communicate?"

"Oh, I see what you mean." Questor smiled. "I am not speaking your language, High Lord—you are speaking mine."

"Yours?"

"Yes, the magic properties of the medallion that permit you passage into Landover also give you the ability to communicate instantly with its inhabitants, either by spoken word or in writing." He fumbled through one of the pouches momentarily and withdrew a faded map. "Here, read something of this."

Ben took the map from him and studied the details. The names of towns, rivers, mountain ranges and lakes were all in English.

"These are written in English!" he insisted, handing the map back again.

Questor shook his head. "No, High Lord, they are written in Landoverian—the language of the country. They only appear to be written in English—and only to you. I speak to you now in Landoverian as well; but it seems to you as if your own language. The medallion's fairy magic permits this."

Ben thought it through for a moment, trying to decide what else he should ask on the matter of language and communication, but decided in the end that there really was nothing further to ask. He changed subjects.

"I've never seen anything like those trees," he informed his guide, pointing to the odd-looking blue pin oaks. "What are they?"

"Those are Bonnie Blues." Questor slowed and stopped. "They grow only in Landover as far as I know. They were

created of the fairy magic thousands of years ago and given
to us. They keep back the mists and feed life into the soil."

Ben frowned dubiously. "I thought sun and rain did that."

"Sun and rain? No, sun and rain only help the process.
But magic is the life source of Landover, and the Bonnie
Blues are a very strong magic indeed."

"Fairy magic, you said—like the magic that enables us to
communicate?"

"The same, High Lord. The fairies gave the magic to the
land when they created it. They live now in the mists about
us."

"The mists?"

"There." Questor pointed in a sweeping motion to the
mountains that ringed the valley, their peaks and forests
shrouded in gray. "The fairies live there." He glanced once
more at Ben. "Did you see faces in the mist when you passed
through the forest from your world to ours?" Ben nodded.
"Those were the faces of the fairies. Only the pathway you
walked upon belongs to both worlds. That was why I was
concerned that you had strayed too far from it."

There was a moment's silence. "What if I had?" Ben
asked finally.

The stooped figure pulled the gray robes free from a trailer
of scrub on which they had caught. "Why, then you might
have wandered too deep into the fairy world and been lost
forever." He paused. "Are you hungry, High Lord?"

"What?" The question startled Ben. He was still thinking
about his brush with the fairy world and the possibility that
one could wander lost in it forever. Until now, this world
into which he had come had seemed fairly safe.

"Food and drink—it occurs to me that you may not have
had either for some time."

Ben hesitated. "Not since this morning, as a matter of
fact."

"Good. Come this way."

Questor walked past him down the slope to a small cluster
of Bonnie Blues at the edge of an oak grove. He waited for

Ben to join him, then reached up and tore free a branch from one of the trees. The branch broke cleanly and soundlessly. The wizard knelt, grasped the base of the branch with one hand, and with the other stripped it of its leaves. The leaves tumbled into the lap of his robe.

"Here, try one," he offered, holding out one of the leaves. "Take a bite of it."

Ben took the leaf, examined it, then cautiously bit into it and chewed. His face brightened with surprise. "It tastes like . . . like melon."

The other nodded, smiling. "Now the stalk. Hold it like this." He held the broken end upright. "Now suck on it— there, at the break."

Ben did as he was told. "Well, I'll be damned!" he whispered. "It tastes like milk!"

"It is the staple of human existence in the valley," Questor explained, chewing a leaf himself. "One can live on only the Bonnie Blues and a small amount of drinking water, if one has nothing else—and there are those who do not. It wasn't always so, but times have changed . . ."

He trailed off, distracted. Then he glanced at Ben. "The Bonnie Blues grow wild everywhere in the valley. Their reproductive capacity is amazing—even now. Look there— look at what has happened."

He pointed to the tree where the limb had been broken off. Already, the break was healing over and beginning to bud anew.

"By morning, a new limb will have begun to grow. In a week's time, it will be exactly as we found it—or should be."

Ben nodded without comment. He was thinking about Questor's carefully phrased qualifications. "Times have changed . . . Their reproductive capacity is amazing—even now . . . In a week's time, it will be exactly as we found it—or should be." He studied the Bonnie Blues behind the one the wizard had chosen. They seemed to be flourishing less successfully, signs of wilt on their leaves and a drooping to their limbs. Something was distressing them.

Questor interrupted his thoughts. "Well, now that we have sampled the Bonnie Blues, perhaps something a bit more substantial would be in order." He rubbed his hands together briskly. "How would you like some ham and eggs, some fresh bread, and a glass of ale?"

Ben turned. "Are you hiding a picnic basket in one of those pouches?"

"A what? Oh, no, High Lord. I will simply conjure up our meal."

"Conjure . . . ? Ben frowned. "You mean use magic?"

"Exactly! After all, I am a wizard. Now, let me see."

The owlish face screwed up, the shaggy brows narrowing. Ben leaned forward. He had eaten nothing since breakfast, but he was more curious than hungry. Could this odd-looking fellow really do magic?

"A bit of concentrated thought, fingers extended so, a quick motion thus, and . . . hah!"

There was a flash of light, a quick puff of smoke, and on the ground before them lay half a dozen scatter pillows, tasseled and embroidered. Ben stared in amazement.

"Oh, well, we will need something to sit upon while we eat, I suppose." The wizard brushed the matter aside as if it were of no consequence. "Must have turned the fingers a bit too far right . . . Now let me see, once again, a bit of thought, fingers, a quick motion . . ."

Again the light flashed, the smoke puffed, and on the ground before them appeared a crate of eggs and an entire pig dressed out and resplendent with an apple in its mouth.

Questor glanced hurriedly at Ben. "The magic is fickle on occasion. But one simply tries harder." He stretched forth his sticklike arms from his robes. "Here, now, watch closely. Thoughts concentrated, fingers turned, a quick motion, and . . ."

The light flashed brighter, the smoke puffed higher, and from out of nowhere a massive tressel table laden with food enough for an army materialized before them. Ben jumped back in surprise. Questor Thews could certainly do magic as he claimed, but it appeared his control of it was rather limited.

"Drat, that is not what I . . . the thing of it is, that . . ." Questor was thoroughly agitated. He glared at the table of food. "I am simply tired, I imagine. I will try once again . . ."

"Never mind," Ben interrupted quickly. He had seen enough of the magic for one sitting. The wizard looked over, displeased. "I mean, I'm really not that hungry after all. Maybe we should just go on."

Questor hesitated, then nodded curtly. "If that is your wish, High Lord—very well." He gave a quick motion with one hand, and the pillows, the pig, the crate of eggs and the entire tressel table with its meal disappeared into air. "You see that I have the magic at my command when I wish it," he announced stiffly.

"Yes, I see that."

"You must understand that the magic I wield is most important, High Lord." Questor was determined to make his point. "You will have need of my magic if you are to be King. There have always been wizards to stand behind the Kings of Landover."

"I understand."

Questor stared at him. He stared back. What he understood above everything, he thought to himself, was that, except for this half-baked wizard, he was all alone in a land he knew almost nothing at all about and he had no desire to alienate his one companion.

"Well, then." Questor's ruffled feathers seemed suddenly back in place. He looked almost sheepish. "I suppose that we should continue on to the castle, High Lord."

Ben nodded. "I suppose we should."

Wordlessly, they resumed their journey.

The afternoon wore on; as it did so, the mists seemed to thicken across the land. The cast of the day dimmed, shadows gathered in dark pools, and the color of the fields, meadows, forests and the lakes and rivers scattered through them lost all hint of vibrancy. There was a sullen feel to the air as if a storm might be approaching, though clearly none was. The sun still shone, and no wind stirred the leaves of the trees. Another moon hung suspended against the skyline, newly risen from beneath the mists.

Ben was still wondering what he had gotten himself into.

It was becoming increasingly apparent to him that Landover was nothing of the sham that Miles Bennett had envisioned. The creatures were not courtesy of the San Diego Zoo and the inhabitants were not supplied by Central Casting. The magic that Questor had performed was not the old rabbit-in-the-hat variety, but magic of a sort imagined in newsstand pulp fantasy. By God, would Miles have been astonished by that table and twenty-course dinner trick! How could anyone possibly conjure something like that up so quickly unless they truly were in a fantasy world where magic was real?

That was the other side of the coin he toyed with, unfortunately. Landover was really not a part of Virginia or the United States or North America or anywhere else on Earth. Landover was a whole other world entirely, and he had somehow stepped through a time zone to reach it.

Damn, it was exciting and terrifying all at once!

He had wanted this, of course. He had made the purchase understanding that he was going to a fantasy world, that he was buying the throne to a fantasy kingdom. But he had never imagined that it could actually be. He had never thought that it would turn out to be just exactly what the promo and old Meeks had said it would be.

He thought suddenly of Annie and wished she were here with him. She would have been able to help him accept what was happening, he thought. But Annie was not here, and it was because he had lost her that he had come in the first place. Landover was his escape from what her loss had cost him.

He shook his head admonishingly. He must remember that he had come to this world to renew his life, to leave behind the old, to find a different existence from what he had known. He had intended to cut all of his ties; he had wanted to begin again. That being so, it was foolish to bemoan the fact that he might have gotten exactly what he had wanted.

Besides, the challenge it presented intrigued him beyond anything he had ever known.

He mulled matters over in silence, letting Questor lead the way. The wizard had not volunteered any further information since the aborted luncheon, and Ben thought that he might be well advised not to ask any more questions of the man for the time being. He concentrated instead on studying the land about them; first, what was visible from the high slope during their descent and, later, what could be seen more closely from the valley floor. They were traveling east, he concluded, if the sun's passage through the skies was an accurate compass. Mountains ringed the valley and the mist lay over everything. Lake and river country comprised the south end of the valley, desert and scrubland the east, hills the north and heavy woods the west. The center of the valley was a green flatland of fields and meadows. There were castles in the central plains; he had glimpsed their towers through the mist. There was a very dark, very unpleasant-looking hollows north and west, a deep bowl that seemed to gather mist and shadows until they stirred like steaming soup. He viewed all this during their descent from the meadow where Questor had found him; when they reached the valley floor he saw his first people. They were an unimpressive bunch—farmers with their families, woodsmen and hunters, a few stray traders with their wares, and a single rider bearing an heraldic banner of some sort. Except for the rider, the rest looked rather downtrodden. Their clothes were poor, their tools and wagons battered, and their stock worn. The homes of the farmers had seen better days and lacked any decent upkeep. Everyone seemed tired.

Ben saw all of this from some distance off, including the

people, so he could not be entirely certain that he was seeing it accurately. Nevertheless, he didn't think he was mistaken.

Questor Thews said nothing about any of it.

It was mid-afternoon when he turned Ben suddenly north. A stretch of wooded hills lay before them, shrouded in trailers of mist that hung across the trees like factory smoke. They passed through in silence, picking their way cautiously where limbs and leaves left the pathway in shadow. They were well north of the lake and river country Ben had seen earlier, yet a sudden cluster of lakes and ponds came into view through the trees, bits of dark water mirroring the muted sunlight in bright splashes. Trailers of mist hung over these as well. Ben glanced about uneasily. There was in these woods a hint of the look and feel that had been present in the fairy world.

They climbed a high ridgeline that rose above the forest trees, and Questor brought Ben to a halt. "Look down there, High Lord," he said and pointed.

Ben looked. Several miles off, ringed in a gathering of trees, mist and shadows was a clearing that shimmered with sunlight. Colors reflected brightly, a rainbow's mix, and there seemed to be flags waving softly in a forest breeze that did not reach to the ridge on which Ben stood.

Questor's arm swept down again. "That is the Heart, High Lord. There you will be crowned King of Landover several days hence when the proclamation of your coming has been sent. Every King that Landover has ever had has been crowned there—every King since Landover came into being."

They stood on the ridgeline a moment longer, staring downward into that single spot of brightness amid the haze of mist and shadows. Neither spoke.

Then Questor turned away. "Come, High Lord. Your castle lies just ahead."

Ben followed dutifully after.

Sterling
Silver

The trees closed about, the mists came up, and Questor Thews and Ben Holiday were back within the forest. Shadows darkened the pathway anew, and the colors and feel of the Heart were gone. Ben pushed his way resolutely forward, keeping pace with the shambling figure of the wizard. It was not easy, for Questor covered ground rapidly despite his odd gait. Ben shifted the duffel from one arm to the other, feeling the muscles cramping with stiffness. He rubbed at his shoulders with his free hand and pushed up the sleeves of the running suit. There was sweat soaking through the back of his pullover.

One would think they could free up an escort and carriage for their new King, instead of making him hike it in, he groused inwardly. On the other hand, maybe they didn't use carriages in Landover. Maybe they flew on winged horses. Maybe Questor Thews should have conjured up a couple of those.

He chewed thoughtfully at his lower lip, remembering Questor's attempts at providing lunch. Maybe he was better off hiking.

They climbed toward a new ridgeline of blue spruce grown so thick that pine needles formed a carpet on the forest earth.

Boughs pushed and slapped at their faces, and they bent their heads against them. Then the trees broke apart, the far side of the ridgeline dropped away into meadow, and the castle stood before them.

Ben Holiday stared. It was the same castle he had seen before—only now he could see it clearly. It sat half a mile distant within a lake upon an island just large enough to support it. The lake was iron gray, the island bare of everything but wintry scrub. The castle was a maze of stone and wood and metal towers, parapets, causeways, and walks that thrust into the sky like fingers of a broken hand. A shroud of mist hung across the whole of the island and the waters of the lake and stirred thickly in a sunless cauldron. There was no color anywhere—no flags, no standards, no banners, nothing. The stone and wood had a soiled look, and the metal appeared to have discolored. Though the mortar and block seemed sound and the bulwarks did not crumble, still the castle had the look of a lifeless shell.

It had the look of something out of Dracula.

"This is the castle of the Kings of Landover?" Ben asked incredulously.

"Hmmmmm?" Questor was preoccupied again. "Oh, yes, this is it. This is Sterling Silver."

Ben dropped his duffel with a thud. "Sterling Silver?"

"That is her name."

"Sterling Silver—as in bright and polished?"

Questor's eyebrows lifted. "She was that once, High Lord."

"She was, was she? Once upon a time, a very long time ago, I'll bet." A well of disappointment opened in the pit of his stomach. "She looks more like Dingy Dungeon than Sterling Silver."

"That is the result of the Tarnish." The wizard folded his arms over his chest and looked out across the meadow. "Twenty years she has been like this, High Lord—not so long, really. The Tarnish has done it. Before, she was bright and polished as the name implies. The stone was white, the wood clean and the metal shining. There were no mists to block the sun. The island was alive with flowers of every color and the lake was crystal blue. It was the most beautiful place in the land."

Ben followed his gaze back to the nightmare that waited below. "So what happened to change all that?"

"The Tarnish. When the last true King of Landover died twenty years ago and no heir ascended to the throne, the discoloration began. It was gradual at first, but quickened as time passed and no King ruled. The life goes out of Sterling Silver, and the Tarnish marks her failing. No amount of cleaning or scrubbing or polishing of stone, wood, and metal can restore her." He glanced over. "She dies, High Lord. She follows her Lord to the grave."

Ben blinked. "You speak of her as if she were alive."

The owlish face nodded. "So she is, High Lord—as alive as you or I."

"But she's dying?"

"Slowly and painfully."

"And that is where you want me to live—in a dying castle?"

Questor smiled. "You must. You are the only one who can heal her." He took Ben's arm and propelled him ahead. "Come along now, High Lord. You will find her quite pleasant on the inside, where her heart is still warm and her life still strong. Things are not really so bad as they might seem. Come, now. You will find her very much a home. Come."

They descended the ridgeline through the meadow to where the waters of the lake lapped softly against a bank of marshy grasses. Weeds grew in thick tufts where the shoreline had eroded and stagnant pools had formed. Frogs croaked and insects hummed, and the lake smelled faintly fishy.

There was a long boat with a curved prow and knight's head, low gunwales, and rudderless stern pulled up upon the banks. Questor motioned, and they climbed aboard. Ben moved to a forward seat while Questor sat in the stern. They had just settled themselves when the boat began to move. It lurched free of the lake shore and slipped quietly into its waters. Ben looked about curiously. He could discover no source of propulsion for the boat.

"The touch of your hands lends it direction," Questor said suddenly.

Ben stared down at his hands as they gripped the gunnels. "My hands?"

"The boat, like the castle, is alive. It is called a lake skimmer. It responds to the touch of those it serves. You are now foremost of those. Will it to carry you and it shall do so."

"Where shall I will it to carry me?"

Questor laughed gently. "Why, to the front door, High Lord."

Ben gripped the gunnels and conveyed the thought silently. The lake skimmer sped swiftly across the dark waters, leaving a white swale in the wake of its passing.

"Slowly, High Lord, slowly," Questor admonished. "You convey your thoughts too urgently."

Ben relaxed his grip and his thoughts, and the lake skimmer slowed. It was exciting, having use of this small magic. He let his fingers brush softly across the smooth wood of the gunwales. It was warm and vibrant. It had the feel of a living thing.

"Questor?" He turned back to the wizard. The sense of life in the lake skimmer bothered him, but he kept his hands in place. "What was it you said before about my healing the castle?"

The fingers of one hand came up to rub the owlish face. "Sterling Silver, like Landover, is in need of a King. The castle fails without one. Your presence within the castle renews her life. When you make her your home, that life will be fully sustained once more."

Ben glanced ahead to the spectral apparition with its dark towers and battlements, its discolored stone walls and vacant eyes. "What if I don't want to make her my home?"

"Oh, I think you will," the wizard replied enigmatically.

Think whatever you want, Ben thought without saying it. His eyes stayed on the approaching castle, on the mist and shadows that shrouded it. He expected at any moment to see something with fangs appear at the windows of the highest tower and to see bats circling watchfully.

He saw, however, nothing.

The lake skimmer grounded gently on the island banks, and Ben and Questor disembarked. An arched entry with raised portcullis stood before them, an open invitation to be swallowed whole. Ben shifted the duffel from one hand to the other, hesitating. If anything, the castle looked worse close up than it had from the ridge crest.

"Questor, I'm not sure about . . ."

"Come, High Lord," the wizard interrupted, again taking his arm, again propelling him ahead. "You cannot see anything worthwhile from out here. Besides, the others will be waiting."

Ben stumbled forward, eyes shifting nervously upward along the parapets and towers; the stone was damp and the corners and crevices a maze of spider webs. "Others? What others?"

"Why, the others who stand in service to the throne—your staff, High Lord. Not all have left the service of the King."

"Not all?"

But Questor either didn't hear him or simply ignored him, hurrying ahead, forcing Ben to walk more quickly to keep pace. They passed from the entry through a narrow court as dark and dingy in appearance as the rest of the castle and from there through a second entry, smaller than the first, down a short hall and into a foyer. Misty light slipped through high, arched windows, mixing with the gloom and shadows. Ben glanced about. The wood of the supports and stays was polished and clean, the stone scrubbed, and the walls and floors covered in rugs and tapestries that had retained some of their original color. There were even a few pieces of stiff-looking furniture. Had it not been for the gray cast that seemed to permeate everything, the room would have been almost cheerful.

"You see, things are much better inside," Questor insisted.

Ben nodded without enthusiasm. "Lovely."

They crossed to a door that opened into a cavernous dining hall with a huge tressel table and high-backed chairs cushioned in scarlet silk. Chandeliers of tarnished silver hung from the ceiling; despite the summer weather, a fire burned in a hearth at the far end of the hall. Ben followed Questor into the hall and stopped.

Three figures stood in a line to the right of the dining table. Their eyes met his.

"Your personal staff, High Lord," Questor announced.

Ben stared. The staff consisted of a dog and two large-eared monkeys—or at least two creatures very like monkeys. The dog stood upright on its hind legs and wore breeches with suspenders, a tunic with heraldic insignia, and glasses. Its coat was golden in color, and it had small flaps for ears that looked as if they might have been tacked on as an afterthought. The hair on its head and muzzle made it appear as if it were half porcupine. The creatures that looked like monkeys wore short pants and leather cross-belts from waist to shoulder. One was taller and spindle-legged. The other was heavy and wore a cook's apron. Both had ears like Dumbo and prehensile toes.

Questor motioned to Ben, and they moved forward to stop before the dog. "This is Abernathy, court scribe and your personal attendant."

The dog bowed slightly and looked at him over the rims of the glasses. "Welcome, High Lord," the dog said.

Ben jumped back in surprise. "Questor, he talks!"

"As well as you do, High Lord," the dog replied stiffly.

"Abernathy is a soft-coated Wheaten Terrier—a breed that has produced a good many champion hunting dogs," Questor interjected. "He was not always a dog, however.

He was a man before he was a dog. He became a dog through a rather unfortunate accident.''

"I became a dog through your stupidity." Abernathy's voice was very close to a canine growl. "I have remained a dog through your stupidity."

Questor shrugged. "Well, yes, it was my fault in a way, I suppose." He sighed, glancing at Ben. "I was trying to disguise him and the magic made him thus. Unfortunately, I have not as yet discovered a way to change him back again. But he does quite well as a dog, don't you, Abernathy?"

"I did better as a man."

Questor frowned. "I would have to dispute that, I think."

"That is because you must find some way to justify what you did, Questor Thews. Had I not retained my intelligence—which, fortunately, is considerably higher than your own—I would undoubtedly have been placed in some kennel and forgotten!"

"That is most unkind." The frown deepened. "Perhaps you would have preferred it if I had changed you into a cat!"

Abernathy's reply came out a bark. Questor started and flushed. "I understood that, Abernathy, and I want you to know that I don't appreciate it. Remember where you are. Remember that this is the King you stand before."

Abernathy's shaggy face regarded Ben solemnly. "So much the worse for him."

Questor shot him a dark look, then turned to the creatures standing next to him. "These are kobolds," Questor advised Ben, who was still struggling with the idea that his personal attendant was a talking dog. "They speak their own language and will have nothing to do with ours, though they understand it well enough. They have names in their own language, but the names would mean nothing to you. I have therefore given them names of my own, which they have agreed to accept. The taller is Bunion, the court runner. The heavier is Parsnip, the court chef." He motioned to the two. "Give greeting to the High Lord, kobolds."

The kobolds bowed. When they straightened, their mouths

parted to reveal rows of sharpened teeth behind frightening smiles. They hissed softly.

"Parsnip is a true kobold," Questor said. "He is a fairy creature who has chosen open service to the household of a human rather than a haunting. His tribe is one of those that drifted out of the fairy world and stayed. Bunion is a wight, more a woods creature than a domestic. Generically, he is a kobold, but he retains characteristics of other fairy creatures as well. He can pass through the mists as they, though he cannot remain. He can cross through Landover with the swiftness of the fairies as well. But he is bound to Sterling Silver in the same fashion as Parsnip and must always return."

"For reasons that man and dog can only surmise," Abernathy interjected.

Bunion grinned at him blackly and hissed.

Ben pulled Questor Thews aside. It was with some effort that he managed to conceal his irritation. "Exactly what is going on here?"

"Hmmmmm?" Questor stared back at him blankly.

"Read my lips. If I'm understanding all of this correctly, the King of Landover lives in a dungeon and is attended by a menagerie. Are there any more surprises in store for me? What have I got for an army—a herd of cattle?"

The wizard looked slightly embarrassed. "Well, as a matter of fact, High Lord, you don't have any kind of army at all."

"No army? Why is that?"

"It disbanded—more than a dozen years ago, I'm afraid."

"Disbanded? Well, what about retainers—workers, servants, people to look after things in general? Who does that?"

"We do—the four of us." Questor Thews made a sweeping gesture back to Abernathy and the two kobolds.

Ben stared. "No wonder the castle is dying. Why don't you bring in some more help, for God's sake?"

"We have no money to pay them."

"What do you mean, you don't have any money? Don't you have a royal treasury or whatever?"

"The treasury is empty. There isn't a coin in it."

"Well, doesn't the throne tax in some fashion so that there should be money?" Ben's voice was getting louder. "How did Kings pay for anything in the past?"

"They taxed." Questor glanced angrily at Abernathy, who was shaking his head in amusement. "Unfortunately, the taxing system broke down some years ago. Nothing has been paid into the treasury since."

Ben dropped his duffel and put his hands on his hips. "Let me get this straight. I bought a kingdom where the King has no army, no staff but the four of you, and no money? I paid a million dollars for that?"

"You are being unreasonable, Ben Holiday."

"That depends on whose shoes you're standing in, I'd say!"

"You must be patient. You have not yet seen all that there is to see nor learned all that there is to learn of Landover. The immediate problems of taxes and retainers and an army can be solved once proper attention is given to the finding of the solutions. You must remember that there has been no King in Landover for more than twenty years. Since that is so, you must expect that not all will be as it should."

Ben laughed without humor. "There's the understatement of the year. Look, Questor, let's get to the heart of the matter. What else should I know about being King of Landover? What other bad news have you got to tell?"

"Oh, I think that is about the worst of it, High Lord." The wizard smiled disarmingly. "We will have time enough to discuss it all later, but I think a bit of dinner is in order first. It has been a long day, a long journey, and I know that you are tired and hungry both."

Ben cut him short. "I am not that tired or that hungry, damn it! I want to know what else you've been . . ."

"All in good time, all in good order—you have your health to consider, High Lord," Questor intoned, ignoring him.

"Parsnip will prepare our meal—the castle's magic still keeps her larder well stocked—and while he is doing so, Abernathy will show you to your rooms where you may wash, take a change of clothes, and rest a bit. Abernathy, please escort the High Lord to his bedchamber and see that he has what he needs. I will be along in a while."

He turned and strode from the room before Ben had a chance to object further. Parsnip and Bunion exited as well. Ben was left staring at Abernathy.

"High Lord?" The dog beckoned to a spiral staircase that wound upward into the castle dark.

Ben nodded wordlessly. He was obviously not going to learn anything more for the moment.

"Lay on, Macduff," he sighed.

Together, they began to climb.

It proved to be a rather healthy trek. They climbed numerous stairs and followed half a dozen shadowed halls before reaching the appointed rooms. Ben spent most of the time lost in thought, pondering the unpleasant news that he was a King without any of the trappings, that he was Lord over Castle Dracula and not much else. He should have been paying closer attention to where he was going, he chided himself when they finally arrived, if for no other reason than to be able to find his way back again without help. He had a faint recollection of stone-block floors and wooden-beamed ceilings, of oak doors and iron fastenings, of tapestries and coats of arms, of muted colors and the discoloration of the Tarnish—but not much more than that.

"Your bath chamber, High Lord," Abernathy announced, halting before a heavy wooden door carved in scroll.

Ben peered inside. There was an iron tub with clawed feet and scrolled sides filled with steaming water, a tray with soaps, a pile of linen towels, with a change of clothing and a pair of boots stacked on a stool.

The bath looked inviting. "How did you manage to keep

the water hot all this time?'' he asked, wondering suddenly at the steam.

"The castle, High Lord. She still retains something of her magic. Food for the larder, hot water for baths—that is about all she has strength enough left for.'' Abernathy cut himself short and started to leave.

"Wait!'' Ben called suddenly. The dog stopped. "I, uh . . . I just want to tell you that I'm sorry that I acted so surprised that you could talk. I didn't mean to be rude.''

"I am quite accustomed to it, High Lord,'' Abernathy replied, and Ben didn't know if he meant the rudeness or the surprise. The dog peered at him from over the rims of his glasses. "In any case, though I am recognized everywhere within Landover as a major curiosity, I doubt that I will prove to be the biggest surprise that you will encounter.''

Ben frowned. "Meaning what?''

"Meaning that you have a lot to learn, and the lessons are likely to be rather astonishing.''

He bowed perfunctorily, backed through the door and closed it silently behind him. Ben's frown deepened. That last comment sounded almost like a warning, he thought. It sounded as if Abernathy was advising him that the worst was yet to come.

He brushed the matter from his mind, stripped off his clothes, lowered himself into the tub of water and lay back blissfully to soak. He remained in the tub for the better part of the hour that followed, thinking over all that had happened to him. Oddly enough, the focus of his concern had shifted completely since his arrival in Landover. Then, his concern had been with whether or not what he was seeing and experiencing was real or induced by clever special effects and the ingenuity of modern science. Now, his concern was with whether or not he should be here at all. Questor's revelations about the condition of the kingship were disheartening at best. He had paid a million dollars for a throne that commanded no retainers, no army, no treasury, and no taxing program. He found himself more inclined to accept that Landover was indeed a world apart from his own, a world in which magic really *did* function, than to accept that he had purchased a throne that commanded nothing.

Still, he wasn't being entirely fair, he chided. He had paid for a throne, but he had also paid for the land—and the land seemed to be exactly as advertised. Moreover, he had to expect that after twenty years with no King sitting on the throne, Landover's monarchy was likely to be floundering somewhat. He couldn't reasonably expect that a working tax system, a standing army, a body of retainers, and a full treasury would survive twenty years of no King. Matters would quite naturally get out of hand after a while. It was logical that there should be some work required of him to get things moving again.

So what was he worried about? When measured against his initial expectations, Landover was far more than he could ever have hoped for, wasn't it?

But Abernathy's veiled warning and his own doubts nagged at him nevertheless, and he could not seem to set the matter to rest. He finished his bath and climbed from the tub, toweling dry. The water in the tub had stayed an even temperature the entire time he was bathing. The room felt comfortable as well—even the stone of the floor was warm against the soles of his bare feet. There was an odd sense of vibrancy in the air, as if the castle were breathing . . .

He cut short the thought, unwilling to pursue it further just then, and began to dress. He pulled on stockings, some loose undergarments that fastened together with stays, a pair of forest green breeches with ties and a belt, and a loose fitting cream tunic with loops that slipped over metal hooks. The makeup of the ensemble seemed strange to him—the whole of it free of the buttons, zippers, Velcro fastenings and elastic bands that he was accustomed to—but the fit was good and he felt comfortable dressed in it.

He had just finished pulling on the pair of soft leather boots and was wondering what had become of Abernathy when the door opened and Questor appeared.

"Well, you seem rested and refreshed, High Lord." The wizard smiled—rather too broadly, Ben thought. "Was the bath satisfactory?"

"Quite." Ben smiled back. "Questor, why don't we cut through all this bull, and get . . ."

"This what?"

"Bull." Ben hesitated, searching for a better word. "Smokescreen."

"Smokescreen?"

"The social amenities of Kingship, damn it! I want to know what I've gotten myself into!"

Questor cocked his head thoughtfully. "Oh, I see. How would it be if I were to show you exactly that?"

Ben nodded at once. "That would be fine. That would be wonderful, in fact."

"Very well." The wizard turned and started from the room. "Come with me, please."

They exited the bath chamber and passed back into the hall. Questor took Ben deep into the castle where a pair of massive scrolled doors opened into a tower well with a staircase that spiraled upward into shadow. Wordlessly, they began to climb. When they had reached the landing at the head of the stairs, Questor had Ben press his palms firmly against a crest of the medallion's image of castle and knight that was graven into a massive oak and metal-bound door seated in the tower wall. The door opened soundlessly, and they stepped inside.

They were in a small, circular room. The wall before them opened halfway around from floor to ceiling into clouds of mist that swirled past the towers of the castle as they rose darkly against the coming night. A silver guardrail on stanchions curved at waist height across the opening. A silver lectern was fastened at its midpoint. Ben looked at it momentarily, then looked at Questor. The room had the appearance of a speaker's platform designed to permit royal addresses to whatever audience could be found in the clouds.

"This is the Landsview," Questor said. "Step over to the rail, please."

Ben did as directed. The silver of the rail and lectern was stained with the Tarnish, but, beneath the discoloring, Ben could see thousands of tiny characters scrolled into the metal, etched by the hand of some enormously patient craftsman. Questor fumbled through the pouches he wore strapped about his waist and after a moment produced the same worn map that he had shown Ben earlier when explaining why it was that Ben could speak and read Landoverian.

He unfolded the map carefully and placed it on the lectern.

"Place your hands upon the railing before you, High Lord," he said.

Ben did so. Questor put his hands upon the railing as well. They stood together that way for a moment, staring out into the darkening mist. It was almost dusk.

Then a sudden warmth spread through the metal, a vibrancy of the sort that Ben had experienced in the bath chamber.

"Keep your hands firmly fixed upon the railing," Questor admonished suddenly. "Look at the map before you and select anything drawn upon it that you wish to see. The Landsview will show it to you."

Ben glanced over at him doubtfully, then looked down at the map. The whole of the valley was inscribed on the parchment, inked in various colors to designate forests, rivers, lakes, mountains, plains, valleys, deserts, towns, territories, and castle keeps, the names of all meticulously marked throughout. The colors were faded, the parchment worn. Ben squinted. His eyes came to rest after a moment on Sterling Silver and then on the dark and forbidding hollows he had seen earlier from the heights. The name of the hollows was smudged and illegible.

"There," he indicated, inclining his head. "That hollows north of here. Show me that."

"The Deep Fell." Questor spoke softly. "Very well. Grip

the railing tightly, High Lord. Take a deep breath. Concentrate on the map."

Ben's hands tightened. His eyes locked on the map and the hollows marked upon it. The mists that shrouded Sterling Silver swirled in murky trailers before him, and the darkness of coming night slipped across the land. Time froze. He glanced curiously at Questor.

"Concentrate on the map, High Lord."

He looked back at the map, concentrating.

Then the whole of the castle fell away beneath him, stone block walls, towers, and battlements dissipating into empty air, the mists faded and the night sky shone clear and starlit all about him. He was flying through space with only the silver railing and lectern wrapped about him for support. His eyes widened in shock, and he stared downward. Below, the valley sped away in a void of shadows and moonlight.

"Questor!" he cried out in terror, arms stiffening to brace his fall.

The wizard was next to him. One hand slid across to squeeze his.

"Do not be frightened, High Lord," he said. His voice was calm and reassuring, so normal in tone that they might still have been standing within the tower. "It is only the magic at work," he continued. "You are in no danger while you hold fast to the railing."

Ben was holding on so tightly that his knuckles had turned white. He was firmly anchored, he discovered. While there was the sensation of movement, he could neither feel nor hear the wind rush past and no air stirred the parchment map. He held his breath and watched the land sweep away hundreds of feet below, a panorama of shadowed forests, jutting mountains and shimmering lakes. Landover's moons had all risen into view now, a gathering of colored spheres dotting the heavens—peach, burnt rose, jade, beryl, sea green, a sort of washed-out mauve, turquoise, and the largest of all, a brilliant white. It was the strangest display that Ben had ever witnessed, a kind of still life fourth-of-July.

He relaxed a bit now, beginning to feel more at ease with what was happening to him. He had ridden in a hot air balloon once. This flight had something of the feel of that.

They circled the valley's mountains in a slow arc, crossing above the mists of the fairy world.

"There is where Landover's magic is born, High Lord." Questor spoke suddenly. "The fairy world is the source of her magic—a place of timelessness and infinite being, of everywhere and always. It borders on all worlds and has access to all. Corridors pass through it, linking the worlds without. Time passages, they are called—pathways that lead from one world to another. You took one of those pathways when you passed from your world into Landover."

"Do you mean that the fairy world lies *between* my world and Landover?" Ben asked, realizing suddenly that he was shouting to be heard and that it was quite unnecessary.

Questor shook his head. "Not exactly. The fairy world is an ephemeral place of non-being, High Lord. It is and at the same time it isn't, being both everywhere and nowhere all at once. It cannot be self-contained nor is it the final source of all things. Do you understand?"

Ben smiled. "Not a word."

"Think of it in this way, then. It is closer to Landover than to any of the other worlds it touches upon. Landover is a sort of stepchild."

An odd comparison, Ben thought and watched the mists slip away. Then they were descending, dropping swiftly toward the Deep Fell. The hollows lay directly below them, a tangled stretch of wilderness forest nestled close to the high mountains that formed the northwest corner of the valley's perimeter, a dismal and forbidding wood that light could not seem to penetrate. Shadows lay over everything, and the mists of the fairy world that ringed the valley seemed to reach downward and drape across it like the corner of a blanket.

"There dwells the witch Nightshade." Questor spoke again. "It is said that she crossed over from the fairy world in a time so distant it has been forgotten by all but her. It is said that she came into the world of mortals to take a lover and that, having done so, she can never go back again."

Ben stared downward into the black. It had the look of a pit that bored all the way to hell.

Once more, they swept away across the land. They sped from horizon to horizon, Ben's eyes picking out names inscribed upon the parchment map, one landmark after the other. He found the country of the River Master, another creature of the fairy world, a spirit who had assimilated into human form and adopted as his home the lakes and rivers that dominated the southern half of the valley, ruling over the sprites and nymphs that dwelt within their waters. Ben explored the hills and steeps north above the smudge of the Deep Fell, where lived numerous tribes of gnomes, trolls, and kobolds. Some were miners, farmers, hunters, and tradesmen, some thieves and cutthroats; some were industrious and honest, some shiftless and malicious; some were friendly and some not. Questor was speaking now. The Lords of the Greensward laid claim to the whole of the central valley, their vast holdings of farmland and stock the wealth of a few families whose lineage could be traced back generations, feudal barons whose subjects were thralls working the crops and animals for their masters.

"Slaves?" Ben interrupted sharply, appalled.

"Thralls!" Questor repeated, emphasizing the word. "These are men and women of free will; but they receive of the land and its bounty only what is allocated to them by the barons."

Slaves, Ben thought to himself. A rose by any other name . . .

Questor's voice droned on, but Ben missed the rest of what he was saying, his attention diverted suddenly to something new. He thought it at first to be nothing more than a peculiar speck of darkness against the silhouette of one of Landover's moons. Then he realized that the speck was moving.

It was moving toward them.

It flew out of the south, a huge, winged shadow that grew

in size against the horizon. Featureless when Ben caught sight of it, it began to take more definite shape as it approached. Leathered wings flared, spined and arched like the struts of a monstrous kite stretched to its breaking point. A barrel-shaped body undulated like a serpent's with the flying motion, its hide covered with scales and plates. Great, clawed feet tucked against its body, and its neck arched snakelike above it, flared behind a head so odious to look upon that Ben flinched in spite of himself.

It was the dragon.

"Questor!" Ben whispered hoarsely, afraid to shout.

The wizard turned, and his head lifted toward the great beast. "Strabo!" he whispered in reply, and there was something almost like reverence in his voice.

They ceased to move then, frozen suddenly in midair. The dragon flew past them, so close that it seemed it would brush against them. It did not see them, for they were not truly to be seen—but it appeared to Ben as if it sensed their presence. The crusted head swept over so that its blooded eyes fixed on them, and its jagged snout split wide. A sharp, frightening hiss ripped through the stillness of the night, lingering and dying slowly into silence.

But the dragon did not slow or change course. Northeast it flew until it had become a distant speck once more. They stared after it until it was gone.

"My God!" Ben said finally, his voice still a whisper. His thirst for adventure was suddenly quenched. He stared down wildly at the empty space that spread away beneath him, the space in which they still hung, unmoving. "Damn it, I've had enough of this, Questor! Take us back to where we came from!"

"The map, High Lord," the wizard said calmly. "Fix your eyes upon the map and seek out Sterling Silver."

Ben did so at once, almost frantic to have his feet back upon solid stone. He found the designation for the castle and concentrated his thoughts upon it. Almost instantly he was back within the tower, standing before the open wall, staring out into the mists.

He released the railing as if it burned him and stepped quickly back. "That beast . . . that was the dragon that I stumbled on in the forest!" he snapped.

"Yes, High Lord, it was," the other agreed, turning away from the railing with him. The owlish face was contemplative. "Strabo is his name. He lives east where the valley is a wasteland of desert, marsh and scrub. He lives alone there, the last of his kind."

Ben folded his arms into his chest, suddenly cold. "He was close enough to touch."

"It only seemed so." Questor's smile was wry. "The magic made it appear that way. In truth, we never left this room."

"Never left?"

"You may try it yourself sometime, High Lord. The magic of the Landsview is yours to wield—and you have seen for yourself how it works."

"All too well, thank you."

"Have you learned enough about Landover for tonight, then? Would you like to have dinner now?"

Ben had regained his composure. "Dinner would be fine." He took a deep breath. "Are there any surprises that go with it? If there are, I would like to know about them now—not after the fact."

The wizard pushed his way back through the tower door. "No, High Lord. There should be no surprises with dinner. It should be quite pleasant. Come along."

They trekked back through the corridors and stairwells of the castle until they had again reached the dining hall. Ben still had questions that needed answers, but he was weary and he was hungry and the questions could wait. He let himself be led to the head of the tressel table and seated. His stomach was beginning to settle again, the chill to leave his body. He had survived after all, with no apparent damage. So if that was the worst that he was to endure . . .

"Would you care for some wine, High Lord?" Questor interrupted his thoughts. The day was gone, and the darkness of the castle was deepening. The wizard lifted his hand and pointed, and the chandeliers came alive with light, a soft golden glow that was flameless and smokeless, yet had no apparent power source. "Another little touch of the magic." The other smiled. "Did you say you wanted wine?"

Ben slumped back in his chair. "Yes—and leave the bottle."

Questor gestured, and the wine appeared at his elbow. The wizard had taken a seat on his right. Abernathy and Bunion appeared and sat on his left. Parsnip would undoubtedly join them after bringing out the dinner. They were just one, big, happy family.

Ben faced the wizard. "I'll say it once more, Questor— no more surprises. I want to know everything. I want to know about the medallion. I want to know about Meeks. I want to know who sold Landover and why. I want to know all of it."

Abernathy put his paws on the table and looked at Ben from over the rims of his glasses. "I would drink the wine first, High Lord, if I were you."

The shaggy face glanced knowingly at Bunion seated next to him. The kobold smiled and hissed and showed all of his teeth.

Ben reached for the wine.

He had consumed a good portion of the bottle before Parsnip reappeared with dinner. The kobold brought a stew made of beef and vegetables, fresh-baked bread, cheeses and pastries. Whatever else was wrong, no one was starving to death, he thought.

He ate a bowl of the stew with pieces of bread and cheese, drank several glasses of wine and thought about Annie and Miles and what he had left behind. Questor and Abernathy argued about everything from the nature of a balanced meal to the role of magic in health care. The kobolds grinned and ate everything in sight. When it came time for seconds, Questor found the stew too cold and suggested it be reheated. Parsnip hissed and showed his teeth, and Abernathy suggested it was better served cold. Questor disagreed. The argument was resolved when Questor used the magic to reheat it where it cooled in its kettle, and the kettle exploded in flames setting fire to the whole of the tressel table and the linen service set upon it. Everyone jumped up, yelling, hissing and barking all at once. Questor used the magic again, and this time it rained inside the dining hall for fifteen minutes.

That was enough for Ben. Wine glass in hand, Abernathy leading, he retired to the royal sleeping quarters, scorched and soaked and woozy. Tomorrow, he decided as he lay back within the coverings of his bed, would be a better day.

Coronation

Tomorrow might indeed have been a better day, but Ben Holiday never had a chance to find out.

He dreamed as he slept, dreams of truth and fantasy. He dreamed of Annie and of finding her alive again, his exhilaration at being with her and loving her blunted by a pervasive sense that she could not stay and he must lose her once more. He dreamed of Miles, bluff and cynical as he reminded Ben at every turn on a journey through a Chicago filled with Bonnie Blues that he had told him so. He dreamed of lawyers and courtrooms in which kobolds hissed from jury boxes and judges had the look of shaggy dogs. He dreamed of high rises and concrete parkways and soaring over all a dragon as black as night. He dreamed of demons and knights, of faces in the mist, and of castles that shone like the sun.

He dreamed, and the world slipped away from him.

When he came awake again, it was morning. He lay within his sleeping quarters, a vast chamber of tapestries and silken hangings, of polished oak and heraldic stone sculptures. He lay within his bed, a great canopied sarcophagus of oak and iron that looked as if it might successfully double as a barge. He knew it was morning by the slant of the light through the high arched windows, though the light remained gray and hazy as the mist without screened away its color. It was quiet within his room and quiet in the rooms without. The castle was like a stone shell.

Yet there was warmth in that castle. Sterling Silver was a dungeon to look upon and it lacked the visual appeal of even the most spartan, avant-garde, chrome-and-steel Chicago high rise, but it had the feel of a home. It was warm to the touch, from the floors that he had walked upon to the walls that he had brushed against. The warmth was in the air, despite the mist and the gray; it flowed through her like a life-blood. She was what Questor Thews had called her. She was a living thing.

Waking up inside of her felt right. It felt secure and comforting, the way it was supposed to feel when one woke within one's own home.

He stretched and glanced over to the nightstand on which he had placed his duffel and found Questor Thews sitting on a high-backed chair, looking at him.

"Good morrow, Ben Holiday," the wizard greeted him.

"Good morning," he replied. The good feelings evaporated in a rush as he remembered the wizard's gloomy revelation of the night before—that he was a King without retainers, army, or treasury.

"You rested well, I trust?" Questor asked.

"Quite well, thank you."

"Wonderful. You have a busy day before you."

"I do?"

"Yes, High Lord." Questor was beaming. "Today is your coronation. Today you shall be crowned King of Landover."

Ben blinked. "Today?" He blinked again. There was a sinking feeling in the pit of his stomach. "Wait a minute, Questor. What do you mean, *today* is the coronation? Wasn't it just yesterday that you were telling me that the coronation would not take place for at least *several* days because you needed time to inform all those that needed informing?"

"Well, ah . . . yes, I did say that, I admit." The wizard

screwed up his owlish face like a guilty child. "The trouble is, it wasn't yesterday that I said that."

"It wasn't yester . . . ?"

"Because this isn't tomorrow."

Ben flushed and sat up quickly in the bed. "Just what in the hell are you talking about?"

Questor Thews smiled. "High Lord, you have been asleep for a week."

Ben stared at him in silence. The wizard stared back. It was so quiet in the room that Ben could hear the sound of his own breathing in his ears.

"How could I have slept for a week?" he asked finally.

Questor steepled his hands before his face. "Do you remember the wine that you drank—the wine I provided?" Ben nodded. "Well, I added a dash of sleeping tonic to its content so that you would be assured of a good night's rest." He gestured with his hands. "It was in the magic I used, just an inflection of the voice and a twist." He demonstrated. "The trouble was, I overdid it. The dash became a thimbleful. So you have been asleep for a week."

"Just a little mistake of the magic, is that it?" Ben was flushed with anger.

Questor fidgeted uneasily. "I am afraid so."

"Well, I am afraid not! What sort of fool do you take me for? You did it on purpose, didn't you? You put me asleep to keep me here!" Ben was shaking, he was so mad. "Did you think I had forgotten the ten-day withdrawal clause in my contract? Ten days were allotted me to return to my own world if I wanted my money back, less the handling fee. Don't tell me you didn't know that! Now eight of those ten days are gone! It's all rather convenient, don't you think?"

"One minute, please." Questor had gone stiff with indignation. "If it were truly my intention to keep you in Landover, High Lord, I would not have bothered to tell you about the sleeping potion or the lost days of sleep *at all*! I would simply have let you think it was still only your second day in Landover and all *ten* days would have passed before you realized differently!''

Ben regarded him silently for a moment and then sat back. ''I guess you're right about that.'' He shook his head in disbelief. ''I suppose I owe you an apology, but frankly I'm too mad to apologize. I've lost a whole damn week because of you! And while I've been sleeping, you've gone right ahead with the plans for making me King—sent out the invitations and everything! Good thing I woke up on time, isn't it, or you would have been faced with a bedside coronation!''

''Oh, I knew you would awake on time after I discovered the problem,'' Questor hastened to assure him.

''You mean you *hoped* you knew,'' Abernathy interjected, appearing through the bedroom door with a tray. ''Breakfast, High Lord?''

He brought the tray over and set it on the nightstand. ''Thank you,'' Ben muttered, his eyes still fixed on Questor.

''I knew,'' the wizard said pointedly.

''Beautiful day for a coronation,'' Abernathy said. He looked at Ben over the rims of the glasses. ''I have your robes of office ready. They have been altered to fit exactly as they ought to.'' He paused. ''I had plenty of time to measure you while you slept.''

''I'll bet.'' Ben chewed angrily on a piece of bread. ''A whole week's worth of time, it appears.''

Abernathy shrugged. ''Not quite. The rest of us drank the wine as well, High Lord.''

''It was an honest mistake,'' Questor insisted, brows knitting.

''You make a lot of those,'' Abernathy sniffed.

''Perhaps it would please you if I simply quit trying to help at all!''

''Nothing would please me more!''

Ben held up his hands pleadingly. ''Hold it! Enough, already!'' He looked from one to the other. ''I don't need another argument. As a lawyer, I got my fill of arguments. I need answers. I said last night that I wanted to know the whole story behind the sale of this Kingdom—well, not last night, but the last time we talked, anyway. So maybe this is the time for it, Questor.''

The wizard rose, cast a dark glance at Abernathy, and looked back again at Ben. "You shall have your explanation, High Lord. But you must settle for hearing it as we travel to the Heart. The coronation must take place at noon, and we must leave at once in order to be there on time.''

Abernathy headed for the door. "His anticipation knows no bounds, I'm sure, wizard. High Lord, I will return with your robes shortly. Meanwhile, try eating a bit more of the breakfast. The castle's magic continues to fail, and we may all soon be foraging the countryside for sustenance.''

He left. Questor glared after him, then turned hastily to Ben. "I will only add, High Lord, that, with two days remaining, you have sufficient time to use the medallion to return to your own world—if that should be your wish.''

He hesitated, then followed Abernathy out. Ben watched them go. "A whole week,'' he muttered, shoved the breakfast tray aside, and climbed from the bed.

They set out within the hour—Ben, Questor, Abernathy, and the two kobolds. They left Sterling Silver and her barren island on the lake skimmer, slipping silently through the murky lake waters to the meadow beyond. From there, they passed back into the forests and the mist.

"It would be best to start at the beginning, I suppose,'' Questor said to Ben after they had entered the forest trees. They walked a step ahead of the others, shoulder to shoulder, the wizard with the studied, swinging gait, shoulders stooped and head lowered. "The problem with the throne began after the death of the old King more than twenty years ago. Things were much different then. The old King had the respect of all of the people of Landover. Five generations of his family had ruled in succession, and all had ruled well. No one challenged the old King's rule—not Nightshade, not even the Mark. There was an army then and retainers and laws to govern all. The treasury was full, and the magic protected the throne. Sterling Silver was not under the Tarnish; she was polished and gleaming like something just crafted, and the island on which she sits was the most beautiful spot in the land. There were flowers and there was sunshine—and no mists or clouds.''

Ben glanced over. He was dressed in a red silk tunic and pants with knee-high boots and silver stays. Abernathy carried his ceremonial robes, crown and chains of office. ''Questor, I hate to have to tell you this but your explanation is beginning to sound like a bad fairy tale.''

''It grows worse, High Lord. The old King died and left but a single son, still a youth, as heir to the throne. The son's guardian was a wizard of great power but dubious principle. The wizard was more father to the son than the old King, having cared for the boy after his mother's death and during the old King's frequent absences from court. The son was a mean-spirited boy, bored with Landover and displeased with the responsibilities his birthright demanded of him, and the wizard played upon this weakness. The wizard had been looking for a way to escape what he viewed as his own limited existence in Landover for some time; he was court wizard then—the position that I now hold—and he thought himself destined for greater things. But a court wizard is bound to the throne and the land by an oath of magic; he could not leave if the throne did not release him. So he employed his considerable skill with words and convinced the boy that they should both leave Landover.''

He paused, and his owlish face turned slightly toward Ben. ''The wizard is my half-brother, High Lord. You know him better as Meeks.''

''Oh-oh.'' Ben shook his head slowly. ''I begin to see the light.''

''Hmmmmm?''

''Just an expression. And will you quit saying *hmmmmmm* like that? My grandmother in her dotage used to do that everytime I said something to her, and it damn near drove me crazy!"

"Sorry. Well, the trouble with leaving Landover is that when you go, you take nothing with you. The magic won't allow it. Neither my half-brother nor the old King's son could stomach that! So they devised a scheme to sell the throne to someone from another world. If someone from another world were to buy Landover, then my half-brother and the old King's son could collect the proceeds in that other world and thwart the laws of this one which would prohibit them from taking anything out. That way, they could live comfortably wherever they were to go."

"How did they decide on my world?" Ben asked.

"Research." Questor smiled. "Yours was a world in which the inhabitants were most likely to be attracted to life here. Landover was the fantasy that they dreamed about."

Ben nodded. "Except that it really isn't."

"Yes, well." Questor cleared his throat. "Time passed while my half-brother subverted the old King's son, while the son grew to manhood, and while they schemed to break their ties with the land. The son never really wanted the throne in any case; he would abandon it quickly enough, whatever the conditions imposed, so long as he could be assured that he would be well looked after. It became the responsibility of my half-brother to find a way to make that happen. That took some thinking and some maneuvering. While all this was happening, the kingdom was falling apart. The magic works on strength of commitment, and there was precious little of that. The treasury emptied. The army disbanded. The laws broke down. The population began to lose its sense of unity and to drift into armed camps. Trade between them all but ceased. Sterling Silver had no master and no retainers to look after her, and she began to fall under the Tarnish. The land was affected as well, withering and turning foul. My half-brother and the old King's son were left with the problem of selling a, ah . . . how do you put it in your world, High Lord? . . . oh, yes, a 'pig in a poke' . . . to some unsuspecting customer.''

Ben stared upward into the trees beseechingly. "You have such a way with words, Questor."

"Yes, but you see, High Lord, it doesn't have to be that way—that's what I have been trying to explain to you. A King of strength and wisdom can restore Landover to the way it once was. The laws can be put back—especially by someone like you, who understands the nature of laws. The treasury can be replenished, the army can be restored, and the Tarnish can be cleansed. That is why I donned the mantle of court wizard when it was discarded by my half-brother. That is why I agreed to help my half-brother seek a buyer for the throne. I even wrote the words for the notice of sale.''

"You wrote that pack of lies for the sale item in the catalogue?" Ben asked in astonishment.

"I wrote it to attract the right kind of person—one with vision and courage!" A bony finger jabbed at Ben. "And it is not a pack of lies!" The finger dropped away and the lean face tightened. "I did what was necessary, High Lord. Landover must be made new again. She has been allowed to waste away with the fragmenting of the old King's rule, and a loss of the magic will destroy her completely."

"We have heard this speech before, Questor," Abernathy muttered from behind them. "Kindly put it to rest."

The wizard shot him an irritated look. "I am speaking only what needs to be spoken. If you are weary of the speech, close your ears.''

"Questor, I'm not following your part in all of this." Ben brought the conversation back around to the subject at hand. "If you feel so strongly about what Landover needs, then why did you let your half-brother and the old King's son run it into the ground in the first place? What were you doing all those years that followed the death of the old King? Where were you while the throne of Landover sat vacant?"

Questor Thews held up his hands imploringly. "Please, High Lord—one question at a time!" He rubbed at his bearded chin fretfully. "You must understand that I was not court wizard then. My half-brother was. And while I don't like to admit it, I am not the wizard that my half-brother is. I am a poor second to him and always have been."

"Where is my quill and scroll," Abernathy exclaimed. "I must have this in writing!"

"I am improving, however, now that I have *become* court wizard," Questor went on, ignoring the other. "I was without position at the court while my half-brother was in service—an apprentice grown too old to stay on, yet unable to find other work in the Kingdom. I traveled quite a bit, trying to learn something of the magics of the fairies, trying to find work to occupy my time. Some years after the old King died, my half-brother called me home again to help with the administration of the court. He advised me of his intention to leave the Kingdom and not return. He advised me that the old King's son had decided to sell the throne and go with him. He appointed me to act as court wizard and advisor to the new King."

He stopped, turning to face Ben. "He thought, you see, that I would cause him little trouble since I was a poor wizard to begin with and something of a failure in life. He thought that I would be so happy to have the position of court wizard that I would acquiesce to anything he wished. I let him believe that, High Lord. I pretended cooperation, because it was the only way I could aid the land. A new King was needed, if matters were to ever be set right again. I was determined to find that King. I even persuaded my half-brother to let me write the words in his sale notice that would bring that King to Landover."

"And here I am," Ben finished.

"Here you are," Questor agreed.

"A million dollars light."

"And a Kingdom richer."

"But my money is gone, isn't it? The contract I signed was a fraud from the beginning? Meeks and the son have walked off with the money, and I'm stuck here for the rest of my life?''

Questor looked at him for a long time, and then he shook his head. "No, High Lord, you are not stuck here for any longer than you choose to be. The contract was valid, the escape clause was valid, and the money awaits you, if you return within ten days.''

Now it was Ben's turn to stare. "I'll be damned," he whispered. He studied Questor wordlessly for a moment. "You didn't have to tell me this, you know. You could have let me think the money was gone and that I must stay.''

The wizard seemed sad. "No, I could never do that, High Lord.''

"Yes, he could," Abernathy chimed in. "And he would, too, if he thought he could get away with it." He squatted and scratched at his neck with his hind leg. "Do you think there are ticks in these woods?" he asked. "I hate ticks.''

They walked on in silence. Ben thought through all that Questor had told him. Old Meeks and the dead King's son conspiring to make a quick killing by selling the throne to the Kingdom and setting themselves up in a new world with the money—it made sense, he guessed. But there was a piece to this puzzle that was still missing. The trouble was, he couldn't figure out what that piece was. He knew it was there somewhere, but he couldn't quite manage to put his finger on it. He exercised his lawyer's skills in an effort to solve the problem, but the missing piece kept eluding him.

He gave up looking for it after a time. He would stumble across it sooner or later and he had a bigger problem just now, in any case. Eight of the ten days allotted him under the terms of the contract had already expired. That left him exactly today and tomorrow to decide whether or not he was going to back out of his purchase and head home again. He could do that, Questor had assured him. He believed Questor. The question was not so much whether or not he could, but whether or not he wanted to. Nothing of Landover had turned out to be the way it was advertised in the catalogue—

except, of course, in the very broadest sense. There were dragons and damsels and all of that, there was magic, and he was King over all—or about to be. But the fantasy was not what he had expected it to be; it wasn't even close. The money he had paid seemed far too much for what he had gotten.

And yet . . . the plaintiff gave way to the defendant . . . and yet there was something indefinable about Landover that appealed to him. Most probably, it was the challenge. He hated to admit it; but if he were to be honest with himself, he had better admit it here and now. He did not like to back away from anything. He did not like to lose. Admitting that he had made a mistake in coming here, in paying one million dollars for a fantasy that truly *was* a fantasy, though not the fantasy he wished, rankled him. He was a trial lawyer with a trial lawyer's instincts and bullheadedness, and he did not like to walk away from any kind of fight. There was surely a fight ahead for him in Landover, for the sovereignty of the throne was in shambles, and it would take one hell of an effort to restore it. Didn't he think that he could do that? Wasn't he capable of matching his skills against those of any of the subjects that he was expected to rule?

Miles would have told him it wasn't worth it. Miles would have thrown up his hands and gone to civilization—to Soldier Field and elevators and taxis. His associates in the profession would have done the same.

Annie would not. Annie would have told him to tough it out and she would have stood with him. But Annie was dead.

He tightened his jaw, frowning. When he got right down to it, he was dead, too, if he gave it up now and went back. That was why he had taken the gamble in the first place and come—to give himself back his life. He still thought he could do that here; he still believed that Landover could be his home. Besides, money was only money . . .

But a million dollars? He could hear Miles' exclamation of disbelief. He could see Miles throwing up his hands in disgust.

He was surprised to discover that he was smiling at the idea.

It was exactly noon when the mist and trees parted almost without warning, and the little company entered a clearing bright with sunshine, its grasses a glimmer of green, gold, and crimson. Bonnie Blues grew all about the edges of the clearing, evenly spaced and perfectly formed, and only those that nestled close against the forest beyond showed signs of the wilt that Ben had observed on his journey in. Burnished timbers of white oak formed a dais and throne at the clearing's center. Polished silver stanchions were anchored at the corners of the dais, and in their holders were tall white candles, their wicks new. Flags of varying colors and insignia lifted from behind the dais, and all about were white velvet kneeling pads and rests.

Questor's arm swept across the sunlit clearing. "This is the Heart, High Lord," he said softly. "Here you shall be crowned King of Landover."

Ben stared at the gleaming oak and silver of the throne and dais, the flags and candles, and the clipped grasses and Bonnie Blues. "It shows nothing of the Tarnish, Questor. It all looks as if it were . . . new."

"The Tarnish has not yet reached the Heart, High Lord. The magic is strongest here. Come."

They crossed in silence, slipping between the lines of velvet kneeling pads and armrests to where the throne and dais waited at the clearing's center. Fragrant smells filled the warm midday air, and the colors of the grasses and trees seemed to shimmer and mix with liquid ease. Ben felt a sense of peace and reverence within the clearing that reminded him of the church sanctuary on Sunday morning when he had been brought to it as a boy. He was surprised to discover that he still remembered.

They reached the dais and stopped. Ben glanced slowly about. The Heart was all but deserted. A few worn-looking herdsmen and farmers, with their wives and children in tow, stood hesitantly at the edges of the clearing, whispering together and looking uncertainly at Ben. Half a dozen hunters in woodsman's garb clustered in a knot in the shadows of the forest, where the sunlight did not reach. A beggar, ragged in fraying leather pants and tunic, sat cross-legged at the base of an oak riddled with wilt.

Other than those few, there was no one.

Ben frowned. There was a hunted, almost desperate look in the eyes of those few that was troubling.

"Who are they?" he asked Questor quietly.

Questor looked out at the ragged gathering and turned away. "Spectators."

"Spectators?"

"To the coronation."

"Well, where is everybody else?"

"Fashionably late, perhaps." Abernathy deadpanned. Behind him, the kobolds hissed softly and showed their teeth.

Ben put his hand on Questor's shoulder and brought him about. "What's going on, Questor? Where is everyone?"

The wizard rubbed his chin nervously. "It *is* possible that those who are coming are simply a bit late arriving, detained perhaps by something that they had not foreseen when they . . ."

"Wait a minute." Ben cut him short. "Run that by me once more—'those who are coming' did you say? Does that mean that some don't intend to come?"

"Oh, well, I was simply using a figure of speech, High Lord. Certainly all who can come will."

Ben folded his arms across his chest and faced the other squarely. "And I'm Santa Claus. Look, Questor, I've been around long enough to know a fox from a hole in the ground. Now, what's going on here?"

The wizard shifted his feet awkwardly. "Ah . . . well, you see, the truth of the matter is that very few will be coming."

"How few is very few?"

"Perhaps only a couple."

Abernathy edged foward. "He means just the four of us,

High Lord—and those poor souls standing out there in the shadows.''

"Just the four of us?" Ben stared at Questor in disbelief. "The four of us? That's all? The coronation of the first King of Landover in more than twenty years, and no one is coming . . ."

"You are not the first, High Lord," Questor said softly.

". . . but the four of us?"

"You are not the first," the wizard repeated.

There was a long moment of silence. "What did you say?" Ben asked.

"There have been others before you, High Lord—other Kings of Landover since the death of the Old King. You are simply the latest of these to ascend the throne. I am sorry that you have to hear this now. I would have preferred that you heard it later when the coronation ceremony was . . ."

"How many others?" Ben's face was flushed with anger. ". . . completed, and we had . . . What did you say?"

"Kings, damn it! How many others have there been?"

Questor Thews squirmed. "Several dozen, perhaps. Frankly, I have lost count."

The sound of thunder rolled from somewhere distant through the forest trees and mist. Abernathy's ears pricked sharply.

"Several dozen?" Ben did not yet hear it. His arms dropped to his sides and the muscles of his neck corded. "I can understand why you might have lost count! I can understand as well why no one bothers to come anymore!"

"They came at first, of course," the other continued, his voice irritatingly calm and his gaze steady. "They came because they believed. Even after they quit believing, they came for a time because they were curious. But eventually they were no longer even curious. We have had too many Kings, High Lord, who were not real."

He gestured roughly toward the few who had assembled at the forest's edge. "Those who come now come only because they are desperate."

The thunder sounded again, louder this time and closer, a deep, sustained rumble that echoed through the forest and shook the earth. The kobolds hissed and their ears flattened back against their heads. Ben looked about sharply. Abernathy was growling.

Questor seized Ben's arm. "Climb onto the dais, High Lord! Go, quickly!" Ben hesitated, frowning. "Go!" the wizard snapped, shoving. "Those are demons that come!"

That was reason enough for Ben. The kobolds were already scampering ahead, and he went after them. The thunder reverberated all about them, shaking trees and earth.

"It appears that you will have your audience after all, High Lord," Abernathy said as he bounded up the dais steps on all fours, nearly losing the ceremonial robes and chains of office.

Ben went up the steps behind him, glancing back over his shoulder anxiously. The Heart was deserted save for the four of the little company. The farmers, herdsmen, their families, the hunters, and the beggar had all scattered into the concealing shadows of the forest. The mist and gloom of the surrounding trees seemed to press in tightly against the sunlit clearing.

"Help the High Lord on with his robes and chains," Questor Thews directed Abernathy, hastening onto the dais to stand with them. "Quickly!"

Abernathy rose up again on his hind legs and began fitting the robes and chains of office about Ben. "Wait a minute, Questor," Ben objected, his eyes darting apprehensively to the black tunnel entrance across from them. "I'm not sure I want to do this anymore."

"It is too late, High Lord—you must!" The other's owlish face was suddenly hard with purpose. "Trust me. You will be safe."

Ben thought that he had ample reason to question that assertion, but Abernathy was already fastening the clasps to the robes and chains. The scribe was surprisingly dexterous for a dog, and Ben found himself glancing downward in spite of the situation. He started. Abernathy's paws had blunted fingers with joints.

"He failed to get even that part right," the scribe muttered on seeing the look on Ben's face. "Let us hope he does better with you."

Shadows and mist joined and swirled like stirred ink at the far side of the clearing, and the stillness turned suddenly to a howling wind. The thunder of the demon approach peaked in a harsh rumble that shook the forest earth. Ben turned, the wind whipping his robes until they threatened to break loose. Abernathy stepped away, growling deep in his throat, and the kobolds hissed like snakes and showed their teeth to the black.

Then the demons broke from the mist and dark, materializing as if a hole had opened in the empty air, an army of lean, armored forms as shadowy as night. Weapons and plating clanked, and the hooves of monstrous, serpentine mounts thudded from rock to earth, reverberated, and died. The army slowed and clattered to a halt. White teeth and red eyes gleamed from the mists, and claws and spines jutted from the mass, as if the whole were tangled into one. The army faced the dais in a ragged line, hundreds strong, pressed between the forest trees and the kneeling pads and rests, the sound of their breathing filling the void left by the passing of the thunder. The wind howled once more and died away.

The clearing was filled with the sound of heavy, clotted breathing. "Questor . . . ?" Ben called softly, frozen where he stood.

"Stand, High Lord," the wizard whispered softly.

The demon horde stirred, weapons lifted as one, and a maddened howl broke from the army's collective throat. Abernathy stepped back, jaws snapping. The kobolds seemed to go mad, hissing and shrieking in fury, crouching to either side of where Ben stood.

"Questor . . . ?" Ben tried again, a bit more urgently this time.

Then the Mark appeared. The demons parted suddenly at

their center, and he came from out of their midst. He sat astride his winged serpent, a thing that was half snake and half wolf, a thing out of the foulest nightmare. The Mark was all in black armor, opaque and worn with use, bristling with weapons and serrated spines. A helmet with a death's head sat on his shoulders, the visor down.

Ben Holiday wished he were practically anywhere other than where he was.

Questor Thews stepped forward. "Kneel, High Lord!" His voice was a hiss.

"What?"

"Kneel! You are to be King! The demons have come to see you made so, and we must not keep them waiting." The owlish face crinkled with urgency. "Kneel, so you may be sworn!"

Ben knelt, eyes locked on the demons.

"Place your hands upon the medallion," Questor ordered. Ben lifted it from beneath his tunic and did so. "Now repeat these words: 'I shall be one with the land and her people, faithful to all and disloyal to none, bound to the laws of throne and magic, pledged to the world to which I have come—King, hereafter.' Say it."

Ben hesitated. "Questor, I don't like . . ."

"Say it, Ben Holiday, if you would truly be the King you have said you would be!"

The admonishment was hard and certain, almost as if come from someone other than Questor Thews. Ben met the other's eyes steadily. He could sense a restless movement from the ranks of the demons.

Ben lifted the medallion until it could be seen clearly by all. His eyes never left Questor's. "I shall be one with the land and her people, faithful to all and disloyal to none, bound to the laws of throne and magic, pledged to the world to which I have come—King, hereafter!"

He spoke the words clearly and boldly. He was mildly surprised that he had remembered them all so easily—almost as if he had known them before. The clearing was still. He let the medallion fall back upon his chest.

Questor Thews nodded, and his hand passed through the air immediately above Ben's head. "Rise, Your Majesty," he said softly. "Ben Holiday, King of Landover, High Lord and Liege."

Ben rose, and the sunlight broke over him as it slipped suddenly through the ceiling of mist. The silence of the clearing deepened. Questor Thews bent slowly and dropped to one knee. Abernathy followed him down and the kobolds knelt with him.

But the demons held their place. The Mark stayed mounted, and none about him moved.

"Show them the medallion one time more!" Questor hissed beneath his breath.

Ben turned and held forth in his right hand the medallion, feeling with his fingers the outline of the mounted knight, the lake, castle, and rising sun. Demons cried softly in the ranks of black forms, and a few dropped down. But the Mark brought his arm back swiftly, beckoning all to stand where they were, to keep their feet. The death's head turned back to Ben defiantly.

"Questor, it isn't working!" Ben breathed from out of the side of his mouth.

There was sudden movement in the demon ranks. Astride his monstrous, winged carrier, the Mark was advancing through the screen of mist and shadows. The demons he led were coming with him.

Ben went cold. "Questor!"

But then there was a flare of light from across the Heart, as if something bright had caught the reflection of the sun. It broke from the edge of the forest shadows between the advancing demons and the dais on which Ben and his companions stood. The demons slowed, eyes shifting. Ben and his friends turned.

A horse and rider appeared from out of the mists.

Ben Holiday started. It was the knight he had encountered

in the time passage between his world and this, the knight whose image was graven on the medallion, a battered and soiled iron statue as he sat astride his wearied horse. His lance rested upright in its boot cradle and his armored form was still. He might have been chiseled from stone.

"The Paladin!" Questor whispered in disbelief. "He has come back!"

The Mark rose in the harness that bound him to his mount, death's head facing toward the knight. Demons shrank back within the mist and shadows all about him, and there were whimpers of uncertainty. Still the knight did not move.

"Questor, what's happening?" Ben demanded, but the wizard shook his head wordlessly.

A moment longer the demons and the knight faced each other across the sunlit span of the Heart, poised like creatures at hunt. Then the Mark brought one arm upward, fist clenched, and the death's head inclined, if only barely, toward Ben. Wheeling his mount, he turned back into the dark, the army he led turning with him. Shrieks and cries broke the stillness, the wind howled and hooves and boots thundered once more. The demons disappeared back into the air out of which they had come.

The mist and the gloom drew back again, and the sunlight returned. Ben blinked in disbelief. When he turned back once more to find the knight and his war horse, they had disappeared as well. The clearing was empty but for the five who stood upon the dais.

Then there was new movement in the shadows. The few farmers and herdsmen and their families, the hunters and the lone beggar slipped back into view, gathering hesitantly at the fringe of the trees. There was fear and wonder in their eyes. They came no further, but one by one they knelt in the forest earth.

Ben's heart was pounding, and he was damp with sweat. He took a deep breath and wheeled on Questor. "I want to know what in the hell is going on, and I want to know right now!"

Questor Thews seemed genuinely at a loss for words for the first time since they had met. He started to say something, stopped, tried again, and shook his head. Ben glanced at the others. Abernathy was panting as if he had been run. The kobolds were crouched close, ears laid back, eyes slitted.

Ben seized Questor's arm. "Answer me, damn it!"

"High Lord, I don't . . . I am at a loss to explain . . ." The owlish face twisted as if caught in a vise. "I would never have believed . . ."

Ben brought his hand up quickly to cut him off. "For God's sake, Questor, get hold of yourself, will you?"

The other nodded, straightening. "Yes, High Lord."

"And answer the question!"

"High Lord, I . . ." He stopped again.

Abernathy's shaggy head craned forward over one shoulder. "This should be interesting," he offered. He appeared to have regained control of himself more quickly than the wizard.

Questor shot him a dark look. "I should have made you a cat!" he snapped.

"Questor!" Ben pressed impatiently.

The wizard turned, took a deep breath, cocked his head reflectively and shrugged. "High Lord, I don't quite know how to tell you this." He smiled weakly. "That knight, the one that appears on the medallion you wear, the one that confronted the Mark—he doesn't exist."

The smile disappeared. "High Lord, we have just seen a ghost!"

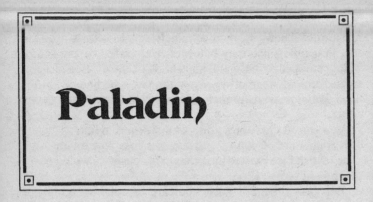

Paladin

Miles used to say that there were lawyers and then there were *lawyers;* trouble was, there were too many of the former and not enough of the latter. He used to say that when he was steamed by some act of incompetence visited upon him by a fellow practitioner of the arts.

Ben Holiday ran that saying through his mind on and off during the hike back to Sterling Silver, altering the words a bit to fit the circumstances of his present dilemma. There were ghosts and then there were *ghosts*, he corrected. There are imagined ghosts and real ghosts, phantoms of the mind and sure-enough live spooks that went bump in the night. He supposed one could safely say that there were indeed too many of the former and not enough of the latter—although maybe everyone was better off that way.

Whatever the case, the knight graven on the medallion he wore, the knight who had twice come between him and the Mark, the knight who materialized and then disappeared as if made of smoke, was certainly one of the latter and not some chemically induced distortion that was the result of eating the food or drinking the water in a strange land. He knew that as surely as he knew that Questor Thews was still holding out on him about the circumstances surrounding the sale of the throne of Landover.

And he meant to learn the truth about both.

But he was not going to learn much of anything right away, it appeared. For Questor, after proclaiming the knight a ghost that no longer existed, refused to say anything more about the matter until they were safely returned to Sterling Silver. Ben protested vehemently, Abernathy tossed off a few barbs about cold feet, the kobolds hissed and showed their teeth to the vanished demons, but the wizard remained firm. Ben Holiday had a right to know the whole story behind the appearance of the ghost—what was it he had called it, the Paladin?—but he would have to wait until they were again within the walls of the castle. The owlish face set itself, the stooped figure turned, and Questor Thews stalked off into the forest without a backward glance. Since Ben had no intention of remaining in that clearing by himself after what had just happened, he hastened after like an obedient duckling following its mother.

Some posture for a King, he chided himself. But then who was he kidding? He was about as much King of Landover as he was President of the United States. He might have been proclaimed King by an inept wizard, a converted dog, and a couple of hissing monkeys and he might have paid a million dollars for the privilege—he set his teeth, thinking of that—but he was still just an outsider who had wandered into a foreign country and who didn't yet know the customs and could barely speak the language.

But that would change, he promised. He would see it change or know the reason why.

It took them the better part of the afternoon to complete the journey back again, and dusk was settling over the misted valley and waterways when they again came in sight of Sterling Silver. The dreary, hollow cast of the fortress dampened Ben Holiday's spirits further, and they scarcely needed that. He thought again about the ten days allotted him to return to his own world under the terms of the contract he had signed—and for the first time the wisdom of doing so seemed clear to him.

Once back within the castle, Questor dispatched Parsnip to prepare dinner and Bunion to lay out a fresh set of clothing for Ben. Then taking Ben and Abernathy in tow, he set out on an expedition that took them deep into the bowels of the castle. They passed down numerous corridors and through countless halls, all musted and stained by the Tarnish, but lit with the smokeless lights and warmed by the life of the castle. Colors shimmered weakly in the gray, and touches of polished wood and stone glimmered. There was a sense of something grand and elegant passing away in the wake of the Tarnish, and Ben was bothered by it. He should not have been, he thought, as he trailed silently after Questor. He had slept only a single time within these walls, and the castle held no special meaning for him. In fact, if it hadn't been for Questor telling him that she was a living thing . . .

He shoved his thoughts aside as they stepped through a massive oak and iron-pinioned door into a small courtyard with a chapel set at its center. The chapel was as dingy and discolored as the rest of Sterling Silver, yet the mists gathered less thickly here, and traces of sunlight still fell upon the stone and wood of roof and walls and the stained glass of high, arched windows. They crossed the courtyard to the chapel steps, climbed to scrolled oak doors that were matched and pegged in iron pins and pushed their way inside.

Ben peered through the failing light. Floors, ceiling, and walls were trimmed in white and scarlet, the colors faded, the whole of the chapel's dim interior musted and gray. There was no altar; there were no pews. Coats of arms hung upon the walls with shields and weapons propped below, and a single kneeling pad and arm rest faced forward toward a dais that occupied the very center of the room. A solitary figure stood upon the dais. It was the knight on the medallion.

Ben started. He thought for an instant that the knight was alive and at watch. Then he realized that it was only an armored shell occupying the dais and that nothing living was kept within.

Questor started forward into the chapel. "Come, High Lord."

Ben followed, eyes fixed on the figure on the dais. Abernathy trailed them. The suit of armor was chipped and battered as if from many battles, the polish gone, the metal stained almost black by the Tarnish. A huge broadsword was sheathed in a scabbard at one hip, and a mace with a wedge-shaped head hung from its leather harness at the other. A great iron-tipped lance rested butt downward from the grip of one metal hand. All three weapons were as debilitated as the armor and crusted over with dirt and grime. There was a crest on the metal breastplate and on the shield that rested beside the lance—an emblem that depicted the sun rising over Sterling Silver.

Ben took a deep breath. He could be certain as he stood before it that the armor was only a shell. Yet he was certain, too, that this was the same armor that had been worn by the knight who had twice now intervened in his encounters with the Mark.

"He was called the Paladin," Questor said at his elbow. "He was the King's champion."

Ben looked over. "He was, was he? What happened to him?"

"He disappeared after the death of the old King, and no one has seen him since." The sharp eyes met Ben's. "Until now, that is."

"It seems, then, that you no longer think I was imagining things when I came through the time passage."

"I never thought that, High Lord. I simply feared that you had been deceived."

"Deceived? By whom?"

They faced each other in silence. Abernathy scratched at one ear.

"This pregnant pause in your digression suggests that some vast and terrible secret is about to be revealed," Ben said finally. "Does this mean I am about to learn the rest of what you still haven't told me?"

Questor Thews nodded. "It does."

Ben folded his arms across his chest. "Fine. But let's have all of it this time, Questor—not just part of all of it like before. No more surprises saved for later, okay?"

The other nodded one time more. "No more surprises, High Lord. In fact, it was your mistrust of me that prompted my request that Abernathy join us. Abernathy is court historian as well as court scribe. He will be quick enough to correct me if I should misspeak myself." He sighed. "Perhaps you will have more faith in his word than in mine."

Ben waited. Questor Thews glanced momentarily at the suit of armor and then looked slowly about the empty chapel. He seemed lost within himself. The silence deepened as the seconds slipped away, and the haze of twilight spread its shadows further into the failing light.

"You may begin whenever you are ready," Abernathy growled impatiently. "Dinner cools on the table while we stand about."

"I find it difficult to know where to begin," Questor snapped. He turned to Ben once more. "It was a different time, you know—twenty years ago. The old King ruled and the Paladin was his champion, as he had been champion of the Kings of Landover since the dawn of her creation. He was born of the magic, created by the fairy people as Landover herself was created, drawn from the mists of their world to become a part of this. No one has ever seen his face. No one has ever seen him other than like this—clad in the suit of armor you see before you, metal head to foot, visor drawn and closed. He was an enigma to all. Even my half-brother found him a puzzle with no solution."

He paused. "Landover is more than just another world that borders on the fairy world—she is the gateway to the fairy world. She was created for that purpose. But where the fairy world is timeless and everywhere at once, Landover is a fixed point in time and place both. She is the end point of the time passages from all of the other worlds. Some worlds she joins more closely than others. Some worlds are but a step through the mists where others, like your own, are a distant passage. The closer worlds have always been those where the magic was real and its use most prevalent. The inhabitants are frequently descendants of creatures of the fairy world who migrated or strayed or were simply driven out. Once gone from the fairy world, they could never return. Few have been happy in exile. Most have sought a way back again. For all, Landover has always been the key."

"I hope all this is taking us somewhere," Ben interjected pointedly.

"It depends on how far you like to travel," Abernathy groused.

Questor hunched his shoulders, arms folding into his robes. "The Paladin was the protector of the King, who in his turn was the protector of the land. There was need for that protector. There were those both within Landover and without who would use her for their own purposes if her King and her protector should falter. But the magic that guarded her was formidable. There was no one who could stand against the Paladin."

Ben frowned, suddenly suspicious. "Questor, you're not going to tell me that . . ."

"I will tell you, High Lord, only what is," the other interrupted quickly. "You wished to be told the whole story, and I am about to accommodate you. When the old King died and his son did not assume the throne, but sought instead for a way to abandon Landover, those who have always laid wait without began to sniff about the gates. The Paladin was gone, disappeared with the passing of the old King, and none could find a way to bring him back again. Months drifted into years as the son grew older and plotted with my half-brother to leave the land, and still no King ruled and the Paladin stayed gone. My half-brother used all of his considerable magic to seek out the absent knight-errant, but all of his considerable magic was not enough. The Paladin was gone, and it seemed unlikely that he would come again.

"Naturally, this encouraged the ones who prowled at Landover's borders. If the Paladin were indeed gone, if the magic were weakened, Landover could be theirs. Remember, High Lord—the gateway to the world of fairy was a prize that some would give anything to own. My half-brother saw this and he knew that he must act quickly or Landover would fall from his control."

The owlish face tightened. "So he devised a plan. The throne of the Kingdom would be sold to a buyer from a very distant world, giving Landover a King and extricating both the son and my half-brother from the laws that bound them to her. But they would sell the throne to a buyer for a limited period of time only—say, six months or a year. That way the throne would revert back to them and they could sell it again. By doing so, they would steadily increase their personal fortune, enabling the son to live as he chose and my half-brother to enhance his opportunities to gain power in other worlds. The difficulty with all of this was in finding interested buyers."

"So he contacted Rosen's?" Ben interjected.

"Not at first. He began by making the sales independently. His customers were mostly unsavory sorts, wealthy but with principles as dubious as his own. Frequently they were men needing to escape temporarily from their own world. Landover was a perfect shelter for them; they could play at being King, live rather well off the comforts of Sterling Silver, and then return to their own world when their tenure was ended."

"Criminals," Ben whispered softly. "He sent you criminals." He shook his head in disbelief, then looked up sharply. "What about the ones who got here and didn't want to leave? Didn't that ever happen?"

"Yes, it happened from time to time," Questor acknowledged. "But I was always there to be certain that they left on time—whether they were ready to do so or not. I had magic enough to accomplish that.'' He frowned. "I have often wondered, though, how my half-brother got the medallion back from such troublemakers once they had returned home again. His magic would advise him of their presence, but how could he have known where to find and how to secure the medallion again . . . ?''

He trailed off thoughtfully, then shrugged. "Never mind. The fact remains that for quite some time he successfully sold Kingships for limited periods and made a good deal of money. But his customers were an unpredictable lot, and the state of affairs in Landover was worsening in the wake of this succession of would-be Kings. More to the point, the money wasn't coming in fast enough. So finally he decided to offer the throne for sale outright—not to the unreliable sorts of people he had been dealing with in the past, but to the general public. He contacted Rosen's, Ltd. He told them that he was a procurer of rare artifacts and unusual service items. He convinced them of his worth by locating through the use of his magic a few treasures and curiosities thought lost. When he was accepted as a legitimate source of such items, he offered them the sale of Landover. I think they must have disbelieved at first, but he found a way to convince them finally. He sent one of them over for a look.''

He grinned fiercely. Then his eyes narrowed. "But there was more to this sale than Rosen's imagined, High Lord. My half-brother and the old King's son had no intention of giving up for good something as valuable as the Kingship of Landover. A pre-condition to the offering gave them exclusive control over the selection of buyers. That way they could sell the throne to someone too weak to hold it, so that it would revert back to them, and they could sell it again. They could even sell options on the side—moving preferred customers to the head of an imaginery list. Rosen's would never know the difference. The difficulty now was not in finding interested customers, but in finding interested customers who possessed both the means of purchase and the requisite lack of character to succeed in staying on as King!''

Ben flushed. "Like me, I gather?"

The other shrugged. "You asked earlier how many Kings of Landover there have been since the old King. There have been more than thirty."

"Thirty-two, to be exact," Abernathy interjected. "Two already this year. You are the third."

Ben stared. "Good God, that many?"

Questor nodded. "My half-brother's plan has worked perfectly—until now." He paused. "I believe he may have made a mistake with you."

"I would withhold judgment on that, if I were you, High Lord," Abernathy spoke up quickly. "Things are more complicated than you perceive. Tell him the rest, wizard."

The owlish face tightened. "I shall, if given half a chance!" He faced Ben. "This last plan was a good one, but there were two problems with it. First, it was obvious to my half-brother that not every buyer would lack sufficient character to overcome the difficulties of governing Landover. Even though he would interview each personally, he might still mistakenly choose one who would not back away from the challenges that the Kingship offered. Should that happen, he might not get Landover back again for sale. The second problem was more serious. The longer the Kingdom languished without a strong King or with a succession of failures, the more disorganized matters would become and the more difficult it would be for any new King to succeed. He wanted that. But he also knew that the more disorganized things became, the greater the chances for usurpation of the crown from those who prowled without. He did not want that."

Questor paused. "So he found a single solution to both problems. He goaded the Mark into challenging for the throne."

"Uh-oh." Ben was beginning to get an inkling of what was to come.

"The Mark rules Abaddon, the netherworld that lies beneath Landover. Abaddon is a demon world, a black pit of exile for the worst of those driven from the fairy world since the dawn of time. The demons exiled there would like nothing better than to get back into the fairy world, and the only way back is through Landover. When my half-brother extended the challenge to the Mark and the Mark became convinced that the Paladin was no longer protector of Landover, the demon lord came out of Abaddon and proclaimed himself King."

The brows of the wizard knit above the sharp, old eyes. "There was a catch to this, of course—and my half-brother knew it. The Mark could not truly be King while another ruled under color of law and while the magic of the medallion gave its protection to the wearer. He could only claim to be King and challenge for the right. So each midwinter, when the Bonnie Blues turn white, the Mark comes out of Abaddon into Landover and asks challenge of the King. As yet, no one has accepted."

"I can imagine," Ben breathed softly. "Just to make certain that I understand all this, Questor, what form does this challenge take?"

The heavy brows lifted. "Strength of arms, High Lord."

"You mean, jousting with lances or something?"

Abernathy touched him on the shoulder. "He means, mortal combat with weapons of choice—a battle to the death."

There was an endless moment of silence. Ben took a deep breath. "That's what I have to look foward to—a fight to the death with this demon?" He shook his head in disbelief. "No wonder no one lasts very long in this position. Even if they wanted to, even if they were willing to try to straighten things out, sooner or later they would have to face the Mark. What's the point of even trying?" He was growing angry all over again. "So what do you expect of me, Questor? Do you expect me to accept a challenge that no one else would? I'd have to be out of my mind!"

The stooped figure shifted from one foot to the other. "Perhaps. But it might be different with you. None of the others had help. Yet twice now after twenty years of absence, the Paladin has come to you."

Ben wheeled at once on Abernathy. "Is he telling me the truth—the Paladin has never come to anyone before?"

Abernathy shook his head solemnly. "Never, High Lord." He cleared his throat. "It grieves me to admit it, but the wizard may have a point. It might indeed be different with you."

"But I had nothing to do with the Paladin's appearance," Ben insisted. "And I don't know that he came to me necessarily. He was simply there. Besides, you said yourself it was a ghost we were seeing. And even if he wasn't a ghost, he looked wrecked to me. The Mark looked the stronger of the two and not in the least intimidated by this so-called champion that the King is supposed to rely upon to protect him. Frankly, I can't believe any of this. And I don't know that I understand it yet. Let's back up a minute. Questor, your half-brother Meeks sells the throne to an outsider like me for a big price, choosing someone who won't last. Even if he mistakenly chooses someone who might tough it out, the Mark is on hand to make sure he doesn't. But the Mark can't be King while someone else holds the medallion—am I right? So what does the Mark get out of all this? Doesn't Meeks keep bringing other candidates in month after month, year after year?"

Questor nodded. "But the Mark is a demon, and the demons live long lives, High Lord. Time is less meaningful when you can afford to wait, and the Mark can afford to wait a long, long time. Eventually, my half-brother and the old King's son will tire of the game and will have accumulated enough riches and power to divert their interest from Landover's throne. When that happens, they will cease bothering with the matter and abandon Landover to her fate."

"Oh." Ben understood now. "And when that happens, the Mark will gain Landover by default."

"That is one possibility. Another is that the demon will find a way in the interim to gain control of the medallion. He cannot seize it by force from the wearer; but sooner or later, one of Landover's succession of Kings will grow careless and lose it—or one will accept the Mark's challenge and be . . ."

Ben held up his hands quickly. "Don't say it." He hesitated. "What about the other predators—the ones whose worlds border on Landover? What are they doing while all this is going on?"

The wizard shrugged. "They are not strong enough as yet to stand against the Mark and the demons of Abaddon. One day, perhaps they will be. Only the Paladin had ever possessed such strength."

Ben frowned. "What I don't understand is why this Paladin simply disappeared after the death of the old King. If he were truly protector of the land and the throne, why would he disappear just because there was a change of Kings? And what's become of the fairies? Didn't you say that they created Landover as a gateway to their world? Why don't they protect it, then?"

Questor shook his head and said nothing. Abernathy was quiet as well. Ben studied them wordlessly a moment, then turned back again to the suit of armor on the dais. It was tarnished and rusted, battered and worn, a shell that resembled nothing so much as the discarded body of a junk car shipped to the salvage yard for scrap. This was all that remained of Landover's protector—of the King's protector. He walked to the kneeling pad and stared up at the metal shell wordlessly. This was what he had seen in the mists of the time passage and again in the mists of the forest that ringed the Heart. Had it been but a part of those mists? He had not thought so, but he was less certain now. This was a land of magic, not exact science. Dreams and visions might seem more real here.

"Questor, you called the Paladin a ghost," he said finally, not turning to look at the other. "How can a ghost be of any help to me?"

There was a long pause. "He was not always a ghost. Perhaps he need not remain one."

"Life after death, is that it?"

"He was a thing created of the magic," Questor answered quietly. "Perhaps life and death have no meaning for him."

"Do you have any idea at all how we can go about finding that out?"

"No."

"Do you have any suggestions for finding a way to get him back again?"

"No."

"That's what I thought. All we can do is hope he shows up before the Mark issues his next challenge and turns me into the latest of a long line of kingly failures!"

"You have another choice. You can use the medallion. The medallion can take you back to your own world whenever you choose to go. The Mark cannot stop you. You need only wish for it, and you will be gone."

Ben grimaced. Wonderful. Just tap the red shoes together three times and repeat, "There's no place like home." Off he would go, back to Kansas. Just wonderful. He had to do it within the next twenty-four hours, of course, if he didn't want to return a million dollars lighter. And whether he chose to do it within the next twenty-four hours or whether he waited until the Mark came riding for him out of the black pit, he would be running in either case, leaving Landover exactly as he had described himself—the latest in a long line of Kingly failures.

His jaw set. He didn't like losing. He didn't like giving up.

On the other hand, he wasn't paticularly keen on dying.

"How did I ever get myself into this?" he muttered under his breath.

"Did you say something?" Questor asked.

He turned away from the dais and the shell of armor, his eyes searching out the stooped figures of the wizard and the scribe through the lengthening shadows of twilight. "No," he sighed. "I was just mumbling."

They nodded and said nothing.

"I was just thinking to myself."

They nodded again.

"I was just . . ."

He trailed off hopelessly. The three of them stared at one another in silence and no one said anything more.

It was almost completely dark out when they left the chapel to retrace their steps through the corridors and halls of the castle. The smokeless lamps spread their glow through the shadows. The flooring and walls were vibrant with warmth.

"What do you gain from all of this?" Ben asked Questor at one point.

"Hmmmmm?" The stopped figure turned.

"Do you get a share of the profits on all these sales of the throne?"

"High Lord!"

"Well, you did say you helped write the sales pitch, didn't you?"

The other was flushed and agitated. "I receive no part of any monies spent to acquire Landover!" he snapped.

Ben shrugged and glanced over at Abernathy. But for once the scribe made no comment. "Sorry," Ben apologized. "I just wondered why you were involved in all of this."

The other man said nothing, and Ben let the subject drop. He thought about it as they walked, though, and decided finally that what Questor gained from these sales was what he had probably wanted all along—the position and title of court wizard. His half-brother had held both before him, and Questor Thews had been a man without any real direction in his life. Now he had found that direction, and it probably made him happy enough just to be able to point to that.

And shouldn't it be like that for me as well, he wondered suddenly?

He was struck by the thought. Why was it that he had purchased the throne of Landover in the first place? He hadn't purchased it with the thought that it would become some other-world version of Sun City where he might retire, play golf and meditate on the purpose of man's existence,

had he? He had purchased the throne to escape a world and
a life he no longer found challenging. He was the wanderer
that Questor Thews had once been. Landover's Kingship
offered him direction. It offered him the challenge he had
sought.

So what was he griping about?

Easy, he answered himself. He was griping because this
kind of challenge could kill him—literally. This wasn't a
court of law with a judge and jury and rules that he was
talking about here. This was a battlefield with armor and
weapons and only one rule—survival of the fittest. He was
a King without a court, without an army, without a treasury,
and without subjects interested in obeying a sovereign they
refused to recognize. He was a King with a castle that was
slowly passing into dust, four retainers straight out of the
brothers Grimm and a protector that was nine-tenths ghost.
He might not have been looking for Sun City, but he sure
as hell hadn't bargained for this, either!

Had he?

He carried the debate with him to dinner.

He ate again in the great hall. Questor, Abernathy and the
two kobolds kept him company. He would have eaten alone
if he had not insisted that the others join him. They were
retainers to the King of Landover now, Questor pointed out,
and retainers did not eat with the High Lord unless they were
invited to do so. Ben announced that until further notice they
all had a standing invitation.

Dinner was less eventful than the previous night. There
were candles and good china place settings. The food was
excellent, and no one felt compelled to improve on its service. Conversation was kept to a minimum; Bunion and Parsnip ate in silence, and Questor and Abernathy exchanged
only mild barbs on the eating habits of men and dogs. Ben
sampled everything on the table, more hungry than he had
a right to be, stayed clear of the wine, and kept his thoughts
to himself. No one said anything about the coronation. No
one said anything about the Mark or the Paladin.

It was all very civilized. It was also endless.

Ben finally sent everyone from the table and sat there alone in the candlelight. His thoughts remained fixed on Landover. Should he stay or should he go? How sturdy was this wall of seemingly unsolvable problems that he was butting his head against? How much sense did it make for him to keep trying.

How many angels could pass through the eye of a needle?

The answers to all of these questions eluded him entirely. He went to bed still seeking them out.

He woke the next morning shortly after sunrise, washed in the basin placed next to his bed, dressed in his running sweats and Nikes, and slipped quietly through the halls of Sterling Silver for the front entry. He was soundless in his movements, but Abernathy had good ears and was waiting for him at the portcullis.

"Breakfast, High Lord?" he asked, his glasses inching down over his furry nose as he looked Ben over.

Ben shook his head. "Not yet. I want to run first."

"Run?"

"That's right—run. I did it all the time before I came to Landover and I miss it. I miss the workouts at the Northside Health Club, I miss the sparring and the speed work and the heavy bag. Boxing, we call it. I guess that doesn't mean anything to you."

"It is true that dogs do not box," Abernathy replied. "Dogs do run, however. Where is it that you plan to run this morning, High Lord?"

Ben hesitated. "I don't know yet. Probably at the valley's rim where there's some sun.

Abernathy nodded. "I'll send someone to accompany you."

Ben shook his head. "I don't need anyone, thanks."

The other turned away. "I wouldn't be too sure of that if I were you," he said and disappeared down the hallway.

Ben stared after him momentarily, then wheeled without

waiting and strode through the portcullis and gates to the lake skimmer. He boarded and his thoughts sent the skiff leaping recklessly ahead through the gray waters. He did not need someone with him everywhere he went, he thought stubbornly. He was not some helpless child.

He grounded the lake skimmer on the far shore, turned, and jogged ahead through the gloom. He worked his way slowly to the valley slope, then started up. When he reached the rim, he turned right and began to follow the forest's edge. Below him, the valley lay wrapped in shadows. Above, the pale golden light of the sun washed the new day in trailers of mist.

He ran easily, his thoughts drifting with the soft padding of his running shoes on the damp earth. His head felt clear and alert, and his muscles felt strong. He hadn't felt like that since he had arrived in Landover, and the feeling was a good one. Trees slipped rapidly away beside him, and the ground passed smoothly beneath. He breathed the air and let the stiffness in his body slowly work itself out.

Last night's questions were still with him, and the search for their answers went on. This was the final day of the ten days allotted him for rescission under the terms of his contract with Meeks. If he didn't rescind now, he would lose the million dollars paid for the purchase of Landover's Kingship. He might also lose his life—although Questor Thews had assured him that the medallion would take him back again at any time with but a moment's thought. In any case, the choices were clear. He could stay and attempt to straighten out the morass of problems he would face as King of Landover, risk a confrontation with the Mark and give up the million dollars, or he could leave, admit that the purchase was the dog that Miles had warned, return to his old life and world, and get back most of the million dollars he had spent. Neither choice held much appeal. Neither choice held much hope.

He was breathing more quickly now, feeling the strain of running begin to wear pleasingly on his muscles. He pushed himself, picking up the pace slightly, working to pass through the wall of his resistance. A flash of something dark caught his eye—something moving through the forest. He glanced over sharply, searching. There was nothing now—only the trees. He kept moving. He must have imagined it.

He thought again about the Paladin, knight-errant of the realm. He sensed somehow that the Paladin was the key to everything that was wrong with Landover's throne. It was too large a coincidence that, with the old King's death, the Paladin had disappeared as well and everything had started to go wrong with the Kingship. There was a link between them that he needed to understand. It might be possible for him to do so, he reasoned, if it were true as Questor had thought that the Paladin had indeed appeared twice now because of him. Perhaps he could find a way to bring the Paladin back yet a third time—and this time discover if he were indeed but a ghost.

The sun rose higher as he ran on, and it was approaching midmorning when he started back down the valley slope for the lake skimmer. Twice more he thought he caught sight of something moving in the trees, but each time he looked there was nothing there. He recalled Abernathy's veiled warning, but dismissed it summarily. They were always telling you to stay off the streets of Chicago, too, but you didn't live life shut away in a box.

He thought about that as he took the lake skimmer back across to Sterling Silver. There were always risks in life. Life was meant to be lived like that because if it wasn't, then what was the purpose of living it at all? Measuring the risks was important, of course, but experiencing them was necessary. It was the same thing he was always trying to explain to Miles. Sometimes you did things because they felt right. Sometimes you did things because . . .

He thought suddenly of the faces of those farmers and herdsmen and their families, those hunters and that beggar who had traveled to the Heart for his coronation. There had been a sort of desperate hope in those faces—as if those

people *wanted* to believe that he could be King. There had
been only a few, of course, and he was hardly responsible
to them, yet . . .

His thinking faltered as the lake skimmer grounded at the
front gates of the castle. He stood up slowly, recapturing
the thoughts, losing himself in them. He barely saw Abernathy appear in the shadow of the portcullis.

"Breakfast, High Lord?"

"What?" Ben was almost startled. "Oh, yes—that would
be fine." He climbed from the boat and moved quickly into
the castle. "And send Questor to me right away."

"Yes, High Lord." The dog trailed after, nails clicking on
the stone. "Did you enjoy your run?"

"Yes, I did—very much. Sorry I didn't wait, but I didn't
think I needed anyone to go along just for that."

There was a moment's silence. Ben sensed the dog looking
at him and glanced back. "I think I should tell you, High
Lord, that Bunion was with you every step of the way. I
sent him to make sure that you were properly looked after."

Ben grinned. "I thought I saw something. But it wasn't
necessary for him to be there, was it?"

Abernathy shrugged. "That depends on how well you
could have handled by yourself the timber wolf, the cave
wight, and the bog wump that he dispatched when he caught
them stalking after you in search of breakfast." He turned
off into an adjoining corridor. "And speaking of breakfast,
yours is waiting in the dining hall. I will send for the wizard."

Ben stared after him. Bog wump? Cave wight? Sweat
beaded on his forehead suddenly. For Christ's sake, he
hadn't seen or heard a thing! Was Abernathy trying to be
funny?

He hesitated, then hurried on. He didn't think Abernathy
was the sort to make jokes about something like this. Apparently he had been in danger out there and hadn't even
known it.

He ate breakfast alone. Parsnip brought it to him and left.
Abernathy did not reappear. Once, halfway through the

meal, he caught sight of Bunion standing in the shadows of an entry off to one side. The kobold grinned so that all of his teeth showed like whitened spikes and disappeared. Ben did not grin back.

He was almost finished when Questor finally appeared. He shoved his plate aside and told the wizard to sit down with him.

"Questor, I want to know exactly how things are now compared to how they were when the old King was alive. I want to know what worked then and what doesn't work now. I want to figure out what has to be done to get things back to where they were."

Questor Thews nodded slowly, brows knitting over his sharp eyes. His hands folded on the table. "I will try, High Lord, though some things may escape my immediate memory. Some of it, you already know. There was an army that served the King of Landover; that is gone. There was a court with retainers; only Abernathy, Parsnip, Bunion and myself remain. There was a treasury; it is depleted. There was a system of taxes and yearly gifts; it has broken down. There were programs for public works, social reforms and land preservation; they no longer exist. There were laws and the laws were enforced; now they are ignored or enforced selectively. There were accords and alliances and pacts of understanding between the peoples of the land; most have lapsed or been openly repudiated."

"Stop right there." Ben rubbed at his chin thoughtfully. "Who among the King's subjects stands allied with whom at this point?"

"No one stands allied with anyone, so far as I can tell. Humans, half-humans, fairy creatures—no one trusts anyone."

Ben frowned. "And none of them has much use for the King, I gather? No, you needn't answer that. I can answer it for myself." He paused "Is there any one of them strong enough to stand up to the Mark?"

The wizard hesitated. "Nightshade, perhaps. Her magic

is very powerful. But even she would be hard pressed to survive a dual with the Mark. Only the Paladin possessed strength enough to defeat the demon.''

"What if everyone were to band together?''

Questor Thews hesitated longer this time. "Yes, the Mark and his demons might be successfully challenged then.''

"But it would take someone to unite them first.''

"Yes, it would take that.''

"The King of Landover could be that someone.''

"He could.''

"But just at the moment the King of Landover can't even draw a crowd for his own coronation, can he?''

Questor said nothing. Ben and the wizard stared at each other across the table.

"Questor, what's a bog wump?'' Ben asked finally.

The other frowned. "A bog wump, High Lord?'' Ben nodded. "A bog wump is a variety of forest wight, a spiney, flesh-eating creature that burrows in marshy earth and paralyzes its victims with its tongue.''

"Does it hunt in the early morning?''

"It does.''

"Does it hunt humans?''

"It might. High Lord, what . . . ?''

"And Bunion—would he be a match for one of these bog wumps?''

Questor's mouth snapped shut on the rest of whatever it was he was going to say. His owlish face crinkled. "A kobold is a match for almost anything alive. They are ferocious fighters.''

"Why are Bunion and Parsnip still here at Sterling Silver when everyone else in the court is gone?''

The owlish face crinkled into a complete knot. "They are here because they have pledged themselves to the service of the throne and its King. Kobolds do not take their pledges lightly. Once made, a pledge is never broken. So long as there is a King of Landover, Bunion and Parsnip will stay on.''

"Is it the same with Abernathy?"

"It is. This is his chosen service."

"And you?"

There was a long pause. "Yes, High Lord, it is the same with me."

Ben sat back. He didn't say anything for a moment, his eyes locking on Questor's, his arms folding loosely across his chest. He listened in the silence for the whisper of the other's thoughts and spun the webbing of his own.

Then he smiled reluctantly. "I have decided to stay on as Landover's King."

Questor Thews smiled back. "I see." He seemed genuinely pleased. "I thought that you might."

"Did you?" Ben laughed. "Then you were more certain than I. I only now made the choice."

"If I might ask, Ben Holiday—what was it that decided you?"

The smile disappeared from Ben's face. He hesitated, thinking momentarily of those few who had come to the Heart to witness his coronation. They were not so different, really, from the clients he had taken an oath to represent, and he not so different from the lawyer who had taken that oath. Perhaps he did owe them something after all.

He said nothing of that to Questor, though. He merely shrugged. "It was a balancing of the equities, I suppose. If I stay, it will cost me a million dollars—presuming, of course, that I can find a way to stay alive. If I go, it will cost me my self-respect. I would like to think that my self-respect is worth a million dollars."

The wizard nodded. "Perhaps it is."

"Besides, I don't like quitting in the middle of something. It grates on me to think that Meeks chose me because he expected that I would do exactly that. I want very badly to disappoint him in his expectation. We have a saying where I come from, Questor: Don't get mad, get even. The longer I stay, the better chance I have of finding a way to do that. It's worth the risks involved."

"The risks *are* substantial."

"I know. And I don't suppose anyone besides me would even think twice about taking them."

Questor thought a moment. "Maybe not. But no one else stands in your shoes, High Lord."

Ben sighed. "Well, in any case, the matter's settled. I'm staying and that's that." He straightened slowly. "What I have to do now is to concentrate on finding ways of dealing with Landover's problems before they bury me."

Questor nodded.

"And the first of those problems is the refusal of any of the King's subjects to recognize me as King. Or themselves as subjects. They have to be made to pledge to the throne."

The other nodded one time more. "How will you do that?"

"I don't know yet. But I do know one thing. No one is going to come here to make that pledge. The coronation would have brought them, were they at all willing. Since they refuse to come here, we'll have to go there—there being wherever they are."

Questor frowned. "I have reservations about such a plan, High Lord. It could prove very dangerous."

Ben shrugged. "Maybe, but I don't see that we have much choice in the matter." He stood up. "Care to make a suggestion as to where we should start?"

The wizard sighed and stood up with him. "I suggest, High Lord, that we start at the beginning."

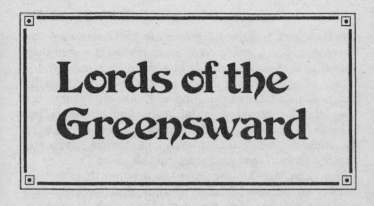

Lords of the Greensward

There had been many who had pledged service to the Kings of Landover—families who for generations had fought in the armies of the High Lords and stood beside their thrones. There had been many who could point with pride to their record of loyal and faithful service. But none had served so well or so long as the Lords of the Greensward, and it was to them that Ben Holiday was advised he should go first.

"The barons trace their bloodlines back thousands of years—some to the time that Landover came into being," Questor Thews explained. "They have always stood with the King. They formed the backbone of his army; they comprised the core of his advisors and court. Some of them were Kings of Landover themselves—though none in the last several hundred years. They were always the first to offer service. When the old King died, they were the last to depart. If you are to gain support anywhere, High Lord, it would be from them."

Ben accepted the suggestion—although it was really less a suggestion than a caution, he thought—and departed Sterling Silver at dawn of the following day for the estates of the land barons. Questor Thews, Abernathy and the two kobolds went with him once again. Ben, the wizard and the scribe rode horseback because the journey to the Greensward was a long one. The kobolds could have ridden, too, had they chosen to do so, but kobolds in general had little use for horses, being quicker of foot and stronger of wind than the best racer that had ever run, and so almost always traveled afoot. Besides, horses were unusually skittish when ridden by kobolds. Ben had no trouble understanding that. Anything that could dispatch a timber wolf, a cave wight, and a bog wump with such ease made him skittish, too.

It was a peculiar-looking group that departed that morning. Questor led the way, his tall, brightly cloaked figure slouched across an old gray that must have been ready for pasture years ago. Ben followed on Wishbone, a sorrel with the oddly shaped white blaze that gave him his name and a propensity for seizing the bit and bolting. He did that twice with Ben hanging on for dear life each time. Questor, after the second incident, whacked him hard across the nose and threatened magic in horse tongue. That seemed to bring Wishbone to his senses. Abernathy followed atop a white-faced bay gelding and carried the King's standard with its by-now familiar insignia of the Paladin riding out from the castle at sunrise embroidered in scarlet on a field of white. It was strange indeed to see a soft-coated Wheaten Terrier with glasses and tunic riding a horse and holding a flag, but Ben kept the smile from his face, because Abernathy obviously saw nothing at all funny about it. Parsnip trailed, leading on a long set of guide ropes a pack train of donkeys with food, clothing, and bedding. Bunion had gone on ahead, sent by Questor to advise the land barons that the King of Landover wished a meeting.

"They will have no choice; they will have to receive you," Questor declared. "Courtesy dictates that they not turn away a Lord whose stature is equal to or higher than their own. Of course, they would have to receive you if you were simply a traveler seeking shelter and food, too, but that is beneath you as King."

"Very little is beneath me at this point," Ben replied.

They rode out through the mists and shadows of the early morning, skirted the shores of the lake until they were turned east, then wound slowly to the valley rim. Several times Ben Holiday glanced back through the gray, watching the stark, colorless projection of Sterling Silver against the dawn sky, her towers, battlements, and walls ravaged as if by some nameless disease. He was surprised to discover that it was hard for him to leave her. She might appear as Castle Dracula to the naked eye, and he might find her loathsome to look upon, but he had felt the warmth of her and he had touched the life within. She had been kind to him. She had made him feel welcome. He found himself wishing that he could do something to help her.

He consoled himself with the thought that one day he would.

Then the castle, the mists, and the valley disappeared behind them as the company rode east through forest and hill country toward Landover's heartland. They traveled steadily for the better part of the day, stopping once for a midday meal and several times to rest, and by dusk they were within sight of the broad sweep of fields, pastures, and farmland that comprised the Greensward.

They made camp that night within a copse of fir on a knoll overlooking pastureland given over to cattle and goats and a cluster of small huts and wooden houses some miles further east. Ben swung down gratefully from Wishbone's back when Questor brought them to a halt. It had been some time since he had ridden a horse. It had been, in truth, the better part of twenty years—and that last time had been on a date in college that he would just as soon have forgotten. Now, a world and a lifetime away, he recalled the feeling that came with a long ride—his body stiff, the land still moving about him as he tried to walk, the sensation of the horse still locked between his knees, though he was dismounted. He knew that by tomorrow he would be sore from the shoulders down.

"Would you walk with me a moment, High Lord?" Questor asked and beckoned to him. Ben wanted to throttle the wizard for even suggesting the idea, but he forced his irritation aside and went.

They walked only a short distance to the edge of the knoll and stood shoulder to shoulder staring out across the flatlands below.

Questor's arm swept the horizon. "The Greensward, High Lord—the estates of the old families, the baronies of Landover. Their domain encompasses more than half of the kingdom. There were but twenty families at last count, and those twenty rule all of the land, its thralls, their villages and families and stock—subject to the King's will, of course."

"Of course." Ben looked out over the valley. "You said twenty families at last count. What do you mean, 'at last count'?"

The wizard shrugged. "Families merge through marriage. Families accept wardship from stronger families. Families die out—sometimes with a little help."

Ben glanced at him from the corner of one eye. "Charming. They don't all get along so well, then, I gather?"

"Just so. United under the old King, they were less disposed to take advantage of one another. Divided under no monarch, they are a suspicious and at times scheming lot."

"A circumstance that I might be able to use to my advantage, you think?"

The owlish face glanced over. "There is that possibility."

Ben nodded. "There is also the possibiity that their suspicions and schemes might result in them trying to do away with me."

"Tch-tch," Questor clucked. "I will be with you, High Lord. Besides, they are unlikely to waste time and effort trying to do away with a King that they regard as essentially worthless. They refused, after all, even to attend your coronation."

"You are a wellspring of inspiration," Ben admonished dryly. "Whatever would I do without your support?"

"Oh, well, that is all part of my service to the throne." Questor either missed the dig entirely or was ignoring it.

"So tell me what else I should know."

"Just this." Questor faced him. "In better times, these lands were fertile, the stock fatted, and there were willing thralls enough to make up a dozen armies to serve Landover's King. Much has changed for the worse, as you will see on tomorrow's journey in. But what has changed can be put right again—if you can find a way to secure the pledge of the Greensward's Lords."

He glanced over once more, turned, and walked back toward the camp. Ben watched him go and shook his head in disbelief. "I'll work on it," he muttered.

It took an hour longer than it should have done to set camp. There were tents to be put up, and Questor took it upon himself to aid the process through use of his magic. The magic inflated the tents like balloons and sent them floating skyward to lodge in the highest tree limbs, and it required all of Parsnip's considerable athletic skill to bring them down once more. The horses bolted from their tether when Abernathy barked—to his acute embarrassment—after catching sight of a stray farm cat, and it was another hour until they could be caught and brought back around. Then supplies were unloaded, the King's standards set, the stock fed and watered, and the bedding placed—all without incident.

Dinner, however, was a disaster. There was a stew with beef and vegetables which smelled delicious while cooking, but lost some of its flavor after Questor fueled the cooking fire with a touch of quickening which created a miniature inferno that left the kettle and its contents black and crusted. The fruit of the Bonnie Blues was moderately satisfying, but Ben would have preferred at least one plate of the stew. Questor and Abernathy carped about the behavior of men and dogs, and Parsnip hissed at them both. Ben began to consider rescinding his standing invitation to have them join him for his meals.

It was nearing bedtime when Bunion returned from his journey to the Greensward to advise them that the land barons would be waiting to receive Landover's new King on his arrival at Rhyndweir. Ben didn't know what Rhyndweir was and he didn't care. He was too tired and fed up to care and he went to sleep without worrying about it.

They reached Rhyndweir by mid-afternoon of the following day, and Ben had an opportunity to see for himself exactly what it was. Rhyndweir was a monstrous, sprawling castle seated atop a broad plateau at the joining of two rivers. Towers and parapets lifted skyward out of fortress walls more than a hundred feet high to lance into the mist-shrouded blue of the mid-afternoon skies. They had been traveling east in the Greensward since sunrise, following the labyrinth roadways that wound down through the valley's lowlands past fields and villages, past farmers' cottages and herdsmen's huts. Once or twice there had been the sight of castle walls in the distance, far from where they traveled and almost miragelike in the shimmer of Landover's sun. But none had been as grand and awesome as Rhyndweir.

Ben shook his head. Sterling Silver was so much the worse by comparison that he hated to think about it.

The homesteads and villages of the common people of the Greensward did not compare favorably either. The fields looked seedy and the crops appeared to be afflicted with various forms of blight. The cottages and huts of the farmers and herdsmen looked ill-kept, as if their owners no longer took pride in them. The shops and stands of the villages looked dingy and weathered. Everything seemed to be falling apart. Questor nodded knowingly at Ben's glance. The Lords of the Greensward spent too much time at each other's throats.

Ben turned his attention back again to Rhyndweir. He studied the castle in silence as the little company approached from the valley it commanded on a roadway running parallel to the northernmost of the rivers. A scattering of village shops and cottages lined the juncture of the rivers in the broad shadow of the castle, forming a threshold to its gates. Thralls watched curiously as the company crossed a wooden bridge spanning to the castle approach, their tools lowered, their heads lifted in silent contemplation. Many had the same worn but expectant look on their faces as those who had come to the Heart.

"They have not seen a King of Landover make this journey to their master's castle in twenty years, High Lord," Questor spoke softly at his elbow. "You are the first."

"No one else made the effort?" Ben asked.

"No one else," Questor replied.

Their horses' hooves clumped off the bridge planks and thudded softly in the dusty earth. Ahead, the roadway lifted toward the walls of the castle and the open gates. Pennants flew from the parapets at every turn, brilliant silks fluttering in the wind. Banners hung from stanchions above the gates, and heralds stepped forward to sound their trumpets in shrill blasts that shattered the afternoon quiet. Lines of knights on horseback formed an honor guard on either side of the gateway, lances lifted in salute.

"This seems a little much, given everyone's attitude about the coronation, don't you think?" Ben muttered. His stomach had the same hollow feeling it always developed before major court appearances.

Questor's owlish face was screwed into a knot. "Yes, this does appear to be a bit overdone."

"When anyone's this overly friendly in my world, it's time to watch your backside."

"You are in no danger, High Lord," the wizard responded quickly.

Ben smiled and said nothing. They had reached the gates, passing down the corridor formed by the honor guard, the blare of the trumpets still ringing across the valley. Ben took a quick count. There were at least a hundred knights in the guard. Armor and weapons glistened brightly. Visored helmets stared straight ahead. The knights were iron statues that kept their place and did not stir. Ben sat rigid atop his mount. Every muscle in his body ached from yesterday's ride, but he refused to let the pain show. This wasn't just a

reception line—this was a show of strength. This looked to
be a case of who could impress whom. He glanced back at
his little entourage of Questor, Abernathy and the kobolds
and wished he had a bit more to work with.

They rode into the shadow of the gateway through the
towering walls and the great woven banners. A delegation
waited in the court ahead, a gathering of men afoot, robed
and jeweled.

"The Lords of the Greensward," Questor breathed softly
to Ben. "The tall one, the one who stands foremost, is Kallendbor, master of Rhyndweir. His is the largest of the estates, and he the most powerful of the Lords. Look for him
to take the lead in what is to follow."

Ben nodded and said nothing. He had forgotten the ache
in his body, and his stomach had settled. Already, he was
considering what he would say—very much as if he were
about to argue a case in court. He supposed that was what
he was going to have to do, in a sense. It was going to be
interesting.

Questor brought the company to a halt a dozen yards from
the assembly of Lords and looked at Ben. Together, they
dismounted. Pages came forward to take the reins. Abernathy remained on his horse, the King's banner hanging limp
from its staff. Parsnip and Bunion stood to either side,
crouched expectantly. No one looked very comfortable.

Kallendbor detached himself from the assemblage and
came forward. Ignoring Ben, he addressed himself to Questor, inclining his head briefly. "Well met, Questor Thews.
I see that you have brought our newest King to visit us."

Ben stepped in front of the wizard at once. "It was my
decision to come here, Lord Kallendbor. I thought it would
be quicker to visit you than to wait for you to visit me."

There was a moment of silence as the two faced each
other. Kallendbor's eyes narrowed slightly, but his face remained expressionless. He was taller than Ben by several
inches, heavier by twenty pounds, red-haired and bearded,

and heavily muscled. He held himself erect, conveying the impression that he was looking down on Ben.

"Coronations occur so frequently these days in Landover that it is difficult to attend them all," he said pointedly.

"I expect the number to undergo a sharp decline," Ben replied. "Mine will be the last for some time."

"The last, you believe?" The other's smile was sardonic. "That may prove a difficult expectation to fulfill."

"Perhaps. But I intend to fulfill it, nevertheless. Please understand this, Lord Kallendbor. I am not like the others who came into Landover and left again at the first hint of trouble. I came here to be King, and King is what I will be."

"The purchase of a crown does not necessarily make one a King," one of the others muttered from the cluster behind Kallendbor.

"Nor does being born into the right family necessarily make one a Lord," Ben shot back quickly. "Nor purchase of an estate, nor marriage into one, nor theft by deception, nor conquest by arms, nor any of a dozen other available schemes and artifices used since the dawn of time—none of these make either Lords or Kings. Laws make Lords and Kings, if there is to be any order in life. Your laws, Lords of the Greensward, have made me King of Landover."

"Laws older than we and not of our making," Kallendbor growled.

"Laws to which, nevertheless, you are bound," Ben answered.

There was quick murmur of voices and angry looks. Kallendbor studied him wordlessly. Then he bowed, his face still expressionless. "You show initiative in coming here to meet with us, High Lord. Be welcome, then. There is no need for us to stand further in this court. Come into the hall and share dinner. Bathe first, if you wish. Rest a bit—you look tired. Rooms have been set aside for you. We can talk later."

Ben nodded in reply, beckoned to the others of the little company, and together they followed the Lords of the

Greensward across the courtyard and into the great hall beyond. Light from high, arched windows that were glassed and latticed flooded the passageways they followed, lending a bright and airy feel to the castle.

Ben leaned close to Questor. "How do you think we are doing so far?"

"They have agreed to board us," the other whispered back. "That is more than I expected them to do."

"It is? That's not what you said earlier!"

"I know. But I saw no reason to worry you."

Ben stared at him momentarily, then shook his head. "You never cease to amaze me, Questor."

"Hmmmmm?"

"Never mind. How far can we trust these people?"

The wizard slouched ahead, smiling. "About as far as piglets hop. I would keep my wits about me at dinner, if I were you."

What followed was a leisurely period of rest and relaxation in the rooms appointed for Landover's King and his entourage. There were sleeping rooms for all, baths with hot water and sweet soaps, fresh clothing, and bottles of wine. Ben took advantage of all but the wine. His experiences with wine thus far had been less than rewarding. Besides, he trusted Kallendbor and the others no farther than Questor, and he wanted a sharp wit about him when it came time to state his case. He left the wine unopened on the serving tray and noticed that the others did the same.

The call to dinner came at sunset. Dinner was a sumptuous affair served in the castle's great hall at a long tressel table filled with foodstuffs and dozens of additional bottles of wine. Ben left the wine alone once more. He was beginning to feel paranoid about it, but that couldn't be helped. He sat at the center of the long dinner table with Kallendbor on his right and a Lord named Strehan on his left. Questor had been placed at one end of the table, Abernathy and the kobolds at another, smaller table. Ben saw at once that he was being deliberately isolated. He thought briefly about arguing the placement, but then decided to let the matter pass. He would be tested sooner or later, and it might as well begin here. It was important that he convince the Lords of the Greensward that he was capable of standing alone.

Conversation was pleasant, but minimal for the first part of the meal, and it was not until the main course of pork roast and young pheasant was nearly gone that the subject of the Kingship was broached once more. Ben was wondering idly if the Lords of the Greensward always ate so well or if this was a deliberate effort to impress him, when Kallendbor spoke.

"You seem a man of some determination, High Lord," the other complimented and lifted his glass in salute.

Ben nodded in response, but left his glass on the table.

Kallendbor drank and set the glass carefully down before him. "We would not poison a King of Landover if we wanted him dead, you know. We would simply wait for the Mark to dispatch him for us."

Ben smiled disarmingly. "Is that what you have planned for me?"

The weathered face creased with amusement. Scars showed white against the tan. "We have nothing bad planned for you. We have nothing planned at all. We are here to listen to what you have planned for us, High Lord."

"We are loyal subjects to the throne, and we stand always with the King," Strehan added from the other side. "But there has been a problem of late knowing just who that King is to be."

"We would serve loyally if we could determine that the King we are asked to serve is a true King and not simply a play King whose interests are his own and not in keeping with ours," Kallendbor continued. "Since the death of the old King and the exile of his son, we have been subjected to a barrage of false Kings who last months or weeks or even days and are gone before we can even learn their names. Pledging loyalty to such as these serves no one's interests."

"Pledging loyalty to such as these is a betrayal of those

Kings that have protected the realm since time began," Strehan said. "What purpose is served in pledging to a King who can do nothing for us?"

Ben looked at him wordlessly and thought, Here comes the pitch.

"You could be another of those Kings," Strehan said.

Ben smiled. Strehan was a thin-faced, angular man, taller even than Kallendbor. "But I'm not," Ben answered.

"Then you must explain what you have planned for us, High Lord," Kallendbor insisted. "You must explain what advantage you have set aside so that we may know our pledge is well given."

Oh-ho, Ben thought. "It seems to me that the advantages of pledging ought to be obvious," he replied. "A King is a figure of central authority who governs over the whole of the land. He gives and enforces laws that are applied fairly to all. He protects against the injustices that would otherwise flourish."

"There are no injustices here in the Greensward!" Strehan snapped.

"None at all?" Ben shook his head wonderingly. "I had been given to understand that even among equals there is always dissension; and quite often, in the absence of central authority, it takes the form of violence."

Kallendbor frowned. "You think that we quarrel among ourselves?"

"I think that, if the opportunity presented itself, you might be tempted to do away with each other like that!" Ben let the shock register in their faces a moment, then bent forward. "Let's get right to the point, shall we? You need a King in Landover. There has always been a King, and there always shall be a King. It is the form of rule that the people recognize and the laws support. If you let the throne remain vacant, or if you continue to refuse to recognize whoever rightfully sits upon it, you risk everything. You are a land of diverse peoples and mounting problems. Those problems need resolution, and you cannot resolve them alone. You do not get along well with each other in the absence of the old King, and you need someone to replace him. I'm the one you need, and I will tell you why."

The rest of the table had gone quiet as the conversation between Ben and the two Lords grew more heated, and now everyone was listening. Ben came slowly to his feet.

"I came here because the Lords of the Greensward have always been the first to pledge their loyalty to Landover's throne. Questor told me that. He said it was here that I should begin, if the loose threads of the Kingship were to be pulled back together again. And it is *your* Kingship. The throne and the laws promulgated by it belong to you and to all of the people of this valley. You have lost both and you need them back before Landover splinters so far apart that, like a broken board, it will never be made whole again. I can do that. I can do that because I do not come from Landover; I come from another world entirely. I have no prejudices to hinder me, no predetermined obligations to honor, no favorites to which I must cater. I can be honest and fair. I gave up everything I had to come here, so you may be certain that I am serious in my intentions. I have a background in the laws of my world that will allow me to interpret yours fairly.

"You need those laws to be in force, Lords of the Greensward. You need them so there can be stability in your lives beyond that brought about by force of arms. Trust comes with mutual reliance and faith—not with threats. I know that all is not tranquil between the estates. I know that all is not tranquil between the peoples of Landover. It will never be so until you agree to stand once more behind a King. History and the law require it."

"We have managed well enough up until now without a King to rule over us," one Lord interjected irritably.

"Have you, then?" Ben shook his head. "I don't think so. The Tarnish that drains the life from Sterling Silver ravages the Greensward as well. I've seen the blighted condition of your crops and the dissatisfied faces of the thralls who work them. The entire valley decays; you need a King! Look at yourselves! You don't begin to feel comfortable with one another—I can sense that much, and I'm an outsider! You are threatened by demons and by others who covet this land. Divided, you won't be able to hold on to what you have for very long, I think.''

Another came to his feet. "Even if what you say is so, why should we pledge to you as High Lord? What makes you think you can do better than your predecessors?''

"Because I can!'' Ben took a deep breath, and his eyes found Questor's. "Because I am stronger than they were.''

"I want nothing to do with this," another Lord growled from across the table. "A pledge to you puts us at risk against the Mark and the demons that serve him!''

"You are already at risk," Ben pointed out. "If no King comes to stand against the Mark, then one day he will come into the land and claim it all. Join with me and we can stop that.''

"*We* can stop that?'' Strehan was on his feet, towering over Ben. "What hope do *we* have, High Lord? Have you fought in battle against demons such as the Mark? Where are your battle scars?''

Ben flushed. "If we stand together, then . . .''

"If we stand together, then it seems we are no better than if we stand alone!'' Strehan snapped. "What use do you serve if you have no battle worth? What you ask is that the Lords of the Greensward put their own lives forward for yours!''

Voices raised loudly in agreement. Ben felt his control over the situation begin to slip.

"I ask no one to risk themselves for me," he said quickly. "I ask for an alliance with the throne, the same alliance that you had with the old King. I will ask such an alliance from all of Landover's subjects. But I ask it first of you.''

"Bravely spoken, High Lord! But what if we were to ask an alliance from *you*?''

The speaker was Kallendbor. He came slowly to his feet,

standing next to Ben, his red-bearded face hard. Strehan slipped back into his seat. The other Lords went silent.

Ben glanced quickly at Questor for help, saw confusion mirrored in the wizard's owlish face, and gave up looking. He turned back to Kallendbor. "What sort of alliance did you have in mind?"

"A marriage," the other said quietly.

"A marriage?"

"Yours, High Lord—to the daughter of any house you choose. Take for a wife the child of one of us, a wife to give you children, a wife to bind you to us with blood ties." Kallendbor smiled faintly. "Then we will pledge to you. Then we will acknowledge you as Landover's King!"

There was an endless moment of silence. Ben was so stunned that for a moment he could not even comprehend what was being asked. When he managed to accept the whole of what Kallendbor had requested of him, he saw as well the truth that lay behind it. He was being asked to provide to the Lords of the Greensward a legitimate heir to the throne of Landover—one that would rule after him. He thought that, once produced, such an heir would not likely have long to wait to ascend to the throne.

"I cannot accept," he said finally. He could see in his mind's eye Annie's youthful face, and the memory of it caused him new pain. "I cannot accept because I have recently lost my own wife, and I cannot take another so soon. I cannot do it."

He saw at once that not one of them understood what he was saying. Angry looks appeared instantly on the faces of all. It might be that in Landover's baronies, as in the baronies of medieval history in his own world, marriage was mostly for convenience. He didn't know, and it was too late now to find out. He had made the wrong decision in the minds of the Lords of the Greensward.

"You are not even a whole man!" Kallendbor sneered suddenly. Shouts rang out from the other Lords in approval.

Ben stood his ground. "I am King by law."

"You are a play-King like the others! You are a fraud!"

"He wears the medallion, Lord Kallendbor!" Questor shouted out from the far end of the table, shuffling away from his seat to come around.

"He may wear it, but it does him little good!" The red-bearded Lord had his eyes fixed on Ben. The shouts from the others continued. Kallendbor played to them, his voice rising. "He does not command the Paladin, does he? He has no champion to fight for him against man or demon! He has no one but you, Questor Thews. You had best come and get him now!"

"I need no one to stand up for me!" Ben stepped between Kallendbor and the approaching wizard. "I can stand for myself against anyone!"

The instant he had said it he wished that he hadn't. The room went still. He saw the smile come immediately to Kallendbor's hard face, the glint to his eye. "Would you care to test your strength against mine, High Lord?" the other asked softly.

Ben felt the dampness of sweat beneath his arms and along the crease of his back. He recognized the trap he had stepped into, but there seemed no way out of it now. "A test of strength seldom proves anything, Lord Kallendbor," he replied, his gaze kept steady on the other.

Kallendbor's smile turned unpleasant. "I would expect a man who relies solely on laws for his protection to say that."

Anger flooded through Ben. "Very well. How would you suggest that I test my strength against yours?"

"High Lord, you cannot allow . . ." Questor began, but was silenced by the shouts of the others gathered about the table.

Kallendbor rubbed his bearded face slowly, considering. "Well, now, there are any number of possibilities, all of them . . ."

He was cut short by a sharp bark from the far end of the table. It was Abernathy who, in his excitement to be heard, had lapsed back momentarily into the form of communica-

tion basic to this breed. "Forgive me," he said quickly as
the snickers began to rise. "Lord Kallendbor, you seem to
have forgotten the etiquette this situation demands. You
were the one to issue the challenge to a contest. It is your
opponent's right, therefore, to select the game."

Kallendbor frowned. "I assumed that because he was
from another world he did not know the games of this one."

"He need only know a variation of them," Abernathy replied, peering at the other over his glasses. "Excuse me for
one moment, please."

He left the table walking upright, head erect. Veiled laughter rose from the gathered Lords as the dog left the room.
Ben glanced quickly at Questor, who shrugged and shook
his head. The wizard had no idea what the scribe was about
either.

A few moments later, Abernathy was back. He carried in
his hands two pairs of eight ounce boxing gloves—the ones
that Ben had brought with him into Landover to keep in
training. "Fisticuffs, Lord Kallendbor," the soft-coated
Wheaten Terrier announced.

Kallendbor threw back his head and laughed. "Fisticuffs?
With those? I would prefer bare knuckles to leather socks
filled with stuffing!"

Abernathy brought the gloves about the table to where the
combatants stood. "High Lord," he bowed deeply, his soft
eyes on Ben. "Perhaps it would be best if you forgave Lord
Kallendbor his rash challenge. It would not do to see him
injured because of his inability to master your weapons."

"No! I do not withdraw the challenge!" Kallendbor
snatched one pair of gloves from the scribe and began to pull
them on. Strehan turned to help him.

Abernathy passed the second pair to Ben. "He is very
strong, High Lord. Watch yourself."

"I thought that you knew nothing of boxing," Ben whispered, working one glove on. Questor appeared at his side,
helping him tighten the laces. "How did you know to find
these?"

"I was responsible for the unpacking of your possessions when you arrived at Sterling Silver," Abernathy answered, giving Ben what might have been a smile coming from anyone else. "These gloves were there along with a magazine that demonstrated your game. I studied the pictures and drawings in the magazine. Our games are much the same. You call yours boxing. We call ours fisticuffs."

"I'll be damned!" Ben breathed.

Kallendbor had his gloves in place and was stripped to the waist. Ben glanced past Questor as he worked. Kallendbor's chest and arms rippled with muscle, and scars from battle wounds criss-crossed his body. He looked like a gladiator from the cast of *Spartacus*.

A space was being cleared at the center of the room, ringed by thralls in service to the castle proper and by the other Lords of the Greensward. The space was a little more than twice the size of a normal boxing ring.

"Any rules to this game?" Ben asked, taking deep breaths to calm himself.

Questor nodded. "Just one. Whoever is still standing at the end of the fight is the winner."

Ben slapped his gloves together to test the tightness of the laces and shrugged the tunic from his back. "That's it, huh? I guess I won't have any trouble remembering, will I?"

He went around the dinner table and into the makeshift ring. Kallendbor was waiting. Ben stopped momentarily at the edge of the crowd; Questor, Abernathy, and the two kobolds crowded in close beside him.

"So much for the lawyer's approach to things," he sighed.

"I will look after you, High Lord," Questor whispered hurriedly.

Ben turned. "No magic, Questor."

"But, High Lord, you cannot . . ."

"No magic. That's final."

The wizard grimaced and nodded reluctantly. "The medallion will protect you anyway," he muttered. But he did not sound all that sure that it would.

Ben shrugged the matter aside and stepped out into the ring. Kallendbor came at him at once, hands cocked, arms spread wide as if he intended to grapple. Ben hit him once with the left jab and sidestepped. The big man turned, grunting, and Ben hit him again, once, twice, a third time. The jabs were sharp and quick, snapping Kallendbor's head back. Ben danced away, moving smoothly, feeling the adrenalin begin to flow through his body. Kallendbor roared with fury and came at him with both arms flailing. Ben ducked, caught the blows on his arms and shoulders, then burrowed into the other's body with a flurry of quick punches, stepped away, jabbed and caught Kallendbor flush on the jaw with a full right hook.

Kallendbor went straight to the floor, a dazed look on his face. Ben danced away. He could hear Questor yelling encouragement. He could hear the oaths and shouts of the Lords of the Greensward. The blood pumped through him, and it seemed to him that he could hear the sound of his heartbeat throbbing in his ears.

Kallendbor climbed slowly back to his feet, eyes glinting with fury. He was as strong as Abernathy had warned. He would not be taken out easily.

He came at Ben once more, cautiously this time, fists held protectively before his face. The fighters feinted and jabbed, circling. Kallendbor's bearded face was flushed and angry. He pushed his gloves into Ben's, knocking them back, looking for an opening.

Then, suddenly, he charged. He was quick, and he caught Ben off balance with his rush. The blows rained into Ben, thrusting through his guard, catching him in the face. Ben danced away, his own fists jabbing back. But Kallendbor never slowed. He bore into Ben like a juggernaut, knocking him to the floor. Ben struggled back to his feet, but Kallendbor's wild blows caught him twice on the side of the head and down he went again.

The shouts of the Lords of the Greensward became a roar in Ben's ears, and there were colored lights dancing before his eyes. Kallendbor was standing over him, hitting at him with both hands, the smell of his sweat heavy in the air. Ben rolled away, careening into the ring of onlookers. Hands shoved him back. Kallendbor's boots and knees struck out at him, and he felt the pain of the blows lance through his body. He curled into a ball, his gloves tight against his face, his forearms against his chest.

He could feel the medallion he wore about his neck pressed against him.

The pain was becoming unbearable. He knew he was going to lose consciousness if he did not do something quickly. He rolled to his knees, bracing. When Kallendbor rushed at him again, he grappled desperately at the other's legs, pulled him off balance and tumbled him to the floor.

Ben came back to his feet at once, shaking the dizziness from his head, gloves cocked before his face. Kallendbor was up as well, his breath hissing from between his teeth. A strange light had appeared from behind the big man and the crowd of onlookers. It was a light that seemed to be growing brighter. Ben shook his head, trying to concentrate on the advancing Kallendbor. But now others were aware of the light as well. Heads had begun to turn and the crowd to part as the light advanced toward them. There was a figure within the light, a knight in battered, worn armor, helmet visor closed.

There was an audible gasp from the crowd of Lords and thralls.

The knight was the Paladin.

The assemblage stared, murmurs rippling through the sudden silence as the figure shimmered in the light. Some dropped to their knees, crying out in the same manner as had the demons when the Paladin had appeared to them in the Heart. Kallendbor stood uncertainly at the center of the circle, hands lowered, eyes turned away now from Ben to view the specter.

The Paladin shimmered a moment longer in the light, and

then he faded back again and was gone. The light died away into evening dark.

Kallendbor wheeled at once on Ben. "What trickery is this, play-King? Why do you bring that ghost into Rhyndweir?"

Ben shook his head angrily. "I brought nothing but . . ."

Questor cut the rest of what he was going to say short. "Lord Kallendbor, you mistake what has happened here. Twice before, the Paladin has appeared when the High Lord's safety was threatened. You are being warned, Lords of the Greensward, that this man, Ben Holiday, is the true King of Landover!"

"We are warned by a ghost in a light?" Kallendbor laughed, spitting blood from his cracked lips. "You have used your magic to try to frighten us, Questor Thews, and you have failed!"

He looked at Ben with disdain. "This game is finished. I want no more of you or your traveling circus. I want no part of you as my King!"

The shouts of the other Lords echoed his declaration. Ben stood where he was. "Whether you want any part of me or not, I am King nevertheless!" he snapped. "You may ignore me as you would ignore any truth, but I will remain a fact of your life! You think to ignore the laws that made me King, Kallendbor, but you will not be able to do so forever! I will find a way to see that you cannot!"

"You need not look far, play-King!" Kallendbor was beside himself with fury. He shrugged out of the boxing gloves and threw them at Ben. "You claim to be King of Landover? You claim to command the services of the Paladin? Very well, prove that you truly are what you claim by ridding us of the one plague on our existence that we cannot ourselves dismiss! Rid us of Strabo! Rid us of the dragon!"

He stalked forward until he was almost on top of Ben. "Twenty years now the dragon has raided our stock and destroyed our property. We have hunted him from one end of Landover to the other, but he has the magic of the old world and we cannot kill him. You are heir to the old magic, too—if you are who you claim! So rid us of the dragon, play-King, and then I will bow to you as High Lord and pledge you my life!''

A roar of approval rose from the throats of all assembled. "Rid us of the dragon!" they cried as one. Ben's eyes remained locked on Kallendbor's.

"Until then, I will ignore you as I would ignore the ants that crawl beneath my feet!" Kallendbor whispered in his face.

He wheeled and stalked from the circle, the other Lords following after. Slowly, the room began to empty. Ben was left alone with Questor, Abernathy, and the kobolds. The four came forward to remove his gloves and to clean the blood and sweat from his face and body.

"What's all this about the dragon?" Ben demanded immediately.

"Later, High Lord," Questor answered, dabbing at a mouse already beginning to form under one eye. "A bath and a night's sleep are in order first."

Ben shook his head. "Not in this place! I wouldn't spend another moment here if it meant hiking out across a damn desert! Pack everything. We're leaving right now. We'll talk about the dragon on the way."

"But, High Lord . . ."

"Now, Questor!"

No one chose to argue the point further. An hour later their little company was back on the road traveling west out of Rhyndweir into the night.

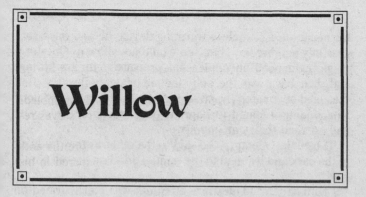

Willow

Ben's decision to leave Rhyndweir so abruptly proved to be a poor one. The company had barely cleared the outskirts of the village shops and cottages lining the castle's approach when it began to rain. The rain came slowly at first, a spattering of drops against their faces, light and teasing. Then the drops became a shower, and the shower became a downpour. Clouds blocked away the land's moons and the distant stars, and everything turned as black as pitch. Wind howled across the flat, empty pastures and fields of the Greensward, thrusting at the travelers like a giant's breath. It took only moments for the company to decide to seek immediate shelter, but they were already soaked to the bone by then.

They spent the night in a dilapidated, empty barn in which stock had once been housed. Rain blew through holes in the walls and roofing, and there were few dry spots to be found. The air turned chill, and the damp clothing seemed colder than before. Ben and his companions huddled together in the dark in a large horse stall at one end of the barn. It was dryer there than anywhere else in the building, and there was straw on which to bed. A fire was out of the question, so everyone had to make do with a quick change of clothing and a sharing of the blankets from their bedding. Questor offered to try

his magic on a flameless warming device he had once successfully conjured up, but Ben would not allow it. Questor's
magic evidenced an unpleasant propensity for backfiring,
and their barn was the only shelter in sight. Besides, Ben
reasoned obstinately, weathering out the storm in such poor
surroundings seemed appropriate punishment for the way he
had botched things at Rhyndweir.

"I blew it, Questor," he said to the other as they huddled
in the dark and listened to the rainfall drum on the old barn's
roof.

"Hmmmmm?" Questor's attention was concentrated on
wiping dirt and blood from the numerous cuts and abrasions
Ben had suffered during his fight with Kallendbor.

"I screwed up. I mishandled the whole thing. I let Kallendbor trick me into accepting his stupid challenge. I lost my
composure; I let the entire affair get out of hand." He sighed
and leaned back against the stall side. "I should have done
a better job of arguing my case. Some lawyer, right? Some
King!"

"I think you handled matters rather well, High Lord."

Ben looked at him skeptically. "You do?"

"It was obviously intended that you should fail in your
attempt to gain a pledge from the Lords of the Greensward
unless you were willing to gain that pledge on their terms.
Had you agreed to marry a daughter of one of their house-
holds, the pledge would have been yours. You would have
had a wife and a dozen in-laws for the balance of your reign
as King—a reign that would have been considerably shorter
than you would have liked." The wizard shrugged. "But you
knew what they intended as well as I, didn't you?"

"I knew."

"So you were right to refuse the offer, and I think you
showed great composure under the circumstances. I think
that if the game had been allowed to continue, you might
have beaten him."

Ben laughed. "I appreciate the vote of confidence. I notice, however, that you left nothing to chance."

"What do you mean?"

"I mean that you ignored my order not to use the magic and conjured up that image of the Paladin when it looked as if I was going down for the count!"

The owlish face studied him, a faint outline in the dark. Questor set aside the bloodied cloths. "I did nothing of the sort, High Lord. That *was* the Paladin."

There was a long silence. "Then he has come three times now," Ben whispered finally, his bewilderment evident. "He came when I was caught in the time passage with the Mark, he came when the demons appeared at the coronation, and now he has come to the Greensward. But he seems just exactly what you called him, Questor—a ghost! He looks as if he's only an image made of light! What is he really?"

The other shrugged. "Maybe what he appears—maybe something more."

Ben hunched his knees up close against his body, trying to stay warm. "I think that he's out there. I think that he's trying to come back again." He looked at Questor for confirmation.

Questor shook his head. "I do not know, High Lord. Maybe so."

"What was it that brought him in the past? There must be something you can tell me about him—about why and how he appeared to the old King."

"He appeared when he was summoned," the other replied. "The summons has always come from the wearer of the medallion. The medallion is a part of the magic, High Lord. There is a link between it, the Kings of Landover, and the Paladin. But only the Kings of Landover have ever fully understood what that link was."

Ben pulled the medallion from beneath his tunic and studied it. "Maybe if I rub it, or talk to it, or just grasp it— maybe that will bring the Paladin. What do you think?"

Questor shrugged. Ben tried all three and nothing happened. He tried wishing for the Paladin's appearance, hands clutched about the medallion so tightly he could feel the impression of its carved surface. Nothing happened.

"I suppose I should have known it wouldn't be that easy." He sighed and dropped the medallion back down the front of his tunic, feeling it catch on the chain that lay looped about his neck. He looked up through a hole in the barn roof as the wind rattled the shingles against their fastenings. "Tell me about the dragon and the Lords of the Greensward."

The wizard's stooped form bent closer still. "You heard most of it from Kallendbor yourself. The Lords of the Greensward are at war with Strabo. The dragon is their nemesis. He has preyed upon them for the better part of twenty years—ever since the old King died. He burns their crops and their buildings; he devours their livestock and occasionally their thralls. He hunts their lands at will, and they are powerless to stop it."

"Because the dragon is part of the magic—isn't that it?"

"Yes, High Lord. Strabo is the last of his kind. He was a creature of the world of fairy until his exile thousands of years ago. He cannot be harmed by mortal weapons, only by the magic from which he was created. That was why Kallendbor felt safe in challenging you to rid him of the dragon—he believes you a fraud. A true King of Landover would command the magic of the medallion and could summon the Paladin to do his bidding."

Ben nodded. "It all comes back to the Paladin, doesn't it? Tell me, Questor, why is it that the dragon hunts the Greensward as he does?"

The wizard smiled. "He is a dragon."

"Yes, I know. But he didn't always hunt like this, I gather—at least, not while the old King lived."

"True. He kept to his own land in times previous. Perhaps he feared the old King. Perhaps the Paladin kept him there until the old King was dead. Your guess is as good as mine."

Ben grunted irritably and leaned back against the stall side. His entire body hurt. "Why is it that you can't manage an answer to any of these questions, damn it? You're supposed to be the court wizard and my personal advisor, but you don't seem to know much of anything!''

Questor looked away. "I do the best I can, High Lord.''

Ben immediately regretted his words. He touched the other on the shoulder. "I know. I'm sorry I said that.''

"I was away from the court when the old King was alive, and my half-brother and I were never close. Had we been close, perhaps I could have learned at least some of the answers to your questions."

"Forget it, Questor. I'm sorry I said anything.''

"It has not been easy for me either, you know.''

"I know, I know.''

"I have had to master the magic practically alone. I have had no tutor, no master to instruct me. I have had to preserve the throne of Landover while shepherding about a flock of Kings who were frightened by the sight of their own shadow and who wanted nothing more challenging than the spectacle of knights at a joust!'' His voice was rising. "I have given everything that I have so that the monarchy might endure, even while beset by miseries that would break the back of an ordinary . . .''

Abernathy's growl interrupted rudely. "Please, wizard, enough of your soliloquies! We are already bored to tears by this account of your sufferings and can bear no more!''

Questor's mouth snapped shut with an audible click of his teeth.

Ben smiled in spite of himself. It hurt his face to do so. "I hope that I do not number among those unfortunate Kings you have just described, Questor,'' he said.

The other's baleful gaze was still turned on Abernathy. "Hardly.''

"Good. Tell me one thing more, then. Can we rely on Kallendbor to be as good as his word?''

Questor looked back now. "About the dragon—yes. He swore an oath.''

Ben nodded. "Then we must find a way to get rid of the dragon.''

There was an endless moment of silence. Ben could sense the others looking at each other in the dark. "Any ideas as to how we go about doing that?" he asked.

Questor shook his head. "It has never been done."

"There is a first time for everything," Ben replied lightly, wondering as he said it just whom it was he was trying to convince. "You said that it would take magic to rid us of the dragon. Who could help us find that magic?"

Questor considered. "Nightshade, of course. She is the most powerful of those come from the world of fairy. But she is as dangerous as the dragon. I think we might have better luck with the River Master. He, at least, has proven loyal to the Kings of Landover in the past."

"Is he a creature of magic?"

"He was, once upon a time. He has been gone from the world of fairy for centuries. Still, he retains something of the knowledge of the old ways and may have help to offer. It was to him that I would have suggested we go next—even if the Lords of the Greensward *had* given their pledge."

Ben nodded. "Then it's settled. Tomorrow we travel to the country of the River Master." He stretched, hunched down into his blankets, hesitated a moment and said, "This may not count for much, but I want to thank you all for standing by me."

There was a mutter of acknowledgment and the sound of the others rolling into their bed coverings. Everything was silent for a moment except for the sound of the rain falling and the soft rush of the wind.

Then Abernathy spoke. "High Lord, would it be asking too much that we refrain from camping out in barns after tonight? I think there are fleas in this straw."

Ben smiled broadly and drifted off to sleep.

Daybreak brought an end to the rain, and a glimmer of sunshine appeared through the haze of mist and clouds that lingered on. The little company resumed the journey through the valley of Landover, this time turning south for the country of the River Master. They traveled all day, Ben, Questor and Abernathy on horseback, the kobolds afoot. Once again, Bunion went ahead to announce their coming. They passed from the lowland estates of the Lords of the Greensward at midafternoon, leaving behind their broad, open stretches of meadow and farmland, and by dusk were deep into the rolling hill country of the River Master.

The color of life was different here, Ben saw. The cast of things was brighter and truer—as if the failing of the magic had not penetrated so deeply. It was a country of lakes and rivers nestled within hollows and valleys, of orchards and woods scattered on gentle slopes, of grasses and ferns that shimmered in the wind like the waves of some ocean. The mists were thicker in the hill country, trapped in pockets like harnessed clouds, stirring and wending their way from hollow to valley and back again. But the greens of grasses and trees and the blues of lakes and rivers were brighter than in the Greensward, and the splashes of pinks, crimsons, and lavenders did not have that wintry tone than marked so distinctly the plains. Even the Bonnie Blues seemed not so blighted, though darkening spots still marred their beauty.

Ben asked Questor why this was.

"The River Master and those who serve him are closer to the old ways than most. Bits and pieces of the magic are still theirs to command. What magic they still retain they use to keep the earth and waters of their homeland clean." Questor gave a cursory glance about and then shrugged. "The River Master's magic protects against a failing of the land's magic only marginally. Already, signs of wilt and graying are evident. The River Master and his followers fight a holding action at best. The land will fail here in the end as it fails everywhere else."

"All because Landover has no King?" Ben still found the corrolation between the two difficult to accept.

"*Had* no King, High Lord—no King for twenty years."

"The thirty-two failures don't count for much, I gather?"

"Against a failing of the magic of the sort you see now? Nothing. You will be the first to count for anything."

Maybe yes, maybe no, Ben thought grimly, reminded of his lack of success with the Lords of the Greensward. "I really don't understand—doesn't anyone recognize the problem? I mean, the land is dying all about them and it's all because they can't get together long enough to settle on a King!"

"I do not think they perceive matters quite that way, High Lord," Abernathy said quietly, edging forward on his horse.

Ben glanced back. "What do you mean?"

"He means that the connection between the loss of a King and the failing of the land's magic is one that only I have made," Questor interrupted, obviously irritated with the scribe. "He means that no one else sees the problem the same way I do."

Ben frowned. "Well, what if they're right and you're wrong?"

Questor's owlish face tightened into a knot. "Then everything you and I are trying to do is a colossal waste of time! But it happens that they are not right and I am not wrong!" Questor glared back at Abernathy momentarily and then faced forward. "I have had twenty years to consider the problem, High Lord. I have observed and studied; I have employed what magic I command to test my theory. It is with some confidence that I tell you that Landover must have a King again if it is to survive!"

He was so adamant in his defense that Ben remained silent. It was Abernathy who spoke first.

"If you have finished momentarily with your attempt at self-vindication, Questor Thews, perhaps you will allow me to get a word in edgewise to explain what I really meant when I said others do not perceive matters as we." He looked down at Questor over the rims of his glasses, while the wizard stiffened in his saddle but refused to turn. "What I *meant* was that the lack of perception on the part of others was not as regards the problem, but the solution to it. Most

see quite clearly that the failing of the magic came about
with the death of the old King. But none agree that coronation of a new King will necessarily solve the problem.
Some believe restrictions should be placed on the solution
sought. Some believe another solution altogether should be
sought. Some believe no solution should be sought at all.''

"No solution at all—who thinks that?" Ben asked
disbelievingly.

"Nightshade thinks that." Questor reined his horse back
to them, his irritation with Abernathy momentarily put aside.
"She cares only for the Deep Fell, and her own magic keeps
the hollows as she wishes them. Should the magic of the land
fail, hers would be the most powerful."

"The Lords of the Greensward would accept one of their
own as King, but no other," Abernathy added to his explanation. "They accept the solution, but would place restrictions on it."

"And the River Master seeks to find another solution altogether—his solution being one of self-healing," Questor
finished.

"*That* was what I meant in the first place," Abernathy
huffed.

The wizard shrugged. "Then you should have said so."

Shadows were gathering rapidly across the land as they
turned their horses into a small grove of poplar to set camp
for the night. A wooded ridgeline crested the skyline west,
and the sun had already settled into its branches, filtering
daylight into streamers of hazy gold. A lake stretched south
of their campsite, a broad stretch of shimmering gray water
over which mist floated in thick clouds while trees screened
away dozens of tiny inlets and coves. Birds flew in wide,
lazy circles against the night.

"The lake is called Irrylyn," Questor told Ben as they
dismounted and handed the reins of their horses to Parsnip.
"It is said that, on certain nights of the high summer, the
sprites and nymphs of the River Master bathe within these
waters to keep their youth."

"That should be exciting." Ben yawned and stretched, wishing nothing more exciting at this point than a good night's sleep.

"Some believe that the waters have the power to preserve youth." Questor was caught up in his musings. "Some believe that the waters can turn back old age and make one young again."

"Some believe anything." Abernathy grunted, shaking himself until his hair ruffled back from beneath the dust that matted it. "I have washed in those waters more than once and gained nothing for my efforts beyond a better smell."

"Something you might give thought to now," Questor advised, wrinkling his nose in distaste.

Abernathy growled in response and padded off into the dark. Ben watched him go, then turned to Questor. "That sounds like a good idea for me, as well, Questor. I feel like somebody's doormat. Is there any reason I can't wash off some of this dirt?"

"No reason at all, High Lord." The wizard was already turning away, searching for Parsnip. "I suppose that I had better see to dinner."

Ben started for the lake and then stopped. "Anything dangerous down there that I ought to know about?" he called back, remembering suddenly the bog wump, the cave wight, and whatever else it was he hadn't even seen during his morning run about Sterling Silver.

But Questor was already out of hearing, his stooped form a vague shadow in the mists. Ben hesitated, staring after him, then shrugged and started for the lake once more. If nymphs and sprites could bathe in the waters of the Irrylyn, how dangerous could it be? Besides, Abernathy was already down there.

He picked his way through the shadows to the water's edge. The lake spread away before him, a sheen of silver that mirrored trailers of mist and the colored spheres of Landover's moons. Willows, cottonwood, and cedar canopied him, like drooping giants against the failing light, and birds called sharply through the twilight. Ben stripped off his clothes and boots, searching the dark for Abernathy. The dog was nowhere in sight, and he could not hear him moving.

Naked, he stepped out into the water. Shock registered in his face. The water was warm! It was like a bath—a soft, pleasant heat that soothed and relaxed the muscles of the body. He reached down and touched it with his hand, certain that the difference in air and water temperature must account for the odd sensation of warmth. But, no, the water was truly warm—as if a giant hot springs.

He shook his head. Cautiously, he stepped out until he was knee-deep in the lake, the shadow of his body stretched back against the waters. Something else was odd. It felt as if he were walking in sand. He reached down again and brought up a handful of the lake bottom. It *was* sand! He checked it carefully in the moonlight to make certain. He was inland at a forested lake where there should only have been mud or rock, and instead there was sand!

He walked ahead, beginning to wonder if perhaps there was indeed some sort of magic at work in the Irrylyn. He glanced about once again for some sign of Abernathy, but the dog was missing. Slowly he lowered himself neck-deep into the water, feeling its warmth soak through him, giving himself over to the sensation. He was several dozen yards from shore by now, the slope from the water's edge a gradual one that receded no more than several inches every ten feet or so. He swam into the dark, stretching his body out, breathing at regular intervals. When he came up for air, he saw a second inlet curve back from his own and swam toward it. It was tiny, barely a hundred feet across, and he swam past it toward a third. He switched from the crawl to a soundless breaststroke, head lifted toward his destination. Moonlight flooded the water with streamers of color, and the mist snaked past in shadowy screens of gray. Ben closed his eyes and swam.

The third inlet was smaller still, barely two dozen yards wide. Rushes screened the shoreline, and cedars and willows canopied above the waters, throwing dark shadows toward the lake. Ben dove beneath the water and swam silently into the cove, pulling his way toward the shallows.

He surfaced a dozen yards from the shoreline—and a woman was directly in front of him. She stood not ten feet away, a little more than ankle-deep in the lake's waters, as naked as he. She made no attempt to turn away or to cover herself. She was like a frightened animal caught in the light, frozen in that split second of hesitation before it would be gone.

Ben Holiday stared, seeing momentarily in his mind someone he had thought forever lost. Water ran down into his eyes and he blinked it away.

"Annie?" he whispered in disbelief.

Then the shadows and the mist shifted where they fell across her, and he saw that she was not Annie—that she was someone else.

And perhaps some*thing* else as well.

Her skin was pale green, smooth and flawless and almost silvery as the waters of the Irrylyn shimmered against it. Her hair was green as well, deep forest green, the tresses tumbling to her waist, braided with flowers and ribbons. But her hair grew in narrow lines along the backs of her forearms as well and along the backs of her calves, silken manes that stirred gently with the whisper of the night wind over the lake.

"Who are you?" she asked softly.

He could not bring himself to answer. He was seeing her clearly now, finding her exquisite beyond anything he would have imagined possible. She was an artist's flawless rendering of a fairy queen brought suddenly to life. She was the most beautiful creature he had ever seen.

She came forward a step in the moonlight. Her face was so youthful that it made her seem hardly more than a girl. But her body . . .

"Who are you?" she repeated.

"Ben." He could barely make himself answer, and it never occurred to him to answer any other way.

"I am Willow," she told him. "I belong to you now."

He was stunned anew. She came toward him, her body swaying with the movement, and now it was he who had become the frightened animal poised to flee.

"Ben." Her voice assumed a sweet, lilting cadence as she spoke to him. "I am a sylph, the child of a sprite become human and a wood nymph stayed wild. I was conceived on the midyear's passing in the heat of the eight moons full, and my fates were woven in the vines and flowers of the gardens in which my parents lay. Twice each year, the fates decreed, I was to steal to the Irrylyn in darkness and bathe in her waters. To the man who saw me thus, and to no other, would I belong."

Ben shook his head quickly, his mouth working. "But that's craz . . . that's not right! I don't even know you! You don't know me!"

She slowed before him, close enough now that she might reach out and touch him. He wanted her to do that. The need for that touch burned through him. He fought against it with everything he could muster, feeling trapped in the emotions that rushed through him.

"Ben." She whispered his name and the sound of it seemed to wrap about him. "I belong to you. I feel that it is so. I sense that the fates were right. I am given, as with the sylphs of old. I am given to the one who sees me thus." Her face lifted, the perfect features radiating back the rainbow colors of the moons. "You must take me, Ben."

He could not force his eyes away from her. "Willow." He used her name now, desperate to turn back the emotions that raged through him. "I cannot take . . . what does not belong to me. I am not even from this world, Willow. I barely know . . ."

"Ben," she whispered urgently, cutting short the rest of what he would say. "Nothing matters but that this has happened. I belong to you." She came a step closer. "Touch me, Ben."

His hand came up. Thoughts of Annie flashed with lightning clarity through his mind, and still his hand came up. The warmth of the waters of the Irrylyn and the air about him wrapped him so close that it seemed he could not breathe. The fingers of her hand touched his.

"Come away with me, Ben," she whispered.

Fire burned through him, a white-hot heat that consumed his reason. She was the need he had never known. He could not refuse her. Colors and warmth blinded him to everything but her, and the whole of the world about him dropped away. His hand closed tightly about hers, and he felt them join.

"Come away with me, now." Her body pressed close.

He reached for her, his arms wrapping her close, the softness of her body astonishing to him.

"High Lord!"

Everything blurred. There was a crashing of underbrush and the sound of footsteps. Rushes stirred, and the silence of the evening was shattered. Willow slipped from his arms.

"High Lord!"

Abernathy shoved his way into view at the shore's edge, panting with near exhaustion, his glasses askew on his furry nose. Ben stared at him in stunned silence, then glanced wildly about. He stood in the tiny inlet alone, naked and shivering now. Willow was gone.

"Goodness, do not wander off like that again without one of us!" Abernathy snapped, a mix of irritation and relief in his voice. "I would have thought that your experience at Sterling Silver would have been lesson enough!"

Ben barely heard him. He was scanning the inlet waters and shoreline for Willow. The need for her still burned through him like fire, and he could think of nothing else. But she was nowhere to be found.

Abernathy sat back on his haunches, grumbling to himself. "Well, I suppose that it is not your fault. It is mostly the fault of Questor Thews. You did tell him that you wished to bathe in the lake and he should have known better than to send you off without Parsnip for company. The wizard seems incapable of understanding the risks this land poses for you." He paused. "High Lord? Are you all right?"

"Yes," Ben answered at once. Had Willow been some sort of bizarre hallucination? She had seemed so real . . .

"You appear a bit distressed," Abernathy said.

"No, no, I'm fine . . ." He trailed off. "I just thought that I . . . saw something, I guess."

He turned then and moved to the shoreline, stepping from the waters of the Irrylyn to dry ground. Abernathy had brought a blanket and wrapped it about him. Ben pulled the blanket close.

"Dinner is waiting, High Lord," the dog advised, studying Ben closely over the rims of his glasses. Carefully, he straightened them. "Perhaps some soup will warm you."

Ben gave a perfunctory nod. "Sounds good." He hesitated. "Abernathy, do you know what a sylph is?"

The dog studied him some more. "Yes, High Lord. A sylph is a sort of woods fairy, the female offspring of sprites and nymphs, I'm told. I have never seen one, but they are supposed to be very beautiful." His ears cocked. "Beautiful in human terms, that is. Dogs might differ."

Ben stared off into the dark. "I suppose." He took a deep breath. "Soup, you say? I could use a bowl."

Abernathy turned and started away. "The campsite is this way, High Lord. The soup should be quite good if the wizard has managed to refrain from trying to improve on it by using his sadly limited magic."

Ben cast a quick glance back at the inlet. The waters of the lake glimmered undisturbed in the moonlight. The shoreline stood empty.

He shook his head and hurried after Abernathy.

The soup was good. It steamed down inside Ben Holiday and took away the chill that had left him shaking when he had discovered he was alone in that inlet. Questor was relieved to see him safely back and quarreled with Abernathy all during the meal as to who should assume responsibility for the High Lord's disappearance. Ben didn't listen. He let them argue, spoke when spoken to, and kept his thoughts to himself. Two bowls of soup and several glasses of wine later, he was comfortably drowsy as he stared into the flames of the small fire Parsnip had built. It hadn't even occurred to him to worry about drinking the wine.

He went to sleep shortly after. He rolled into his blankets and turned away from the fire, his gaze directed to the silver waters of the lake, the trailers of mist that hovered and swirled above them, and the night beyond. He listened to the silence that settled quickly over the hill country. He searched the darkness for shadows.

He slept well that night and, while he slept, he dreamed. He did not dream of Annie or Miles. He did not dream of the life he had left when he crossed over into Landover, nor of Landover or the myriad problems he faced as her King.

He dreamed instead of Willow.

River Master

Bunion returned at dawn. The morning was chill and damp; mist and shadows settled thick across the forest like a gray woolen blanket pulled close about a still-sleeping child. The remainder of the little company was at breakfast when the kobold appeared from the trees, a phantasm slipped from the dreams of last night. He went directly to Questor, spoke to him in that unintelligible mix of grunts and hisses, nodded to the others, and sat down to finish off what was left of the cold bread, berries, and ale.

Questor advised Ben that the River Master had agreed to receive them. Ben nodded wordlessly. His thoughts were elsewhere. Visions of Willow still lingered in his mind, images so real that they might have been something other than the dreams they were. Waking, he had sought to banish them, feeling them a betrayal somehow of Annie. But the visions had been too strong and he had been strangely anxious to preserve them in spite of his guilt. Why had he dreamed of Willow? he pondered. Why had the dreams been so intense? He finished his meal wrapped in his private reverie and saw nothing of the looks exchanged by Questor and Abernathy.

They departed the campsite shortly thereafter, a ragged

little procession of ghosts, winding silently through the half-light. They made their way single file about the Irrylyn, following the shoreline along a pathway barely wide enough for one. It was a journey through fantasia. Steam lifted snakelike from the valley floor in a mix of warm earth and cool air to mingle with the trailers of mist that swirled about the forest. Trees stood dark and wet against the gray, a tangle of huge, black-barked oaks, elms, gnarled hickories, willows, and cedars. Wraiths of the imagination whisked into view and were gone in the blink of an eye, lithe creatures that teased and taunted. Ben found himself numbed by the intransiency of it all—feeling as if he could not come fully awake from last night's sleep, as if he had been drugged. He rode in a fog that shrouded mind and eyes both, straining for a glimpse of what was real through the maze of shadow pictures. But only the mist-dampened trees and the flat, hard surface of the lake were certain.

Then the lake was gone with the rest of the world, and only the trees remained. Morning lengthened, and still the mist and shadows wrapped the land close and would do no more than whisper of hidden secrets. Sounds filtered softly through the deep haze, bits and pieces of other lives and other happenings that Ben could only guess at. He searched the haze at every turn for a glimpse of Willow, a prodding voice within him whispering that she was there somewhere among the sounds and shadows, watching. He searched, but he did not find her.

It was shortly thereafter that the wood sprite appeared to them.

They had turned their horses down a draw formed by a series of fallen trees, Bunion leading the way on foot, when the sprite slipped from the mists at the kobold's shoulder. He was a lean, wiry figure, barely taller than Bunion, skin as brown and grainy as the bark of a sapling, hair grown thick down the back of his neck and along his arms. Earth-colored clothing hung loosely against his body; his sleeves and pantlegs were cut short, his feet slipped into a boot that laced about the calves with leather. He barely slowed the procession as he appeared, falling in beside Bunion, moving forward through the haze in an almost birdlike manner, quick and restless.

"Questor!" Ben's voice was a rough hiss, louder than he had intended it to be. "Who is that?"

The wizard, riding just ahead, leaned back in his saddle, a finger to his lips. "Gently, High Lord. Our guide is a wood sprite in service to the River Master. There are others all about us."

Ben's gaze shifted quickly to the mist. He saw no one. "Our guide? Our guide to what?" His voice had dropped to a whisper.

"Our guide to Elderew, the home of the River Master."

"We need a guide?"

Quester shrugged. "It is safer to have one, High Lord. Marsh lies all about Elderew and more than a few have been lost to it. The lake country can be treacherous. The guide is a courtesy extended us by the River Master—a courtesy extended to all guests upon their arrival."

Ben glanced once more into the opaque curtain of the fog. "I hope the same courtesy is extended to guests upon their departure," he muttered to himself.

They moved ahead into the trees. Other forms appeared suddenly from the mist, lean, wiry shapes like their guide, some with the same wood-grained appearance, some stick-like and gnarled, some smooth and sleek with skin that was almost silver. They fell in silently on either side of the column, hands grasping the reins of the horses, guiding the animals ahead. Pools of water and reed-grown marsh materialized all along the trail they followed, vast patches of swamp in which nothing moved but the fog. The trail narrowed further and at times disappeared altogether, leaving them in water that rose to their guides' waists and the horses' haunches. Creatures swam in the water, some with fins, some with reptilian scales, some with faces that were almost human. Creatures darted through the mist, dancing across the mire's surface like weightless skip-flies. They surfaced far out in the fog, and there were only flashes before they were gone again. Ben felt himself waking now, the dreams of last night dissipated finally, no more than faint memories and disconnected feelings. His mind sharpened as he peered through the gloom and studied the beings about him with mingled incredulity and disbelief. He was enveloped in a sudden, biting sense of hopelessness. Sprites, nymphs, kelpies, naiads, pixies, elementals—the names came back to him as he watched these marsh creatures appear and fade again. He recalled his early, exploratory reading of fantasy and horror fiction, an almost forbidden trespass, and relived his wonder at the strange beings he had encountered. Such creatures could only exist in the writer's mind and come to life through his pen, he had believed—wishing secretly at the same time that it could be otherwise. Yet here those creatures were, the inhabitants of the world into which he had come, and he knew less of them than he did of those make-believe writer's creations he had encountered in his youth—and they, in turn, knew nothing at all of him. How, in God's name, could he convince them then to accept him as their King? What could he say that would persuade them to pledge to him?

The hopelessness of the task was appalling. It terrified him so that for a moment he was paralyzed with indecision. The lean, shadowy figures of the River Master's people slipped through the mist all about him, and he saw them as alien beings for whom he was nothing more than a curiosity. It had been different with the Lords of the Greensward. There had been a similarity in appearance, at least, a sense of sameness. But there was nothing of that with the people of the River Master.

He shoved the indecision and the fear from his mind. He swept back into its cubicle the hopelessness he felt. He banished them with a fury that was surprising. Such feelings were merely excuses to quit, and he would never do that. Bridges could be built between beings of any kind. There had been Kings that had served these people before; he could serve them just as well. He would find a way to make them see that. He would do whatever was necessary, but he would never quit. Never.

"High Lord?"

Abernathy was at his elbow, liquid brown eyes questioning. Ben looked down. His hands were gripping the pommel of his saddle so tightly that the knuckles were white. Sweat dampened the back and underarms of his tunic. He knew his face reflected the intensity of his feelings.

He took a deep breath and steadied himself, hands releasing their death-grip. "It was just a chill," he alibied, forced his gaze away, and kicked Wishbone ahead so that Abernathy was safely behind him once more.

A great gathering of hoary cypress loomed darkly through the mist ahead, trailers of moss hanging from their branches, gnarled roots digging into the marshy soil like claws. The little company and their wraithlike guides passed into their midst, swallowed in shadows and the smell of fetid earth. Their path was snakelike through the ancient trees, circumventing black pools that mirrored, like opaque glass, and patches of marsh that steamed. The grove of cypress was massive, and they became lost within it. The minutes slipped away, and daylight took on the guise of fading dusk.

Then the sheltering trees thinned and the ground began to rise. Slowly the company worked its way upward through the forest to where the mist burned away and the day brightened with sun. Marsh gave way to hardened earth, cypress to oak and elm. The raw smell of the lowland lake country filtered out into sweeter smells of pine and cedar. The faces in the mist became distinct now as elusive figures darted all about, but had the substance of real beings. Voices lifted out of the forest ahead. Ben sensed the end of their journey was at hand, and his pulse quickened.

A rush of color filtered through the trees, garlands of flowers strung from limbs and swaybars, and the sound of rushing water filled the air. The trees parted before them, the trail broadened, and a massive open-air amphitheater stood cradled in the light. Ben stared. The amphitheater was formed of living trees wrapped in a three-quarter circle about an arena of grasses and flowers; there were lines of walkways and seats constructed of limbs and sawn logs, fastened and shaped about the framework of the amphitheater's bowl. Branches from the trees canopied overhead to form a natural covering, and traces of sunlight broke through the mist where it thinned at the roof of the forest, falling in long, rainbow streamers to the grasses below in the manner of light in a rain forest when the monsoons have passed.

"High Lord," Abernathy called softly back to him. "Look."

He pointed—not to the amphitheater, but to what lay beyond. Ben felt his breath catch in his throat. What he was seeing was something almost surreal. Trees twice the size of those which framed the amphitheater lifted skyward in the forest beyond, pillars of such monstrous proportions that they dwarfed even the redwoods he had once visited when traveling with Annie through California. Great, angular branches laced together, binding one tree to the next, creating a complex and intricate network of limbs that joined each to the other until all were one.

An entire city lay cradled within and below those branches.

It was a magnificent, sprawling artist's rendering of an imagined fairy homeland. Cottages and shops sat high within the branches of the giant trees, interconnected by lanes and walkways that descended gradually toward the forest floor where the greater part of the city sat astride a series of canals fed by a river that cut through the center of the city. It was the soft rush of the river's waters that they had heard before. The forest's leafy roof screened away the sky, but sunlight broke through in scattered patches. Color from flowers and bushes brightened homes and shops, gardens and hedgerows, waterways and treelanes. The mists shrouded the city

like a soft filter, and the gray, wintry cast that characterized
so much of the valley was banished.

The fairy-born people of the River Master filled the treelanes and waterways, angular faces and bodies bits and
pieces of the land's shadows as they passed through the mist.

"That is Elderew," Questor announced needlessly, for
Ben had already surmised that much.

The members of the little company turned into the amphitheater, the slight forms of their guides slipping from them
one by one until only the guide who had appeared first to
them remained. They passed through the open quarter section to the arena bowl—Bunion in the lead, stride for stride
with their guide; Questor and Ben next; Abernathy a few
paces behind, bravely hoisting aloft once more the scarlet
and white King's standard with the armored figure of the
Paladin; Parsnip and the pack animals trailing. A reception
committee was waiting, just emerged from one of several
tunnels leading into the amphitheater from beneath its seats,
gathered now in a knot at the tunnel's entrance. There were
men and women both in the group; while Ben could not discern faces from so great a distance, he could easily identify
items of forest clothing similar to that worn by their guide
and swatches of the same wood-grained skin.

They drew to a halt at the center of the arena, dismounted,
and walked forward to where the reception committee
waited. The kobolds and Abernathy trailed Ben and Questor
now, and the guide had remained behind with the animals.
Ben cast a quick glance over at the wizard.

"If you have any last minute advice, Questor, I would
appreciate it," he whispered.

"Hmmmmm?" The wizard's thoughts were elsewhere
once again.

"About the River Master? About what sort of person he
is?"

"What sort of creature, you mean," Abernathy interjected
acidly from behind them.

"A sprite, High Lord," Questor answered. "A fairy who

become half-human when he crossed into Landover and adopted this valley as his home, a woods and water being, a . . . a, uh . . ." The wizard paused thoughtfully. "He is really quite hard to describe, when you come right down to it."

"Best that he discover for himself," Abernathy declared pointedly.

Questor thought a moment, then nodded in agreement. "Yes, perhaps so."

They were too close to the gathering that awaited them for Ben to discuss the matter further—though in light of what had just been implied, he would have dearly loved to do so— and he turned his attention instead to a quick study of his hosts. He identified the River Master at once. The River Master stood central and foremost among those gathered, a tall, lean figure garbed in pants, tunic and cloak that were forest green, polished boots and leather cross-belts, and a slim silver diadem bound about his forehead. His skin was of a silver cast and grained like that of their guide—almost scaled—but his hair was black and thick about the nape of his neck and forearms. There was an odd, chiseled appearance to his eyes and mouth, and his nose was almost non-existent. He had the look of something carved of wood.

The remaining members of the gathering stood grouped about him, younger for the most part, men and women of varying shapes and sizes, a scattering of faces as nut-brown and grained as that of their guide, one or two silver like the River Master, one sticklike and almost featureless, one covered with fur that was a russet color, one reptilian in looks and coloring, one a ghostly white with deep black eyes, and one . . .

Ben slowed abruptly, fighting to keep from his face the sudden shock that raced through him. One of those gathered, the one standing at the River Master's left hand, was Willow.

"Questor!" His voice was a low hiss. "The girl on the left—who is she?"

Questor stared over at him. "Who?"

"The girl on the left! The one with the green skin and hair, damn it!"

"Oh, the sylph?" Questor smiled benignly to those ahead, speaking to Ben out of the side of his mouth. "Her name is Willow. She is one of the River Master's children." He paused. "What difference does . . ."

Ben hushed him into immediate silence. They kept walking, Ben's mind working frantically, his eyes flitting from the faces of the others gathered to Willow's. She stared back at him boldly, her own eyes challenging.

"Welcome, High Lord," the River Master greeted as Ben and his companions reached him. He bowed briefly, little more than a nod, and those with him bowed as well. "Welcome to Elderew."

Masking his surprise at seeing Willow, Ben drew his scattered thoughts together with a vengeance. "I appreciate the greeting. I appreciate as well your receiving me in your home on such short notice."

The River Master laughed. It was a big, hearty laugh that filled the amphitheater with its sound, but the grainy, chiseled face was like stone. "The fact that you come at all does you much credit, High Lord. You are the first to do so since the old King died. I would be a poor host indeed if I were to refuse to receive you after so long a wait!"

Ben smiled politely, but the smile gave way to shock when he noticed that the River Master had gills at the side of his neck. "Apparently it has been a long wait for everyone," he managed.

The River Master nodded. "Quite long." He turned. "This is my family, High Lord—my wives, my children, and my grandchildren. Many have never seen a King of Landover and asked to be in attendance."

He introduced them one by one, the gills at the side of his neck fluttering softly as he spoke. Ben listened patiently, nodding to each, nodding to Willow as to the others as she was brought forward, feeling the heat of her eyes burn

through him. When the River Master had finished, Ben in
troduced those in his own company.

"All are welcome," the River Master announced in response, and he gave his hand to each. "There will be a celebration in your honor this evening and a processional. You
are to think of Elderew as your home while you are with
us." He gave Ben what was meant to pass for a smile. "And
now I think that you and I should speak of what has brought
you here, High Lord. It is the way of things in the lake country to dispose of business directly and with expedience.
While your companions are boarded in the village, you and
I shall have our conference—just the two of us. Will you
consent to that?"

Ben nodded. "I will." He did not even glance at Questor
to see if the wizard approved. Questor could not help him
in this. He knew what it was that he had to do, and he knew
that he had to do it alone. Besides, the River Master did not
seem a bad sort, Abernathy's cryptic comments
notwithstanding.

The River Master dispatched his family with instructions
to conduct Questor, Abernathy, and the kobolds to their
lodgings. Then he turned to Ben. "Would you like to see
something of the village while we talk, High Lord?" he
asked.

It was more a suggestion than a question, but Ben nodded
agreeably nevertheless. The River Master beckoned him
down into one of the tunnels that cut beneath the amphitheater and he followed wordlessly. He had a last glimpse
of Willow staring after him from the misty sunlight and then
the shadows closed about.

When he emerged at the far end of the tunnel, the River
Master took him along a canal bank lined with flowerbeds
and hedgerows, carefully trimmed and tended, into a park
that bordered the perimeter of the amphitheater. There were
children playing in the park, small darting forms of varying
sizes and shapes that reflected the diversity of their paren-
tage, their voices bright and cheerful in the comparative still-

ness of the afternoon. Ben smiled wistfully. It had been a
long time since he had listened to the sound of children playing; except for their different appearance, they might have
been the children of his own world.

But, of course, *this* was his world now.

"I know that you have come to Elderew to ask my pledge
to the throne, High Lord," the River Master informed him
suddenly, his silver face a tight, expressionless mask. It
seemed that his face never altered, reflecting nothing of his
thoughts. "I know, as well, that you went first to the Lords
of the Greensward with this same request and that the request was refused." Ben glanced quickly at him, but the
River Master brushed the look aside with a shrug. "Oh, you
needn't be surprised that I know such things, High Lord. I
am once and always of the fairy world, and I still have something of the magic I once wielded. I have eyes in most corners
of the valley."

He paused, digressing momentarily on the construction of
the park and the canal system that ran through Elderew. Ben
listened patiently, seeing that he meant to conduct the dis-
cussion at his own pace, content to let him do so. They
walked from the park into a grove of elm bordering the giant
trees that were the framework of the village.

"I respect the initiative and the courage that you have
shown in undertaking your journey to the peoples of the valley, High Lord." The River Master returned now to the matter of Ben's visit. "I believe you to be a stronger man than
those who laid claim to the throne of Landover before. Your
actions at Rhyndweir would suggest that you are, in any
case. I think you are also a straightforward and decisive man,
so I will spare you the evasive maneuverings of diplomacy.
I have considered your request—knowing what it is, as I
have said—and I must reject it."

They walked on in silence. Ben was stunned. "May I ask
why?" he said finally.

"I can see no advantage to granting it."

"I would argue that you should see many advantages."

The River Master nodded. "Yes, I know. You would argue that there is strength in numbers—that a central government would benefit the whole of the people of the land. You would argue that the people of the land cannot trust one another while there is no King. You would argue that we are threatened from without by neighboring worlds and from within by the Mark and his demons. You would argue that the land is stricken with a blight that is caused by a failing of the magic that made her, and that eventually she will die." He looked over. "Have I correctly stated the arguments that you would make?"

Ben nodded slowly. "How would you answer them?"

"I would tell you a story." The River Master slowed and led Ben to a bench chiseled from a massive rock. They sat. "The people of the lake country came from the fairy world, High Lord—most in a time long since forgotten by everyone but us. We are a fairy people who choose to live in a world of humans. We have become mortals by choice, affected by time's passage where once we were virtually immortal. We are elementals—creatures of wood, earth, and water—sprites, nymphs, kelpies, naiads, pixies, and dozens more. We left the fairy world and claimed the lake country as our own. We made it what it is—a country of beauty, grace, and health. We made it so because that was our purpose for coming into Landover in the first place. We came to give her life—not simply the lake country, but all of the valley."

He paused. "We have that power, High Lord—the power to give life." He bent close, an earnest teacher instructing his pupil. "We have not lost all of the magic, you see. We still possess the power to heal. We can take a land that suffers from sickness and blight and make it whole again. Come with me a moment. See what I mean."

He rose and walked a short distance to a gathering of brush nestled at the perimeter of the elm grove. The leaves were showing signs of wilt and spotting, much as the Bonnie Blues Ben had observed on his journey to Sterling Silver.

"See the sickness in the leaves?" the River Master asked.

He reached down and placed his hand upon the brush, close to where it rooted in the earth. There was concentration in his face. His breathing slowed and his head bent until his chin rested on his chest. Slowly the brush stirred, responding to his touch. The wilt and spotting disappeared, the color returned, and the brush grew straight again in the afternoon light.

The River Master rose. "We have the power to heal," he repeated, the intensity still visible in his eyes. "We would have used it to benefit the whole of the land had we been allowed to do so. But there are many who distrust us. There are many more who care nothing for the work that we do. They prefer us confined to the lake country, and we have honored their wishes. If they chose to think us dangerous because we are different, then so be it. But they will not leave well enough alone, High Lord. They continue to harm the land through their use of it. They cause sickness to spead through their carelessness and disregard. They bring sickness not only to their own homes in the valley, but to ours as well—to the rivers and the forests that belong to us!"

Ben nodded. Perhaps they shared common ground after all. "Your world is really not so different from my own, River Master. There were many who pollute the land and water in my world as well, and they disregard the safety and health of others in doing so."

"Then, High Lord, you will understand the ending that I put to my story." The River Master faced him squarely. "The lake country belongs to us—to the people who live within and care for it. This is our home. If the others in the valley choose to destroy their homes, that is of no concern to us. We have the power to heal our rivers and forests, and we will do so for as long as it is necessary. The loss of the magic that came with the death of the old King caused no greater problem for us than had already existed. The Lords of the Greensward, the trolls, kobolds, gnomes, and all of the others had spread their sickness through Landover long before that. Nothing has changed for us. We have always been a separate people, and I suspect that we always will be."

He shook his head slowly. "I wish you success, High Lord, but I will not pledge to you. Your coming to the throne of Landover changes nothing for the people of the lake country."

Ben glanced down again at the bit of brush the River Master had healed and then folded his arms across his chest solemnly. "I was told by Questor Thews that the River Master and his people worked to cure the sickness that spreads through Landover. But isn't it true that your work to keep the sickness out grows more difficult each day? The loss of the magic spreads the sickness too quickly, River Master. There will come a day when even your skill will not be enough, a day when the blight is so strong that the magic of the land itself will die."

The River Master's face was a stone. "The others may perish because they lack the skills to survive, High Lord. That will not happen with us."

Ben frowned. "That declaration of independence seems rather overoptimistic, don't you think? What of the Mark and his demons? Can you survive them?" There was a trace of irritation in his voice.

"They cannot even see us if we do not wish it. We can disappear into the mist in a moment. They pose no danger to us."

"They don't? What if they occupy Elderew?"

"Then we would build again. We have done so before. The land always offers the means to survive when you possess the magic."

His placid certainty was infuriating. He was a mirror image of the proverbial scholar who lived inside of his books and saw nothing of the world that was not printed there. It appeared that Abernathy's cynicism had some foundation in fact after all. Ben's mind raced, sorting through arguments and discarding them just as quickly. The River Master had obviously decided that he would not pledge to *any* King of

Landover, and it did not seem that there was anything that could make him change his mind. Yet Ben knew that he must find a way.

A light clicked on inside his head. "What of the reason that you came to Landover in the first place, River Master? What of your work here?"

The chiseled face regarded him thoughtfully. "My work, High Lord?"

"Your work—the work that brought all of your people out of the fairy world and into Landover. What of that? You left paradise and timeless, immortal life to cross into a world with time and death. You accepted that you would be human. You did that because you wanted to cleanse Landover, to make her earth, trees, mountains, and waters healthy and safe! I don't know why you made that choice, but you did. Now you seem to be telling me that you have given up! You don't seem that sort of man to me. Are you willing to sit back and let the whole valley turn sick and wither away into nothing just to prove a point? Once the sickness spreads far enough and deep enough, how will you ever find the magic to drive it out!"

The River Master stared at him wordlessly, a small frown appearing, a hint of doubt in his eyes.

Ben charged quickly ahead. "If you pledge to me, I will put an end to the pollution of the waterways and the forests. I will stop the spread of the sickness—not just here, in the lake country, but throughout the valley."

"A noble ambition, High Lord." The River Master seemed almost sad. "How will you do that?"

"I will find a way."

"How? You lack even the small magic of the old King, the magic that gave him mastery over the Paladin. You wear the medallion—I see it beneath your tunic—but it is little more than a symbol of your office. High Lord, you are a King in name only. How can you do any of what you promise?"

Ben took a deep breath. The words stung, but he was

careful to keep the anger from his voice. "I don't know. But I will find a way."

The River Master was silent a moment, lost in thought. Then he nodded slowly. His words were slow and carefully measured. "Very well, High Lord. Nothing is lost by letting you try. You make a promise I will hold you to. Put an end to the pollution. Put a stop to the spreading of the sickness. Extract a promise from the others who inhabit this valley that they will work with us to preserve the land. When you have done that, then I will give you my pledge."

He extended his hand. "A bargain, High Lord?"

Ben gripped the hand firmly in his own. "A bargain, River Master."

They shook. The sound of the children's laughter rang softly in the distance. Ben sighed inwardly. Another conditional pledge extracted. He was a man building a house of cards.

He gave the River Master his best courtroom smile. "You wouldn't happen to know a way to keep the dragon out of the Greensward, would you?"

Elderew

The River Master did not know a way to keep the dragon out of the Greensward. No one did, so far as he knew. Nightshade might, he speculated as he guided Ben back through the grove of elm and into the park with its children. The witch of the Deep Fell had magic more powerful than that of any other creature in the valley—although even Nightshade had never dared offer challenge to Strabo. In any case, Nightshade would never agree to help him, even if she had the means to do so. She had always hated the Kings of Landover because they commanded the services of the Paladin, and the Paladin was more powerful than she.

Times change, Ben thought dismally.

There were the fairies, of course, the River Master added almost as an afterthought. The fairies had always been able to control the dragons. That was why the dragons had fled from or been driven out of their world and come over into the valley. But the fairies would not help Ben either. The fairies helped no one, unless it was their idea first. They stayed within the mists, hidden in their timeless, ageless world, and lived their own lives according to their own rules. Ben could not even go to them to ask their help. No one ever went into the fairy world and came out again.

They walked down together through Elderew, the River Master describing the history of his city and its people, Ben wondering how on God's green earth—or this one, for that matter—he was ever going to make a success out of being King. The afternoon slipped away; while the city was a marvelous and exciting creation, the tour was wasted on Ben. He listened dutifully, commented in all of the appropriate places, asked the proper questions, and waited with a saint's patience for a chance to excuse himself.

The chance never came. Dusk settled, and the River Master deposited him at his lodging for the night—a ground-level cottage with several open-air porches and walkups, secluded gardens and an impressive stand of Bonnie Blues. Overhead, the brightly lighted treelanes of the city spiraled through the mist of the forest roof in arcs of hazy gold. Laughter and light banter echoed through the shadows. For some, the day's work was finished.

Ben trooped into the cottage, the daylight fading quickly to nightfall behind him, the River Master's promise of an evening of celebration hanging over him like a pall. The last thing he felt like doing was celebrating.

The others of the little company were waiting for him as he entered. He gave them a cursory hello and plopped down in a comfortably cushioned wicker rocker.

"I struck out again," he announced wearily.

Questor took a seat across from him. "He refused his pledge, High Lord?"

"More or less. He promised to give it only after I've found a way to put a stop to the pollution of the valley by the others who live here. I have to extract their sworn vow to work with the lake country people to keep the valley clean."

"I warned you he would be difficult, High Lord," Abernathy declared triumphantly. Ben glanced over. He remembered his scribe's admonishment somewhat differently, but there was nothing to be gained by arguing the point.

"I think you have done rather well, High Lord," Questor informed him, ignoring Abernathy.

Ben groaned. "Questor, please . . ."

"I am quite serious about this, I assure you," the wizard added quickly. "I was worried he would refuse you unconditionally. He was loyal to the old King out of a sense of respect for a monarchy that had governed hundreds of years and out of a desire not to provoke trouble by refusing obeisance. But the lake country people have never truly had a sense of belonging; there has never been an acceptance of them by the others."

"The River Master said something along those same lines. Why is it such a problem?"

Questor shook his head. "Mostly, it is a lack of understanding. The people of the lake country are fairies and they command magic the others in the valley do not and never will. The people of the lake country chose self-exile from a world viewed by most as perfect, a world that is timeless and changeless, a world where one can be immortal. The people of the lake country live differently from the others, and their conception of life's priorities is different. All of that breeds mistrust, jealousy, envy—a lot of very destructive emotions."

"There is another side to the story, of course," Abernathy interjected from behind Questor. "The people of the lake country have always had difficulty associating with the others of Landover. They remain aloof for the most part, arguing that their values should be imposed while they as a people remain apart. They rail against the others for spreading sickness and blight through poor management of the land and waters, yet they stay hidden within their mist and forest."

Ben frowned. "Is the pollution they complain about really that bad?"

Questor shrugged. "Bad enough. The Lords of the Greensward strip the land for their fields and livestock and hunt the forests for food. The trolls mine the mountains north for ores and their smelts poison the streams that feed the valley. Others contribute their share as well."

"It is difficult to accommodate everyone, High Lord," Abernathy added quietly, eyes blinking thoughtfully beneath his shaggy brows.

"Words of wisdom." Ben found himself thinking suddenly of the life he had left behind him in Chicago. "The more things change, the more things stay the same," he muttered.

Questor and Abernathy looked at each other. "High Lord?" Questor asked.

Ben rose, stretched and shook his head. "Forget it. How soon do tonight's festivities commence?"

"Quite soon, High Lord," the wizard replied.

"A bath, High Lord?" Abernathy asked quickly. "A change of clothes?"

"Both. And some ideas, if anyone has any, on how we can go about pleasing everyone long enough to persuade them all to acknowledge the damn throne!"

Bunion and Parsnip hissed and grinned eagerly from across the room. Ben gave them a dark look, started from the room, then stopped. "You know, I wouldn't mind tonight so much if I thought I could find a way to change the River Master's mind—but I don't see it happening." He paused, considering. "Still, how much time do I have to work with?"

"These celebrations usually last all night, High Lord," Questor replied.

Ben sighed wearily. "Terrific," he muttered and left the room.

Questor's prediction proved to be right on target. The celebration began shortly after sunset and lasted until dawn. It was ostensibly held in honor of Landover's visiting High Lord, but Ben was left with the distinct impression that the people of the lake country would have been willing to hold a celebration for almost any reason. Certainly neither pace nor order, orchestration nor duration, was in any way dictated by him.

The festivities began with a processional. Ben was seated in the amphitheater with the members of his little company, the River Master and his family, Willow among them, and several hundred others, as children and young people with torches and colored banners streamed through the open quarter section and circled the arena in a kaleidoscope of color and light, singing songs as they came. Concentric circles formed and turned slowly about one another, and the cheers and shouts of the people gathered lifted in appreciation. Music from flutes, horns, stringed instruments, and pipes rose from a band of players gathered directly below where Ben sat. The music was high and lilting, whisking the processional along, increasing its tempo as the minutes slipped past.

Soon the broad concentric circles dissolved into smaller wheels, and the marchers became dancers who spun and whirled in the grasses, torches and banners fluttering above them as the music quickened. Wine and ale passed freely about the arena and the amphitheater seats above, and all joined in the clapping and singing. The sound rose to echo through the great forest trees of Elderew, filling the night until no other sound could be heard. Mist dissipated and the moons of Landover filled the skies, bright spheres of color that hung suspended like oversized balloons. Streamers of rainbow light filtered down through the trees to mingle with the fire of the torches and cast back the shadows.

Ben quickly gave up looking for an opportunity to talk further with the River Master about pledging to the throne. No one was interested in doing anything except having a good time. The singing and shouting drowned out all efforts at normal conversation, and the wine was consumed with a speed he found astonishing. He accepted a glass warily and as a courtesy and found it quite good. He drank another—because what the hell difference did it make?—then several more; in no time at all, he was three sheets to the wind and having one hell of a good time. Questor and the kobolds drank with him, seemingly as relaxed as he, and only Abernathy abstained, muttering something about wine not being good for animals. Soon they were all singing and clapping, and it didn't really matter what the singing and the clapping was for.

The River Master seemed pleased that Ben was having such a good time. He came over often, his chiseled, expressionless face flushed and dark eyes bright, welcoming Ben once again to Elderew, wishing him well, asking him if there was anything he might need. Ben was tempted to give him the obvious answer, but held his tongue. The River Master clearly meant well, and the merriment was infectious. He had not enjoyed himself this much since long before he had come into this strange land.

The night slipped on, the festivities grew heightened, and the people in the amphitheater seats began to pour down into the arena to mingle with the those who had made up the processional. The singing and dancing became more frenzied, the fairies of the lake country flitting through the shadows and light as if they were yet the magical people they had once been. The River Master took the hand of one of his several wives, a slender river sprite, and pulled her after him toward the field. He called to Ben and the others, to the members of his family, and to his people to join him. Most went. Ben rose, hesitated, looked back to where Willow had been seated, found her gone, and sat down again. What was he thinking? What cause had he to celebrate? The wine's effects wore off with astonishing swiftness as he faced the unpleasant truths of his efforts at Kingship, and he lost his taste for celebrating.

He rose again, still unsteady, excused himself hastily to the others, and hurried toward the closest amphitheater exit. Abernathy came after him, but he sent the scribe scurrying with a sharp admonishment. Sprites, nymphs, kelpies, naiads, and pixies milled past him, dancing and singing, caught up in the spirit of the celebration. Ben brushed quickly past them. He had had enough of people for one day, and he wanted to be alone.

Shadows closed about him in the tunnel beneath, and then he was back in the forest. Lights winked from the treelanes overhead, and the sounds of the celebration began to diminish. He pushed ahead into the dark, anxious to be returned to his lodging and to be away from the festivities he had abandoned. His stomach churned with the wine, and suddenly he was sick at the pathside. He straightened, waited for his head and stomach to clear, and went on. When he reached the cottage, he climbed the walkway to an open-air side porch and slumped down in a high-backed wicker chair.

"Aren't you wonderful?" he congratulated himself.

He felt depressed and discouraged. He had believed so strongly in himself in the beginning. He knew he could be King of Landover. He possessed intelligence and ability, he was compassionate, he had experience working with people, and he understood the application of laws in society. Most important of all, he needed this challenge and he had thought himself ready for it. But all of that seemed to count for nothing in the greater scheme of things. His progress toward gaining even the minimal amount of recognition a King required had met with no success whatsoever—just a lot of conditional bargains. The old King's closest allies had rebuffed him; the others had ignored him. He had lost the services of the King's protector, now become something very much akin to a ghost haunting a deserted house, and the Mark and his demons were footsteps creeping up on him with the passing of each day.

He stretched and stared out into the night. Well, what the hell? he thought obstinately. Nothing at stake here but his self-respect, was there? All he had to do was use the medallion and he'd go back to Chicago, a million dollars lighter, but safe and sound. He had failed before at things, and he would undoubtedly fail again. Face it—this might be one of the failures.

He played with the idea in his mind a moment, then found himself thinking of the faces of those few who had come to his coronation, the farmers and their families, the hunters, the ones who still looked for a King they might believe in. Too bad for them, of course, he thought, wondering even as he did so how he could be so damn flip.

"So maybe you're not so wonderful after all," he muttered wearily.

Something moved in the shadow of the trees close beside the porch, and he jerked about.

"Ben?"

It was Willow. She slipped from the trees and came toward him, a ghostly figure in white silk, her green hair shimmering in the light. She was like a bit of moonlit mist crossing a midnight lake, ephemeral but impossibly beautiful. She came up to him, the silk hanging close against her body.

"I followed you, Ben," she told him softly, but with no apology in her voice. "I knew you would tire and come to sleep. But do not sleep yet. Come first with me. Come with me and watch my mother dance."

He felt his throat tighten as she neared him. "Your mother?"

"She is a wood nymph, Ben—so wild that she will not live among the people of Elderew. My father has never been able to bring her to him. But the music will draw her and she will yearn to dance. She will come to the old pines and she will look for me. Come, Ben. I want you there."

She came onto the porch, reached down for his hand and stopped. "Oh, your face! You have been hurt!" He had almost forgotten the beating Kallendbor had administered. Her hand touched his forehead softly. "I did not see your injuries at the Irrylyn. Here."

She swept her fingers swiftly about his face and at once the pain was gone. He could not hide the astonishment in his eyes.

"The small hurts can be healed, Ben," she whispered. "The ones that can be seen."

"Willow . . ." he began.

"I will not ask you to come away with me again—not until

you are ready." Her fingers lingered on his cheek, warm and
gentle. "I know who you are now. I know you to be of another world and not yet at peace with ours. I will wait."

He shook his head. "Willow . . ."

"Come, Ben!" She grasped his hand firmly and pulled him
from the chair. "Come, hurry!" She led him from the porch
and into the trees. "My mother will not wait!"

Ben no longer thought to resist. They ran into the forest,
she a vision of something he had not believed could exist
and he the shadow she drew after her. They darted through
the trees, his hand in hers, and soon he was hopelessly lost
and did not care. The heat of her touch burned through him,
and the need for her began to grow anew within him.

They slowed after a time, deep in a woods become misted
and shadowed far beyond that of Elderew. The sounds of
the celebration still echoed through the trees, but distant and
soft. Colored slivers of moonlight slipped downward from
the forest roof and dappled the earth like paint spots. Willow
held Ben's hand tightly in her own, the warmth of her like
a fire that drew him. The mane of hair from her forearm
brushed against his wrist like corn silk. She crept now
through the trees and brush, soundlessly skirting the giant
sentinels and their offspring, a bit of fragmented night.

Then the hardwood trees gave way to pine, evergreens
that were giant and aged. Willow and Ben pushed through
their needled boughs, and a clearing opened before them.

There Willow's mother danced in a prism of colored
moonlight.

She was a tiny thing, barely larger than a child, her features
delicate and fine. Silver hair hung below her waist, and the
skin of her slender body and limbs was pale green, like her
daughter's. She was clothed all in white gauze, and a radiance emanated from her that seemed born of some self-gen-
erated inner light. Spinning and leaping as if she were driven
by a madness peculiar to her alone, she danced through the
moonlit clearing to the rhythm of the distant music.

"Mother!" Willow breathed softly, and there was excitement and happiness reflected in her eyes.

The wood nymph's eyes met her own for just an instant, but she did not slow her dance. Willow knelt wordlessly at the clearing's edge, pulling Ben down gently beside her. Together they sat in silence and watched the phantasm before them do magic.

How long she danced and how long they watched, Ben did not know. Time seemed to come to a standstill in that clearing. All that had troubled him on his return from the amphitheater lost significance and was forgotten. There was only Willow and he and the lady who danced. He felt them made one by the grace and beauty of that dance. He felt them bond in a way he did not understand, but desperately needed. He fet the bonding take place, and he did not resist.

Then the dance was finished. There was a sudden stillness, a hush, and it seemed that the music had ceased to play. Willow's mother turned for a fleeting moment to view them and was gone. Ben stared, hearing again the music of the celebration. But the wood nymph had disappeared as if she had never been.

"Oh, Mother!" Willow whispered, and she was crying. "She is so beautiful, Ben. Isn't she beautiful?"

Ben nodded, feeling her small hand grasping his own. "She is very beautiful, Willow."

The sylph rose, drawing him up with her. "Ben," she spoke his name so softly he almost missed it. "I belong to you now. High Lord and the daughter of fairies, we shall be one. You must ask my father to allow me to go with you when you leave. You must tell him that I am needed—for I truly am, Ben—and when you have told him that, he will let me go."

Ben shook his head quickly. "Willow, I cannot ask for . . ."

"You are the High Lord, and your request cannot be refused." She hushed him, a finger resting on his lips. "I am but one of my father's many children, one whose mother will not even live with the man she lay with to give me birth, one whose favor in her father's eyes varies with his moods. But you must ask for me, Ben.''

Annie's face flashed in his mind, a counterpoint to the fire that this girl kindled within his body. "I can't do that."

"You do not understand the magic of the fairy people, Ben. I see that in your eyes; I hear it in your voice. But Landover *is* the heart of that magic, and you must accept what that means."

She released his hand and stepped softly away. "I must go now. I must nourish in the soil that my mother has graced. Leave me, Ben. Go back through the forest; the way will open up to you."

"No, wait, Willow . . ."

"Ask for me, Ben. My father must give me up." Her delicate face lifted to the colored streamers of moonlight that bathed the clearing. "Oh, Ben, it is as if my mother were all about me, wrapping me close, drawing me to her. I can feel her still. The essence of her reaches to me from the soil. This night I can be with her. Leave now, Ben. Hurry away."

But he stood rooted before her, stubbornly refusing to do as she asked. Why was she insisting that she belonged to him? Why couldn't she see that what she was seeking was impossible?

She spun in the clearing's center, beautiful, sensuous, delicate. He wanted her so badly in that instant that tears came to his eyes.

"Willow!" he cried out, starting forward.

She came out of her spin and faced him, feet planted firmly in the clearing's earth, arms raised skyward, face lifted. Ben stopped. A sudden radiance began to emanate from the sylph, the same radiance that her mother had given off while dancing. Willow shimmered, turned transparent in the light and began to swell and distort. Ben shielded his eyes, dropping to one knee in shock. Willow was changing before him, turning into something different entirely, arms and legs darkening and turning gnarled, sweeping outward like a canopy, splitting and lengthening . . .

He blinked, and Willow was gone. A tree had taken her place. It was the tree from which she took her name. She had become that tree.

Ben stared. He felt a wave of shock and repulsion wash through him. He fought to deny it, but it would not give way. She had said she would nourish in the soil. She had said she could feel her mother reaching up to her. My God, what manner of being was she?

He waited for the answer to come to him, a solitary figure in the mist and shadows of the forest. He waited, but the answer would not come.

He might have waited there all night if Bunion had not appeared, stepping suddenly from the trees to take his arm and lead him away like a disobedient child. He went with the kobold without argument, too stunned to do anything else. Conflicting emotions raged through him, battering him. Willow was so beautiful and vibrant, and the need for her within him was impossibly strong. Yet at the same time he was repulsed by her, a creature who gave every appearance of being amorphous, who could become a tree as easily as a human.

He did not look back as he left the clearing; he could not bear to. He was too ashamed of what he was feeling. He pushed his way through the ancient pines, trailing after Bunion in silence. The kobold must have followed after him, he realized. Questor or Abernathy must have sent him. They were taking no chances after his disappearance at the Irrylyn.

He wished suddenly that they had not found him that night. He wished that he had disappeared. He wished a thousand other things that might have happened and now never would.

The journey back was a short one. The others were waiting

for him at the cottage, anxious looks on their faces. They sat him down and gathered around him.

"You should have told us of the sylph, High Lord," Questor said quietly, after exchanging a few brief words with Bunion. "We could have warned you what to expect."

"I warned him once already that the people of the lake country were not like us," Abernathy advised, and Ben didn't know whether to laugh or cry. Questor hushed the scribe quickly.

"You have to understand something, High Lord," the wizard went on, turning back to Ben. "Willow is the child of a sprite and a wood nymph. Her father is only half human. Her mother is less so, more a part of the forest than a part of man, an elemental who finds life within the soil. Something of that was passed on to Willow at birth, and she requires the same nourishment. She is a changeling; she owes her life to both plant and animal forms. It is natural for her to take the form of each; she could be no other way. But it must seem strange, I know, to you."

Ben shook his head slowly, feeling some of the conflict within dissipate. "No stranger than anything else that's happened, I guess." He felt sick at heart and weary; he needed to sleep.

Questor hesitated. "She must care deeply for you."

Ben nodded, remembering. "She said that she belongs to me."

Questor glanced quickly at Abernathy and away again. The kobolds stared at Ben with bright, questioning eyes. Ben stared back.

"But she doesn't," he said finally. "She belongs to the lake country. She belongs to her family and to her people."

Abernathy muttered something unintelligible and turned away. Questor said nothing at all. Ben studied them wordlessly a moment, then climbed to his feet. "I'm going to bed," he announced.

He started from the room, and their eyes followed after

him. Then he stopped momentarily at the doorway to his bedroom. "We're going home," he told them and waited. "Tomorrow, at first light."

No one said anything. He closed the door behind him and stood alone in the dark.

G'home
Gnome

They left Elderew the next morning shortly after daybreak.
Mist hung across the lake country like a shroud, and the
dawn air was damp and still. It was the kind of day in which
ghosts and goblins came to life. The River Master was there
to see them off and looked to be neither. Questor had summoned him, and he appeared without complaint. He could
not have slept, for the festivities had barely ended, but he
looked fresh and alert. Ben extended his thanks on behalf
of the company for the hospitality they had been shown, and
the River Master, his grainy, chiseled face still as expressionless as flat stone, bowed briefly in acknowledgment. Ben
glanced about several times for Willow, but she was nowhere
to be seen. He considered again her request that she be allowed to accompany him back to Sterling Silver. Part of him
wanted her with him; part of him would not allow it. Indecision gave way to expediency; time ran out on the debate.
He left without speaking of it to her father.

The company rode north for the remainder of the day,
passing out of the lake country and its mists into the gray,
open expanse of the western end of the Greensward and from
there to the forested hills surrounding Sterling Silver. Sunlight barely pierced a clouded sky that stretched above them

the whole of the journey back, and there was the smell of rain in the air. It was nightfall when they stepped once more from the lake skimmer and walked the final few yards to the gates of the castle. A smattering of raindrops was just beginning to fall.

It rained all that night. The rain was steady and hard and it blotted out the entire world beyond the immediate walls. That was perfectly all right with Ben. He fished out the bottle of Glenlivet he had been saving for a special occasion, gathered Questor, Abernathy, and the two kobolds at the table in the dining hall, and proceeded to get roaring drunk. He got drunk alone. The other four sipped gingerly from their tumblers as he consumed nearly the whole of the bottle by himself. He talked to them as he drank about life in his world, about Chicago and its people, about his friends and family, about anything and everything but Landover. They responded politely, but he had no memory later of what they said and frankly didn't care. When the scotch was gone and there was no longer anything left to talk about, he rose to his feet and stumbled off to bed.

Questor and Abernathy were both at his bedside when he awoke the next morning. He felt like hell. It was still raining.

"Good morning, High Lord," they greeted together, faces somber. They had the look of pallbearers at a funeral.

"Come back when I'm dead," he ordered, rolled over and went back to sleep.

He came awake a second time at noon. This time there was no one there. The rain had stopped, and the sun was sending a few faint streamers of light earthward through a veil of mist. Ben pushed himself into a sitting position and stared into space. His head throbbed and his mouth tasted of cotton. He was so angry with himself that he could barely keep from screaming.

He washed, dressed and trooped down the castle stairs to the great hall. He took his time, studying the stone walls, the tarnished silver trappings, the worn tapestries and drapes. He felt the warmth of the castle reaching out to him, a comforting mother's touch. It had been a long time since he had felt that touch. His hands brushed the stone in response.

Questor, Abernathy, and the kobolds were all gathered in the great hall, engaged in various make-work tasks. All looked up quickly as he entered. Ben came up to them and stopped.

"I'm sorry about last night," he apologized immediately. "I guess that was just something that I had to get out of my system. I hope you all rested well, because we have a great deal of work to do."

Questor glanced at the others, then back to Ben. "Where are we going now, High Lord?" he asked.

Ben smiled. "We're going to school, Questor."

The lessons began that afternoon. Ben was the student; Questor, Abernathy, Bunion, and Parsnip were his teachers. Ben had thought it all through—much of it in fits and starts while in various stages of inebriation and repentance—but carefully. He had spent most of his time since his arrival in Landover running about pointlessly. Questor might argue that the visits to the Greensward and Elderew had served a good purpose—and perhaps they had. But the bottom line was that he was floundering. He was a stranger in a land he had never dreamed could exist. He was trying to govern countries he had not even seen. He was trying to bargain with rulers and headmen he knew nothing about. However competent, hard-working, and well-intentioned he might be, he could not expect to assimilate as rapidly as he was trying. There were lessons to be learned, and it was time that he learned them.

He began with Sterling Silver. He took the remainder of the afternoon and toured the castle from cellar to turret, Questor and Abernathy at his side. He had the scribe relate the history of the castle and her Kings from as far back as his records and memory would record. He had the wizard fill in the gaps. He learned everything he could of what had transpired in and about those halls and chambers, towers and parapets, grounds and lakes. He used eyes and nose and touch to ingest her life, and he made himself feel as one with her.

He ate dinner late that night in the great hall and spent the dinner hour and two hours after with Parsnip learning to recognize the consumables and poisons of the valley. Questor stayed with him, interpreting everything Parsnip said.

The next day he used the Landsview. He took Questor with him the first several times out, traversing the valley from one end to the other, studying the geography, the provinces, the towns, the fortresses and castles, and the people who inhabited them all. By midafternoon, he was making the trip alone, feeling more comfortable with the magic, learning to expand the vast range of the Landsview to suit his needs, and replaying in his mind the bits and pieces of information imparted to him by the wizard.

He went out by Landsview again the following day, and each day after that, his attention focused now on the history of the valley, matching events with places and people. Questor was his teacher once again, and the wizard proved infinitely patient. It was difficult for Ben to match dates and times to places and things where he had so little previous background in either. Questor was forced to repeat the lessons over and over. But Ben had a good memory and he was determined. By the end of the first week of lessons, he had a decent working knowledge of Landover.

He engaged in outings closer to Sterling Silver as well, journeys made afoot and not through the magic of the Landsview. Bunion was his guide and mentor on these excursions. The kobold took him from the valley into the forests and hills about the castle to study more closely the life forms that inhabited the region. They tracked down a timber wolf, hunted to his lair a cave wight, and uncovered a pair of bog wumps. They unearthed tunnel rats, snakes, and reptiles of various forms, treed a variety of cats, and spied upon the distant, rock-sheltered eyries of hunting birds. They studied the plantlife. Questor went with them on the first outing to interpret; after that, he was left behind. Ben and the kobold found that they could communicate well enough on their own.

Ten days later, Ben used the Landsview to seek out Strabo. He went alone. He intended this outing to be a measure of his progress in learning to control the magic. He had thought at first to seek out Willow, but it would be as if he were spying on her and he did not want that. So he settled on the dragon instead. The dragon terrified him, and he wanted to see how he could handle his fear. He searched most of the day before finding the monster engaged in devouring half a dozen cattle at the north end of the Greensward, gnawing and crunching on carcasses shredded and broken almost beyond recognition. The dragon seemed to sense his presence as he brought himself to within a dozen yards of the feast. The crusted snout raised and jagged, blackened teeth snapped at the air before him. Ben held his ground for a long five count, then pulled quickly away, satisfied.

He wanted to make a foray alone into the forests about Sterling Silver to test what he had learned from Bunion, but Questor put his foot down. They compromised on a daytime hike in which Bunion would trail and not interfere if Ben was not threatened. Ben trooped out at dawn, trooped back again at dusk and never saw Bunion once. He also never saw the cave wight and the tree adder that the kobold dispatched as they were about to make a meal of him. He consoled himself with the knowledge that, while he had seen neither of these, he had seen and avoided several bog wumps, wolves, other wights and reptiles, and a big cat, all of whom would have made a meal of him just as quickly.

Two weeks later, he could recite from memory recent history, geographical landmarks and routes to and from the same, consumables and poisons, the creatures inhabiting the valley, the workings of the social orders that dominated the major races, and the rules that any manual of basic survival in Landover would include. He was still working on the

Landsview. He had not yet developed his confidence in its magic to undergo the final test that he had set for himself— a search for the witch Nightshade in the hollows of the Deep Fell. Nightshade never ventured out of the oppressively dark confines of the Deep Fell, and he did not yet trust himself to attempt an intrusion.

He was still wrestling with his uncertainty when a more immediate problem appeared at the castle gates.

"You have visitors, High Lord," Abernathy announced.

Ben was bent over a worktable in one of the lower sitting rooms, perusing ancient maps of the valley. He looked up in surprise, seeing first the scribe and then Questor a few discreet steps behind him.

"Visitors?" he repeated.

"Gnomes, High Lord," Questor advised him.

"G'home Gnomes," Abernathy added, and there was a hint of disdain in his voice.

Ben stared at them. He shoved back the maps. "What in the world are G'home Gnomes?" His lessons with Questor had never gotten this far.

"A rather pathetic species of gnome, I am afraid," Questor replied.

"A rather worthless species, you mean," Abernathy corrected coldly.

"That is not necessarily so."

"It is definitely so."

"I am sorry to say that you reflect only your own prejudices, Abernathy."

"I reflect a well-reasoned opinion, Questor Thews."

"What is this—Laurel and Hardy?" Ben broke in. They stared back at him blankly. "Never mind," he told them, impatiently brushing the reference aside with a wave of one hand. "Just tell me what G'home Gnomes are."

"They are a tribe of gnomes living in the foothills north below the high peaks of Melchor," Questor answered, his owlish face shoving forward past Abernathy. "They are burrow people; they inhabit tunnels and dens they dig out of the earth. Most of the time they stay in the ground . . .''

"Where they ought to stay," Abernathy interjected.

". . . but now and again they forage the surrounding countryside." He gave Abernathy a withering glance. "Do you mind?" His eyes shifted back to Ben. "They are not well liked. They tend to appropriate things that do not belong to them and give back nothing in exchange. Their burrowing can be a nuisance when it encroaches on pastureland or grain fields. They are extremely territorial and, once settled in, will not move. It doesn't matter who owns the land they have settled on—once there, they stay."

"You have not told him the worst!" Abernathy insisted.

"Why not tell him yourself," Questor huffed, stepping back.

"They eat dogs, High Lord!" Abernathy snapped, unable to contain himself any longer. His muzzle drew back to reveal his teeth. "They are cannibals!"

"Unfortunately, true." Questor shoved forward once more, crowding Abernathy aside with his shoulder. "They eat cats as well, however, and I have never heard you complain about that!"

Ben grimaced. "Terrific. What about the name?"

"An abbreviation, High Lord," Questor said. "The gnomes became so vexatious with their burrowing and their thieving that everyone began to express openly their wish that they would simply 'go home' to wherever it was they had come from. After a while, the admonishment 'go home, gnomes' became the nickname by which they were known— G'home Gnomes."

Ben shook his head in disbelief. "Now there's a story right out of the Brothers Grimm. The G'home Gnomes. Well, what brings these gnomes to us?"

"They will speak of that only with you, High Lord. Will you see them?"

Abernathy looked very much as if he wanted to bite Questor, but he managed to refrain from doing so, his shaggy muzzle frozen in a half-snarl. Questor rocked back on his heels, eyes fixed on Ben expectantly.

"The royal appointment calendar isn't exactly bulging at the seams," Ben answered, looking first at Abernathy, then at Questor. "I can't see where meeting someone who has taken the trouble to come all this way can hurt anything."

"I trust you will remember later that it was you who said that, High Lord." Abernathy sniffed. "There are two of them waiting. Shall I show both in?"

Ben had to fight to keep from grinning. "Please do."

Abernathy left and was back a few moments later with the G'home Gnomes.

"Fillip and Sot, High Lord," Abernathy announced, teeth showing.

The gnomes came forward and bowed so low their heads touched the castle stone. They were the most miserable-looking creatures Ben had ever seen. They were barely four feet tall, their bodies stout and covered with hair, their faces ferretlike and bearded from neck to nose. They wore clothes that the lowliest bum would have refused, and they looked as if they hadn't bathed since birth. Dust coated their bodies and clothing; dirt and grime were caked in the seams of their skin and under fingernails that looked dangerously diseased. Tiny, pointed ears jutted from either side of skull caps with red feathers stuck in the bands, and toes with curled nails peeked out from the ends of ruined boots.

"Great High Lord," one addressed him.

"Mighty High Lord," the other added.

They took their heads off the floor and faced him, eyes squinting. They looked like moles come to surface for a glimpse of daylight.

"I am Fillip," one said.

"I am Sot," the other said.

"We have come to offer our pledge of fealty to the High Lord of Landover on behalf of all of the G'home Gnomes," Fillip said.

"We have come to offer felicitations," Sot said.

"We wish you long life and health," Fillip said.

"We wish you many children," Sot said.

"We extend to you our skills and our experience to be used in whatever manner you may choose," Fillip said.

"We extend to you our services," Sot said.

"But first we have a small problem," Fillip said.

"We do," Sot agreed.

They waited, their presentation apparently finished. Ben wondered if they had simply run out of gas. "What sort of problem do you have?" he asked solicitously.

They glanced at each other. Sharp mole faces crinkled and tiny, pointed teeth showed liked daggers.

"Trolls," Fillip said.

"Crag Trolls," Sot said.

Again they waited. Ben cleared his throat. "What about them?" Whereas he had known nothing of the G'home Gnomes, he did know something of the Crag Trolls.

"They have taken our people," Fillip said.

"Not all of our people, but a rather substantial number," Sot corrected.

"They missed us," Fillip said.

"We were away," Sot said.

"They raided our burrows and dens, and they carried our people off with them," Fillip said.

"They seized everyone they found," Sot said.

"They took them to Melchor to work the mines and the furnaces," Fillip said.

"They took them to the fires," Sot grieved.

Ben was beginning to get the picture. The Crag Trolls were a rather primitive race of beings living in the mountains of Melchor. Their primary business was mining ores from the rock and converting them in their furnaces to weapons and armor which they sold to the other inhabitants of the valley. The Crag Trolls were a reclusive and unfriendly bunch, but they seldom provoked trouble with their neighbors and had never used slave labor.

He glanced past the gnomes to Questor and Abernathy.

The wizard shrugged and the scribe gave him one of his patented 'I told you so' looks.

"Why did the Crag Trolls seize your people?" Ben asked the gnomes.

Fillip and Sot glanced at each other thoughtfully, then shook their heads.

"We do not know, great High Lord," Fillip said.

"We do not," Sot said.

They were without doubt the worst liars Ben had ever encountered. Nevertheless, he decided to be tactful. "Why do you *think* the Crag Trolls seized your people?" he pressed.

"That would be difficult to say," Fillip said.

"Very difficult," Sot agreed.

"There could be any number of reasons," Fillip said.

"Any number," Sot echoed.

"It is possible, I suppose, that in foraging we might have appropriated property which the trolls felt belonged to them," Fillip speculated.

"It is possible that we might have claimed property we believed abandoned but which, in truth, still belonged to them," Sot added.

"Mistakes of that sort sometimes do happen," Fillip said.

"Sometimes," Sot said.

Ben nodded. He didn't believe for a minute that any foraging from the Crag Trolls had been anything short of deliberate. The only mistake had been in the gnomes' belief that they could get away with it.

"If a mistake of this sort were to happen," Ben observed carefully, "wouldn't the Crag Trolls simply have asked for the missing property back?"

The gnomes looked decidedly uncomfortable. Neither said anything.

Ben frowned. "What sort of property might have been misappropriated, do you think?" he asked them.

Fillip glanced down at his boots, and the toes wriggled

uneasily. Sot's ferret features twisted about and looked as if they might like to disappear into his fur.

"The trolls like to keep pets," Fillip said finally.

"The trolls are very fond of pets," Sot added.

"They like the furry tree sloths most of all," Fillip said.

"They give them to their children to play with," Sot said.

"How can one tell wild furry tree sloths from pet furry tree sloths?" Fillip queried.

"How can one know which is which?" Sot queried.

A terrible suspicion crossed Ben's mind. "You can always give back misappropriated pets, can't you?" he asked them.

"Not always," Fillip said, somehow managing to look mortified.

"No, not always," Sot agreed.

Ben caught a glimpse of Abernathy out of the corner of his eye. His scribe's hackles were raised up like the spikes of a cornered porcupine.

He looked back at the gnomes. "You ate those tree sloths, didn't you?" he demanded.

Neither said a word. They looked down at their boots. They looked aside at the walls. They looked everywhere but at Ben. Abernathy gave a low, menacing growl, and Questor hushed him into silence.

"Wait outside, please," Ben told the gnomes.

Fillip and Sot turned about quickly and scurried from the room, small rodent bodies swaying awkwardly with the movement. Fillip glanced back once as if he might say something more, then reconsidered and hurried out. Questor followed them to the door and closed it tightly behind them.

Ben looked at his aides. "Well, what do you think?"

Questor shrugged. "I think it is easier to catch and devour a tame furry tree sloth than a wild one."

"I think someone should eat a few of them and see how they like it!" Abernathy snapped.

"Would such a meal interest you?" Questor asked.

Ben stepped forward impatiently. "I'm not asking what

you think about what they did. I'm asking what you think about helping them.''

Abernathy was appalled. His ears flattened back and his glasses slipped askew on his nose. "I would sooner bed down with fleas, High Lord! I would sooner share lodging with cats!''

"What about the fact that the trolls have forced these people into slavery?" Ben pressed.

"It seems clear to me that they brought it on themselves!'' his scribe answered stiffly. "In any case, you have far more important concerns than the G'home Gnomes!''

Ben frowned. "Do I?''

"High Lord,'' Questor interrupted and stepped forward. "The Melchor is dangerous country and the Crag Trolls have never been the most loyal of the King's subjects. They are a tribal people, very primitive, very unreceptive to intervention from anyone not of their own country. The old King kept them in line primarily by staying out of their business. When he had to intervene, he did so with an army to stand behind him.''

"And I have no army to stand behind me, do I?" Ben finished. "I don't even have the services of the Paladin.''

"High Lord, the G'home Gnomes have been nothing but trouble for as long as anyone can remember!'' Abernathy stepped over to join Questor. "They are a nuisance wherever they go! They are cannibals and thieves! Why would you even consider helping them in this dispute?''

Questor nodded in agreement. "Perhaps this kind of request is one best refused, High Lord.''

"No, Questor,'' Ben replied at once. "This is exactly the kind of request that I cannot refuse.'' He looked at the wizard and the scribe in turn and shook his head. "You don't understand, do you? I came into Landover to be King. I cannot pick and choose when I will be King and over whom. I am King now and always and for everyone who needs me. That is the way it works with monarchies. I know that much from the history of my own world. A King must proclaim and administer the laws of the Kingdom fairly and equally to all of his subjects. There can be no favorites; there can be no exceptions. What I would do for the Lords of the Greensward and the sprites and nymphs of Elderew I must do for the G'home Gnomes. If I back away once, I set a precedent for doing so the next time and the time after that and so on any time it seems convenient."

"But you have no support in this, High Lord," Questor argued.

"Perhaps not. But if I am successful in helping the gnomes, then I might have that support the next time out. The gnomes have given their pledge, which is one pledge more than I had before they made the journey here. They deserve something for that. Maybe the others will pledge as well if they see that the throne can be of use even to the G'home Gnomes. Maybe they will reconsider their position."

"Maybe cows will fly over the castle," Abernathy grumbled.

"Maybe," Ben agreed. "I've seen stranger things since I arrived."

They stared at each other wordlessly for a moment.

"I do not care for this idea at all," Questor said, his owlish face lined with doubt.

"Nor I," Abernathy echoed.

"Then we agree," Ben concluded. "I don't like it either. But we are going anyway. We are going because that's what we have to do. School's out, as the saying goes. It's time to face life in the real world again. Now let's have the gnomes back in here."

Questor and Abernathy bowed in acknowledgment and left the room muttering to themselves.

The G'home Gnomes returned with protestations of good intent spilling forth. The furry tree sloths were a favorite food of their people, Fillip insisted. Yes, the furry tree sloths were quite delicious, Sot agreed. Ben cut them short. Their request would be granted, he told them. He would go with them to the Melchor to see what could be done to gain the release of those taken by the Crag Trolls. They would depart Sterling Silver at dawn. Fillip and Sot stared at him, then fell to their knees before him, groveling in a most disgusting manner. Ben had them removed at once.

He went up to the Landsview alone that evening after dinner. The gnomes had been sequestered in their rooms by Abernathy (who refused to trust them anywhere else in the castle), and the others were occupied with preparations for the journey north. Ben had time to use as he chose. He decided to take a quick peek into the lake country.

The night was misted and dark, no different from dozens of others, seven of Landover's brightly colored moons faintly visible over the line of the horizon, stars a distant sprinkling of street lights through a midnight fog. The Landsview took him instantly to the lake country, and he descended slowly into Elderew. The city was bright with torchlight atop treelanes and along roadways, and her people were still abroad. The sound of laughter and light conversation made him feel uneasy somehow—more an intruder that he already was. He slipped over the amphitheater, down across the city dwellings and shops, past the cottage that had been his lodging, and into the deep woods. He found the old pines where Willow's mother had danced. They were deserted. The tree into which Willow had transformed herself was gone. Willow was nowhere to be found.

He let himself remain in the deep woods for a time, thinking of Annie. He could not explain why, but he needed to think of her. He needed to be with her, too, but he knew that Annie was gone and it was pointless to dwell on it. He felt alone, a traveler come far from home and friends. He was adrift. He felt that he had cut himself off from everything, and that his reasons for doing so were proving to be poor ones. He needed someone to tell him that it would all work out, that he was doing the right thing, that there were better times ahead.

There was no one to do that, however. There was only himself.

Midnight came and went before Ben finally refocussed on Sterling Silver. He took his hands reluctantly from the railing of the Landsview and he was home again.

Crag
Trolls

Morning followed night, as it always does, but Ben awoke
questioning the assumption that it necessarily must. His
mood was dark, and his nerves were on edge after a sleep
troubled with a vicious and depressing dream of death and
personal futility. There had been people dying in his dream;
they had died all about him, and he had been powerless to
save them. He had known none of them in his waking life,
but they had seemed quite real in his sleep. They had seemed
his friends. He had not wanted them to die, but he had been
unable to prevent it. He had tried in desperation to come
awake so that he could escape what was happening, but he
could not. There had been in his sleep that frightening sense
of timelessness that occurs when the subconscious suggests
that waking will never come, that the only reality is in the
dream. When his eyes finally slipped open, he saw the dawn
filtering down, misted and gray, through the windows of his
sleeping chamber. It had been misted and gray in the world
of his dream, too—a twilight in which neither day nor night
could seize upon the other.

He found himself wondering then if there were some
worlds where morning could not follow night—where there
was only the one or the other or a constant mix of both. He

found himself wondering if, with the failing of the magic, Landover might not become one.

The prospect was too dark to contemplate, and he dismissed it with a flourish of activity. He rose, washed, dressed, finished gathering up his gear for the journey north, greeted Questor, Abernathy, Bunion, Parsnip, Fillip, and Sot at breakfast, ate, saw his possession to the pack animals on the far side of the lake shore, mounted Wishbone, and gave the command to ride. He had been careful not to permit himself time to think back on the dream. It was nearly forgotten now, a fading memory better gone. Landover's King, with the members of his court and the G'home Gnomes in tow, sallied forth once more.

They journeyed north through the hill country all that day, traversing forested steeps, scrub-covered hollows and glens, and the shores of thicketed lakes. They passed west of the Greensward, east of the Deep Fell. The sun shone above them, veiled by clouds and mist, a fuzzy white ball of light that barely cast out night's shadows. The land they traveled looked wintry and ill. Leaves and brush were dark and spotted with wilt, grasses looked dried and burned as if by frost, and trees were blanketed with fungus that sapped away their juices. The land was growing sicker; its life was seeping away.

Strabo passed over the little company toward evening. The dragon appeared from out of the west, a massive winged shadow darker than the skies he flew. The G'home Gnomes saw him at the same moment and together scrambled from the back of the horse they shared and disappeared into the brush. The remainder of the company watched in silence as the dragon passed east. It took fifteen minutes after he was gone for Ben and his companions to persuade the gnomes to surface from their hiding place and continue the journey.

They camped that night in a glen sheltered by apple trees and clumps of birch. The light disappeared quickly in the dusk, and they ate their evening meal in darkness. No one had much of anything to say. Everyone seemed preoccupied with his own thoughts. They finished eating and went directly to sleep.

The following day was much the same as the first—gray, misted, and unfriendly. They crossed from the borders of the Greensward into the foothills leading upward to the Melchor. The mists of the fairy world which rimmed the valley seemed to have drifted far down across the shoulders of the Melchor, forming a mantle of gray that obscured everything. They rode toward it and then into it. It was past midday when they were swallowed.

Bunion guided them ahead, sure-footed and unswerving, his eyes sharper than those of his companions. They followed a rock-strewn road that quickly became a pathway and then a narrow, rutted trail. Cliff walls and shadows closed about. They were within the Melchor. The light began to fail rapidly with the coming of dusk. They were forced to walk their horses now, the way forward too uncertain to risk a fall. Fillip and Sot clung to each other as the company pressed ahead, mumbling to themselves, their uneasiness apparent. Ben squinted through the mist and darkness, trying to see whay lay beyond. He might as well have been peering through paint.

There was a growing sense of desperation in Ben Holiday. He had been struggling to deny it all day, but it was persistent and claimed him in the end. This expedition into the country of the Crag Trolls to secure the release of the captured G'home Gnomes was more important than he had been willing to admit. It was, quite possibly, his last chance. He had failed to gain the pledge of a single ally to the throne. He had failed to accomplish a single positive act since assuming the Kingship. If he failed again here—with these universally disdained and pitifully dependent gnomes—where would he go next? The word of his failure would travel quickly. No one else was likely to seek his help. He would become the play-King that the Lord Kallendbor had labeled him.

Night settled in. The way forward grew more uncertain and the pace slowed to a walk. There was thunder in the distance, a low rumbling punctuated by the sharp crack of lightning. A dull, reddish glow began to stain the darkness. Ben peered at the glow uncertainly. The thunder and lightning took on new tones, no longer the sounds of a storm approaching, but of something else.

Bunion brought the company to a halt. He exchanged a few words with Questor, and the wizard turned to Ben. The reddish glow was the fire of the troll furnaces. The thunder and lightning wcrc thc sounds of bellows being pumped and metal being forged.

Ben had Abernathy unfurl the King's banner and hoist it over them. The little company went forward.

Minutes later they crested a rise, the narrow trail broadened as the defile ended, and they found themselves poised at the entrance to Hell. At least, that was how it appeared to Ben. Hell was a valley surrounded by great, towering cliffs that disappeared into a ceiling of mist and darkness. Fires burned everywhere. They burned in monstrous rock kilns, the stone so hot that it glowed, in iron kettles, molten ore bubbling and stcaming, in pits dug out of the rock and earth, flames licking at waste and fuel, and in iron stanchions set to give light to the valley perimeter and to aid in the keeping of the watch. The fires burned red, so that everything was bathed in crimson light. A narrow river wound its way through the valley basin, its waters the color of blood. Shadows flickered like chained beings across the cliffs and boulders, thrown against the stone by the flames. Squat houses of stone blocks and tiles lay scattered between the fires, and close beside them were the pens. The pens were formed of iron stakes and wire. The pens held living beings—livestock, but humans as well. The center pen contained a gathering of some fifty odd gnomes, ragged, frightened-looking creatures, their ferret faces buried in bowls of food and pails of water. There were gnomes outside the pen as well, these engaged in feeding the fires. Backs bent, heads lowered, their furry bodies singed and blackened, they hauled fuel, fed raw ore, stoked the kilns, and hammered molten metal. They were the damned of the earth, sent to their eternal reward.

The trolls were there to see that this reward was properly bestowed. There were hundreds of them, dark, misshapen forms that slouched purposefully about the valley from fire to fire, some engaged in the work allotted, some engaged in directing its course. The trolls were sullen, heavy-limbed beings, their faces closed and virtually featureless, their bodies muscled and disproportionately fashioned. Limbs were long and rangy, heavier than the lean bodies. Torsos were bent at the spine, shoulders too broad for the ligaments and sinew that bound them, heads oblong and sunk down into chests matted with wiry hair. Their skin had the look of burned toast, an uneven cast that failed to reflect the fires' light but seemed only to absorb it. Gnarled, splayed feet gripped rock and earth with the sureness of a mountain goat's hooves.

Ben felt the air go out of his lungs as if it had been sucked away by the fires. Despite the suffocating heat that washed over him, he turned cold. Heads swung about and misshapen bodies lumbered forward. The little company had already been seen. Bright, yellowed eyes fixed on them as the Crag Trolls advanced.

"Dismount," Ben ordered quietly.

He climbed down, Questor and Abernathy beside him. Parsnip came forward to stand with Bunion, and the kobolds hissed in warning at the trolls, their teeth showing white against the fires' crimson light. Fillip and Sot cowered behind Ben, their small bodies pressed down close against his legs.

Two dozen Crag Trolls were in front of them almost immediately. They crowded to within several yards, slouched forms bumping mindlessly, yellow eyes decidedly unfriendly. A geyser of fire erupted from one of the waste pits in the valley behind them, exploding in a booming cough. Not a head turned.

"Show them the flag," Ben ordered Abernathy.

The scribe dropped the flag forward at an angle so that its

insignia rolled clear of the folds. The trolls studied it without interest. Ben waited a moment, glanced briefly at Questor and stepped forward.

"I am Ben Holiday, High Lord of Landover!" he shouted. His voice reverberated from the rock walls and died. "Who is your headman?"

The trolls studied him. Not a one moved. There was a headman of this tribe; Ben knew that much from his studies with Questor. "Who speaks for you?" he demanded, keeping his voice steady and commanding.

Other Crag Trolls had joined the first gathering. They parted now, and a single troll slouched forward, a rugged, battered creature with a collar of silver studs. He spoke quickly, a tongue that Ben did not recognize.

"He wants to know what we are doing here, High Lord," Questor interpreted the response. "He sounds irritated."

"Does he understand what I'm saying?"

"I do not know, High Lord. Possibly."

"Speak to him in his own language, Questor. Tell him again who I am. Tell him that because he failed to attend the coronation when summoned I have come to see him instead, and that now he must give me his pledge."

"High Lord, I don't think . . ."

Ben's face was hard. "Tell him, Questor!"

Questor spoke briefly to the troll, and there was a rumble of discontent through the ranks of those gathered behind him. The troll lifted one arm and the rumble ceased. The troll said something more to Questor.

Questor turned to Ben. "He says that he knows nothing of any coronation, that there is no King of Landover and hasn't been since the old King died. He says that he will give his pledge to no one."

"Wonderful." Ben kept his eyes on the headman. Slowly he extracted the medallion from beneath his tunic and held it out where it could be seen. There was a murmur of recognition. The Crag Trolls glanced at one another and shuffled back uneasily. "Tell them I command the magic, Questor,"

Ben ordered. "And be ready to give them a show of proof if I call for it."

Questor's owlish face tightened sharply as he glanced at Ben, hesitating.

"Do it, Questor," Ben said softly.

Questor spoke again. The trolls mumbled among themselves, still shifting about. The headman looked confused. Ben waited. The heat from the fires washed over him; sweat soaked through his clothes. He could feel the faces of the G'home Gnomes pressed up against his pant legs, peering past them at the trolls. The seconds slipped by, and nothing happened. He knew he had to do something quickly or he would lose whatever small advantage he might have gained.

"Questor, tell the headman again that he must give his pledge to the throne. Tell him that he must give over to me as a show of good faith the G'home Gnomes he has taken so that they might serve me instead. Tell him he must do so immediately, that I have little time to waste on him, that I go next to the witch of the Deep Fell. Tell him not to challenge me."

"High Lord!" Questor breathed in disbelief.

"Tell him!"

"But what if he challenges you and I cannot summon the magic?"

"Then we fry in the fire with the gnomes, damn it!" Ben's face was flushed and angry.

"Caution, High Lord!" Abernathy warned suddenly, his muzzle shoving into view.

"The hell with being cautious!" Ben wheeled on him. "Bluff or no bluff, we have to try something . . . !"

Abernathy cut him short with a hiss of warning. "High Lord, I think he understands what you have both been saying!"

Ben froze. The headman was studying him, his yellow eyes suddenly cunning. He *had* understood everything; Ben knew it instantly. The troll gave a quick command to those behind him and they began to fan out about the little company.

"Use the magic, Questor," Ben whispered.

The wizard's face was gray with uncertainty. "High Lord, I do not know if I can!"

"If you don't, we are in big trouble!" Ben kept his eyes fixed on Questor's. "Use it!"

Questor hesitated, his tall, rainbow-colored form a statue against the fires and the night. Then abruptly he wheeled on the Crag Trolls, his arms lifting. The trolls shrieked. Questor's arms windmilled, words poured forth from his throat and the air exploded with light.

It began to rain flowers.

They showered down from out of nowhere—roses, peonies, violets, lilies, daisies, chrysanthemums, orchids, daffodils and every other kind of flower under the sun. They descended on the little company and the Crag Trolls in buckets, tumbling off them and bouncing to the ground.

It was difficult to decide who was the most surprised. It was certain that everyone had expected something else—including Questor, who made a valiant effort to recover after his initial shock, arms lifting a second time as he tried again to engage the magic. He was far too slow. The Crag Trolls had already recovered. They launched themselves at the members of the little company somewhat in the manner of linebackers in a full blitz. They looked monstrous. Ben shouted in warning to the others. He saw the kobolds leap up, heard them hiss, heard Abernathy's teeth snap, felt the gnomes Fillip and Sot grappling at him for protection, and smelled an instant's mix of charred ash and smoke.

Then the Crag Trolls piled into him. He was hammered back—thrown from his feet with the force of the rush. His head struck the hard earth, and the air before him exploded instantly into blinding light. Then everything went dark.

He came awake a prisoner in Dante's *Inferno*. He was chained to a post in the central holding pen, heavy bracelets and locks fastened to his wrists and ankles. He sat slumped against the post, the faces of dozens of furry gnomes peering at him through a haze of smoke. His head throbbed and his body was bathed in sweat and grime. The stench of the kilns and waste pits filled the air and made him instantly nauseous. The fires burned all about, crimson light falling like a mantle across the valley rock.

Ben blinked and turned his head slowly. Questor and Abernathy were chained to posts close by, awake and whispering together guardedly. The kobolds were trussed hand and foot by chains and bound to iron rings fixed to spikes driven into the stone floor. Neither appeared conscious. Crag Trolls patrolled the perimeter of the compound, their misshapen forms little more than shadows drifting silently through the night.

"Are you awake, High Lord?"

"Are you unhurt, High Lord?"

Fillip and Sot edged forward out of the sea of faces peering at him. Ferret eyes regarded him solicitously, squinting. Ben wanted nothing so badly at that instant as to break free long enough to throttle them both. He felt like the prize exhibit at the zoo. He felt like a freak. Most of all, he felt like a failure. It was their fault that he felt like that. It was because of them that he was here in the first place. Damn it, all of this had happened because of them!

But that wasn't true, and he knew it. He was here because it had been his choice to come, because this was where he had put himself.

"Are you all right, High Lord?" Fillip asked.

"Can you hear us, High Lord?" Sot asked.

Ben shoved his misplaced anger aside. "I can hear you. I'm all right. How long have I been unconscious?"

"Not long, High Lord," Fillip said.

"Not more than a few minutes," Sot said.

"They seized us all," Fillip said.

"They threw us into this pen," Sot said.

"No one escaped," Fillip said.

"No one," Sot echoed.

So tell me something I don't know, Ben thought bitterly.

He glanced about the compound. They were caged by wire fences that were six foot high and barbed. The gates were of heavy wood lashed with chains. He tugged experimentally at the chains secured to his ankles and wrists. They were firmly locked and fixed in their rings. Escape was not going to be easy.

Escape? He laughed inwardly. What in the hell was he thinking about? How was he going to escape from this place?

"High Lord!" He turned at the sound of his name. Questor had discovered that he was awake. "Are you hurt, High Lord?"

He shook his head no. "How are you and Abernathy? And the kobolds?"

"Quite well, I think." The owlish face was black with soot. "Bunion and Parsnip got the worst of it, I am afraid. They fought very hard for you. It took more than a dozen trolls to subdue them."

The kobolds stirred in their chains, as if to substantiate the wizard's claim. Ben glanced at them a moment, then turned again to Questor. "What will they do to us?" he asked.

Questor shook his head. "I really do not know. Nothing very pleasant, I would think."

Ben could imagine. "Can you use the magic to free us?" he asked.

Questor shook his head once more. "The magic does not work when my hands are chained. It has no power when iron binds me." He hesitated at moment, his long face twisting. "High Lord, I am sorry that I have failed you so badly. I tried to do as you asked—to invoke the magic to aid us. It simply would not respond. I . . . cannot seem to master it . . . as I would wish." He stopped, his voice breaking.

"It's not your fault," Ben interjected quickly. "I'm the one who got us into this mess—not you."

"But I am the court wizard!" Questor insisted vehemently. "I should have magic enough at my command to deal with a handful of trolls!"

"And I should have brains enough to do the same! But it would appear that this time we both came up a bit short, so let's just forget it, Questor. Forget the whole business. Concentrate on finding a way out of this cattle yard!"

Questor Thews slumped back in dejection. He seemed broken by what had happened, no longer the confident guide that had brought Ben into the land. Even Abernathy made no response. Ben quit looking at them.

Fillip and Sot edged closer to where he was chained.

"I am thirsty," Fillip said.

"I am hungry," Sot said.

"How soon can we leave this place, High Lord?" Fillip asked.

"How soon?" Sot asked.

Ben stared at them in disbelief. How about the twelfth of never? How about next decade? Did they think that they were just going to walk out of here? He almost laughed. Apparently they did.

"Let me give it some thought," he suggested and smiled bravely.

He turned away from them and stared out over the pen yard. He found himself wishing he had brought some sort of weapon with him from the old world. A bazooka, maybe? A small tank, perhaps? Bitterness welled up within him. That was the trouble with hindsight, of course—it gave you perfect vision when it was too late to be of any use. It had never occurred to him when he had decided to come into Landover that he would ever have need of a weapon. It had never occurred to him that he would ever find himself in this sort of predicament.

He wondered suddenly why the Paladin had failed to appear when the trolls had come at him. Ghost or not, the Paladin had always appeared before when he was threatened. He would have welcomed an appearance on this occasion as well. He mulled the question over in his mind for a moment before deciding that the only difference between this time and the others was that this time he had failed to think about the medallion when threatened. But that seemed a tenuous link. After all, he had tried to summon the Paladin by willing his appearance when he was testing the medallion's power, and absolutely nothing had happened.

He sagged back against the holding post. The throbbing was beginning to ease in his head. Hell wasn't as bad as it had been five minutes ago. Before it had been intolerable; now it was almost bearable. He reflected momentarily on his life, dredging up all the bad things that had gone before to hold up in comparison to this. The comparison failed. He thought of Annie, and he wondered what she would say if she were alive to see him like this. Annie would probably have dealt with the situation much better than he; she had always been the more flexible, always the more resilient.

There were tears in his eyes. They had shared so much. She had been his one true friend. God, he wished he could see her just once more!

He brushed furtively at his eyes and straightened himself. He tried thinking of Miles, but all he could think about was Miles telling him "I told you so" over and over. He thought about his decision to come to Landover, to the fairy-tale Kingdom that couldn't exist. He thought about the world he had left to come here, about all of the little amenities and irritations he would never experience again. He began to catalogue the wishes and dreams that he would never see fulfilled.

Then he realized what he was doing. He was giving up on himself. He was writing himself off as dead.

He was immediately ashamed. The iron-hard determination that had carried him through so many fights reasserted itself swiftly. There would be no quitting, he swore. He would win this fight, too.

He smiled bitterly. He just wished he knew how.

Two familiar ferretlike faces shoved into view once more.

"Have you had enough time to think about it yet, High Lord?" Fillip asked.

"Yes, have you decided when we will leave, High Lord?" Sot asked.

Ben sighed. "I'm working on it," he assured them.

The hours slipped away. Midnight passed, and the Crag Trolls began to shuffle off to bed. A few stayed on duty to tend the kilns and watchfires, but the rest disappeared into their stone huts. Questor and Abernathy dropped off to sleep. Most of the G'home Gnomes joined them. Fillip and Sot curled up at his feet. Only the kobolds remained awake with Ben. They lay on their sides, unable to get to a sitting position, their narrow eyes fixed on him watchfully, their white teeth showing through those maddening grins. Ben smiled back at them once or twice. They were tough little creatures. He admired them and he regretted getting them into this mess. He regretted getting them all into this mess.

It was nearing morning when he felt a hand lightly touch his face. He had been dozing, and he came awake with a start. Mist and smoke hung like a pall across the valley floor. Shadows cast by the fires chased one another through the haze, red and black wraiths. There was a chill in the air; the fires burned low.

"Ben?"

He looked around and Willow was there. She was crouched directly behind him, huddled close to the chaining post. Slate and earth-colored clothing concealed her slim form and a hooded cloak shadowed her face and hair. He blinked in disbelief, thinking her a part of some half-remembered dream.

"Ben?" she repeated, and her sea-green eyes stared out at him from beneath the hood. "Are you all right?"

He nodded mechanically. She was real. "How did you find me?" he whispered.

"I followed you," she answered, moving closer. Her face was inches from his own, the shadows drawn clear of her exquisite features. She was so impossibly beautiful. "I told you that I belonged to you, Ben. Did you not believe me?"

"It was not a question of believing you, Willow," he tried to explain. "You cannot belong to me. No one can."

She shook her head determinedly. "It was decided long ago that I should, Ben. Why is it that you cannot understand that?"

He felt a wave of helplessness wash through him. He remembered her naked in the waters of the Irrylyn; he remembered her changing into that gnarled tree within the pines. She excited and repelled him both, and he could not come to terms with the mix of feelings.

"Why are you here?" he asked in frustration.

"To set you free," she answered at once. She slipped from beneath the cloak a ring of iron keys. "You should have asked my father for me, Ben. He would have given his permission if you had asked. But you did not ask, and because you did not, I was forced to leave anyway. Now I cannot go back again."

"What do you mean, you can't go back?"

She began working the keys into the locks of his chains, trying each in turn. "It is forbidden for any to leave the lake country without my father's permission. The penalty is exile."

"Exile? But you're his daughter!"

"No longer, Ben."

"Then you shouldn't have come, damn it! You shouldn't have left, if you knew that this would happen!"

Her gaze was steady. "I had no choice."

The third key fitted and the chains fell away. Ben stared at the sylph in anger and frustration, and then in despair. She slipped from his side and moved to Questor, Abernathy, and the kobolds. One by one, she set them free. Daylight was beginning to lighten the eastern sky across the mountains. The trolls would be waking soon.

Willow slipped back to him. "We must go quickly, Ben."

"How did you get in here without being seen?" he asked.

"There are none who can see the people of the lake country if they do not wish it, Ben. I slipped into the valley after midnight and stole the keys from the watch. The gates stand open, the chain only draped through its rings. But we must leave at once; the deception will be discovered.''

She passed the ring of keys to him, and he took them. His fingers brushed hers. He hesitated, thinking suddenly of what she had risked to come after him. She must have shadowed him since he had left the lake country. She must have been watching over him all that time.

Impulsively he reached for her and hugged her close. ''Thank you, Willow,'' he whispered.

Her arms wrapped about his body and she hugged him back. He felt the warmth of her body burn into him, and he welcomed it.

''High Lord!'' Questor was pulling urgently on his arm.

He released Willow and glanced about hurriedly. The G'home Gnomes were stirring in their sleep, rubbing their eyes and stretching their furry limbs. Some were awake already.

''Is it time to leave, High Lord?'' Fillip asked, coming drowzily to his feet.

''Yes, is it time, High Lord?'' Sot echoed, rising with him.

Ben stared at them, remembering what had brought him here in the first place. Abernathy suddenly leaned close. ''High Lord, it will be difficult enough for five of us to slip away unnoticed. We cannot hope to take an entire company of gnomes in the bargain!''

Ben glanced about once more. Mist and smoke were beginning to dissipate. The sky was growing lighter. There were signs of life in several of the stone huts. The entire village would be awake in the next few minutes.

He looked down at the anxious faces of Fillip and Sot. ''Everyone goes,'' he said quietly.

''High Lord . . .!'' Abernathy tried to protest.

''Questor!'' Ben called softly, ignoring his scribe. Questor stepped close. ''We need a diversion.''

The wizard went pale. The owlish face twisted into a knot. ''High Lord, I have already failed you once . . .''

"Then don't do so again," Ben cut him short. "I need that diversion—as soon as we're through the gates of this cattle pen. Do something that will distract the Crag Trolls. Explode one of their kilns or drop a mountain on them. Anything—but do it!"

He took Willow's arm and started across the compound. Bunion and Parsnip were ahead of him at once, clearing the way, creeping through the fading dark. Furry, ferret-faced forms squirmed and bunched close as he went.

He caught a glimpse of a lean, misshapen figure approaching the compound gates. "Bunion!" he warned with a hiss.

The kobold was through the gate in an instant, shoving free the chains from their rings. He caught the surprised troll before the creature knew what was happening and silenced him.

Ben and Willow rushed from the compound, Questor and Abernathy a step behind. The G'home Gnomes poured through after. Shouts of alarm broke through the stillness almost immediately, deep-throated cries that shattered the sleep of the Crag Trolls. The trolls stumbled from their huts, grunting. The gnomes scattered, stocky forms moving much faster than Ben would have thought possible. He drew up short. There were Crag Trolls at every turn.

"Questor!" he yelled frantically.

Brilliant white light exploded overhead, and Strabo appeared. The dragon flew across the valley breathing fire everywhere. Crag Trolls scrambled frantically for cover, and G'home Gnomes screamed in terror. Ben stared in disbelief. Where had the dragon come from?

Then he caught sight of Questor, arms thrust out of his robes and windmilling madly as the wizard stumbled back. He saw at the same instant that Strabo had only one leg, that the wings were not centered properly on the barrel-shaped body, that there were odd clumps of feathered plumage about the leathered neck, and that the dragon's fire lanced earthward but burned nothing. The dragon was a fake. Questor had given them their diversion.

Willow saw it, too. She seized his arm, and together they broke for the valley pass that had brought the little company in the previous night. The others followed, Questor bringing up the rear. Already the illusory dragon was beginning to fade, bits and pieces of his body disintegrating as he flew back and forth above the astonished trolls. Ben and his companions dashed through their midst. Twice they were intercepted, but Bunion dispatched the attackers with a swiftness that was frightening. They gained the defile in moments, the way before them clear.

Ben risked a final glance back. The dragon had come apart completely, pieces of magic falling into the mist and smoke like a broken puzzle. The trolls remained in a state of complete confusion.

The little company dashed into the shadows of the defile, and the trolls, the fires, the valley, and the madness were left behind.

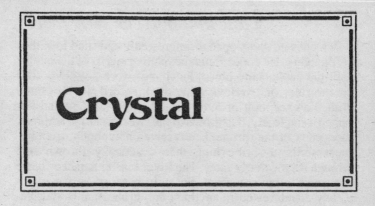

Crystal

It was nearing midmorning when Ben and his companions finally ended their flight. They were safely out of the Melchor by then, well below the shadowed, misted cliffs and defiles, back within the foothills from which the G'home Gnomes had originally been taken. The gnomes had long since disappeared, the Crag Trolls appeared to have lost interest in the matter, and there no longer seemed to be any reason to continue running.

Make no mistake, Ben thought, lowering himself gingerly to rest his back against an oak trunk—they had been running. It was an ignominious admission. It would have been far more satisfying to couch their flight in terms of making an escape, or some such. But the truth of the matter was that they had been running for their lives.

Willow, Questor, Abernathy, and the kobolds gathered about him, seating themselves in a circle on a patch of wintry saw grass colored a faint pink. Clouds rolled overhead in a thick blanket of gray, and the smell of rain was in the air. They ate a brief meal of leaves and stalks from Bonnie Blues that grew close at hand, and they drank the water of a spring that ran down out of the mountains. They had nothing else to eat or drink. All of their possessions, horses included, had been lost to the trolls.

Ben chewed and sipped disinterestedly and tried to gather his thoughts. He could argue the relative merits of the matter until the cows came home, but things were not going well for the ruler of Landover. His track record was abysmal. With the exception of those seated about him, he had not gained a single ally. The Lords of the Greensward, traditional supporters of the throne, had received him coolly, tried unsuccessfully to bribe him, then practically thrown him through Rhyndweir's gates. The River Master had been more congenial in his reception, but only because he was completely disinterested in anything the throne said or did, believing the salvation of his people lay entirely in his own hands. The Crag Trolls had imprisoned him and would have undoubtedly fried him had he not managed to escape their cattle pens—thanks, he reminded himself, not to anything he had done but to Willow's perserverance and to a fortuitous turn of events that finally enabled Questor to conjure up the magic in more or less the right way for a change.

There were the G'home Gnomes, of course. Fillip and Sot had pledged for them. But what was that worth? What good was the pledge of a burrow people who were despised by everyone for being thieves and scavengers and worse?

"So what exactly do we have here?" he asked aloud, and everyone looked up in surprise. "We have this. The Lords of the Greensward—Kallendbor, Strehan and the rest—will pledge to the throne on the day I rid them of the dragon, something that no one has ever been able to do. The River Master will pledge to the throne on the day that I gain the promise of the Lords of the Greensward and various others to cease pollution of his lands and waters and to work with him to keep the valley clean. Fat chance. The Crag Trolls will pledge to the throne on the day I can walk back into the Melchor without fear of being offered up for roast beef. Good luck there, as well." He paused. "I'd say that about covers the situation, doesn't it?"

No one said anything. Questor and Abernathy exchanged uncertain glances. Willow looked as if she did not understand—which, indeed, she might not, he conceded. The kobolds stared at him with their bright, knowing eyes and grinned their needle-sharp smiles.

He flushed with a mix of sudden embarrassment and anger. "The truth of the matter is I have made absolutely no progress whatsoever. Zero. Nil. Zip. Any arguments?" He hoped someone would try.

Questor obliged him. "High Lord, I think you are being entirely too hard on yourself."

"Am I? What part of what I said was untrue, Questor Thews?"

"What you said was true as far as it went, High Lord. But you overlook an important consideration in your appraisal."

"I do? What consideration is that?"

Questor held his ground. "The difficulty of your position. It is not easy to be King of Landover under the best of circumstances."

The others nodded in agreement. "No," Ben shook his head at once. "I can't accept that. I can't blame this on the circumstances. You take the circumstances as you find them and make the best of them."

"Why do you think that you have not done this, Ben?" Willow wanted to know.

The question confused him. "Because I haven't! I couldn't persuade the Lords of the Greensward or your father or those damned trolls to do any of the things that I wanted them to do! I almost got us killed back there with the trolls! If you hadn't followed us and if Questor hadn't managed to get his magic working, we would probably all be dead!"

"I would not make too much out of any help you gained from my magic." Questor muttered softly, owlish face twisting uncomfortably.

"You did succeed in freeing the gnomes, High Lord," Abernathy reminded him stiffly. His brown eyes blinked. "I personally consider it wasted effort, but such value as their lives might hold is owed now entirely to you. You were the one who insisted that we take them with us."

The others nodded once more. Ben glanced from face to face, frowning. "I appreciate the vote of confidence, but I think it's misplaced. Why don't we just accept what we all know—I'm just not doing the job.''

"You are doing the best that you can, High Lord," Questor replied at once. "No one can ask anything more."

"Nor do anything more," Abernathy added.

"But maybe someone else *can* do more," Ben declared pointedly. "Maybe someone else *should*."

"High Lord!" Abernathy rose stiffly. He pushed his glasses back on his long nose and his ears cocked back. "I have been scribe to the throne for more years than you have lived. Perhaps that is difficult to realize given my present form," he cast a withering glance at Questor, "but I ask you to accept my word nevertheless. I have witnessed Kings of Landover come and go—the old King and those many who followed after him. I have observed them all in their attempts to govern. I have seen them exercise their wisdom and their compassion. Some have been capable; some have not." His right paw pointed dramatically. "But I will tell you now, High Lord, that none—not even the old King—have ever shown more promise than you!"

He finished and sat back on his haunches slowly. Ben was stunned. He would not have expected in his wildest dreams to receive such a ringing endorsement from the cynical scribe.

He felt Willow take his hand. "Ben, you must listen to him. The part of me that is my mother senses something very special about you. It tells me that you are different. I think that you are meant to be King of Landover. I think no one else should even try."

"Willow, you cannot make that judgment . . ." he started to tell her, but a sudden hissing from the kobolds cut him short. They spoke between themselves a moment, and then Bunion said something quickly to Questor.

The wizard looked at Ben. "The kobolds agree with the sylph. There is something different about you, they feel. You show courage and strength. You are the King they wish to serve."

Ben sagged back weakly against the tree trunk, shaking

his head reprovingly. "What do I have to do to convince you that you are mistaken about me? There is nothing different about me, nothing special, nothing that would make me a better King than the next guy. Don't you see? You're doing the same thing I did when I took the kingship—you're deceiving yourselves! This may be a fantasy kingdom on paper, but it is real enough in the flesh—and we have to accept the fact that no amount of wishing or make-believe is going to solve its problems!"

No one responded. They stared at him silently. He thought about saying something further to persuade them, but decided against it. There wasn't anything else worth saying.

Finally, Questor rose. He came to his feet as if the weight of the world were suddenly on his shoulders. His owlish face was screwed up so tightly that he appeared to be in pain. Slowly, he straightened.

"High Lord, there is something that you should know." He cleared his throat nervously. "I told you before that my half-brother chose you quite deliberately as buyer of the throne of Landover. I told you that he chose you because he believed that you would fail as King and that the Kingship would revert once again to him—just as it has each time it has been sold since the old King's death. He believed you one of life's more obvious failures, High Lord. He depended on it, in fact."

Ben folded his arms defensively across his chest. "Then I guess he won't be disappointed when he discovers the way things are working out, will he?"

Questor cleared his throat again, shifting his weight uncomfortably. "As it happens, High Lord, he knows exactly how things are working out and he is extremely disappointed."

"Well, frankly, Questor, I don't give a . . ." Ben stopped short. He stared hard at the other man. "What did you say? Did you say he knows how things are working out—*exactly* how they're working out?"

He came to his feet and faced the wizard. "How can that be, Questor? His magic doesn't reach into this world anymore, does it? You said he couldn't take anything with him when he left Landover except the medallion. Everything else had to be left behind. If that's so, then how does he know what's happening back here?"

Questor was eerily calm, his face composed like a death mask. "I tell him what is happening, High Lord," he said quietly.

There was an endless silence. Ben could not believe what he had just heard. "You tell him?" he repeated in astonishment.

"I must, High Lord." Questor's eyes dropped. "It was the bargain I made with him when he departed Landover with the old King's son. I could be court wizard in his absence, but I had to agree to report to him on the progress of the would-be Kings of Landover sent over from your world. I was to let him know of their failures, and should they occur, of their successes. He planned to use this information in his selection process of candidates for future sales of the throne; he would look for weaknesses that the information revealed."

The others had come to their feet as well. Questor ignored them. "I want no more secrets between us," he went on quickly. "There have been too many secrets already, I fear. So I will tell you the last of what I have kept from you. You asked once how many Kings of Landover there have been since the death of the old King. I told you more than thirty. What I did not tell you was that the last eight came from Rosen's, Ltd.—all within a span of less than two years! Five of those lasted less than the ten-day trial period permitted under the terms of your agreement. Consider for a moment what that means, High Lord. It means that five times, at least, the store would have had to refund to the customer the money paid—five times my half-brother would have lost his sale. One million dollars each time, High Lord. Bad publicity, bad business. I think that neither the store nor my brother would have tolerated such losses. That suggests to me the losses were never discovered. I think that most, if not all, of those sales were kept hidden from the store. And I think that the subsequent dissatisfaction of the customers was covered up in the most expeditious way possible."

He paused deliberately. "Questor, what are you saying?" Ben whispered.

"That were you to use the medallion now to return to your own world, High Lord, you would find your money gone and your life expectancy shortened considerably."

Abernathy was furious, his muzzle drawn back to reveal all of his numerous teeth. "I *knew* you were not to be trusted, Questor Thews!" he growled ominously.

Ben brought his hand up quickly. "No, wait a moment. He didn't have to tell me this; he chose to do so freely. Why, Questor?"

The wizard's smile was strangely gentle. "So that you would know how much I believe in you, High Lord Ben Holiday. The others have argued their belief persuasively and eloquently, but you appear unwilling to listen. I am hoping that this admission to you will accomplish what they, apparently, have not and make you believe in yourself. I think you the King that Landover has waited for. I think that my half-brother fears this as well. He has shown more than a little concern over your refusal to give up when so many before you would have done so long ago. He worries that you will find a way to keep the throne. He is frightened of you, High Lord."

Willow seized Ben's arm tightly. "Listen to him, Ben. I believe him."

Questor sighed wearily. "I had what I believed to be good reason for doing as my half-brother asked. I would not have been given the position of court wizard had I refused. I knew that I could do nothing to help the land if the position were not mine. I believed that the help I could give as court wizard would outweigh any damage my reports might do. It was not until just recently that I began to surmise the fate of those who had purchased the Kingship and failed to stay on. By then it was too late to help them . . ."

His voice broke. "My half-brother made a further bargain with me, High Lord—a bargain that, I am ashamed to admit,

I could not bring myself to refuse. His books of magic, the secrets of the conjuring acquired by wizards since the dawn of the land, are concealed within the Kingdom. Only he knows where. He could not take them out with him, and he has promised them to me. Each time a new King fails, he gives me a bit more of the magic with which to work. I do nothing to aid his plan, High Lord—but the need for the magic is an irresistible lure. Bits and pieces aid me in my learning. I know that he will never give the books to me; I know that he uses me as his pawn. But I believe that sooner or later he will say one word more than he should or give up one secret too many, and I will be able to find the books without him and use them to put an end to him!"

The owlish face twisted sharply in on itself, lines cutting to the bone. "I let myself be used, High Lord, because I saw no other way. My intentions have always been good ones. I want this land restored to what it was. I would do anything to achieve that. I love this land more than my own life!"

Ben studied him silently, conflicting emotions washing through him. Willow still grasped his arm, her fingers insistent, their pressure telling him that she thought Questor spoke the truth. Abernathy still looked wary. The kobolds stood mute beside him, and he could read nothing in their dark faces.

He looked back again at the wizard. His own voice was rough. "Questor, you suggested to me more than once that I could use the medallion to return safely to my own world."

"It was necessary that I test the depth of your commitment, High Lord!" the other whispered fiercely. "It was necessary that you be given the choice!"

"And if I had elected to use the medallion?"

The silence was endless. "I would like to believe, High Lord . . . that I would have stopped you."

There were sudden tears in the other's eyes. Ben read the mix of shame and hurt reflected there. "I would like to believe so, too, Questor," he said softly.

He thought a moment, then put his hand on the wizard's

shoulder. "How do you communicate with Meeks, Questor? How do you speak with him?"

Questor took a moment to compose himself, then dug into the folds of his clothing and pulled something free. Ben stared. It was the crystal that Questor had been wearing when Ben had first crossed into Landover. Ben had all but forgotten it. He had seen it several times since, but had never given it more than a passing thought.

"The crystal is his, High Lord," Questor explained. "He gave it to me when he departed Landover. I warm it with my hands, and his face appears within it. I can speak with him, then."

Ben studied the crystal wordlessly for a moment, looking into the depthless facets, peering through the rainbow of colors that shimmered within. The crystal hung from a silver chain fastened to a ring screwed into its apex.

He looked at Questor. "Has Meeks any other source of contact with Landover?"

The wizard shook his head. "I think not."

Ben hefted the crystal experimentally. "Do you have enough faith in me to give the crystal up, Questor?" he asked, his voice almost a whisper.

"The crystal is yours, High Lord," the wizard replied at once.

Ben nodded and smiled faintly. He passed the crystal back to Questor. "Summon up Mr. Meeks for me, would you, please?"

There was a moment's hesitation, and then Questor placed the crystal within his palms and cupped them together. Willow, Abernathy, and kobolds pressed close. Ben felt his heart race. He had not expected to encounter Meeks so soon again; but now that it was about to happen, he looked forward to it eagerly.

Questor opened his palms carefully and picked the crystal up by its chain. Meeks peered out of the crystal's center, surprise mirrored in his sharp eyes.

Ben bent down so that his eyes were even with those of

Meeks. "Good day, Mr. Meeks," he greeted. "How are things in New York?"

The craggy old face went dark with anger, the eyes baleful as they stared back. Ben had never seen such hatred.

"Don't feel like talking?" Ben smiled his best courtroom smile. "Can't say that I blame you. Things aren't working out all that well for you, are they?"

The black-gloved hand came up in warning as Meeks tried to say something.

"No, don't bother answering," Ben cut him short. "Nothing you have to say would interest me. I just want you to know one thing." He took the crystal from Questor and held it up before him. The smile disappeared. "I just want you to know that the wheels are about to come off your wagon!"

Then he carried the crystal to a stand of rocks that jutted through the earth of a nearby hillside and smashed the orb against them until it was reduced to fragments. He ground the fragments into the earth with his boot.

"Good-bye, Mr. Meeks," he said quietly.

He turned. His companions were watching him, standing in a knot where he had left them. He walked slowly back to where they waited. Their eyes remained riveted on him.

"I guess that's the last of Mr. Meeks," he offered. "It appears that we are back to square one."

"High Lord, please allow me to say something," Questor asked. He was agitated, but he composed himself. "High Lord, you cannot give up." He glanced awkwardly at the others. "Perhaps I have lost everyone's trust because of what I have done. Perhaps it would be best if I were to go no further with you. I accept that. But you, at least, must go on. Abernathy, Bunion, Parsnip, and Willow, too, will stay with you. They believe in you, and they are right to do so. You have the wisdom, compassion, strength, and courage of which they spoke. But you have something else, High Lord Ben Holiday. You have something that no other King of Landover has shown for many a year—something a King of Landover must have. You have determination. You refuse to quit when another man would. A King needs that quality most of all.''

He paused, his stooped form straightening. "I did not lie when I told you that my half-brother sees that determination in you and is frightened by it.'' He shook his head admonishingly. "Do not quit now, High Lord. Be the King that you have wished to be!''

He had finished, and he waited for Ben's response. Ben glanced at the others—at Willow, the fire in her eyes a reflection of more than her trust; at Abernathy, sardonic and wary; at Parsnip and Bunion, their monkey faces sharp and cunning with hidden knowledge. Each face was like an actor's mask in some bizarre piece of theater, and the play a thing not yet finished. Who were they really, he wondered—and who was he?

Suddenly he was a lifetime away from everything that had come before his journey into this strange world. Gone were the corporate high rises, the lawyers, the judicial system of the United States of America, the cities, the governments, the codes, and the laws. It was all gone, everything that had ever been. There was only what never was—dragons, witches, fairy creatures of all sorts, castles and knights, damsels and wizards, things of magic and things of enchantment. He was starting life over, and all of the rules were new. He had jumped into the abyss, and he was still falling.

Quite unexpectedly, he started to grin. "Questor, I have no intention of quitting.'' The grin broadened. "How could I possibly quit in the face of such an eloquent testimonial of faith? How could I possibly quit with friends such as you to stand with me?'' He shook his head slowly, as much at his own madness as at theirs. "No, the beat goes on, and so do we.''

Willow was smiling. The kobolds hissed their approval. Questor looked relieved. Even Abernathy nodded his agreement.

"One condition, however,'' The grin disappeared from his face. He stepped forward and put his hand gently on Questor's shoulder. "We started together, and we finish together. What's past is past, Questor. We need you with us."

The wizard stared at him in disbelief. "High Lord, I would do anything you asked of me, but . . . I cannot . . ." He glanced at the others self-consciously.

"A vote," Ben called out at once. "Does Questor go with us? Bunion? Parsnip?" The kobolds nodded. "Willow?" The sylph nodded as well.

He paused and looked at Abernathy. "Abernathy?"

Abernathy faced him silently and made no gesture either way. Ben waited. The scribe might have been chiseled out of stone. "Abernathy?" he repeated softly.

The dog shrugged. "I think he knows less about character than he does about magic, but I also think he meant no real harm. Let him come."

Ben smiled. "Well done, Abernathy," he commended. "We are a company once more." He looked at Questor. "Will you come with us?"

Flushing, a smile tugging at the corners of his mouth, the wizard nodded eagerly. "Yes, High Lord, I will."

Ben glanced at each of them in turn, thinking momentarily that they were all nuts, then turned to study the sky. The sun was a fuzzy white glow through the mist and clouds, its center directly overhead. It was nearing midday.

"I suppose that we had better be going, then," he said.

Abernathy's teeth clicked sharply. "Umm . . . going where, High Lord?" he asked hesitantly.

Ben came up to him and put his hands on the dog's furry shoulders. He glanced conspiratorially at the others. "Where I told the Crag Trolls we were going, Abernathy; where we should have been going all along."

The scribe stared at him. "And where is that, High Lord?"

Ben smiled solemnly. "To the Deep Fell, Abernathy. To Nightshade."

Deep Fell

They thought Ben Holiday mad. They thought it to varying degrees, perhaps, but the vote was unanimous. The kobolds expressed it with a quick hiss and frightening, humorless grins. Willow's green eyes mirrored it, and she shook back her waist-length hair in disapproval. Questor and Abernathy were aghast, and both began talking at once.

"You have taken leave of your senses, High Lord!" the scribe exploded.

"You cannot risk placing yourself in the hands of the witch!" the wizard admonished.

Ben let them go on a bit, then sat them all down and patiently explained himself. He had not taken leave of his senses, he assured them. On the contrary, he knew exactly what he was doing. He might be taking some risk in going down into the Deep Fell and confronting Nightshade, but there was risk in almost any alternative left to him at this point and no other alternative made as much sense or offered the same opportunities.

Think about it, he urged. The key to every door closed against him lay in use or acquisition of magic. It was magic that had given life to the land and those who lived upon it in the beginning; it was loss of magic that threatened to steal that life away now. The medallion was a thing of magic, enabling him to pass from his world into theirs and—if need be—out again. The Paladin was a thing of magic, and magic was needed to bring him back to them. The castle at Sterling Silver was a thing of magic, and magic was needed to save it. Most of the land's creatures were creatures of magic, and magic was what they understood, respected and feared. The Lords of the Greensward wanted Ben to rid them of the dragon, and it would take magic to do that. The River Master wanted the land's inhabitants to work with him to heal the land, and that would probably take some form of magic as well. The Mark and his demons were a dark magic that threatened to destroy them all, and it would take a very powerful form of white magic, indeed, to prevent that from happening.

He paused. Who was most likely, then, to have access to the magic that he needed in order to begin to put things right again? Who possessed magic that the others did not?

Sure, there was risk. There was always risk. But no one had gone to Nightshade in many years; no one had even thought to try. No King of Landover had sought her allegiance since the death of the old King. Since before that, Abernathy interjected firmly—the old King wanted nothing to do with her either. All the more reason to see her now, Ben insisted. She could be talked to. Perhaps she could be persuaded. Possibly, if all else failed, she could be tricked.

His companions stared at him in horror.

He shrugged. Very well, forget the part about tricking her. She was still their best bet. She was possessor of the land's most powerful magic—Questor had said as much in their lessons. The others fixed accusing eyes on the wizard. A bit of that magic might turn things about for him. He wouldn't need much; enough to solve just one of the problems facing him would be plenty. Even if she refused her own magic, she might agree to arrange a meeting with the fairies; perhaps he could enlist their help.

He saw Willow cringe slightly at mention of the fairies,

and for an instant he was no longer quite so sure of himself. But he shrugged the feeling off and went on with his argument. He had reasoned it through, and the solution to his problem was unmistakable. He had need of an ally to help bring the other inhabitants of Landover to terms. He would not find a more powerful ally than Nightshade.

Nor a more dangerous one, Questor pointed out bluntly.

But Ben was not to be dissuaded. The matter was decided and the journey about to commence. They were off to the Deep Fell. Anyone who didn't care to go with him could stay behind—he would understand.

No one stepped back. But there were a lot of uneasy looks.

It was midday by now, and they traveled south through the hill country until nightfall. The weather remained foul, the clouds continuing to mass, the onslaught of rain to draw closer. Mist turned to fog as night descended, and it began to drizzle. The company made camp beneath an outcropping of rocks below a ridgeline draped by a grove of weathered ash. The damp and the dark closed about quickly, and the six travelers hunched down together in their shelter and ate a sparse meal of spring water, Bonnie Blues, and some odd roots collected by the resourceful Parsnip. The air turned chill, and Ben found himself wishing for a shot of his now-departed Glenlivet.

Dinner was completed rather quickly, and they began to give thought to their sleeping accommodations. They were without bedding of any kind; everything had been lost in their flight from the trolls. Questor volunteered his use of the magic, and this time Ben agreed. The kobolds seemed hardy enough, but the rest of them might well catch pneumonia by morning if they didn't have something to help ward off the cold. Besides, Questor had shown improved control over the magic at the Melchor.

Such was not the case this night, however. The magic sparked and poofed, and several dozen flowered hand towels materialized. Questor grumbled about the weather and tried again. This time he produced burlap sacks. Now Abernathy was grumbling as well, and tempers were heating up faster than bodies. On the third try, the wizard conjured up a colorfully striped pavilion tent complete with sitting cushions and dressing boards, and Ben decided that they would settle for that.

They settled themselves in and one by one drifted off to sleep. Abernathy kept watch as he slept, his nose pointed out the tent flap, not entirely convinced that the trolls had given up on them.

Only Ben remained awake. He lay in the dark and listened to the sound of the rain as it drummed against the tent. He was beset with uncertainties that until now he had successfully ignored. He felt time slipping inexorably from him. Sooner than he wished, he knew, it was going to run out altogether. Then the Mark would have him or some other evil that he had no real protection against. Then he would be forced to use the medallion to save himself, even though he had sworn that he would not. What choice would he make then? What would he do when his life was *really* threatened—not by manor lords looking to box his ears or trolls looking to pen him up, but by some monster that could snuff his life out with nothing more than a thought? Such monsters were out there, he knew. Nightshade was out there.

He forced himself to think about the witch of the Deep Fell for a time. He had not let himself do so earlier; it was easier not to. He knew he had to go to her. It did not help matters to think about how dangerous that might be. Nightshade frightened the others badly, and nothing besides the Mark had done that. He might be biting off more than he could chew once again; he might be putting them all in a worse predicament than the one they had experienced in the camp of the Crag Trolls. He chewed his lower lip thoughtfully. He could not afford to do that. There might be no one to rescue them this time. He would have to be more careful; he would have to take steps to protect them.

Especially Willow, he thought. He glanced over to where she lay in the dark, trying to follow the line of her sleeping form. She had not transformed herself into and taken root as a tree this night. Evidently, she did so only periodically. He found that he was less repelled by the idea than he had previously been. Perhaps it was only the strangeness of the change that had bothered him so at first, and now he was used to the idea. Sometimes familiarity bred acceptance, not contempt.

He shook his head admonishingly. What you really mean, Holiday, is that she saved your skin, so now you can accept her. Bully for you.

His breathing evened out and his eyes closed. He wished she hadn't given up so much to follow him. He wished that she had been a little less impulsive. It made him feel responsible for her, and he didn't want that. She wanted it, of course. She saw things the way some child would see them— their fate told in the winding of vines on a bridal bed, their lives joined by a chance meeting at some midnight swim. She expected things from him that he wasn't prepared to give to anyone.

His thoughts wandered, and his obstinacy slowly diffused. Perhaps the problem was not with her at all; perhaps it was with him. Maybe the real problem was that he simply didn't have the things to give her that she was asking for. Perhaps he had lost everything good about himself when Annie had died. He didn't want to think that, but perhaps it was so.

He was surprised to find tears in his eyes. He brushed them silently away, grateful that no one could see.

He let his thoughts slip away then, and he drifted down into himself. His dreams overtook him, and he slept.

He was awake early, the daylight still a faint blush against the eastern horizon where the mist rolled across the hills. The others of the little company were awake as well, stretching muscles cramped from sleeping in the damp and chill, yawning against the too quick passing of the night. The rain had died away to a spattering of drops from the leaves of the trees. Ben stepped from the pavilion tent into the half-light and walked to where a trickle of water spilled down out of the rocks through a gathering of heavy brush. He was bending down to catch a drink in his cupped hands when a pair of ferretlike faces poked out suddenly from the brush.

He jumped backward, water flying up into his face, a startled oath on his lips.

"Great High Lord," a voice greeted quickly.

"Mighty High Lord," a second voice echoed.

Fillip and Sot. Ben recovered his composure, forced himself with considerable effort to discard his impulse to throttle them both, and waited patiently as they worked their way free of their concealment. The G'Home Gnomes were a bedraggled pair, their clothing ripped and their fur matted with the rain. They appeared even dirtier than usual, if that was possible.

They waddled forward, eyes peering up at him in the near dark.

"We experienced some difficulty eluding the Crag Trolls, High Lord," Fillip explained.

"We were hunted until dark, and then we could not determine where you had gone," Sot added.

"We were frightened that you had been taken again," Fillip said.

"We were afraid that you had not escaped," Sot said.

"But we found your trail and followed it," Fillip continued.

"We see poorly, but we have an excellent sense of smell," Sot added.

Ben shook his head helplessly. "Why did you bother coming at all?" he asked, kneeling down so they were all at eye-level. "Why didn't you simply go on home with the rest of your people?"

"Oh, no, High Lord!" Fillip exclaimed.

"Never, High Lord!" Sot declared.

"We gave our promise to serve you, if you should aid us in freeing our people," Fillip said.

"We gave our word," Sot said.

"You kept your part of the bargain, High Lord," Fillip said.

"Now we intend to keep ours," Sot finished.

Ben stared at them in disbelief. Loyalty was the last thing he had ever expected from these two. It was also the last thing he needed. Fillip and Sot were more likely to prove a source of trouble than a well of relief.

He almost told them so, but then he caught the look of determination on their faces and in their half-blind eyes. He reminded himself that the G'home Gnomes were the first to step forward and offer their pledge to Landover's throne—the first, when no one else would. It seemed wrong to dismiss their offer of help out of hand when they were so willing to serve.

He straightened slowly, watching as their eyes followed him up. "We are going to the Deep Fell," he advised them. "I plan to meet with Nightshade."

Fillip and Sot looked at each other expressionlessly and nodded.

"Then we can be of service to you, High Lord," Fillip said.

"Indeed, we can," Sot agreed.

"We have gone into the Deep Fell on many occasions," Fillip said.

"We know the hollows well," Sot said.

"You do?" Ben didn't even try to hide his amazement.

"Yes, High Lord," Fillip and Sot said together.

"The witch pays little attention to creatures such as us," Fillip said.

"The witch does not even see us," Sot said.

"We will guide you safely in, High Lord," Fillip offered.

"Then we will guide you safely out again," Sot added.

Ben extended his hand and shook heartily each grimy paw. "You have yourselves a deal." He grinned. The gnomes beamed. He drew back. "One question. Why did you wait until now to show yourselves? How long have you been crouching back there in the brush?"

"All night, High Lord," Fillip admitted.

"We were afraid of the dog," Sot whispered.

Ben brought them into the camp and announced to the others that the gnomes would be accompanying them to the Deep Fell. Abernathy was thoroughly dismayed and expressed the fact in no uncertain terms. It was one thing to agree to accept the wizard back into their company on the theory that he might prove useful—though he questioned how much use he would, in fact, be—but the gnomes were clearly of no use at all. He growled, and the gnomes shrank back uneasily. The kobolds hissed at them, and even Willow looked doubtful. But Ben was firm in his decision. The G'home Gnomes were coming with them.

They resumed their journey shortly after sunrise. They ate a quick breakfast of stems and leaves from the Bonnie Blues, Questor made the pavilion tent disappear in a flash of light and a puff of smoke, frightening the gnomes half to death in the process, and they were on their way. They traveled south and west on a meandering course that took them down out of the hill country and back into the forestland and lakes bordering the Greensward. Bunion led and the rest followed. It rained on and off, frequently misting like a veil of cold steam. The valley lay socked in by clouds and fog that formed an oddly bluish haze that rolled and mixed against the treetops and the dark, distant walls of the mountains. Flowers bloomed in the rain, and Ben found that odd. The flowers were pastel in color, fragile blooms that lasted only minutes and then withered. Rain flowers, Questor called them—evidencing a sorry lack of originality. They came with the rain and then they were gone. Once, in better times, they had enjoyed a lifespan of a dozen hours or more. But now, like everything else in the valley, they were stricken by the sickness. The magic no longer gave them more than a brief life.

The little company took a short break at mid-morning, settling themselves beside a spring grown thick with reeds, lilies, and cypress. The spring had a greenish-brown cast to it and nothing growing near looked healthy. Bunion set off in search of drinking water. It had begun to rain again, and the others clustered in twos and threes beneath the branches of the trees. Ben waited for a time, then caught Willow's eye and took her aside where they could be alone.

"Willow," he said gently. He knew this was going to be difficult. "I have been thinking about your coming with us into the Deep Fell—and wherever else we end up going. I don't think that you should go any further. I think that you ought to return to your home in Elderew."

She looked at him steadily. "I do not want to return home, Ben. I want to stay with you."

"I know that. But I think that it is too dangerous for you to do so."

"It is no more dangerous for me than it is for you. It may be that you will have need of my help again. I will stay."

"I will write a letter explaining to your father that I wished you with me until now so that you will not be in trouble with him," he went on. "I will come later to explain it to him myself."

"I don't want to go, Ben," she said again.

The green cast of her face was darkened by the shadows of the cypress, and she seemed to Ben almost a part of the tree. "I appreciate your willingness to take the same risks that I take," he said, "but there is no reason for you to do so. I cannot allow it, Willow."

Her face tilted back slightly, and now there was sudden fire in her green eyes. "You have nothing to say about it, Ben. The decision is mine." She paused, and it seemed as if she were staring right through him. "Why not tell me what is really on your mind, High Lord of Landover."

He stared back at her in surprise, then slowly nodded his agreement. "Very well. I'm not sure how to say this. If I could keep you with me and be honest with myself, I think I would do so. But I cannot. I don't love you, Willow. It may be that the fairy people discover love in a single sighting, but it doesn't happen that way with me. I don't believe in what the vines and the portents told you about how this would happen. I don't believe that you and I are meant to be lovers. I think you and I are meant to be friends, but I can't let you risk your life for me because of that!''

He stopped, feeling her hands catch up his own and gently hold them.

"You still do not understand, do you, Ben?" she whispered. "I belong to you because that is what is meant to be. It is truth woven in the fabric of the land's magic, and though you may not see it, nevertheless it will come to pass. I feel love for you because I love in the way of the fairies—at first sighting and by promise. I do not expect that of you. But you will come to love me, Ben. It will happen.''

"Maybe so," he acknowledged, gripping her hands tightly in response in spite of himself, finding her so desirable that he could almost admit that she might be right. "But I do not love you now. I find you the most beautiful creature I have ever seen. I find myself wanting you so badly that I have to fight back the need for you.'' He shook his head. "But, Willow, I cannot believe in the future that you seem to see so clearly. You don't belong to me! You belong to yourself!''

"I belong to nothing if I do not belong to you!" she insisted fiercely. Her face leaned close to his. "Are you frightened of me, Ben? I see fear in your eyes, and I do not understand it.''

He took a deep breath. "There was someone else, Willow—someone who truly belonged to me and I to her. Her name was Annie. She was my wife, and I loved her very much. She was not as beautiful to look at as you, but she was pretty and she was . . . special. She died two years ago in an accident and I . . . I haven't been able to forget her or to quit loving her or or to love anyone else.''

His voice broke. He hadn't realized it would be so difficult talking about Annie after all this time.

"You have not told me why are you afraid, Ben," Willow pressed, her voice gentle, but insistent.

"I don't know why I'm afraid!" He shook his head, confused, "I don't know. I think it's because when Annie died I lost something of myself—something so precious that I'm not sure I'll ever get it back again. Sometimes I think I can't feel anymore. I just seem to pretend . . ."

There were sudden tears in her eyes, and he was shocked. "Please don't cry," he asked her.

Willow smiled bitterly. "I think you are afraid to let yourself love me, because I am so different from what she was," the sylph said softly. "I think you are afraid that if you let yourself love me, you will somehow lose her. I wouldn't want that. I want what you were and are and will be—all that is you. But I cannot have that because you are afraid of me."

He started to deny it, then stopped. She was right when she said that he was frightened of her. He saw her in his mind as she danced in the clearing of aged pines at midnight, changing from sylph to willow tree, rooting in the soil that her mother had danced upon. The transformation repelled him still. She was not human; she was something beyond and apart from that.

How could he ever love a creature so different from Annie . . . ?

Her fingers brushed at the tears that were slipping now from his own eyes. "I am life of the magic and subject to its will, Ben. So must you be; so will you be. Earth mother and heaven father made us both, and the land binds us." She bent forward and kissed him on his check. "You will lose your fear of me and one day you will love me. I believe that." Her breath was soft against his face. "I will wait for as long as that takes, Ben, but I will not leave you—not if you beg me, not if you command me. I belong to you. I belong with you. I will stay with you, though the risk is ten times as great as it is now. I will stay, though my own life be given up for yours!"

She rose, a rustle of long hair and clothing in the mid-morning stillness. "Do not ever ask me to leave you again," she told him.

Then she walked quickly away. He stared after her word-lessly and knew that he would not.

The little company arrived at the Deep Fell shortly before midday. The rain had passed and the day brightened, though clouds still screened the whole of the sky. The smell of damp hung thick in the air, and the morning chill had sharpened.

Ben stood with his companions at the edge of the Deep Fell and stared downward. All but the rim of the bowl was screened away by a blanket of mist. The mist hung over everything, swirling sluggishly across a scattering of tree tops and ridges that poked through the haze like jagged bones from a broken corpse. Scrub choked the rim and upper slopes of the hollows, brambles and thickets that were wintry and stunted. Nothing moved in the pit. No sound came out of it. It was an open grave that waited for an occupant.

Ben eyed it uneasily. It was frightening to look upon—the more so from its edge than from the safety of the Lands-view. It appeared monstrous to him, a sprawling, misshapen chasm carved from the earth and left to gather rot. He glanced momentarily at a stand of Bonnie Blues that grew close to the rim. They were blackened and withered.

"High Lord, it is not too late to rethink your decision," Questor advised softly, standing at his elbow.

He shook his head wordlessly. The decision had been made.

"Perhaps we should wait until morning," Abernathy muttered, glancing uneasily at the clouded sky.

Ben shook his head a second time. "No. No more delays. I'm going in now." He turned to them, glancing from one face to the next as he spoke. "I want you to listen carefully and I don't want any arguments. Fillip and Sot will go with me as guides. They say that they know the Deep Fell. I will take one other. The rest of you will wait here."

"High Lord, no!" Questor exclaimed in disbelief.

"You would trust yourself to those . . . those cannibals!" Abernathy raged.

"You may have need of our protection!" Questor went on.

"It is madness for you to go alone!" Abernathy finished.

The kobolds hissed and bared their teeth in unmistakable disapproval, the G'home Gnomes chittered and shrank from the conflict, and the scribe and the wizard kept arguing, both at the same time. Only Willow said nothing, but she stared at Ben so hard that he could feel it.

He put up his hands to quiet them. "Enough, already! I told you that I didn't want any arguments, and I don't! I know what I'm doing. I've thought it through pretty carefully. We're not going to have a replay of what happened in the Melchor. If I don't come out when I should, I want some-one free to come in after me."

"It may be far too late for you by then, High Lord," Abernathy pointed out bluntly.

"You said you were taking one other, High Lord," Questor interjected quickly. "I assume you meant me. You may have need of my magic."

"I may, indeed, Questor," he agreed. "But not unless I run into trouble with Nightshade and need my chestnuts pulled out of the fire. You're staying here with Abernathy and the kobolds. I'm taking Willow."

The sylph's hard stare turned to one of surprise.

"You would take the girl?" Questor exclaimed. "But what protection can she offer you?"

"None." Ben watched her eyes turn introspective. "I'm not looking for protection. I'm looking for common ground. I don't want the witch to think the King of Landover *needs* protection, and that is what she is likely to think if I descend on her with all of you. Willow is not so threatening. Willow is a fairy creature like the witch. They share a common background, and together Willow and I may be able to find the means to enlist Nightshade to our cause."

"You do not know the witch, High Lord!" Questor insisted vehemently.

"You certainly do not!" Abernathy agreed.

Willow came forward then, and she took his arm gently. "They may be right, Ben. Nightshade is not likely to offer her help simply because of me. She cares nothing more for the lake country people than for the court at Sterling Silver. She cares nothing for anyone. This is very dangerous."

He noticed that she did not offer to remain behind. She had already stripped away boots and forest cloak and stood next to him, barefoot in a pair of short pants and sleeveless tunic. "I know," he answered her. "That is why Questor, Abernathy, and the kobolds will remain here—to come to our rescue if we need it. If we all go in at once, we all risk falling victim to the same treachery. But if the strongest of us remain behind, the chances of rescue are improved." He looked at the others. "Do you understand?"

There was a general grumbling of acknowledgment. "I respectfully submit that this whole idea is both dangerous and foolish, High Lord," Abernathy declared.

"I would prefer to be there to advise you," Questor argued.

Ben nodded patiently. "I respect your feelings, but I've made up my mind. Whatever risk there is, I don't want anyone sharing it with me who doesn't have to. If I could do this myself without endangering anyone, that's what I would do. Unfortunately, I can't."

"No one has ever asked you to, High Lord," Questor replied quietly.

Ben met his eyes. "I know. I could not have had better friends than you have been." He paused. "But this is where it all ends, Questor. You have done for me all that you can. Time and choices are running out. I have to make something happen if I wish to be Landover's King. I have that responsibility—to you, to the land, and to myself."

Questor said nothing. Ben glanced briefly at the others. No one spoke. He nodded and reached for Willow's hand. He fought back against the chill that had suddenly settled through him.

"Lead on," he ordered Fillip and Sot.

Together, they started down into the pit.

Nightshade

It was like stepping off into a pool of blackened, fouled water. The mist rose to greet them, lapping anxiously at their boots. It climbed to their thighs and curled to their waists. It tugged at their shoulders and finally their necks. A moment later, they were submerged in it completely. Ben had to suppress a sudden urge to hold his breath against its suffocating tide.

His hand gripped Willow's tightly.

The mist was an impenetrable screen, closing about them as if a blanket that would smother them. It clung to their skin with fingers of damp insistence, and its touch was an itch that scratching would not cure. The smell of rotting wood and earth filled the air, permeating the mist, giving it the texture of toxic liquid splashed upon the skin. An unpleasant warmth issued out of it, as if something huge were trapped within the murk and sweating in terror as its life-blood was sucked steadily away.

Ben sensed the terror to be his own, and he fought back against it. The back and underarms of his tunic were damp, and his breathing was ragged. He had never been so frightened. It was worse than when the Mark had come for him in the time passage. It was worse than his encounter with the dragon. It was a fear of something felt and not seen. His feet picked their way mechanically down the scrub-choked slope; he was barely aware of their movement. He could see the stocky forms of the gnomes a few feet ahead of him as they doggedly worked their way forward. He could see Willow beside him, her green-skinned form ghostlike, the corn-silk hair on her head, calves and forearms trailing out behind her as if stirred by the mist. He could see bits and pieces of the scrub and rock about him, and of trees and ridges somewhere far ahead. He saw them and was blind to them. It was what he could not see and could only feel that commanded the focus of his attention. It was what was hidden that he seemed suddenly to see best.

His free hand searched for the medallion tucked within his tunic, and he fingered it reassuringly through the cloth.

The minutes dragged on as the four companions groped their way through the haze, eyes searching sightlessly. Then the slope leveled out, the mist thinned, and scrub turned to brush and forest. They had reached a plateau several dozen feet above the hollows floor. Ben blinked. He could see again. Trees spread away before him in a tangle of trunks, limbs, and vines, and ridges thrust upward sharply into their mass, cresting against a skyline that was canopied in roiling mist. The hollows rim had disappeared. Everything beyond was gone.

Ben pushed past the gnomes to stand on a small promontory that jutted out from the slope, and he stared into the wilderness. His breath caught sharply in his throat.

"Oh, my God!" he whispered.

The hollows spread away for as far as the eye could see—farther than was conceivably possible. The Deep Fell had mushroomed into something so vast that its walls could no longer contain it. The Deep Fell had grown as big as all of Landover!

"Willow!" he whispered urgently.

She was beside him at once. He pointed out into the forest, into the vast, endless tract of it, terror reflected in his eyes as he struggled to comprehend what he was looking at. She understood at once. Her hands closed about his, squeezing. "It is only illusion, Ben," she said quickly. "What you see is not really there. It is only Nightshade's magic at work. She has mirrored back a thousand times the whole of the hollows to frighten us away."

Ben looked again. He saw nothing different, but he nodded as if he did anyway. "Sure—just a trick with magic to scare us off." He took a deep breath. He was calm again. "Want to know something, Willow? It works pretty well."

He gave her a quick smile. "How is it that you aren't fooled?"

She smiled a pixie grin back. "The fairy in me senses such tricks."

They continued their descent toward the hollows floor. Fillip and Sot seemed unbothered by the illusion. That was probably because their eyesight was so poor that they were unaware of the illusion, Ben decided. Sometimes ignorance *was* bliss.

They reached the hollows floor and paused. The tangle of the wilderness spread away before them, seemingly endless. Gnarled trunks and limbs twisted like spiders' webs against the ceiling of mist, vines clung like snakes, and brush choked on itself in thick tangles. The earth was damp and yielding.

Fillip and Sot sniffed the air a moment, then started forward. Ben and Willow followed. They pushed ahead through the wilderness, finding paths where it seemed there could be none. The hollows wall disappeared behind them and the jungle closed about. It was eerily still. They neither saw nor heard another living thing. No animals called, no birds flew, no insects hummed. The light was weak, sunlight screened into a dim gray haze by the clouds of mist. Shadows lay over everything. There was a sense of having been swallowed whole. There was a feeling of having been snared.

They had not gone far when they encountered the lizards.

They were at the edge of a deep ravine and about to start down when Ben saw movement at the bottom. He brought the others to a hurried halt and peered cautiously into the shadows. Dozens of lizards clustered together in the pit of the ravine, their scaled, greenish black bodies slithering across one another, their wicked-looking tongues flicking at the misted air. They were all sizes, some as large as alligators, some as small as frogs. They blocked all passage forward.

Willow took Ben's hand and smiled. "Another illusion, Ben," she assured him.

"This way, High Lord," advised Fillip.

"Come, High Lord," invited Sot.

They descended into the pit and the lizards disappeared. Ben was sweating again and wishing he didn't feel like such a fool.

Other illusions awaited them, and Ben was fooled each time. There was a monstrous old ash tree clustered thick with giant bats. There was a stream filled with piranhalike fish. Worst of all, there was the clearing in which vaguely human limbs stretched from the broken earth, clawed fingers grasping at anything that sought to pass through. Each time Willow and the gnomes led him resolutely foward, and the imagined dangers evaporated into the mist.

More than an hour slipped by before they reached the swamp. It was past midday. A vast marsh of reeds and quicksand stretched across their path for as far as the eye could see. Steam lifted from the marsh, and the quicksand bubbled as if fed by gasses from the earth below.

Ben glanced quickly at Willow. "Illusion?" he asked, already prepared for the answer she would give.

But this time she shook her head. "No, the swamp is real."

The gnomes were sniffing the air again. Ben glanced out across the swamp. A crow sat on a branch of deadwood halfway across, a large, ugly bird with a streak of white cresting its head. It stared at him with its tiny, dark eyes, and its head cocked reflectively.

Ben glanced away. "What now?" he asked the others.

"There is a trail further on, High Lord," Fillip answered.

"A pathway across the marsh," Sot agreed.

They waddled ahead, following the line of the swamp, ferret faces lifted, testing the air with their noses. Ben and Willow trailed slowly after. A hundred feet further on, the gnomes turned into the swamp and proceeded to cross. The swamp looked no different here than anywhere else, but the ground was firm enough to hold them, and they were safely past in a few minutes time. Ben glanced back at the crow. It was still watching him.

"Let's not get paranoid," he muttered to himself.

They pressed on into the jungle. They had gone only a short distance further when Fillip and Sot became suddenly excited. Ben pushed quickly forward and found that the gnomes had discovered a nest of forest mice and flushed the family out. Fillip slipped into the brush on his belly, snaked through it soundlessly and emerged with one of the unfortunates firmly in hand. He bit off its head and gave the body to Sot. Ben grimaced, kicked Sot in the backside, and angrily ordered them both to get moving. But the memory of the headless mouse stayed with him.

He forgot about the mouse when they came up against the wall of brambles. The brambles lifted better than a dozen feet into the air, mingling with the trees and vines of the forest, stretching away into the distance. Again, Ben glanced at Willow.

"The brambles are real, too," she announced.

Fillip and Sot tested the air, walked up and down the wall both ways, then turned right. They had gone about fifty feet when Ben saw the crow. It was sitting on the crest of the wall of brambles just above them and staring down. Sharp eyes fixed on Ben. He stared back momentarily and could have sworn the bird winked.

"Here, High Lord," Fillip called.

"A passage, High Lord," Sot announced.

The gnomes pushed through the brambles as if they didn't exist, and Ben and Willow followed. The brambles parted easily. Ben straightened on the other side and glanced back. The crow was gone.

He saw the crow several times after that, sitting in trees or perching on logs, motionless as it watched him with those same secretive eyes. He never saw it fly and he never heard it call. Once he asked Willow if she saw it, too—none too certain that this wasn't just another illusion. She said that she did see it, but that she had no idea what it was doing there.

"It seems to be the only bird in the hollows," he pointed out doubtfully.

She nodded. "Perhaps it belongs to Nightshade."

That was not a very reassuring thought, but there was nothing Ben could do about it, so he put the matter out of his mind. The jungle had begun to thin, the trunks, limbs, and vines giving way to small clearings in which pockets of mist hung like tethered clouds. There was a brightening in the sky ahead, and a hint of the jungle's end. But there was no sign of the walls of the hollow as there should have been, and the Deep Fell was as sprawling and endless as it had first seemed.

"Can you tell where we are or how far we've come?" he asked the others, but they shook their heads wordlessly.

Then abruptly the jungle gave way and the four companions stood on the threshold of a castle fortress that dwarfed anything Ben had ever seen or even imagined could exist. The castle rose up before them like a mountain, its towers lifting into the clouds and mist so that they were screened from view, its walls receding into the distant horizon for miles. Turrets, battlements, parapets, and ramparts were constructed one upon the other in dazzling geometrical designs, the whole so vast in scope that it might have enclosed an entire city within its stone-block shell. It sat upon a great plateau with the jungle grown thick at its base. A rock-strewn trail led from where they stood to the open castle gates and a raised portcullis.

Ben stared at the castle in disbelief. Nothing could be this huge, his instincts told him. Nothing could be of such monstrous size. It had to be an illusion—a trick of magic, like his vision of the hollows and the things they had encountered. . . .

"What is this place, Willow?" he blurted out, cutting short

his speculation, and the disbelief and awe he felt were apparent in his voice.

"I do not know, Ben." She stood with him, her own gaze fixed on the monstrosity. She shook her head slowly. "I do not understand it. This is not an illusion, Ben—and yet it is. There is magic at work, but the magic accounts for only part of what we see."

The G'home Gnomes, too, were confused. They shifted about uneasily, their ferretlike faces casting about for a scent they could rely upon. They failed to find one and began mumbling in guarded tones.

Ben forced his gaze away from the castle and looked carefully about for anything that would give him a clue as to its origin and purpose. He saw nothing at first, save for the jungle and the mist.

Then he saw the crow.

It was perched on a tree limb several dozen yards away, wings folded carefully in, eyes fixed on him. It was the same crow—glossy black feathers crested in white. Ben stared at it. He could not explain it, but he was certain that the crow knew what was this was all about. It infuriated him that the bird was sitting there so placidly, as if waiting to see what they would do next.

"Come on," he told the others and started up the trail.

They walked cautiously ahead and the castle loomed closer. It didn't shimmer and disappear as Ben had expected it might. Instead, it took on an ominous, grim appearance as the weathered rock grew more detailed and the sound of wind whistling through towers and ramparts grew pronounced. Ben was leading now, with Willow a step behind. The gnomes had fallen back, their paws fastened to Ben's pants, their furry faces apprehensive as they peered out from behind his legs. Dry leaves and twigs rustled across the stone pathway, and the warmth of the jungle had faded to a chill.

The entrance to the castle gaped open before them, a black hole with iron teeth. Shadows wrapped everything beyond in an impenetrable shroud. Ben slowed at the gates and peered guardedly into the gloom. He could just make out

whut uppeured to be a kind of courtyard with a few scattered
benches and tables, a cluster of blackened stanchions and a
weather-beaten throne covered with dust and spiderwebs.
He could see nothing beyond that.

He went forward once more, the others trailing. They
passed beneath the shadow of the portcullis and entered the
courtyard. It was massive, unkempt, and empty. Their footsteps rang in hollow cadence through the stillness.

Ben was halfway across when he saw the crow. Somehow
it had gotten there before them. It sat upon the throne, eyes
fixed directly on him. He slowed and stopped.

The crow's eyes blinked and suddenly turned blood-red.

"Nightshade!" Willow whispered quickly in warning.

The crow began to change. It seemed to expand against
the gloom, shimmering with an aura of crimson light, its
shadow rising up against the throne like a wraith set free.
Blackened stanchions flared and caught fire, and light exploded through the darkness. The G'home Gnomes gasped
in dismay, bolted back through the gates of the castle, and
were gone. Willow stood next to Ben, her hand gripping his
as if it were a lifeline that kept her from drowning. Ben
watched the crow transform into something darker still, and
he was suddenly afraid that he had made an awful mistake.

Then the crimson aura died away and there was only the
light from the fires that burned in the iron stanchions. The
crow was gone. Nightshade sat upon the crumbling throne.

"Welcome to Deep Fell, great and mighty High Lord,"
she greeted, her voice barely more than a soft hiss.

She was not what Ben had expected. She didn't really look
much like a witch at all—although it never crossed his mind
even for an instant that she wasn't. She was tall and sharp-
featured, her skin white and flawless, her hair raven black
except for a single streak of white that ran down its center.
She was neither old nor young, but somewhere in between.
There was an ageless look to her features, a sort of marble
statue quality that suggested an artist's creation that might
survive all human life. Ben didn't know what artist had cre-

ated the witch, whether god or devil, but some thought had gone into the sculpting. Nightshade was a striking woman.

She rose, black robes falling all about her tall, spare form. She came down off the throne and stopped a dozen feet in front of Ben and Willow. "You show more determination than I had thought possible for a pretender. The magic does not frighten you as it should. Is that because you are stupid or merely reckless?"

Ben's mind raced. "It's because I'm determined," he replied. "I didn't come into the Deep Fell to be frightened off."

"More's the pity for you, perhaps," she whispered, and the color of her eyes seemed to change from crimson to green. "I have never liked the Kings of Landover; I like you no better. It matters nothing to me that you are from another world, and it matters nothing why you have come. If you wish something of me, you are a fool. I have nothing I wish to give."

Ben's hands were sweating. This was not going well at all. "What if I have something I wish to give to you?"

Nightshade laughed, black hair shimmering as her body rocked. "You would give something to me? Landover's High Lord would give something to the witch of the Deep Fell?" The laughter stopped. "You are a fool after all. You have nothing that I want."

"Perhaps you are mistaken. Perhaps I do."

He waited and would say nothing more. Nightshade came nearer, her ghostly face bent down to view him more closely, her sharp features taut against the bones of her face. "I know of you, play-King," she said. "I have watched you travel from the Greensward to the lake country to the Melchor and finally to here. I know you seek the pledge of the valley's people and can command nothing more than the misguided loyalty of this girl, that charlatan Questor Thews, a dog, two kobolds, and those pathetic gnomes. You hold the medallion, but you do not command the magic. The Paladin stays gone from you. The Mark hunts you. You are a single step from being yesterday's memory!"

She loomed over him, a head taller, her dark form hanging like death's specter. "What can you give to me, play-King?"

Ben edged a step in front of Willow. "Protection."

The witch stared at him speechlessly. Ben kept his eyes fixed on hers, trying to back her away from him by sheer force of will, the closeness of her dark form suffocating. But Nightshade did not move.

"I am King of Landover, Nightshade, and I intend to remain King," he said suddenly. "I am not the play-King that you believe me, and I am not a fool. I may not be of this world, and I may not yet know everything about it I should. But I know enough to recognize its problems. Landover needs me. You need me. If you lose me, you risk losing yourself."

Nightshade stared at him as if he were mad, then glanced at Willow as if to ascertain whether or not the sylph thought him mad as well. Her eyes glittered as they sought his again. "What risk is there to me?"

Ben had her close attention now. He took a deep breath. "The magic goes out of the land, Nightshade. The magic fails. It fails because there is no King as a King was meant to be. Everything fragments, and the poison settles deeper. I see it happening, and I know its cause. You need me. The Mark claims the land, and sooner or later he will have it. The demon will not tolerate you. He will drive you out. He will not abide strength greater than his own."

"The Mark will not challenge me!" she sneered and there was fury in her eyes.

"Not yet, he won't," Ben pressed quickly. "Not in the Deep Fell. But what happens when the rest of the land has withered into an empty husk and only the Deep Fell remains? You'll be all alone. The Mark will have everything. He'll have strength enough to challenge you then!"

He was guessing, but something in the witch's eyes told him he was guessing right. Nightshade straightened, her black form rising up against the gloom. "And you believe that you can protect me?"

"I do. If the valley's people pledge to me, the Mark will

not be so quick to challenge. He cannot stand against all of us. I don't think he will even try. And if you pledge first, the others must do the same. You are the most powerful, Nightshade; your magic is the strongest. If you give your allegiance to me, the others will follow. I ask nothing else from you. I promise in return to guarantee that the hollows will belong to you alone—always. No one shall bother you here. Not ever."

She almost smiled. "You offer nothing that I do not already have. I don't need you to stand against the Mark. I can do that whenever I choose. I can call the others to me and they will come because they are afraid!"

Oh, brother, Ben thought. "They won't come, Nightshade. They will hide or run from you or they will fight you. They will not allow you to lead them as they might allow me."

"The lake country will never accept you, Nightshade," Willow whispered in agreement.

Nightshade's brow furrowed. "The River Master's daughter would say as much," she sneered. "But you mistake whom you deal with, sylph. My magic would sicken ten times over what your father's would cure—and more quickly than this!"

Her hand shot out, seized Willow's wrist and turned the sylph's arm black and withered. Willow shrieked, and Ben yanked the stricken arm free. Instantly, the arm was restored, the sickness gone. Willow was flushed and there were angry tears in her eyes. Ben faced the witch.

"Seize me as you did her!" he challenged, and his hand closed about the medallion.

Nightshade saw the movement and drew back. Her eyes veiled. "Do not threaten me, play-King!" she warned darkly.

Ben held his ground. He was as angry now as she. "Nor you me or those who are my friends, witch," he replied.

Nightshade seemed to retreat within her robes. Her sharp face lowered into her raven hair, and one hand lifted slowly to point at Ben. "I grant you your determination, play-King.

I grant you a measure of courage. But I do not grant you my pledge. If you would have that, you must first prove to me that you deserve it. If you are weaker than the Mark, then I ally myself to my disadvantage. I might as easily ally myself with the demon and bind him in a pledge of magic that he could not break. No, I will not risk myself for you until I know what strength you possess."

Ben knew he was in trouble. Nightshade had made a decision about him that she was not likely to alter. His mind worked frantically. The darkness of the castle, the vastness of its chambers, seemed to weigh down upon him. Nightshade was his last chance; he could not afford to lose her. He felt his hopes begin to fade, and he fought to hold on to them.

"We need each other, Nightshade," he argued, searching for a way out. "How can I convince you that I possess the strength necessary to be King?"

The witch seemed to think the matter through for a moment, her pale face lost again within her hair. Then slowly she looked up. There was an unpleasant smile on her thin lips. "Perhaps we do need each other—and perhaps there is something that can help us both. What if I were to tell you that there is a magic that could rid the Greensward of the dragon?"

Ben frowned. "Strabo?"

"Strabo." The smile stayed fixed. "There is such a magic—a magic that can make you master of the dragon, a magic that can give you command over everything that he does. Use it, and he will do as you say. You can send him from the Greensward, and then the Lords must give you their pledge."

"So you know of that as well," Ben mused, trying to give himself time to think. He studied the pale face carefully. "Why would you agree to give such a magic to me, Nightshade? You've already made it clear how you feel about me."

The witch smiled with the intensity of a wolf eyeing dinner. "I said nothing about *giving* the magic to you, play-King. I

said, what if I were to *tell* you of such a magic. The magic
is not in my possession. You must retrieve it from where it
is hidden and bring it to me. Then we will share the magic,
you and I. Bring it to me, and I will believe in your strength
and accept you as King. Do so, and you will hold the promise
of your own future.''

"Ben . . ." Willow began, a note of caution in her voice.

Ben dismissed her with a shake of his head. He had already
committed himself. "Where is this magic to be found?" he
asked Nightshade.

"It will be found in the mists," she answered softly. "It
will be found in the fairy world."

Willow's hand clamped on Ben's. "No, Ben!" she
exclaimed.

"The magic is called Io Dust," Nightshade continued, ignoring the girl. "It grows from a midnight-blue bush with
silver leaves. It nurtures in pods the size of my fist." She
clenched her hand before Ben's face. "Bring two pods—one
for me, one for yourself. The dust from a single pod will be
enough to give you mastery over the dragon!"

"Ben, you cannot go into the fairy world!" Willow was
frantic. She wheeled on the witch. "Why not go yourself,
Nightshade? Why send Ben Holiday when you will not go
yourself?"

Nightshade's head lifted in disdain. "I am admonished by
one whose people left the fairy world for this valley when
the choice to remain was theirs? You are quick to forget,
sylph. I cannot go back into the fairy world. I was cast out
from it and am forbidden to return. It is certain death for me
if I go back." She smiled coldly at Ben. "But perhaps this
one will have better fortune than I. He, at least, is not forbidden entry."

Willow yanked Ben about to face her. "You cannot go,
Ben. It is death if you do. No one can go into the fairy world
and survive who is not born to and kept by it. Listen to me!
My people left that world because of what it was—a world
in which reality was a projection of emotion and thought,
abstraction and imagery. There was no reality apart from

what we were, and no substantive truth apart from ourselves!
Ben, you cannot survive in such an environment. It requires
disciplines and familiarities that you lack. It will destroy
you!"

He shook his head. "Maybe not. Maybe I'm more capable
than you think."

Tears glistened in her eyes. "No, Ben. It will destroy
you," she repeated tonelessly.

There was an intensity in her face and voice that was
frightening. Ben stared into her eyes and hardened himself
against the plea that was mirrored there. Slowly he pulled
her close against him. "I have to go, Willow," he whispered
so that only she could hear. "I have no other choice!"

"She tricks you, Ben!" Willow whispered back, her face
hard against his. "This is a trap! I hear the deception in her
voice!" She was shaking. "I see now what this castle is!
This castle is a projection of the magic against the wall of
the mists! Journey far enough through it and you stand within
the fairy world! Ben, she arranged this deception! She knew
you were coming to her and she knew why! She has known
all along!"

He nodded and pushed her gently away. "That doesn't
change anything, Willow. I still have to go. But I'll be careful, I promise. I'll be very careful." She shook her head
wordlessly, and the tears ran down her cheeks. He hesitated,
then leaned forward and kissed her gently on the mouth. "I'll
be back."

She seemed to find herself again in that instant. "If you
go, so do I."

"He goes alone," Nightshade interjected coldly, her face
impassive. "I want no aid being given by a creature born of
the fairy world. I want no interference from anyone. I want
to see for myself whether the play-King possesses the
strength he claims. If he brings the pods of Io Dust to me,
I will have my proof."

"I have to go," Willow insisted, shaking her head slowly.
"I belong to him."

"No," Ben told her gently. He struggled to find the right

words. "You belong to Landover, Willow—and I don't yet. Maybe I never will. But I have to belong to the land before I can ever even think of belonging to her people. I haven't earned that right yet, Willow—and I have to!" His smile was tight. "Wait for me here. I will come back for you."

"Ben . . ."

"I will come back," he insisted.

He stepped away, turning again to find Nightshade. He felt empty and directionless, as if some tiny bit of life was turned loose in a sea of debris and blowing winds. He was about to be alone for the first time since he had come into Landover, and he was frightened almost beyond reason.

"Where do I go?" he asked Nightshade, fighting to keep his voice calm.

"Follow the corridor—there." She pointed behind her, and torchlight glimmered along a shadowed corridor in which mist swirled like a living thing. "You will find a door at its end. The fairy world lies beyond."

Ben nodded and walked past her without a word. His mind reeled with whispered warnings that he was forced to ignore. He slowed at the corridor entrance and glanced back. Willow stood where he had left her, her slender form a pale green shadow, her strange, beautiful face streaked with tears. He was filled with sudden wonder. How could this girl care so much for him? He was just a stranger to her. He was just someone she had happened across. She had blinded herself to the truth with fables and dreams. She imagined love where there was none. He could not understand.

Nightshade stared after him, her cold face expressionless.

He turned slowly away and walked into the mists.

Fairy

Everything disappeared at once. The mists closed about like a shroud, and Ben Holiday was alone. The corridor tunneled ahead, coiling snakelike through pairs of torches that gave off dim halos of light in a haze of shadows and gloom. Ben followed it blindly. He could barely see the passage walls against which the halos cast their feeble glow, blocks of stone charred by flame and stained by damp. He could hear only faintly the sound of his boots as they thudded against the flooring. He could see or hear nothing else.

He walked for a long time, and the fear which had already taken seed within him spread like a cancer. He began to think about dying.

But the corridor ended finally at an iron-bound, wooden door with a great curved handle. Ben did not hesitate. He gripped the handle and twisted. The door opened easily, and he stepped quickly through.

He was standing in an elevator facing forward. A panel of lighted buttons to the right of the closed doors told him he was going up.

He was so astonished that for an instant he could only stare at the doors and the buttons. Then he wheeled about, searching for the door through which he had passed. It was gone. There was only the rear wall of the elevator, simulated oak with dark plastic trim. He felt along the edges with his fingers, testing for a hidden latch. There was none.

The elevator stopped on the fifth floor, and a janitor got on.

"Morning," he greeted pleasantly and punched button eight.

Ben nodded wordlessly. What in the hell was going on? He stared at the control panel, finding it oddly familiar. He glanced hurriedly about the interior and realized that he was on the elevator that serviced the building where his law offices were situated.

He was back in Chicago!

His mind spun. Something had gone wrong. Something *must* have gone wrong. Otherwise, what was he doing here? He braced himself against the wall railing. There was only one explanation. He had gone back through the mists completely; he had passed right through the fairy world into his own.

The elevator stopped at eight, and the janitor got off. Ben stared after him as the doors slipped closed. He had never seen the man before in his life, and he thought he knew all of the help that serviced the building—by sight, if not by name. They cleaned the offices on Sundays; that was the only time they were permitted to ride the elevators. He was always there, too, catching up on his paperwork. But he didn't know this man. Why didn't he?

He shook his head. Maybe it was someone new, he decided—someone the building supervisor had just hired. But new help wouldn't work the offices on Sunday alone, not when they had access to . . . He caught himself. He smiled, suddenly giddy. Sunday! It must be Sunday if the janitors were using the elevators! He almost laughed. He hadn't thought to ask the day of the week since he had crossed into Landover!

The elevator began to rise. He saw the panel buttons blink

in front of him and watched them climb toward fifteen. The elevator was taking him to his office. But he hadn't punched the button, had he? He glanced down in confusion and jumped. He was no longer wearing the clothes he had worn when Nightshade had sent him into the mists. He was wearing the running suit and Nikes he had worn when he had gone into the Blue Ridge.

What was happening?

The elevator stopped at fifteen, the doors slid open and he stepped out into the hallway. A jog left and he was at the glass doors that fronted the lobby to the offices of Holiday and Bennett, Ltd. The doors were open. He pushed through and stepped inside.

Miles Bennett turned from the reception desk, a sheaf of papers in his hands. He saw Ben, and the papers slipped from his fingers and tumbled to the floor. "Doc!" he whispered.

Ben stared. It was Miles who stood before him, but not the Miles he had left behind. This Miles was a shell of that other man. He was no longer simply heavy; he was bloated. His face was florid in the manner of a man who drinks too much. His dark hair had gone gray and thin. Worry lines marked his face like an etching.

The shock faded from his partner's eyes and was replaced with undisguised rancor. "Well, well—Doc Holiday." Miles spoke his name with distaste. "Goddamn if it isn't old Doc."

"Hello, Miles," he greeted and stuck out his hand.

Miles ignored it. "I can't believe it. I can't believe its really you. I thought I'd never see you again—thought no one ever would. Goddamn. I thought you long since gone to hell and shoveling brimstone, Doc."

Ben smiled, confused. "Hey, Miles, it hasn't been that long."

"No? You don't call ten years a long time? Ten goddamn years?" Miles smiled as he saw the stunned look on Ben's face. "Yeah, that's right, Doc—ten years. Not a living soul has heard a word from you in ten years. No one—me, least

of all, your goddamn partner, in case you'd forgot!" He
stumbled over the words, swallowing. "You poor, dumb
jerk! You don't even know what's happened to you while
you've been off in your fairy world, do you? Well, let me
clue you in, Doc. You're broke! You've lost everything!"

Ben felt a chill settle through him. "What?"

"Yeah, everything, Doc." Miles leaned back against the
desk top. "That's what happens when you're presumed le-
gally dead—they take everything away and give it to your
heirs or to the state! You remember your law, Doc? You
remember how it works? You remember anything, goddamn
it?"

Ben shook his head disbelievingly. "I've been gone ten
years?"

"You always were a quick study, Doc." Miles was sneer-
ing openly at him now. "The great Doc Holiday, courtroom
legend. How many cases was it you won, Doc? How many
shootouts did you survive? Doesn't much matter anymore,
does it? Everything you worked for is gone. It's all gone."
The veins on his cheeks were red and broken. "You don't
even have a place with this firm anymore. You're just a collection of old stories I tell the young bucks!"

Ben wheeled about and looked at the lettering over the
glass entry doors. It read, Bennett and Associates, Ltd.
"Miles, it seemed like only a few weeks . . ." he stammered
helplessly.

"Weeks? Oh, damn you to hell, Doc!" Miles was crying.
"All those dragons of the law you thought you'd slay, all
those witches and warlocks of injustice that you thought
you'd take on and straighten out—why the hell didn't you
stay here and do it? Why'd you leave here for your goddamn
fairy land? You weren't a quitter before, Doc. You were too
stubborn to quit. Maybe that's why you were such a good
lawyer. You were, you know. You were the best I'd ever
seen. You could have done anything. I'd have given my right
arm just to help you do it, too. I admired you that much.
But, no, you couldn't survive in the same world with the

rest of us. You had to have your own goddamn world! You had to jump ship and leave me with the rats! That's what happened, you know. The rats came out of their holes and took over—the rats, sniffing around the old cheese. I couldn't handle it alone! I tried, but the clients wanted you, the business couldn't function without you, and the whole goddamn mess went down the tubes!''

He sobbed. ''Look at you, damn you! You don't look like you've aged a day! And look at me—a boozed-up, burned-out wreck . . .'' He shoved forward, neck muscles straining against the collar of his shirt. ''You know what I am, Doc? I'm dead weight, that's what I am. I'm something that takes up space—something the younger bucks are trying to find a way to shove quietly out the door!'' He sobbed again. ''And one day, they're gonna do it, Doc! They're gonna shove me right out of my own damn office . . .''

He broke down completely. Ben felt sick inside as he watched his old friend's composure disintegrate completely. He wanted to step forward, to go to him, but he was unable to move. ''Miles . . .'' he tried.

''Get out, Doc,'' the other cut him short, his voice breaking. He motioned roughly with his arm. ''You don't belong here. They took everything you had long ago. You're a dead man, Doc. Get the hell out!''

He left the reception room in a rush and stumbled down the hall into his office. Ben stood rooted in place for an instant, then followed. When he reached Miles' office, the door was closed. He grasped the handle and stepped inside.

Mist swirled past his face . . .

The mist disappeared. He stood in an orchard of apple trees ripe with fruit. Green grasses waved gently in the summer breeze, and the smell of honeysuckle was in the air. A pasture fenced with board rail painted white was visible in the distance, and horses grazed in its enclosure. A stables sat close by, and a sprawling ranch house of brick and stained fir overlooked it all from a tree-shaded knoll.

He wheeled about in shock, already knowing that Miles,

the office, and the elevator would all be gone. They were. There was nothing left. Had he imagined them? Had he imagined everything? The terrible confrontation with Miles was still replaying itself hatefully in his mind, the emotions it had triggered razor sharp as they cut against his memory. Had he imagined the whole thing?

He glanced quickly down at his clothing. The running suit and Nikes had been replaced by slacks, a short-sleeved shirt and loafers.

What in the hell was happening?

He fought to control the fear that raced through him and brought what was left of his common sense to bear. Had he jumped through time, he wondered? He didn't think so. But he might have imagined that he had. It could have all been just an illusion. It hadn't seemed an illusion, but it could have been. The mists could have blinded him. His passage through the fairy world could have deceived him somehow. He could have gone nowhere at all. But if he had gone nowhere and if everything he had seen was an illusion, then what was he seeing now . . . ?

"Ben?"

He turned, and there was Annie. She looked exactly as he remembered her, a small, winsome girl with huge brown eyes, button nose, and shoulder-length auburn hair. She was dressed in white, a summer frock with ribbons at the waist and shoulders. Her skin was pale and freckled, and the air about her seemed to shimmer in the flush of the sun's midday light.

"Annie?" he whispered in disbelief. "Oh, my God. Annie, is it really you?"

She smiled then, that unaffected little-girl smile she always gave him when she found something amusing in his expression, and he knew that it truly was her. "Annie," he repeated and there were tears in his eyes.

He started toward her, the tears almost blinding him, but her hands came up quickly in warning. "No, Ben. Don't touch me. You mustn't try to touch me." She stepped back a pace, and he stopped, confused. "Ben, I'm not alive any-more," she whispered, tears in her own eyes. She tried to smile through them. "I'm a ghost, Ben. I'm only an image of what you remember. If you try to take hold of me, I will disappear."

He stood before her, confused all over again. "What . . . what are you doing here if you're a ghost?"

She laughed gaily and it was as if he had never lost her. "Ben Holiday! Your memory is as selective as ever. Don't you remember this place? Look about you. Don't you know where we are?"

He glanced about, seeing again the pastureland, the sta-bles, the horses, the ranch house on the knoll—and suddenly he did remember. "Your parents' home!" he exclaimed. "This is your parents' country home, for Christ's sake! I'd forgotten about it! I haven't been out here for . . . oh, I don't remember how long!"

Her laughter crinkled the corners of her eyes. "It was your special hideaway when the rigors of city life became too much. Remember? My parents used to kid you about being a city boy who didn't know a horse's front end from its hind. You used to say there wasn't much difference. But you loved it here, Ben. You loved the freedom it gave you." She glanced about wistfully. "That's why I still come here, you know. It reminds me of you. Isn't that odd? We spent so little time here, but still it's the place that reminds me most of you. I think it was the sense of freedom it seemed to give you that made me feel so good about it—that more so than my own love of the country."

She wheeled about, pointing back toward the ranch. "Re-member the dormer passageways that connected the sleeping rooms through their closets? We used to laugh about those, Ben. We used to talk about gremlins living there—as in the movie. We used to threaten to board them up if anything strange ever happened while we were staying over. You said we'd own that house someday, after my parents were gone, and then we'd board them up for sure!"

Ben nodded, smiling. "Annie, I did always love it here—always."

She folded her arms across her breast, her smile fading. "But you didn't keep the house, Ben. You don't even come back to visit."

He winced at the pain in her eyes. "Your parents were gone, Annie. It . . . hurt too much to come back after losing you, too."

"You should have kept the home, Ben. You would have been happy here. We could have still been with each other here." She shook her head slowly. "At least you should have come to visit. But you never came even once. You still don't come. I wait for you to come, but you never do. I miss you so much, Ben. I need to have you by me . . . even though I can't touch you or hold you as I once did. Just having you near helps me . . ." She trailed off. "I can't make you see me in the city, Ben. You don't see anything there. I don't like the city. If I must be a ghost, I would much prefer to haunt the country where everything is fresh and green. But it is no good living here either when you never come."

"I'm sorry, Annie," he apologized quickly, anxiously. "I never thought that it would be *possible* for me to see you again. I would have come had I known that you were here."

She smiled. "I don't think you would have, Ben. I don't think I mean anything to you anymore. Even your coming now was an accident. I know what you are about in your life. Ghosts have better sight than the living. I know that you have chosen to leave me and travel to another world—a world where I will become only a memory. I know of the girl you have met. She is very pretty—and she loves you."

"Annie!" He almost reached for her in spite of the warning. He had to force his hands to remain at his sides. "Annie, I don't love this girl. I love you. I have always loved you. I left because I couldn't stand what was happening to me with you gone! I thought I had to try something or I would lose everything that was left of me!"

"But you never came looking for me, Ben," she insisted,

her voice soft and filled with hurt. "You gave up on me.
Now I've lost you forever. You've gone into this other
world, and I can never have you back. I can't come to you
there. I can't have you close to me like this and I need that,
Ben. Even a ghost needs the closeness of the one she loves."

Ben felt his grip on his emotions start to slip. "I can still
come back, Annie. I have the means to do so. I don't have
to stay in Landover."

"Ben," she whispered, her brown eyes sad and empty.
"You no longer belong in this world. You chose to leave it.
You can't come back. I know that you have spoken with
Miles Bennett. What he told you was true. Ten years have
passed, Ben. You've nothing to come back to. Everything
you once had is gone—your possessions, your position with
the firm, your standing with the bar, everything. You made
a choice ten years ago, and you have to accept the fact that
it's too late to change it now. You can never come back."

Ben's struggled in vain to respond. This was madness!
How could it be happening? Then he caught himself sharply.
Maybe it wasn't happening. Maybe it was all part of the
illusion he had suspected before, a trick of the mists and the
fairy world, none of it real. The enormity of that possibility
stunned him. Annie seemed real, damn it! How could she
not be?

"Daddy?"

He turned. A small child stood a dozen feet away in the
shadow of a giant apple tree, a little girl no more than two,
her tiny face a mirror of Annie's. "This is your daughter,
Ben," he heard Annie whisper. "Her name is Beth."

"Daddy?" the little girl called to him, and her small arms
reached up.

But Annie intercepted her, pulled her back, and held her
close. Ben dropped slowly to one knee, his tall form stooped
over, his arms folded against his chest to stop himself from
shaking. "Beth?" he repeated dully.

"Daddy," the little girl said again, smiling.

"She lives with me, Ben," Annie told him, swallowing

against her own pain. "We visit the country, and I try to teach her what life would have been like for her if . . ."

She couldn't finish. She bent her head into Beth's shoulder, hiding her face. "Don't cry, Mommy," the little girl said softly. "It's all right."

But it wasn't all right. Nothing was all right, and Ben knew that it never would be again. He felt himself breaking apart inside, needing to be with them, wanting to hold them both, unable to do anything but stand there helplessly.

"Why did you leave us, Ben?" Annie was asking again, her eyes searching his. "Why did you cross over into that other world when we needed you so badly in ours? You should never have quit on us, Ben. Now we've lost you—and you've lost us. We've lost each other forever!"

He was on his feet then, a cry breaking from his throat, stumbling blindly toward where they knelt, arms outstretched. He saw Beth's small arms trying to reach back.

Mist swirled past his face . . .

He stumbled, pitched forward, and fell sprawling to the ground. There was a moment of dizziness as he fought to regain the breath that had been knocked from his body. A rush of cool air swept over him, and the sunlight was gone. He blinked against the dusk that closed about, and his hands clutched at an earth turned barren and hard.

Annie and Beth—where were his wife and child?

Slowly he pushed himself back to his feet. He stood at the rim of a valley that was shrouded in mist and twilight. The valley had the look of a dying creature whose death had been a long and painful ordeal. Forests were stripped of their leaves and vines, the limbs and trunks of the trees gnarled and rotting. Plains had turned wintry, the grasses stunted, the flowers sapped of their color. Mountains crested against the misted skyline, but their slopes were stark and barren. A scattering of dwellings and castles hunched down against the earth, ill-kept and worn. Steam rose from lakes and rivers turned foul, their waters sluggish with filth.

Ben caught his breath in horror. He recognized the valley.

It was Landover. He looked down at his clothing. It was the clothing that he had been wearing when he had gone down into the Deep Fell.

"No!" he whispered.

Annie and Beth were forgotten. He searched frantically for some sign of life upon the ravaged land. He sought out movement about the dwellings and castles, but found none. He sought out Sterling Silver and found only an empty island in a lake of black water. He sought out the Deep Fell, Rhyndweir, the lake country, the Melchor, and all of the landmarks he had come to know. Each time, he found nothing but devastation. Everything had disappeared.

"Oh, my God!" he breathed.

He stumbled forward, breaking quickly into a run as he dashed down the slope of the hillside, still searching for something of the valley he had left behind him when he had ventured into the fairy world. Grasses rustled dry and stiff against his legs as he ran, and the brittle branches of dying scrub snapped off their stems like gunshots. He passed a stand of Bonnie Blues turned black, their leaves withered and curled. He scanned the trees of the nearest fruit grove and found them bare. No birds flew against the twilight. No small animals scattered at his approach. No insects hummed or darted past.

He grew quickly winded and slowed to a staggering halt. The valley lay blackened and empty before him. Landover was a graveyard.

"This can't be . . ." he started to protest softly.

Then a shadow materialized within the mist before him. "So Landover's King has finally found his way back to us," a caustic voice greeted.

The speaker stepped into view. It was Questor Thews, the gray robes and gaily colored silk scarfs shredded and soiled, the white hair and beard ragged and unkempt. One leg was gone, and he hobbled forward on a crutch. Welts and scars marked his face and arms. His fingers were black with disease, and his eyes were bright with fever.

"Questor!" Ben whispered, horrified.

"Yes, High Lord, Questor Thews, once court wizard and advisor to the Kings of Landover, now a homeless beggar wandering in a land where only the forgotten still live. Are you pleased to see me so?"

His voice was so bitter that Ben shrank from it. "Pleased? Why would I be pleased?" he managed finally. "What happened, Questor?"

"What happened, High Lord? Do you truly not know? Look about you, then. That which you see is what happened! The land died for lack of the magic which a King could have given it! The land died. When the land died, her people died as well. There is nothing left, High Lord—everything is gone!"

Ben shook his head in confusion. "But how could that happen . . . ?"

"It could happen because Landover's King abandoned her!" the other cut him short, fury and pain in his voice. "It could happen because you were not here to prevent it! You were off in the fairy world in pursuit of your own ends, and we were left to manage as best we could! Oh, we tried to find you and bring you back; but once within the fairy world, you were lost to us. I warned you, High Lord. I told you that no one could go safely into the fairy world. But you did not listen to me. No, you listened only to your own foolish reasoning and you wandered into that world of mists and dreams and were lost to us. You were gone an entire year, High Lord. An entire year! No one could find you. The medallion was lost. All hope of finding a King was lost. It was the finish for us!"

He stumbled closer, hunching brokenly against the crutch. "The magic faded quickly, High Lord; the poison spread. Soon the creatures of the land, human and otherwise, began to sicken and die. It happened so fast that no one could defend against it—not the River Master with all his healing magic, not Nightshade with all her power. Now all are dead or scattered. Only a few remain—a few like me! We live only because we cannot manage to die!'' His voice shook. ''I thought that you would come back to us in time, High Lord. I kept hoping that you would. I was a fool. I believed in you, when I should have known you were not worth believing in!''

Ben shook his head sharply. ''Questor, don't . . .''

A mottled hand brushed his protest aside. ''It remains only for the Mark and his demons to come now, High Lord. There is no one left to stand against them, you see—no one. All are dead. All are destroyed. Even the strongest could not survive the passing of the magic.'' He shook his head in anguish. ''Why did you not come back to us sooner, High Lord? Why did you stay gone so long when you knew you were needed? I loved this land and her people so! I thought it was the same with you. Oh, if I had strength enough left in me, I would take this crutch and . . .''

His body trembled, and he lifted the crutch threateningly. Ben stepped back in horror, but Questor could lift the crutch only inches, and the effort brought him to ground, a collapsed rag doll. Tears streamed down his ravaged face.

''I hate you so much for what you have done!'' he cried. Slowly his face lifted. ''Do you know how much I hate you? Do you have any idea? Let me show you!'' There was madness in his eyes. ''Do you know what became of your beloved sylph after you abandoned her? Do you know what became of Willow?'' His face was a mask of fury. ''Do you remember her need to nourish within the land's once fertile soil? Look down into the valley, close by that lake! Look down where the shadows lie deepest! Do you see that twisted, blackened trunk with its roots rotted away into . . . ?''

Ben could listen no more. He turned and ran. He ran without thinking, consumed with anger and horror that he could not control, desperate to escape the words of this hateful old man who blamed him for all that had happened. He ran, heedless of direction, pushing mindlessly forward through shadows and mist. Screams echoed after him, whether from within his own mind or outside, he could not tell. His world was collapsing about him like a house of cards brought down by an errant wind. He had lost everything—his old world, his new, his old friends, his new, his past, and his future. Familiar faces pushed in about him—Miles, Annie, Questor—their accusing voices whispering of his failures, hurt and anger in their eyes. Words pummeled him, insidious warnings of the losses he had caused.

He ran faster, his own cries strident against the beating of his heart.

Then suddenly he quit moving altogether. He was still running, but the ground had been taken out from under him and he was suspended in air. There was sudden pain. He jerked about violently, searching for the cause . . .

Taloned feet had fastened on his shoulders, digging deep into clothing and flesh. A massive, twisted form hovered above him, scaled body smelling fetid and rank, the disease of the land sunk deep within it. Ben stared upward wildly, and Strabo's maw gaped open as the dragon reached down for him.

He screamed.

Mist swirled past his face . . .

It was happening again. Time and place were shifting. He closed his eyes instantly and kept them closed. The act was accomplished almost before the directive was issued. Something was terribly wrong. His instincts told him so. His instincts told him that the swift changes of time and place that he had been experiencing were impossible. They seemed to be happening, but in reality they were not. They were illusions or dreams or something very close. Whatever they were, they were taking over his life and tearing him apart. He had to stop them now before he was destroyed.

He hid quietly in the darkness of his mind, eyes tightly shut, his voice stilled. He forced himself to concentrate on the sound of his heart beating within his body, on the feeling of the blood coursing through his veins, on the silence that shrouded him. Be at rest, he whispered. Be at peace. Do not give way to what seems to be happening.

Slowly he regained control of himself. But still he kept his eyes closed. He was afraid that if he opened them some new horror would await. He must understand what had been happening to him first.

Meticulously, he reasoned it through. He had gone nowhere, he decided. He was still within the fairy world, still within the mists. Nor had ten years or even one year lapsed. They couldn't have. The shifts in time and place were illusions brought about by the fairy world or its inhabitants or his reaction to either or both. What he needed to do now was to discover what was causing this. He just needed to understand why.

He built the foundation for his understanding one block at a time. Nothing he had seen was real—that was his beginning premise. If nothing was real, then everything must be false, and if everything was false, there had to be a reason for it taking the form that it had. Why was he seeing these particular visions? He retreated deep into his mind, down into its blackest, most silent regions, where there was nothing beyond the sound of his own thinking. Questor, Miles, and Annie—why had he seen them depicted as he had? He let himself relax in the inky darkness. Willow had warned him of the dangers of the fairy world. What was it that the sylph had said? She had said that in the fairy world reality was a projection of emotion and thought. She had said that there was no reality, no substantive truth apart from what you were. If that were so, what he had seen was what he had projected from within himself. What he had seen was a manifestation of his emotions . . .

He took a long, slow breath and let it out again. His understanding was beginning to take shape. His visions were the creation of his emotions—but which emotions? He replayed in his mind what he had seen of Miles, Annie and Beth, and Questor Thews. All had been angered or disappointed by what he had caused them to suffer. All had blamed him for their misfortunes. Illusions, but that was the way he had seen them. He had seen them as victims of his own poor judgment and inaction. Why had he seen them so? His mind raced through the possibilities, and suddenly he had his answer. He was afraid that what he had envisioned might really happen! He was afraid that it might all be true! Fear! Fear was the emotion that had shaped his thinking!

It made perfect sense. Fear was the strongest emotion of all. Fear was the least controllable emotion. That was why he had jumped through time and space to witness the horrors that had seemed to befall his friends and loved ones—the fear was breathing life into his worst imaginings. He had been frightened that he would fail in what he had undertaken from the moment he had made his decision to cross into Landover. The natural result of such a failing would be the scenarios he had just experienced. He would be cut off from his old life entirely with no chance to return, he would be stripped of all that he had believed he would gain in his new life, and he would fail his friends and family alike. He would be a man who had lost everything.

A sense of relief rushed through him. Now he understood. Now he knew what to do. If he could control his emotions, he could prevent the nightmares. If he could shut off the fear, conscious or subconscious, he could bring himself back into the present. It was a tall order, but it was his only chance.

He took several long moments to collect his thoughts and to focus them on the task at hand. He told himself to remember the kind of lawyer he had once been, to remember the courtroom skills that had made him so. He told himself to remember that everything he had experienced before was a lie, an imagining of his own making. He pictured instead the world he had seen when traveling through the time passage that had brought him to Landover—the forest with its shroud of mist.

Then slowly he opened his eyes. The forest was back again, deep, solitary, primeval. Mist swirled gently through

its trees. Faint visions danced upon the mists, but they did
not trouble him. The nightmares were gone, the lies banished. His reasoning had not failed him. He breathed deeply,
letting himself drift through the cool, peaceful darkness, in
and out of the substanceless visions. Cautiously, he began
to search for the magic he had come here to find, for the Io
Dust. He thought he caught glimpses of silver and midnight-
blue, but nothing whole. He continued to drift, and suddenly
he was fragmenting like ice shattered on stone. He was
breaking apart, splitting into separate pieces that would not
rejoin. Frantically, he forced the feeling down within himself
to feel the solidity of the earth beneath his feet.

The sense of dissipation faded. The mist closed about.

He was no longer alone. Voices whispered.

—You are welcome, High Lord of Landover—

—You have found yourself and in doing so you have found
us—

He struggled to speak, but found he could not. Faces
crowded close, lean and sharp, their features somehow mud-
died in the twilight. They were the faces he had seen when
he had crossed into Landover through the time passage.
They were the faces of the fairies.

—Nothing is lost that we do not first see as lost, High
Lord. Believe it saved, and it may be. Visions born of fear
give birth to our failing. Visions born of hope give birth to
our success—

—What is possible lives within us, and it only remains for
us to discover it. Can you give life to the dreams that live
within you, High Lord? Look into the mists and see—

Ben stared deep into the mists, then watched them swirl
and part before him. A land of incredible beauty appeared,
sunlight spreading out across it like a golden mantle. Life
flourished in the land, and it was filled with boundless en-
ergy. There was excitement and promise beyond anything
he would have believed possible. He felt himself cry out at
the sight and feel of it.

Then slowly the vision faded and was gone. The voices whispered.

—Another time and place for such visions, High Lord. Another life. Bondings such as this must wait their birthings—

—You are a child among elders, High Lord, but you are a child who shows promise. You have seen the truth behind the lies that would deceive you and know it to be your own. You have earned the right to discover more—

Then show me, he wanted to shout! But he could not, and the voices whispered on.

—You have unmasked the fear that would have destroyed you, High Lord. You have shown great presence. But fear has many disguises and assumes many forms. You must learn to recognize them. You must remember what they truly are when next they come for you—

Ben's throat worked soundlessly. He didn't understand. What was the fairy's meaning?

—You must go back now, High Lord. Landover needs your help. Her King must be there to serve her—

—But you may take with you that which you came to find—

Ben saw a bush materialize within the mist before him—a bush of midnight-blue with silver leaves. He felt something pressed into the palm of each hand. He looked down and found that he was holding a pair of oblong pods.

The voices whispered.

—Io Dust, High Lord. Inhale it, and you belong to the giver until released. A single breath is all it takes. But beware. The witch Nightshade seeks the dust for uses of her own and plans to share nothing of it with you. Once you have secured it for her, you will have no further value—

—Be quicker than she, High Lord. Be swift—

Ben nodded mutely, determination etched into the lines of his face.

—Go now. One day only has been lost to you—but that day must remain lost. To bring you back more quickly would cause you harm that could not be repaired. Understand, therefore, that things must necessarily be as you find them—

—Come back to us, High Lord, when the magic is found again—

—Come back to us when the need is there—

—Come . . . —

— . . . back—

Voices, faces, and slender forms faded into the mist and were gone. The mist drew back in a tight swirl and disappeared.

Ben Holiday blinked in disbelief. He stood once more in the twilight of the Deep Fell, a pod of Io Dust gripped tightly in each hand. He glanced about cautiously and found that he was alone. Fragments of his imagined encounters with Miles, Annie, and Questor Thews darted momentarily through his memory, cutting like tiny knives. He winced at the pain they caused and quickly brushed them away. They had never been real. They had been lies. His meeting with the fairies had been the only truth.

He lifted the pods of Io Dust and stared thoughtfully at them. He could not help himself. He began to smile like the Cheshire Cat. He had done the impossible. He had gone into the fairy world and, despite everything, he had come out again.

He felt as if he had been reborn.

Io
Dust

The Cheshire Cat smile and the good feelings that went with it lasted about thirty seconds—the time it took Ben Holiday to remember the fairies' warning about Nightshade.

He glanced hurriedly about, eyes sweeping the misted gloom of the Deep Fell. There was no sign of the witch, but she was out there somewhere, waiting for him, planning to dispose of him the instant she got her hands on the Io Dust. That must have been her intention from the beginning—to send him into the fairy world to do what she could not and then to do away with him on his return. He frowned. Had she known that he *would* return? Probably not. It would make no difference to her if he didn't. It cost her nothing to let him try. But the fairies had spoken as if she expected that he would come back. That bothered him. How could the witch have known that he would succeed in doing something that no one else could?

His hands closed reassuringly about the pods and he took a deep breath to steady himself. There wasn't time just now to worry about what the witch did or didn't know. He had to find Willow and escape the Deep Fell as quickly as he could. He was frightened for the sylph; Nightshade was unlikely to treat her any better than she had treated Ben. Anything might have happened to the girl in his absence, and whatever happened would most certainly be his fault. A whole day lost, the fairies had said. That was far too much time for the girl to have been left alone. Willow was no match for Nightshade. Worse, the others from the little company might have come down into the Deep Fell looking for their missing King and run afoul of the witch as well.

Gritting his teeth angrily against the unpleasant possibilities, he cast about a second time in a effort to get his bearings. Mist and forest rose about him like a wall, and one direction looked the same as another. Clouds hung low across the forest roof, concealing sun and sky. There was nothing to tell him where he was or where he should go.

"Damn!" he whispered softly.

Throwing caution to the winds, he began walking. A lot had happened to Ben Holiday since he had come into Landover from his own world, and most of it had been bad. Each time he had tried to take a step forward, he had been forced to take two steps back. It seemed as if nothing could go right. But all that was about to change. For once, he was going to succeed. He had gone into the fairy world and come out again with the Io Dust when every shred of logic said he couldn't. He had the means to rid the Greensward of the dragon Strabo and gain the pledge of his most important ally. It would be a giant leap forward toward accomplishing everything he had set out to accomplish—never mind the single steps he had been experimenting with so far. He didn't care if there were a dozen Nightshades lurking about in the forest mist; he was not about to let this opportunity slip through his fingers.

A pair of furry faces pushed through the brush directly in front of him, and he jumped back with a startled cry.

"Great High Lord!"

"Mighty High Lord!"

It was Fillip and Sot. Ben exhaled sharply and waited for his heart to drop back out of his throat. So much for his brave determination!

The G'home Gnomes stepped out of the bushes guardedly,

their ferret faces hawking the forest scents, noses twitching expectantly.

"High Lord, is it really you? We never thought to see you again!" Fillip said.

"Never! We thought you lost in the mist!" Sot said.

"Where have you two been?" Ben asked, remembering that they had fled the castle at the witch's transformation from the crow.

"Hiding!" Fillip whispered.

"Watching!" Sot whispered.

"The witch looked for us long and hard," Fillip said.

"But she couldn't find us," Sot said.

"Not when we went underground," Fillip said.

"Not in our burrows," Sot said.

Ben sighed. "Bully for you." He glanced about. "Where is she now?"

"Back where you left her in that clearing, High Lord," Fillip said.

"Still waiting for your return," Sot said.

Ben nodded. "And Willow?"

Fillip glanced quickly at Sot. Sot looked at the ground.

Ben knelt before them, a hollow feeling opening in the pit of his stomach. "What happened to Willow?"

Furry faces wrinkled uncomfortably and grimy paws twisted together.

"High Lord, we don't know," Fillip said finally.

"We don't," Sot agreed.

"When you failed to return, the others came looking for you," Fillip said.

"They came down from the valley's rim," Sot said.

"We didn't even know they were in the valley," Fillip said.

"If we had, we would have warned them," Sot said.

"But we were hiding," Fillip said.

"We were frightened," Sot said.

Ben brushed the explanations aside with an impatient wave of his hand. "Will you just tell me what happened!"

"She took them all prisoner, High Lord," Fillip said.

"She took them all," Sot echoed.

"Now they have disappeared," Fillip finished.

"Not a trace of them," Sot agreed.

Ben sat back slowly on his heels; the color drained from his face. "Oh, my God!" he said quietly, his worst fears realized. Willow, Questor, Abernathy, and the kobolds—Nightshade had them all. And it was his fault. He took a long moment to consider the dilemma, then came back to his feet. There could be no thought of escape now—not without his friends. Io Dust or no Io Dust, he wasn't about to leave them behind.

"Can you take me to Nightshade?" he asked the gnomes. Fillip and Sot regarded him with undisguised horror.

"No, High Lord!" Fillip whispered.

"No, indeed!" Sot agreed.

"She will make you a prisoner as well!" Fillip said.

"She will make you disappear with the others!" Sot said.

Entirely possible, Ben thought to himself. Then he gave the G'home Gnomes an encouraging smile. "Maybe not," he told them. He pulled one of the pods of Io Dust from beneath his tunic and held it up thoughtfully. "Maybe not."

He took five minutes or so to prepare for his encounter with Nightshade. Then he explained the plan he had devised to the gnomes, who listened dutifully and regarded him with perlexed stares. They seemed uncertain what it was he was talking about, but there was no point in trying to explain it further.

"Just try to remember what it is that you're to do and when you're to do it," he cautioned finally and gave up on the matter.

They set out through the forest, the gnomes in the lead, Ben trailing. The afternoon light was fading, passing slowly toward dusk. Ben glanced about uneasily, pausing briefly at the sight of shadows that flickered through the mists behind him. The fairy world was back there somewhere and with it the ghosts of his imagination. He could feel their eyes on him yet, the living and the dead, the past and the present, the old world and the new. What he had seen had been lies, his own fears brought to life. But the lies lingered, whispers of truths that might yet be. He had failed no one in the ways the fairy mists had shown. But he might, if he were not as swift as the fairies had warned that he must be. He might fail them all.

The minutes slipped by. Ben felt them pass with agonizing swiftness. He wanted to urge the gnomes to hurry faster, to quicken their studied pace through the forest maze. But he kept his peace; Fillip and Sot were taking no chances with Nightshade and neither should he.

Then a clearing opened ahead through a screen of pine and heavy brush, barely visible in the gloom. Fillip and Sot dropped into a crouch and glanced hurriedly back at Ben. He crouched with them, then inched ahead cautiously for about another yard or so and stopped.

Nightshade sat statuelike on the webbed, dust-covered throne where she had first appeared to him, eyes fixed on the ground before her. Weather-beaten tables and benches were scattered about before her, ringed by a line of blackened stanchions in which tiny fingers of flame licked at the shadows. The courtyard, the portcullis, and the entire castle were gone. There was only the forest and these few ruined bits of furniture sheltering the witch.

Blood-red eyes blinked, but did not lift.

Ben crept slowly back again, taking the G'home Gnomes with him. When they were safely out of ear-shot, he dispatched them to carry out their assignment. Soundlessly, they disappeared into the trees. Ben watched them go, lifted his eyes skyward in a silent prayer, and settled back to wait.

He let fifteen minutes pass, judging the time as best he could, then stood up and started forward boldly. He passed through the screen of pine and brush and stepped into the clearing where Nightshade waited.

The witch looked up slowly, head and eyes lifting to watch his approach. Her stark, sharp-featured face reflected a mix ot pleasure and surprise—and something else. Excitement. Ben came toward her cautiously, knowing he must be careful. He was still a dozen paces off when she stood up and signaled for him to stop.

"Do you have it?" she asked softly.

He nodded, saying nothing.

Her thin hand ran back through her raven hair, smoothing out the white streak like a trail of foam stirred in dark waters. "I knew you to be better than the play-King I called you," she whispered, her smile suddenly dazzling. She was tall and majestic standing there before him, robes spread against the forest, marble skin flawless. "I knew you to be . . . special. I have always had the sight." She paused. "The Io Dust— show it to me."

He glanced about, as if searching. "Where is Willow?"

The red eyes narrowed almost immeasurably. "Waiting, safely kept. Now show me!"

He started forward, but her hand came up like a shield and her voice was a hiss. "From there!"

Both hands were in his pockets. Slowly he extracted the left, producing an oblong pod for her inspection.

Her face came alive with excitement. "Io Dust!" She was shaking as she beckoned him closer. "Bring it to me. Carefully!"

He did as he was told, but stopped just out of reach, glancing about once again. "I think you ought to tell me where Willow is first," he hedged.

"First the Dust," she insisted, reaching.

He let her take the pod, saying, "Oh, that's all right, I see her now, back there in the trees." He started past her, looking anxiously. "Willow! Over here!"

His call and the fervent prayers that accompanied it were both answered on cue. There was a rustling within the brush and a glimpse of someone coming into view. Nightshade turned in startled surprise, red eyes narrowing, following Ben's gaze. Words of disclaimer were already forming on her lips.

Ben's right hand came out of his pocket and he flung a handful of the concealed Io Dust directly into Nightshade's face. The witch gasped in surprise—inhaling the dust as she did so. Surprise and fury twisted her thin features with a look of sudden horror. Ben threw a second fistful of the dust into her face—and again she inhaled it, tripping over her robes as he pushed her roughly back. The pod flew from her hands and she sprawled back upon the earth in a tangle.

Ben was on her like a cat. "Don't touch me!" he cried in warning. "Don't even think about hurting me! You belong to me; you will do anything and everything I tell you and nothing else!" He saw her lips draw back in a snarl of rage, and felt the sweat soak the back and underarms of his tunic. "Tell me that you understand," he whispered quickly.

"I understand," she repeated and her hatred for him burned in her eyes.

"Good." He took a deep breath and slowly climbed back to his feet. "Stand up," he ordered.

Nightshade stood, straightening herself slowly, her body stiff and unyielding, as if constricted from within by some iron will that she fought to resist and could not. "I will destroy you for this!" she snarled. "I will see you suffer in ways that you could not imagine!"

"Not today, you won't," he muttered, more to himself than to her. He glanced hurriedly about. "Fillip! Sot!"

The G'home Gnomes crept cautiously from the bushes where they had been hiding, waiting for Ben's signal to pretend that they were Willow answering his call. They emerged with looks of apprehension etched into their furry faces, their ferret eyes peering almost blindly toward the witch.

"Great High Lord," Fillip whispered.

"Mighty High Lord," Sot whispered.

Neither sounded quite so certain he was either, inching forward like rats prepared to bolt at the slightest move. Nightshade swung her gaze on them like a hammer and they cringed from its blow.

"She can't hurt you," Ben assured them—working at the

same time at assuring himself. He walked over to pick up
the discarded pod and brought it back. He held it up for
Nightshade to inspect. "Empty," he said, pointing to a tiny
hole he had carved in its bottom. "I took out all the dust
and put it in my pocket to use on you. Just about what you
had planned for me, wasn't it? Answer me."

She nodded. "It was." The words were laced with venom.

"I want you to stand here and do only what I tell you.
We'll start with some questions. I'll ask them and you'll
answer them. But tell me the truth, Nightshade—no lies.
Understand?" She nodded wordlessly. Ben reached into his
tunic front and extracted the second pod of Io Dust. He held
it out to her. "Will the dust contained in this pod be enough
to gain control of the dragon?"

She smiled. "I don't know."

He hadn't expected that. A suspicion of doubt tugged at
his mind. "Have I given you enough dust that you must do
as I say?"

"Yes."

"For how long?"

She smiled again. "I don't know."

He kept his expression neutral. There would be little mar-
gin for error, it appeared. "If you feel your need to obey me
fading, you must tell me. Do you agree?"

The hatred in her eyes burned deeper. "I agree."

He didn't trust her, Io Dust or no Io Dust. He wanted to
get this over with and get out of the Deep Fell. Fillip and
Sot looked as if they were at least a dozen steps ahead of
him already. They were crouched down in the shadow of
one of the ruined tables, snouts buried in their chests like
confused ostriches.

His eyes returned to Nightshade. "What have you done
with Willow and the others who came with me?"

"I took them prisoner," she said.

"Questor Thews, Abernathy the scribe, the two kobolds?
All of them?"

"Yes. They came looking for you, and I took them."

"What have you done with them?"

"I kept them for a time and then I sent them away."

She looked almost pleased with the way this was going, and Ben hesitated in spite of himself. "What do you mean, you sent them away?" he pressed.

"I had no use for them, so I sent them away."

Something was wrong. Nightshade had not planned to release him. She would never have released his friends. He stared at her, watching her eyes change suddenly from crimson to green. "Where did you send them?" he asked quickly.

Her eyes glittered. "To Abaddon. To the Mark."

He went cold all over. The lies he had imagined had become truths. He had failed his friends after all. "Bring them back!" he ordered sharply. "Bring them back now!"

"I cannot." She sneered openly. "They are beyond my reach!"

He seized the front of her dark robes, enraged. "You sent them there—you can bring them back again!"

She was smiling in delight. "I cannot, play-King! Once sent to Abaddon, they are beyond my power! They are trapped!"

He released her and stepped back, fighting to regain control of himself. He should have foreseen this! He should have done something to prevent it from happening! He stared about the shadowed clearing futilely, anger and disgust coursing through him as he considered and discarded possibility after possibility in rapid succession.

He wheeled back on her. "You will go into Abaddon and bring them back!" he ordered triumphantly.

Her smile was a thing of near ecstasy. "I cannot do that either, play-King! I have no power in Abaddon! I would be as helpless as they!"

"Then I'll go myself!" he said. "Where is the entrance, witch!"

She laughed, her face taut. "There *is* no entrance, fool! Abaddon is forbidden! Only a few . . . !"

Her triumph was so complete that she failed to catch herself in time. Her mouth snapped shut, but she was already too late. Ben seized the front of her robes.

"A few? What few? Who besides the demons can go there? You?" Her head twisted back and forth wordlessly. "Then who, damn it? Tell me!"

She shuddered and stiffened as if jerked by a hook embedded deep within. Her reply came out almost a scream. "Strabo!"

"The dragon!" he breathed, seeing now. He released her and walked away. "The dragon!" He wheeled and came back again. "Why can the dragon enter and not you?"

Nightshade was beside herself with rage. "His magic . . . encompasses a greater range than mine, reaches farther . . . !"

And is more powerful, Ben finished what she could not bring herself to say. He felt himself go limp, sweat soaking through him, weariness sapping at his strength. It made sense. He had first encountered Strabo at the fringes of the mists, still within the fairy world. If the dragon could pass into the fairy world, it stood to reason that he could pass into Abaddon.

And he could take Ben with him.

He almost smiled. The sudden coming together of circumstance and need was frightening. He had thought to use the Io Dust simply to send the dragon out of Landover. That would have been difficult and dangerous enough. Now he must use the Io Dust to force Strabo to carry him down into Abaddon where his friends were trapped and then carry them all out again. The enormity of the task was staggering. He must do this without direction or guidance. He must do this alone. But there was never any question of his not doing it. Willow, Questor, Abernathy, Bunion, and Parsnip had risked themselves for him time and time again. It was an imperative beyond that of Kingship that required he do the same for them.

His eyes found those of the witch. He could see an undisguised satisfaction mirrored there. "You have sworn to destroy me, Nightshade, but it is I who ought to destroy you," he whispered in fury.

Fillip and Sot had slipped from behind the table and were tugging tentatively at his legs.

"Can we go now, High Lord?" Fillip asked.

"Can we leave this place, High Lord?" Sot echoed.

"She frightens me," Fillip said.

"She wants to hurt us," Sot said.

Ben glanced down at them, saw the fear in their eyes, and watched their noses twitch expectantly. They looked like dirty children about to be punished, and he felt sorry for them. They had been through a lot.

"Just a moment more," he promised. He looked back at Nightshade. "How long has it been since you sent my friends into Abaddon?"

The witch narrowed her green eyes. "I disposed of them this morning—quite early."

"Did you harm them in any way?"

Her face pinched sharply. "No."

"They are well, then?"

She laughed. "Perhaps—if the demons haven't tired of them."

He wanted to throttle her, but he managed to keep control of himself. "Once I am within Abaddon, how can I find them?"

Nightshade's body seemed to fold itself deeper into the dark robes. "The dragon can find them for you—if he still obeys!"

Ben nodded wordlessly. There was that problem on top of everything else. How long would the Io Dust render the dragon helpless against him? How long before the effects of its magic wore off? There was only one way to find out, of course.

He shrugged the thought aside. "Where will I find the dragon?" he asked the witch.

Nightshade smiled darkly. "Everywhere, play-King."

"I'm sure." He rethought the question. "Where is he certain to go that I can wait for him to come?"

"The Fire Springs!" Her voice was a thin hiss. "He makes his home in the flame-waters!"

Ben remembered the Springs from his studies at Sterling Silver. Lava pools or oil pits or some such, they lay east beyond the Greensward, deep within the wastelands.

"High Lord!" Fillip called urgently, interrupting his thoughts.

"High Lord!" Sot tugged at his leg.

Ben nodded in response one time more. The day was coming to a close, the sun's light giving way to darkness, the shadows of dusk lengthening through the trees. He did not want to be caught in the Deep Fell after dark.

He stepped forward and stood directly before Nightshade. "I am King of Landover, Nightshade. You may not think so and others may not think so, but, until I decide otherwise, that's the way it is. A King has certain responsibilities. Among them is a responsibility to protect his subjects. You took it upon yourself to interfere with that responsibility and to place people who were not only subjects, but friends, in extreme danger—so extreme that I may never see any of them again!"

He paused, watching the hate glitter in her eyes as they turned from green back to red again. "You have passed judgment on yourself, Nightshade. What you have done to my friends, I now do to you. I command you to transform yourself into that crow and to fly back into the mists of the fairy world. Do not deviate from your course. Fly until you are once again within the old world and keep flying until . . . whatever happens, happens."

The witch shook with rage and frustration, and a sudden glimmer of fear crept into her eyes. "The fairy magic will consume me!" she whispered.

Ben was unmoved. "Do what I have told you, Nightshade. Do it now!"

Nightshade went rigid, then shimmered with crimson light.

Flames exploded skyward in the iron stanchions. The witch and the light disappeared and in their place was the crow. Shrieking, it spread its wings against the dusk and flew away into the forest.

Ben stared after her, half expecting that she would return again. She did not. Nightshade was gone. She would fly as he had commanded until she entered the mists and the fairy world that was forbidden to her. He didn't know what would happen to her when she arrived, but he doubted that it would be pleasant. Too bad. He had given her at least as much chance to survive as she had given his friends. Fair was fair.

He shook his head. He had a bad feeling about it nevertheless.

"Let's find our way out of here," he muttered to Fillip and Sot, and the three of them hurried from the clearing.

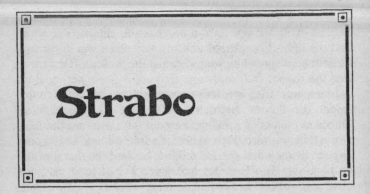

Strabo

Ben slept that night in a poplar grove a few miles south of
the rim of the Deep Fell. When he awoke at sunrise, he began
his journey east to the Fire Springs.

He took Fillip and Sot with him, despite their obvious
reluctance to go. He had no choice. He was afraid that without them he might become lost or sidetracked. He knew the
country reasonably well from his studies at the castle, but
there was always the possibility of encountering something
those studies had missed or becoming stymied through ignorance, and he couldn't risk letting either happen. Time
was something that he didn't have to waste, and the G'home
Gnomes would have to bear with him a little while longer.

As it was, the journey took the better part of three days.
It would have taken longer if Fillip and Sot hadn't appropriated a pair of plow horses whose day had clearly come
and gone. They were so swaybacked and rough-gaited that
it jarred his bones just to watch them amble about the campsite. Riding them was worse, but the pace of travel improved
and they covered more distance, so he kept his peace. He
never asked the gnomes where they got the horses. Moral
principle took a backseat to expediency on this occasion.

They came down out of the forested hill country below

the Deep Fell, skirted the broad plains of the Greensward, and passed east into the wasteland that stretched to the far rim of the valley. Their journey seemed endless. It dragged with the weight of a millstone tied about their necks. Ben was consumed by fear for his missing friends; too much could happen, all of it bad, before he would be able to reach them. Fillip and Sot were consumed by fear for their own skins; they believed themselves sacrificial lambs being led to the dragon's dinner table. The three talked to one another as little as possible, uncomfortable with the journey, its purpose, and each other.

Ben thought frequently of Nightshade as they traveled, and his thoughts were not pleasant ones. It was bad enough that he had left Willow alone and unprotected when he had gone into the mists, bad enough that Questor and the others had come down into the hollows looking for him when he had failed to return that first day, and worse than bad that all of them had been whisked off to Abaddon and the demons on a whim, while Nightshade idled about waiting for his return. But it was unforgivable that he hadn't made better use of the witch when he had held her captive under the power of the Io Dust. There were any number of things he should have done and hadn't. He should have had her use her magic to bring the dragon to him—to lure it there, if nothing else. Had she been unable to do that, he should have had her use the magic to send *him* to the dragon. That would have saved three days of traipsing all over the valley on a plow horse! He should have had her supply him with some of her magic. A little extra protection wouldn't have hurt. And he never should have let her off so easy—not after what she had done. He should have made certain she would cause him no further problems. Or at least he should have made her pledge to him in case she did escape.

But as the journey wore on, such thoughts fragmented, faded and died away. Should have, could have—what the hell difference did it make now? He had done the best he could; he simply hadn't thought of everything. A pledge

made under duress was probably worthless. Unknown magic
was probably more dangerous than no magic. Things were
better as they were; he would find a way to make do with
what he had.

They reached the Fire Springs late on the third day out.
The gnomes had taken him deep into the wasteland east of
the Greensward, a country of mixed horrors—barren plains
of desert sand and dust, hills of saw grass, scrub, and gnarled
short trees, sucking swamp that oozed red mud and quicksand, and petrified forests where the trees were tangled, broken bones that jutted from the earth. The land had a wintry
cast beyond anything that Ben had seen in the other parts
of the valley, a washed and colorless mix from dying vegetation and broken earth. Even the Bonnie Blues did not
grow here. The three had worked their way through hills and
ridges grown thick with stunted briar and tangled brush to
a forest of deadwood, cresting a deep ravine. They walked
their horses, unable to ride them through the heavy undergrowth. Mist floated in thick clouds over everything, a blanket that smelled of the land's death.

"There, High Lord!" Fillip cried suddenly, bringing Ben
to a halt with a hasty tug on one sleeve.

"The Fire Springs, High Lord!" Sot announced, pointing
into the distance.

Ben peered through the mist and trees. He couldn't see a
thing. He peered harder. Now he caught a glimpse of something flickering against the gloom—a sort of light that reflected on the mist.

"Let's get a bit closer," he urged. "I can't see anything
from here."

He started forward again and then stopped. Fillip and Sot
were not moving. They glanced at each other, then at him,
then at each other again. Their furry faces lowered and their
noses twitched.

"This is close enough, High Lord," Fillip advised.

"As close as we're going, High Lord," Sot agreed.

"We have no protection against the dragon."

"No protection at all."

"He would eat us without thinking twice about it."

"He would burn us to the bone!"

Fillip hesitated. "The dragon is too dangerous, High Lord. Leave him and come away."

Sot nodded solemnly. "Let the dragon be, High Lord. Let him be."

Ben studied them a moment, then shook his head. "I can't let him be, fellows. I need him." He smiled ruefully and walked back. He placed a hand on the shoulder of each. "Will you wait here for me? Until I come back?"

Fillip looked up at him, eyes squinting. "We will wait for you, High Lord. Until you come back."

Sot rubbed his paws together absently. "*If* you come back," he muttered.

Ben left them with the plow horses and forged ahead into the tangled undergrowth. He picked his way cautiously, trying to be as quiet as possible. He could see geysers of steam rising from beyond the ridgeline to mingle with the mist. The flickering light shone more clearly, a shimmer of brightness dancing against the sky. He could smell something as well—something unpleasantly reminiscent of spoiled meat.

Sweat and dust streaked his face and arms, but he was cold inside. He had been anxious for this until now.

One hand stole to the pockets of his tunic. What remained of the Io Dust from the emptied pod was in his right pocket. The full pod was in his left. He really hadn't devised a plan yet for using the dust. He didn't have any idea at all what sort of plan would work. His sole objective was to get as close to the dragon as possible and hope that an opportunity presented itself.

A King of Landover ought to have a better plan than that, he thought gloomily, but he couldn't seem to come up with one.

He crested the ridgeline and peered over. A broad, misshapen ravine sprawled away before him, pitted with craters

of all sizes and shapes, their bowls filled with an unidentifiable bluish liquid on which yellowish flames danced and
burned, casting flickers of light against the shroud of mist.
Tangled thickets and mounts of earth and rock clogged the
floor of the ravine between craters, a formidable array of
obstacles to anyone who sought to enter.

Ben looked the ravine over carefully. The dragon was nowhere to be seen.

"It figures," he muttered.

He debated for a time what to do next. He could either
wait where he was until Strabo returned or make his way
down into the ravine and wait there. He opted for the second
choice. He wanted to be as close as possible to the dragon
when he finally faced it.

He slipped over the crest of the ridge and started down.
A voice somewhere deep inside kept whispering that he was
crazy. He fully agreed. He could not believe he was doing
this. He was terrified of the dragon; he would have preferred
to turn tail and run out of there as quickly as his shaking
legs could manage it. He was not particularly brave; he was
just desperate. He hadn't realized until this moment exactly
how desperate he was.

But I won't let them down, he promised himself, thinking
of Willow and the others. Whatever happens, I won't.

He reached the bottom of the ravine and glanced about.
Steam geysered sharply from a crater close at hand, a
whooshing sound that startled him. Flames lifted with the
explosion and flickered hungrily against the mist. He could
barely see where he was going this close to the springs, but
he made his way forward resolutely. He supposed that some-
place in the middle of the Fire Springs might be the best
place to wait—although not *too* far out in the middle. His
breathing was quick and ragged. He wished he had command
of the Paladin. He wished Questor and the kobolds were with
him. He wished *anyone* was with him. He wished he were
somewhere else.

Steam and heat seared his nose and mouth, and he wrinkled his face in distaste. The smell was terrible. There were bones on the floor of the ravine, some of them quite new. He forced himself to ignore them. Brush and scrub blocked his way, but he pushed steadily through. He skirted a pile of broken rock, a boulder cluster, and the skeleton of a rather large animal. He thought he had come far enough. There was a massive earth mound just ahead with a curl of rock at one end. It appeared a good hiding place. He would wait there for the dragon to return.

He wondered suddenly how long that might be. The Fire Springs might be Strabo's home, but that didn't mean he came there all that often. Maybe he came only once a year, for pete's sake! His impatience with himself flared. He should have asked the witch, damn it! He should have . . .

He came to an abrupt and startled halt. He was less than a dozen feet from his chosen hiding place, the curl of rock against the massive earthen mound—and the mound had just moved.

He stared. No, he must have imagined it.

The mound moved again.

"Oh, my God," he whispered.

A tiny cloud of dust rose from just above what he had believed to be the tip of the rock curls and a huge, lidded eye slipped open.

Ben Holiday, lawyer extraordinaire, intrepid adventurer, and would-be King of Landover had just made a very big mistake.

The dragon stirred lazily, shaking off the layer of earth and dust that covered it, and uncurled from its sleep. It kept its eyes on Ben, watching him the way a snake watches its cornered prey. Ben was frozen where he stood. He should have used the Io Dust. He should have turned and run. He should have done something—anything!—but he could not move an inch. It was all over but the shouting. He found himself wondering in a rush of black humor if he would be fried or sautéed.

Strabo blinked. The crusted head swung slowly about and

the long snout split wide. Blackened teeth slipped free, and a long, split tongue flicked at the misted air.

"I know you from somewhere, don't I?" the dragon asked.

Ben was floored. He had expected a good many things from the dragon, but talking wasn't one of them. The fact that the dragon talked changed everything. It took the edge off the fear he felt for the beast. It revised in an instant's time his whole perspective on what was happening to him. If the dragon could be talked to, maybe the dragon could be reasoned with! He forgot about being fried or sautéed. He forgot about defending himself. He searched instead for something to say in reply.

Strabo's head snapped up. "The mists at the edge of the fairy world—that's where I saw you. Several weeks ago wasn't it? I was asleep and you wandered past me. Stared at me so hard you woke me. Rude of you to do that, I might add." He paused. "That was you, wasn't it?"

Ben nodded mechanically, an image flashing in his mind of the dragon blowing him away head-over-heels like a feather caught in the wind. He brushed the image aside. He was still unable to believe that he was actually hearing the beast talk. The dragon had an odd voice, a sort of machinelike hiss that reverberated as if released from an echo chamber.

"Who are you?" the dragon asked, head lowering again. "What were you doing in the mists?" He showed his teeth as his lips curled back from his gums. "Are you one of the fairies?"

Ben shook his head. "No, I'm not." He gathered his wits quickly now. "I'm Ben Holiday, from Chicago. From another world, really. I'm Landover's new King."

"Are you?" The dragon seemed unimpressed.

"Yes." Ben hesitated, his courage slowly returning. "You know, I didn't think dragons talked."

Strabo shifted his bulk slightly, undulating his long, serpentine body so that his backside rested against a series of smaller pools, the flames dancing close against his scaled hide. "Oh, one of those," he sniffed.

Ben frowned. "One of which?"

"One of those humans who think dragons are illiterate, mindless beasts who spend their time wreaking havoc on poor, hard-working, simple folk until some champion appears to do them in. You're one of those, aren't you?"

"I suppose I am."

"You read too many fairy tales, Holiday. Who do you think spreads those stories about dragons? Not the dragons, you can be sure. No, humans spread those stories, and humans are not about to characterize themselves as the bad folk and the dragon as the one mistreated, are they? You must consider the source, as they say. It is much easier to cast the dragon as the villain—burning fields, devouring livestock and peasants, seizing beautiful princesses, and challenging knights in armor. It all makes great reading, even if it isn't the truth."

Ben stared. What kind of dragon was this?

"There were dragons before there were humans, you know. There were dragons before most of the fairy creatures came into being." Strabo bent down. His breath was terrible. "The trouble didn't start with the dragons; it started with the others. No one wanted the dragons around. The dragons took up too much space. Everyone was frightened of the dragons and what they were capable of doing—never mind that it was only a few giving the rest a bad name! And our magic was so much stronger than theirs that they could not control us as they wished."

The crusted head shook slowly. "But there are always ways of getting what you want if you work hard enough at it, and they worked very hard at getting rid of us. We were exiled, hunted, and destroyed, one after the other, until now there is only me. And they would destroy me as well, if they could."

He didn't specify who "they" were, but Ben guessed he meant everyone in general. "Are you saying you aren't re-

sponsible for any of the things for which you are blamed?"
he asked, looking a bit doubtful.

"Oh, don't be stupid, Holiday—of course I'm responsible! I'm responsible for practically all of them!" The voice
hissed softly. "I kill the humans and their tame animals when
I wish. I burn out their crops and homes if I choose. I steal
their mates because it pleases me. I hate them."

The tongue flicked. "But it wasn't always so, you see. It
wasn't so until it became easier for me to be the thing they
thought me than to try to survive as the creature I once
was . . ." He trailed off, as if remembering. "I've been alive
for almost a thousand years, you know, and all alone for the
past two hundred of those. There are no more dragons.
They're all legends. I'm all there is—like the Paladin. You
know of him, Holiday? We're both the last of our kind."

Ben watched the dragon nuzzle at a Fire Spring, drinking
the burning waters, inhaling the flames slowly. "Why are
you telling me all of this?" he asked, genuinely puzzled.

The dragon looked up. "Because you're here." The snout
dipped. "Why are you here, by the way?"

Ben hesitated, remembering suddenly what had brought
him. "Well . . ."

"Oh, yes." The dragon cut him short. "You're Landover's newest King. Congratulations."

"Thanks. I haven't been at it very long."

"No, I assume not—otherwise you wouldn't be here."

"I wouldn't?"

"Hardly." The dragon bent closer. "When the old King
was alive, he kept me exiled here in this wasteland. I was
forbidden the rest of the valley. The Paladin was used to
keep me here because the Paladin was as strong as I. I flew
the skies at night, sometimes, but could not let myself be
seen by the humans nor interfere in their lives. . ." The dragon's voice had grown hard. "I promised myself that one day
I would be free again. This valley was as much mine as anyone's. And when the old King died and the Paladin disap-

peared, I *was* free, Holiday—and no King of Landover shall ever put me back again.''

Ben was aware of a none-too-subtle shift in the atmosphere between them, but he pretended not to notice. ''I'm not here for that,'' he said.

''But you *are* here to ask for my pledge to the throne, aren't you?''

''I'd thought about it,'' Ben admitted.

Strabo's snout split wide with a low, hissing laugh. ''Such courage, Holiday! Wasted, though. I have never given my pledge to Landover's Kings—never, in the thousand years of my life. Why should I? I am not as those others who live here! I am not confined to Landover as they! I can travel anywhere I choose!''

Ben swallowed. ''You can?''

The dragon shifted, tail curling back behind Ben. ''Well . . . not anywhere, I suppose. But almost anywhere. I cannot travel deep into the fairy world nor into worlds where they do not believe in dragons. Do they believe in dragons in your world?''

Ben shook his head. ''I don't think so.''

''That explains why I have never been there. I travel only to lands where dragons are real—or, at least, where dragons once were real. I frequent half a dozen worlds close at hand. Most I have hunted. I had to hunt them when the old King forbid me the valley.'' His look turned sly, eyes lidding. ''But hunting beyond the valley is more work than I care to do. It is easier to hunt here. It is more *satisfying!*''

The atmosphere had now gone decidely chilly. The dragon could be talked to, but it looked doubtful that he could be reasoned with. Ben felt doors closing all about him. ''Well, I don't suppose that there's much point in my suggesting that you do anything else then, is there?''

Strabo lifted slightly on his hindlegs, dust rising from his massive body. ''I have enjoyed our conversation, Holiday, but it appears to be at an end. Unfortunately, that means the end of you.''

"Oh, wait a minute, let's not be so hasty." Ben couldn't get the words out fast enough, his mind racing. "Our conversation doesn't have to be over, does it? I think we should talk a bit more!"

"I can understand why you would might want to," the dragon hissed softly. "But I grow bored."

"Bored! Okay, let's change the subject!"

"That wouldn't help."

"No? Well, how about if I just leave, then—just walk away, say good-bye, so long?" Ben was desperate now.

The dragon loomed above him, a huge, scaled shadow. "That just postpones the inevitable. Eventually you would come back again. You would have to, because you are Landover's King. Face it, Holiday—I am the enemy. Either you have to destroy me or I have to destroy you. I much prefer the latter."

Ben glanced about wildly. "For God's sake, why does one of us have to destroy the other?"

"Why? Because that's the way it is between dragons and Kings. That's the way it's always been."

Ben's frustration had reached the breaking point. "Well if that's the way it's always been, then why the long dissertation on the disservice being done to dragons by storytelling humans? Why did you waste time telling me all that if you planned to fry me right after?"

The dragon actually laughed. "What a quaint way of putting it!" He paused. "Yes, why bother telling you anything under the circumstances? Good point." He thought about it for a moment, then shrugged. "I suppose because it was something to do. There's not a lot do do out here, you know."

Ben felt the last of his hope drain away. This was the end. He had dodged one silver bullet in the mists of the fairy world and a second in his confrontation with Nightshade. But this third one was going to do him in. He watched the dragon lift higher above him and begin to inhale slowly. One blast of fire and that would be it. His mind worked frantically. He had to do something! Damn it, he couldn't just stand there and let himself be incinerated!

"Wait!" he called out sharply. "Don't do it!" His hand reached into his tunic front and yanked free the medallion. "I still have this! I'll use its magic if I have to."

Strabo exhaled slowly, steam, smoke and flame singing the misted air. He stared at the medallion and his tongue licked out. "You don't command the magic, Holiday."

Ben took a deep breath. "You're wrong. I do. I'll bring the Paladin if you don't let me go."

There was a long moment of silence. The dragon studied him thoughtfully and said nothing. Ben sent up a silent prayer. This was his last hope. The Paladin had come to him before when he was in trouble. Maybe . . .

His hand tightened about the face of the medallion, feeling the engraved surface press against his palm. A sudden, unexpected revelation came to him. What was he thinking? He could escape right now, if he chose! He had forgotten momentarily that the medallion gave him the means to do so! The medallion would take him back to his old world in an instant—all he had to do was take it off!

But that would mean leaving his friends trapped in Abaddon. That would mean leaving Landover forever. That would mean giving up.

That would also mean staying alive. He weighed the prospect, undecided. "I think you're lying, Holiday," the dragon said suddenly and began to breathe in again.

Good-bye, world, Ben thought and prepared to make a futile dash for safety.

But suddenly there was a sharp glimmer of light through the mist and steam that rose above the flames of the springs, and the Paladin *did* appear! Ben could not believe it. The knight materialized out of nothingness, a solitary, battered form atop his aging mount, lance hoisted in the crook of one arm before him. Strabo turned at once, clearly startled. Flames burst from his maw in an explosive roar, enveloped the knight and horse, and died into smoke. Ben flinched, feeling the backlash of the tremendous heat. He turned away, shielding his eyes, then quickly looked back again.

The Paladin was unharmed.

Strabo rose slowly on his massive hindlegs, wings lifting like a shield, lidded eyes casting about to find Ben again. "Twenty years—it's been twenty years!" he whispered in a low hiss. "I thought him gone forever! How did you bring him back, Holiday? How?"

Ben started to stammer something in reply, as surprised as Strabo by the Paladin's reappearance, then quickly caught himself. This was the opportunity he had been waiting for.

"The medallion!" he exclaimed at once. "The medallion brought him! The words of magic are inscribed here—on the medallion's back! Look for yourself!"

He held the disk out obligingly, dangling it from its silver chain so that the misted light reflected brightly from its surface. Strabo bent down, serpentine neck angling from his massive body, crusted head drawing close. The huge maw split open, the long tongue licking. Ben caught his breath. The dragon's shadow fell over him, blocking away the light.

"Look—you can see the writing!" Ben urged and thought, *just a little closer . . .*

One hooked foreleg reached for the medallion.

Ben's free hand jerked clear of his tunic pocket, and he flung a fistful of the Io Dust directly into Strabo's nostrils. The dragon inhaled in surprise, then sneezed. The sneeze nearly blew Ben off his feet, but somehow he held his ground. He snatched back the medallion, reached into his other pocket and produced the pod. Strabo's head was already swinging about to find him, jaws widening. Ben hurled the pod into the open maw. The dragon was quick, catching the pod in midair, biting down on it in fury, grinding it into pulp.

Too late Strabo realized his mistake. Io Dust flew everywhere, expoding from the dragon's mouth in jets of white smoke. Strabo gave a dreadful roar and flames burst forth. Ben threw himself aside, rolled twice, scrambled to his feet again and raced for the clump of boulders he had passed coming in. He gained it half a dozen yards ahead of the fire and dove frantically behind it. Strabo had gone completely beserk. He was thrashing above the floor of the Fire Springs in a frenzy, his massive body smashing earth and rock alike. A crater of flames geysered skyward with a booming cough. The dragon roared and breathed fire everywhere. Flames and smoke filled the afternoon air, obscuring everything. The Paladin disappeared. The springs disappeared. Ben huddled in his shelter and prayed he had been quick enough that the dragon had lost sight of him.

After a time, the thrashing and the flames ceased, and it grew quiet again. Ben waited patiently in his shelter, listening to the muffled sounds of the dragon as he moved slowly about. The booming explosions of the Fire Springs faded back into a soft hissing.

"Holiday?"

The dragon's voice was harsh with anger. Ben stayed where he was.

"Holiday? That was Io Dust, Holiday! That was an entire pod of Io Dust! Where did you get it? You said you weren't one of the fairies! You lied!"

Ben waited. He hadn't heard anything he liked yet. He listened as Strabo moved somewhere off to his left—listened to the heavy sound of his body dragging.

"Do you know how dangerous such magic is, Holiday? Do you know the harm you could have caused me? Why did you trick me like that?"

The moving stopped. Ben heard the dragon shift himself, then heard the sound of drinking. Maybe he had made a mistake, he thought suddenly. Maybe an entire pod of Io Dust was too much for anyone. Maybe the dragon was hurt.

There was a lengthy sigh. "Holiday, why have you done this to me? What is it that you want of me? Tell me and be done with it!"

The dragon sounded more hurt than angry. Ben decided

to risk it. "I want your word that you will do nothing to harm me!" he called out.

The dragon's reply was a soft hiss. "You have it."

"I want you to tell me that you will do whatever I tell you to do and nothing else. You have to anyway, you know."

"I know, Holiday! I agree! Tell me what it is that you want!"

Ben slipped cautiously from behind the shelter of the boulders. Streamers of mist and smoke still hung over the pit of the Fire Springs, casting everything in an eerie half-light. Strabo crouched several dozen yards away between a series of burning craters, looking like an angry, trapped animal. His ugly, crusted head swung slowly about, lidded eyes catching sight of Ben. Ben tensed, prepared to dive back behind the boulders. But the dragon only looked at him and waited.

"Come over here," Ben ordered.

The dragon came—meekly. There was undisguised hatred in his eyes. Ben watched the monster approach. The barrel-shaped body hunched along above thick, armored legs. Wings flapped with the movement, and the long tail snaked about restlessly. Ben felt like Fay Wray with King Kong.

"Set me free!" Strabo demanded. "Set me free, and I'll let you live!"

Ben shook his head. "I can't do that."

"You mean you won't!" the dragon whispered, his voice like sandpaper rubbed across slate. "But you can't keep me like this forever, and when I do get free of you . . ."

"Let's just skip the threats, shall we?"

". . . there won't be enough left of you to fill a gnome's thimble goblet, not enough to feed the smallest cave wight— and I'll cause you such pain that you won't believe . . ."

"Are you ready to listen to me?"

The dragon's head lifted disdainfully. "I won't pledge to you, Holiday! It would mean nothing given this way!"

Ben nodded. "I understand that. I don't want your pledge."

There was a long moment of silence as the dragon studied him. The hatred in the beast's eyes had given way to curiosity. It appeared that the worst was over. The dragon was his—for the moment, at least. Ben felt a welcome easing of tension within himself, a dissipation of the fear and sharp anticipation. He had dodged silver bullet number three. He still held the medallion clasped tightly in one hand, and he slipped it back into his tunic now. He glanced about momentarily for the Paladin, but the knight had disappeared again.

"Like a ghost . . ." he murmured.

He turned back to the dragon. Strabo was still studying him. The wicked tongue licked nervously at the misted air. "Very well, Holiday. I give up. What *do* you want from me?"

Ben smiled. "Why don't you make yourself comfortable, and I'll tell you."

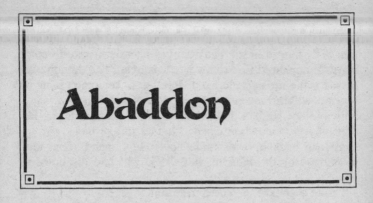

Abaddon

It was nearing dusk when Ben tightened the last of the straps on the makeshift leather riding harness he had fashioned, ordered Strabo to kneel down and climbed aboard. He settled himself carefully in the seat that rested at the juncture of several clusters of bony spikes that ribbed the dragon's spine, tested the cinch straps for slippage and fitted his boots into the iron stirrups.

At least he had the riding harness. He was lucky to have that. It was an unwieldy apparatus, constructed from traces, straps, buckles, and rings that had belonged to various field animals fallen victim to the dragon and brought to the Fire Springs for leisurely consumption. He had picked it out from among the bones and fastened it all together. It was bound about the dragon's neck just above and behind the forelegs, the saddle on which he sat settled forward of the haunches. Reins ran to the neck just behind the crusted head. Ben didn't think for a moment that he would be able to guide the dragon as he would a horse; the reins were just one more precaution to keep him from falling off.

"If you fall, you're in trouble, Holiday," the dragon had warned him earlier.

"Then you'd better make sure that I don't," Ben had replied. "You are *ordered* to make sure that I don't."

He wasn't convinced, however, that Strabo could do that, Io Dust or no Io Dust. They were descending into the netherworld of Abaddon, and both lives would be at risk. Strabo would have difficulty keeping them safe under the best of circumstances—and the proposed rescue of his missing friends from the realm of the demons did not promise the best of anything.

He paused momentarily, seated atop the dragon, and gazed out across the wasteland. They had moved to the rim of the Fire Springs, clear of the burning craters and the thick undergrowth. The day was dying into evening; as the sun slipped down behind the distant mountains, mist and gloom settled over the valley. Landover was a murky gathering of shadows and vague shapes. Ben could almost watch the failing of the daylight from one moment to the next. It was as if the valley were disappearing before his eyes. He had the uneasy sensation that it was, the unpleasant feeling that he would never see it again.

He straightened himself in the stirrups, hardening his resolve against such thoughts. He forced a grim smile. Ben Holiday was about to sally forth, a knight atop his steed, off to the rescue. He almost laughed. Don Quixote, off to tilt with windmills—what a picture he could send home again if he had his camera! Damn, but he had never thought—never believed—that he would be doing anything like this with his life! All those years of living behind concrete and steel walls; all those stuffy courtrooms and musty law libraries; all those sterile pleadings and legal briefs; all those lawbooks and statutes and codes—how far removed from that he was now!

And he knew, with a certainty that surprised him, that he could never go back again to any of it.

"What are you doing up there, Holiday—admiring the view?" Strabo's hiss of displeasure interrupted his thoughts. "Let's be on our way!"

"All right," Ben agreed softly. "Take me up."

The dragon's wings spread wide, and he lifted from the ground with a lurch. Ben held tightly to the reins and harness

straps, watching the land drop away quickly beneath him.
He had a momentary glimpse of bramble, thicket, and deadwood forests fading into trailers of mist and dusk's lengthening shadows, and then there was only gloom. Fillip and
Sot were down there somewhere, hidden from view. He had
gone back to them long enough to let them know that he was
riding Strabo down into Abaddon to rescue the others. He
had dispatched them back again to Sterling Silver to await
his return. They had been only too quick to go, their horror-
stricken faces clearly reflecting their unspoken conviction
that they had seen the last of him.

Maybe they had, he mused. Maybe he should have told
them to go on home and forget about him. They probably
wouldn't have done that, though. They still took their pledge
to him quite seriously.

He reflected momentarily on all the help they had given
him—a pair of larcenous, grimy little cannibals. Who would
have thought it? Silently, he wished them well.

Strabo flew into the coming night, passing from the eastern
wasteland to the fringes of the Greensward and then west.
The daylight failed completely, darkness descended, and
Landover's moons began to shine. They were all visible on
this night—white, peach, washed-out mauve, burnt rose, sea
green, beryl, turquoise, and jade—their colors unobstructed
by the mists that shrouded the valley below. They were like
giant balloons, Ben thought and wondered where the party
was.

The minutes slipped rapidly past. Strabo's massive body
undulated rhythmically beneath Ben as the leathered wings
beat against the night winds and carried them westward. Ben
gripped the reins and harness and hung on for dear life. Air
currents buffeted and chilled him. Landover was a vast bowl
of steaming soup over which he hung suspended. He was
exhilarated by the sensation of flying like this, but he was
frightened, too. He hadn't liked horseback riding and he
didn't like dragon riding any better. The dragon kept a steady
pace and that helped, but Ben still distrusted the situation.

He knew the Io Dust could wear off at any time and that would be the end of him.

"This is a foolish venture!" Strabo called back to him moments later, as if reading his thoughts. The crusted, misshapen head swung about, eyes glinting. "All this for a handful of humans!"

"My friends!" Ben shouted in reply, the wind whipping the words back into his face.

"Your friends mean nothing to me!"

"Fair enough—you mean nothing to them! Except Questor Thews, I suppose—he thinks you special!"

"The wizard? Pah!"

"Just do what I told you to do!" Ben ordered.

"I hate you, Holiday!"

"Sorry—I don't care!"

"You will! Sooner or later, I'll get free of you and when I do you'll be sorry you ever decided to use me this way!"

The head swung back again, the cold, mechanical voice dying into the rush of the wind. Ben said nothing. He gripped the reins and the harness straps tighter.

They flew deep into the Greensward toward the center of the valley. Ben did not know where they were going. He knew the dragon was taking him to Abaddon, but he had no idea where Abaddon was. Abaddon was the netherworld of Landover, but its gates were time passages of the sort that had brought him from his own world. They were not, however, the *same* time passages. They were not to be found within the mists that ringed the valley. They were hidden somewhere within the valley, Strabo had told him—somewhere only the demons and the dragon could reach . . .

Strabo slowed suddenly and began a long sweep back that became a widening circle. Ben looked down. The valley was a shroud of mist and gloom. Strabo's wings spread wider, and the dragon began to bank sharply on the night winds.

"Hold tight to me, Holiday!" the dragon cried back to him.

Strabo dipped suddenly and started down. Wings flattened back and the long neck stretched forward. They began to pick up speed as the dragon's dive steepened. The wind rushed past Ben Holiday's ears in a vicious roar that drowned out everything. The ground began to come into focus, a shapeless blur sharpening with the passing of each second they dropped. Ben was cold all the way through. They were going too fast! They were going to dive right into the middle of the Greensward!

Then abruptly the dragon fire exploded from Strabo's throat, a huge, brilliant arc of crimson flame. The air seemed to melt before it, cellophane that wrinkled and expanded at its edges, leaving a jagged hole. Ben squinted against the rush of the wind and saw the blackness of the hole open out of the night. Dragon fire died away, but the hole remained. They were passing through it, flying into the empty dark. Landover disappeared; the misted Greensward was gone. There was a sucking noise as the hole closed behind them and then sudden stillness.

Strabo leveled off within the black. Ben lifted slightly from where he had crouched down against the dragon's spine and stared about, awestruck. The world had undergone a radical change. Moon and stars were gone. There was a sky of inky black, canopied over a sprawling mass of jagged peaks and deep gorges. Flashes of lightning danced at the juncture of earth and sky, filling the fringes of the horizon with a bizarre light show. Volcanos growled in the distance, their reddish fires glimmering from out of mountainous cones of rock; streams of lava flowed in long red trailers like blood. The earth shook and grumbled with the eruptions, and geysers of flame and molten rock exploded skyward against the blackness.

"Abaddon!" Strabo advised, his voice a slow hiss.

He dropped downward with sickening speed, and Ben felt the pit of his stomach lurch. Mountain peaks rushed past, and the fire from the volcanos burst skyward all about. Ben was terrified. Abaddon was the realization of his worst nightmare. He had never seen anything so inhospitable. Nothing could survive in such a world.

A shadow rocketed past, winged and elusive. Strabo

hissed in warning. Another shadow slipped past, then another. There were sharp hisses and flashes of teeth. Dragon fire burst suddenly from Strabo's maw, and one of the shadows screamed and dropped earthward. Ben flattened himself within the nest of spikes that protected the dragon's spine. The fire burst forth again and again. Another of the shadows exploded into ash and fell. Strabo was weaving evasively as more of the shadows appeared. He stretched out his massive body and increased his speed. The black things fell behind and were gone.

A series of rugged peaks whipped past, and then the dragon slowed once more. "Gnats!" he growled contemptuously. "No match for me!"

Ben was drenched with sweat and could barely catch his breath. "How much farther?"

The dragon's laugh was harsh. "A bit, Holiday. What seems to be the matter? Is this more than you bargained for?"

"I'll be fine. You do what you were told to do and get to my friends!"

"Temper, Holiday."

The dragon flew on through the fire-streaked blackness. The "gnats" came at them twice more, and twice more Strabo burned a handful of them before flying past. The world of Abaddon stretched on below, unchanging in its look, a world of rock and fire. White light danced frantically on the horizons all about, and lava flared within the craters of the mountain peaks, but in the valleys and gorges below all remained impenetrably black. If there was something living down there, it could not be seen from the air.

Ben began to experience a growing sense of futility. His friends had been trapped in this world for almost five days!

Strabo banked left between two monstrous volcanic peaks and started down. Wind rushed past, and trailers of fire laced the mountain rock on both sides. Ben peered down into the lava. Things were swimming in the fire! Things were playing there!

A monstrous black shadow heaved up from out of the

shadows on one peak, tentacled arms reaching. Strabo hissed and the dragon fire burned at the arms. The arms shuddered and drew back. The shadow disappeared.

Then they were through the mountains and within a valley ringed by jagged peaks. Strabo dove sharply and leveled off less than fifty feet above its floor. Pools of fiery lava bubbled at the fringes of the valley, throwing rocks and flame skyward in small bursts. Cracks and crevices split the barren floor, dropping away into blackness. Creatures scurried everywhere, small and misshapen in the crimson half-light, things barely human. Cries rose up at the sight of the dragon, shrieks that disappeared as quickly as they sounded in the distant roar of the volcanos. Ben heard the dragon screech in reply.

The "gnats" reappeared, dozens strong. Other things winged into view, larger and more fearsome-looking. Strabo leveled out and flew faster. Ben was hunched down so close to the dragon's spine that he could feel the pulsing of his hide. Straps and cinches strained with the effort of the dragon's flight. Ben could feel things beginning to loosen.

Then a monstrous pit of fire appeared before them, its throat thousands of feet deep. A tiny slab of rock hung suspended by chains across that throat—a disk of stone that measured no more than a dozen feet across. The slab of rock danced and bobbled unsteadily on its webbing of iron, and the fire licked up at it hungrily from far below.

Ben caught his breath sharply. There were a handful of tiny figures crouched on that slab of rock, fighting to keep their balance.

His friends!

Strabo dove for them, gnats and other flying demons in pursuit. Other demons still, hundreds strong, were gathered about the fire pit, throwing rocks at the figures crouched upon the slab and shaking the chains that secured it. All were yelling gleefully. It was a game they were playing, Ben realized in horror. The demons had trapped or placed his friends on that slab and were waiting now to see them fall into the fire!

The pit drew closer. The demons turned, seeing the dragon now, crying out. Hands reached for the pins that fastened the chains to the pit wall. The demons were trying to drop the slab and his friends into the fire before he could reach them!

Ben was frantic. Chains fell away quickly, one after another, and the slab of rock buckled and shook. Strabo breathed fire at the demons and burned dozens to ash, but the rest continued to work at the chains. Ben screamed in fury as he saw clearly now the faces of Questor Thews, Abernathy, the kobolds—and Willow! Strabo rocketed clear of the rim of the pit, past the demons working to release the chains that bound the rock slab. Too late, Ben thought. They were going to be too late!

There was an instant then in which time froze. There was no time and all the time in the world. Ben seemed to see everything that happened with a frightening detachment that held him suspended in the instant of its happening. The chains at one section fell away completely and the slab of rock buckled and sagged. His friends dropped to their hands and knees and began to slide toward the pit.

Strabo dove sharply, dragging Ben with him toward the fire. He reached the slab of rock as the people on it slipped away. Clawed feet snatched two out of midair. With a quick snap of his jaws, he caught another, and his great head twisted back to deposit a kobold in front of Ben. The second kobold flung himself at the harness and grasped the straps.

The final figure dropped into the pit. It was Questor Thews.

Ben saw him fall, watching in horror as the gray robes with their rainbow-colored sashes flared and billowed like a failing parachute. Strabo arced downward, then rose quickly again into the night. He was too far away to reach the wizard. He could not save him.

"Questor!" Ben screamed.

Then something truly magical happened, something so bizarre that even with all that had happened in the few moments past, it left Ben stunned. Questor's plunge into the fire seemed to slow and then to stop altogether. The wizard's arms spread wide against the crimson light of the flames and slowly the sticklike figure began to rise from the pit.

Ben caught his breath, his mind racing. There was only one possible answer. Questor Thews had finally conjured up the right spell! He had made the magic work!

Strabo arced downward quickly, bursts of fire incinerating the "gnats" and other flying demons that sought to intercede. He reached Questor Thews just as the wizard levitated above the rim of the pit, flew under him, and caught him on his back so that he was settled just behind Ben.

Ben turned hurriedly and stared. Questor sat there like a statue, his face ashen, his eyes bright with astonishment. "It . . . it was all in a proper twist of the fingers, High Lord," the wizard managed before fainting.

Ben reached back and secured him, one hand firmly fixed to the gray robes as Strabo began to climb. Shrieks rose from the demons, a cacophony of epithets that faded quickly as the dragon outdistanced them. The ground dropped away below, transformed into a rumpled black shroud rent by jagged holes and cracks of flame. The lightning at the edges of the world danced wildly, streaking across the horizon's sweep, and all of Abaddon seemed to shake and rumble.

Then Strabo breathed dragon fire into the air before them, and once again the sky melted and gave way. Edges frayed and crinkled about a jagged hole, and the dragon and his passengers passed through.

Ben had to squint against a sudden change of light. When he opened his eyes wide again, stars and colored moons brightened a misted night sky.

They were back in Landover once more.

It took Ben several moments to regain his bearings. They were in Landover, but not over the Greensward. They were north, almost to the wall of the valley. Strabo circled for a time, winging over thick forestland and barren ridgeline, then eased down gently into a deserted meadow.

Ben scrambled down from the dragon's back. Bunion and

Parsnip greeted him with hisses and gleaming teeth, so agitated they could barely contain themselves. Abernathy dropped rudely to the ground, picked himself up, brushed himself off, and denounced the day he had ever let himself become mixed up with any of them. Questor, conscious again, lowered himself gingerly along the harness straps and stumbled over to Ben, barely aware of what he was doing, his eyes fixed on the dragon.

"I had never believed I would see the day that *anyone* would rule this . . . this marvelous creature!" he whispered, awestruck. "Strabo—last of the old dragons, the greatest of the fairy creatures, brought to the service of a King of Landover! It was the Io Dust, of course, but still . . ."

He stumbled into Ben and suddenly remembered himself. "High Lord, you are safe! We thought you lost for certain! How you found your way clear of the fairy world, I will never know! How you accomplished what you did . . ." His enthusiasm left him momentarily speechless, and he reached for Ben's hand and pumped it vigorously. Ben grinned in spite of himself. "We came looking for you after you failed to return that first day, and the witch took us," the wizard went on hastily. "She sent us to Abaddon and dropped us on that slab of rock for the demons to play with. Almost five days, High Lord! That's how long we have been trapped there! Days of being teased and taunted by those loathsome, foul . . ."

The kobolds hissed and chittered wildly, pointing.

Questor nodded at once, his enthusiasm fading. "Yes, you are correct to intercede—I had indeed forgotten." He took Ben's arm. "I ramble, High Lord, when there are more pressing concerns. The sylph is very ill." He hesitated, then pulled Ben after him. "I am sorry, High Lord, but she may be dying."

Ben's smile was gone instantly. They hurried forward of where Strabo crouched, watching them with lidded eyes. Abernathy was already kneeling in the grass next to Willow's inert form. Ben knelt with him, and Questor and the kobolds gathered close.

"Her time for joining with the earth came when she was trapped in Abaddon," Questor whispered. "She could not deny the changeling need, but the rock would not accept her."

Ben shuddered. Willow had tried to transform, unable to resist the need, and the attempt had been only partially completed. Her skin had gone wrinkled and barklike, her fingers and toes had turned to gnarled roots, her hair had become slender branches, and her body had twisted and split. She was so hideous to look upon that Ben could barely manage to do so.

"She still breathes, High Lord," Abernathy said softly.

Ben fought down his revulsion. "We have to save her," he replied, trying desperately to think of what to do. He stared in horror as Willow's body convulsed suddenly, and more roots split from the skin beneath one wrist. The sylph's eyes fluttered blindly and closed again. She was in agony. Anger coursed through Ben like a fire. "Questor, use your magic!"

"No, High Lord." Questor shook his head slowly. "No magic that I possess can help. Only one thing can save her. She must complete the transformation."

Ben wheeled on the wizard. "Damn it, how is she supposed to do that? She's barely alive!"

No one said anything. He turned back to the girl. He should never have left her alone with Nightshade. He should never have permitted her to come with him in the first place. It was his fault that this had happened. It would be his fault if she died . . .

He swore softly and thrust the thought aside. His mind raced.

Then suddenly he remembered. "The old pines!" he exclaimed. "The grove in Elderew where her mother danced and she transformed herself that last night! It was special to her! Perhaps she could complete the transformation there!" He was already on his feet, directing the others. "Here, help me carry her! Strabo—bend down!"

They bore the sylph to the dragon and bound her to his

back. Then they climbed up beside her, fastening themselves where they could to the makeshift harness. Ben rode in front of the unconscious girl, Questor and Abernathy behind, the kobolds to either side at the stirrups.

Strabo grunted irritably in response to a command from Ben and then lifted into the night sky. They flew south, the dragon leveling out and straining to increase his speed, the wind threatening to tear them all loose from the creaking harness. The minutes slipped past, and the hill country north gave way to the plains of the Greensward. Ben's hand reached back to touch the body of the sylph and found the barklike skin cold and hard. They were losing her. There wasn't enough time. The Greensward passed away and the forests and rivers of the lake country appeared, dim patches of color through the haze of mist. The dragon dropped lower, skimming the treetops and the ridgelines. Ben was shaking with impatience and frustration. His hand still clasped Willow's arm, and it seemed as if he could actually feel the life passing from her.

Then Strabo banked sharply left and dove downward into the forest. Trees rushed up to greet them, then there was a small clearing through the wall of branches; as quick as that, they were on the ground once more. Ben scrambled down wordlessly, the others with him, all working frantically to free Willow. The forest loomed about them like a wall, trailers of mist swirling through the rows of dark trunks. Bunion hissed at them and led the way, his instincts sure. They moved into the trees, slipping and groping their way through the near black, carrying the rigid form of the girl.

They reached the pine grove in seconds. The pines stood empty and silent in the mist, sentinels against the dark. Ben directed the procession to the grove's center, the earthen stage on which Willow's mother had danced the last night before he had departed Elderew.

Gently, they laid Willow down. Ben felt the girl's wrist above the mass of roots and tendrils that had broken the skin. The wrist was cold and lifeless.

"She is not breathing, High Lord!" Questor whispered in a low hiss.

Ben was frantic. He lifted the stricken sylph in his arms and held her close against him. He was crying. "Damn it, you can't die, Willow, you can't do this to me!" He cradled her, feeling the roughness of her skin chafe his face. "Willow, answer me!"

And suddenly he was holding Annie, her body broken and bloodstained from the accident that had taken her life, another piece of wreckage to be swept from the scene. The sensation was so sharp that he gasped. He could feel bone and blood and torn flesh; he could feel the small, frail life of his unborn child. "Oh, God, no!" he cried softly.

He jerked his head up, and the image faded. He was holding Willow again. He bent close, kissing the sylph's cheek and mouth, his tears running down her face. He had lost Annie and the child she carried. He could not stand it if he were to lose Willow, too. "Don't die," he begged her. "I don't want you to die. Willow, please!"

Her frail body stirred, responding almost miraculously, and her eyes opened to his. He looked into those eyes, past the ravaged face and body, past the devastation wrought by the half-completed transformation. He reached for the flicker of life that still burned within.

"Come back to me, Willow!" he begged her. "You must live!"

The eyes closed again. But the body of the sylph stirred more strongly now, and convulsions became spasms of effort to regain muscle control. Willow's throat swallowed. "Ben. Help me up. Hold me."

He brought her quickly to her feet, and the others stepped back from them. He held her there, feeling the lifeblood work itself through her, feeling the transformation begin again. Her roots snaked deep into the forest soil, her branches lengthened and split, and her trunk stretched and hardened.

Then everything went still. Ben looked up. The change was complete. Willow had become the tree that was her namesake. It was going to be all right.

His eyes squeezed tightly shut. "Thank you," he whispered.

He lowered his head, wrapped his arms about the slender trunk, and cried.

The demon appeared toward dawn, materializing out of the gloom, a black and misshapen thing wrapped in armor. It happened very suddenly. The wind whispered, the mist swirled, and the demon was there.

Ben was awake almost instantly. He had been dozing, sleeping in fits and starts, cramped from leaning against Willow, from holding her. Strabo was presumably still back in the clearing where Ben had left him.

The demon approached, and Ben rose to meet it. The kobolds interposed themselves instantly, moving to block the demon's way. Abernathy jerked awake and kicked Questor roughly. The wizard awoke as well and scrambled to his feet. The demon's helmeted head swung slowly about, and its crimson eyes surveyed the company and the pine grove with studied caution.

Then it spoke. Ben could not understand anything of what was said, and the speech was over almost before it began. Questor hesitated, then looked back at him. "The Mark issues you a challenge, High Lord. He demands that you meet him in combat three dawns from now at the Heart."

Ben nodded wordlessly. What had been promised from the beginning was finally here. Time had run out. He was only half awake, still near exhaustion from his ordeal of the past several days, but he grasped the significance of the challenge instantly.

The Mark had had enough of him. The demon was angry. But perhaps—just perhaps—the demon was worried, too. Questor had once told him that the demon always challenged at midwinter—and it was nowhere near midwinter yet. The demon was rushing things.

He thought about it a moment, tried to reason it through, then shook his head numbly. It didn't matter. He had made the decision to stay long ago, and nothing would change that decision now. It surprised him that his resolve was so strong. It gave him a good feeling.

He nodded to the messenger. "I'll be there."

The demon was gone in a swirl of mist. Ben stared after it a moment, then gazed off into the trees where the first light of dawn was still a faint silver tinge against the far horizons. "Go back to sleep," he told the others gently.

He settled down again by Willow, rested his cheek against her roughened trunk and closed his eyes.

Dawn had broken when he came awake once more. He was stretched full length upon the earth in the shadow of the aged pines. His head rested in Willow's lap and her arms cradled him. She had transformed back again.

"Ben," she greeted softly.

He looked at her slender arms, her body and then her face. She was just as she had been when he had seen her that first night bathing in the waters of the Irrylyn. The color, the beauty, and the vibrancy had been restored. She was the vision he had wanted and been afraid to seek. Yet it was no longer the vision that mattered to him; it was the life inside. The repulsion, the fear, and the sense of alienation he had once felt were gone. They had been replaced by hope.

He smiled. "I need you," he whispered and meant it.

"I know, Ben," she said to him. "I have always known."

She bent her face to his and kissed him, and he reached up to draw her close.

Iron Mark

The first thing Ben did that morning was to release Strabo from the spell of the Io Dust that bound the dragon to him. He gave Strabo his freedom on the condition that the dragon not hunt the Greensward or any other settled part of the valley or any of its citizens so long as Ben was King.

"The duration of your rule in Landover amounts to a splash of water in the ocean of my lifetime, Holiday," the dragon advised him coldly, eyes lidded against his thoughts. They stood together in the clearing where Strabo had waited the night.

Ben shrugged. "Then the condition should be easy to accept."

"Conditions from a human are never easy to accept—especially when the human is as deceitful as you."

"Flattery will gain you nothing more than I have already offered. Do you agree or not?"

The crusted snout split wide, teeth gleaming. "You risk the possibility that my word means nothing—that extracting it while the magic binds me renders it worthless!"

Ben sighed. "Yes or no?"

Strabo hissed, the sound rising up from deep within. "Yes!" He spread his leathered wings and arced his long neck skyward. "Anything to be free of you!" Then he hesitated and bent close. "Understand—this is not finished yet between you and me, Holiday. We will meet again another day and settle the debt owed me!"

He rose with a rush of beating wings until he was atop the trees, banked eastward, and disappeared into the rising sun. Ben watched him go and then turned away.

Questor Thews could not understand. First he was astonished, then angry, and finally just mystified. Whatever could the High Lord have been thinking? Why would he release Strabo like that? The dragon was a powerful ally, a weapon that none would dare to challenge, a lever which could be used to exact the pledges the High Lord so desperately needed!

"But that's precisely what's wrong with keeping him," Ben tried to explain it to the wizard. "I'd end up using him like a club; I'd have my pledges not because the people of Landover felt they should give them but because they were terrified of the dragon. That's no good—I don't want loyalty from fear! I want loyalty from respect! Besides, Strabo is a two-edged sword. Sooner or later the effects of the Io Dust are going to wear off anyway, and then what? He'd turn on me in a minute. No, Questor—better that I let him go now and take my chances."

"Aptly put, High Lord," the wizard snapped. "You will indeed take your chances. What happens to you when you face the Mark? Strabo could have protected you! You should at least have kept him until then!"

But Ben shook his head. "No, Questor," he answered softly. "This isn't the dragon's fight; it's mine. It always has been, I think."

He left the matter there, refusing to discuss it further with any of them. He had thought it through carefully. He had made up his mind. He had learned a few things he had not known earlier and deduced a few more. He saw clearly what a King of Landover must be if he were to have any value at all. He had come full circle in many respects from the time he had first entered the valley. He wanted his friends to understand, but he did not think he could explain it to them. Understanding would have to come another way.

Happily, there was no further opportunity to dwell on the subject right then. The River Master appeared, alerted by his people that something strange was going on in the grove of the old pines. Strabo had flown in toward midnight and flown out again that dawn. He brought with him a handful of humans, including the man named Holiday who claimed Landover's throne, the wizard Questor Thews, and the River Master's missing daughter. Ben greeted the River Master with apologies for the intrusion and a brief explanation of what had befallen them all during the past several weeks. He told the River Master that Willow had followed him at his invitation, that it was his oversight in not advising the sprite earlier, and that he wished the sylph to remain with him for a few days more. He asked that they meet again three dawns hence at the Heart.

He said nothing of the challenge issued by the Mark.

"What purpose will be served, High Lord, in meeting with you at the Heart?" the River Master asked pointedly. His people were all about them, faint shapes in the mist of the early dawn, eyes that glimmered in the haze of the trees.

"I will ask again your pledge to the throne of Landover," Ben answered. "I think that this time you will want to give it."

Skepticism and a hint of alarm reflected in the sprite's chiseled features, and the gills on his neck ceased their steady flutter. "I have given you my conditions for such a pledge," the River Master said softly. There was a warning note in his voice.

Ben kept his gaze steady. "I know."

The River Master nodded. "Very well. I will be there."

He embraced Willow briefly, gave his permission for her to stay on with Ben and was gone. His people disappeared with him, melting back into the forest gloom. Ben and the members of his little company were left alone.

Willow moved close, her hand closing about his. "He does not intend to give you his pledge, Ben," she whispered, lowering her voice so that the others could not hear.

Ben smiled ruefully. "I know. But I'm hoping that he won't have any choice."

It was time to be going. He dispatched Bunion to Rhyndweir castle with a message for Kallendbor and the other Lords of the Greensward. He had done as they had asked and rid them of Strabo. Now it was their turn. They were to meet him at the Heart three dawns hence and give him their pledge of loyalty.

Bunion disappeared into the forest wordlessly, and Ben and the remaining members of the little company turned homeward toward Sterling Silver.

It took them longer returning from Elderew and the lake country this time than it had before, because this time they traveled afoot. Ben didn't mind. It gave him time to think, and he had a great deal to think about. Willow walked with him as they traveled, staying close, saying little. Questor and Abernathy questioned him repeatedly about his plans for dealing with the Mark, but he put them off. The truth of the matter was he didn't have any plans yet, but he didn't want them to know that. It was better if they thought that he was simply being closemouthed.

He spent much of his time surveying the country they traveled through and imagining how it had been before the failing of the magic. His memory of the vision shown him by the fairies recalled itself often, a gleaming, wondrous painting where the mists, the gloom and the wilting of the land's life were absent. How long ago had this valley been like that, he wondered? How long before it could be made that way again? The vision of the fairies had been more than a memory; it had been a promise. He pondered the sluggish swirl of the deep mists that screened the sunshine and shrouded the mountains, the thinning groves of Bonnie Blues dotted with wilt and spotting, the lakes and rivers turned gray and clouded, and the meadows and grasslands grown sparse and wintry. He pondered the valley's people and their lives in a world turned suddenly harsh and unproductive. He thought again of the faces of those few that had appeared for his coronation—of the many who had lined the roads leading into Rhyndweir. That could all be changed if the failing of the magic could be halted.

A King to serve the land and lead her people would accomplish that end, Questor Thews believed. Twenty years of no King upon Landover's throne had caused the problem in the first place.

But the concept was a difficult one for Ben to grasp. Why would such a simple thing as the loss or gain of a King have so great an effect upon the life of this valley? A King was just a man. A King was just a figurehead. How could one man make such a difference?

It could, he decided finally, where the land took its life from the magic that had created it, and the magic was sustained by the rule of a King. Such a thing might not be possible in a world governed solely by natural laws, but it could be so here. The land took its life from the magic. Questor had told him so. Perhaps the land took its life from the King as well.

The implications of that possibility were staggering, and Ben could not begin to comprehend all of the ramifications that they suggested. Instead, he reduced their number to those relevant to his most immediate problem—staying alive. The magic failed without him; the land failed without the magic. There was a bond among the three. If he could understand it, he could save himself. He knew it instinctively. The fairies had not created Landover one day to see it fall apart the next simply because of the loss of a King. They had to have foreseen and provided a way to bring that King back again—a new King, a different King, but a King to rule and keep the magic strong.

But what provision had they made?

The first day for the journey back seemed endless. When night finally descended and the others of the little company slept, Ben lay awake, still thinking. He was awake a long time.

The second day passed more quickly, and by midday they had reached once more the island castle of Sterling Silver. Bunion was waiting at the gates, already returned from his journey to the Greensward. He spoke rapidly, punctuating his sentences with sharp gestures. Ben couldn't begin to follow him.

Questor interceded. "Your message was delivered, High Lord." His voice was bitter. "The Lords of the Greensward reply that they will come to the Heart as commanded—but they will postpone until then any decision as to whether or not they will pledge to the throne."

Ben grunted. "Hardly surprising." He ignored the look exchanged by the wizard and Abernathy and moved ahead through the entry. "Thanks for the effort, Bunion."

He walked quickly down the connecting passageway to the inner court and crossed, the others trailing. He had just stepped inside the front hall when a pair of bedraggled apparitions darted frantically from the shadows of an alcove and threw themselves at his feet.

"Great High Lord!"

"Mighty High Lord!"

Ben groaned in recognition. The G'home Gnomes Fillip and Sot fell to their knees before him, grovelling and whimpering so pitifully that it was embarrassing. Their fur was matted and spiked, their paws were caked with mud, and they had the look of something dredged from the sewers.

"Oh, High Lord, we thought you devoured by the dragon!" Fillip wailed.

"We thought you lost in the depths of the netherworld!" Sot cried.

"Ah, you have great magic, High Lord!" Fillip praised him.

"Yes, you have returned from the dead!" Sot declared.

Ben wanted to kick them into next week. "Will you kindly let go of me!" he ordered. They had fastened themselves to his pant legs and were kissing his feet. He tried to shake free, but the gnomes would not release their death grip. "Let go, already!" he snapped.

They fell back, still hugging the stone flooring, their lidded eyes peering up at him expectantly.

"Great High Lord," Fillip whispered.

"Mighty High . . ." Sot began.

Ben cut him short. "Parsnip, Bunion—get these two mud bunnies into a bath and don't let them up for air until you can tell what they are again." The kobolds dragged the G'home Gnomes from the foyer, still groveling. Ben sighed, suddenly weary. "Questor, I want you and Abernathy to take one last look through the castle histories. See if there is anything—anything at all—that refers to the way that Landover, her Kings and the magic are joined." He shook his head sadly. "I know we've been this route before; I know we haven't found anything, but . . . well, maybe we missed something . . ." He trailed off.

Questor nodded bravely. "Yes, High Lord, it is possible that we missed something. It doesn't hurt to look again."

He disappeared down the hallway with Abernathy in tow. Abernathy looked doubtful.

Ben stood alone in the foyer with Willow for a few moments after the others had gone, then took the sylph gently by the hand and climbed the tower stairs to the Landsview. He felt a need to explore the valley one last time—he bit his tongue at the thought—and he wanted the girl to go with him. They hadn't spoken much since her recovery from the transformation, but they had stayed close to each other. It helped him having her there. It gave him an assurance that he didn't entirely understand. It gave him strength.

He tried to tell her. "I want you to know something, Willow," he said as they stood together on the platform of the Landsview. "I don't know how all this is going to turn out, but I do know that, whichever way it goes, I'm the better by a long sight for having had you for a friend."

She did not reply. Her hand closed tightly over his. Together they grasped the railing, and the castle walls fell away into the clouded gray skies.

They were gone all afternoon.

Ben slept soundly that night and did not wake until midday. Questor met him on his way downstairs. The wizard looked exhausted.

"Don't tell me." Ben smiled sympathetically. "Let me guess."

"Guessing is not required, High Lord," Questor replied. "We worked all night, Abernathy and I, and we found nothing. I am sorry."

Ben put his arm around the sticklike frame. "Nothing to be sorry for—you tried. Go get some sleep. I'll see you for dinner."

He ate some fruit and cheese and drank some wine in the kitchen while Parsnip watched silently, then went alone to the chapel of the Paladin. He stayed there for some time, kneeling in the shadows, wondering what had become of the champion and why he would not return, trying to draw some small measure of understanding and strength from the armored shell that rested on the pedestal before him. Dreams and wishes paraded before his eyes, vague images in the musted air, and he let himself feel the sweetness of the life he had enjoyed. Old world and new, the good things recalled themselves and gave him peace.

He walked back through Sterling Silver in the late afternoon hours. He took his time, trailing silently through her halls and passageways, brushing her stone with his hands, feeling the warmth of her body. The magic that gave her life still burned somewhere deep within, but it was weakening. The Tarnish had grown worse; the discoloration had moved deeper within the castle walls. She was failing rapidly. He remembered the promise he had made to himself—that one day he would find a way to help her. He wondered now if he ever would.

He gathered his friends in the dining hall for dinner that evening—Willow, Questor, Abernathy, Bunion, Parsnip,

Fillip, and Sot. There was little to eat. The castle larder was nearly empty and the magic could no longer produce the needed food. Everyone pretended the meal was fine. Conversation was subdued. No one complained; no one argued. They all worked very hard at avoiding any mention of what lay ahead.

When the meal was almost ended, Ben stood up. He had difficulty speaking. "I hope that you will excuse me, but I should try to get at least a few hours sleep before I, uh . . ." He stopped. "I thought I'd leave around midnight. I don't expect any of you to go with me. In fact, it might be better if you didn't. I appreciate the way you've all stood by me up to this point. I couldn't ask for better friends. I wish there was something I . . ."

"High Lord," Questor interrupted gently. He came to his feet, thin arms folding into his gray robes. "Please don't say anything more. We all decided earlier that we would come with you tomorrow. Good friends could do no less. Now why don't you go on to bed?"

They stared silently at him—the wizard, the scribe, the sylph, the kobolds, and the gnomes. He nodded slowly and smiled. "Thank you. Thank you all again."

He walked from the room and stood alone for a moment in the hall beyond. Then he climbed the stairs to his bedroom.

Willow came to wake him at midnight.

They stood together in the darkness of the bedroom after Ben had risen and held each other. Ben's eyes closed wearily and he let the warmth of the girl seep through him.

"I'm afraid of what's going to happen, Willow," he whispered to her. "Not of what might happen to me . . ." He cut himself short. "No, that's a lie—I'm scared to death of what might happen to me. But I'm more afraid of what might happen to Landover if the Mark kills me. If I fail to survive this confrontation, Landover may be lost. And I'm afraid I *will* fail, because I still don't know how to prevent him from winning!"

She hugged him tightly, and her voice was fierce. "Ben! You have to believe in yourself! You have accomplished so much more than anyone ever imagined that you would. The answers you need are there. You have found them before when you needed them; I think you can do so again."

He shook his head. "I don't have enough time left to find them, Willow. The Mark hasn't left me enough time."

"You will find the answers in the time that you have."

"Willow, listen to me." Ben moved his face away from hers. "Only one thing can prevent the Mark from killing me—only one. The Paladin. If the Paladin appears to defend me, I have a chance. It's possible that he might. He's saved me several times now since I came into the valley."

He bent close again. "But, Willow, he's a ghost! He lacks substance and strength! He's a shadow, and shadows don't frighten anyone for very long! I don't need a ghost—I need the real thing! And, damn it, I don't even know if the real thing still exists!"

Her green eyes were calm in the aftermath of his fury. "If he has come to you before, Ben, he will do so again." She paused. "Do you remember when I told you that you were the one promised me by the fates woven in the marriage bed of my parents? You did not believe me, but you have seen since that it was so. I told you something more, Ben. I told you I sensed you were different; I told you I believed you were meant to be King of Landover. I still believe that. And I believe that the Paladin will come to you again. I believe that he will protect you."

He looked at her for a very long time without speaking. Then he kissed her lightly on the mouth. "Guess there's only one way to find out."

He gave her a brave smile and took her hands in his. Together, they started for the door.

Dawn stalked the Heart on cat's feet; the first faint tinges of silver were beginning to lighten the eastern skies above the tree line. Ben and the members of his little company had arrived several hours earlier and were gathered now on the dais. Others had been arriving all night. The River Master was there, standing close against the screen of the forest, surrounded by dozens of his people, all faint shadows in the mist and night. The Lords of the Greensward were there as well, dressed in battle harness, bristling with arms. War horses stamped and knights stood close like iron statues. Fairy people and humans, they faced one another across the rows of white velvet kneeling pads and armrests, eyes watchful in the gloom and half-light.

Ben sat quietly on the throne at the center of the dais, Willow at one hand, Questor and Abernathy at the other. The kobolds crouched directly in front of him. Fillip and Sot were nowhere to be seen. The G'home Gnomes had vanished once more.

Tunneled down about twenty feet, Ben surmised with faint amusement.

"Abernathy." Ben turned abruptly to find his scribe.

The dog jumped at the sound of his voice, then collected himself and bowed stiffly. "Yes, High Lord?"

"Go to Kallendbor and the Lords of the Greensward, then to the River Master. Ask that they join me before the dais."

"Yes, High Lord."

He went immediately. Abernathy hadn't quarreled once with Questor since they had left the castle. Both were on their best behavior—both walking on eggshells. It made Ben more nervous than he would have been if they had simply acted normal.

"High Lord." Questor bent close, his voice a whisper. "It nears dawn. You wear no armor and you have no weapons. Let me suggest that you allow me to equip you with some of each—now."

Ben looked up at the scarecrow figure with his gray robes and colored scarfs, his wispish hair and beard, and his lined, anxious face and he smiled gently. "No, Questor. No weapons and no armor. They wouldn't do me any good against a creature like the Mark. I can't defeat him that way. I have to find another."

Questor Thews cleared his throat. "Do you happen to have such a way in mind, High Lord?"

Ben felt the cold that had settled deep within him burn sharply. "I might," he lied.

Questor stepped back. The shadows that cloaked the clearing were beginning to fade with the coming of daylight. Figures appeared from out of the gloom to either side—the Lords of the Greensward and the River Master and members of his family. Ben stood up and walked to the edge of the dais, stepping past the watchful kobolds. The iron forms of the Lords and the slim shadows of the fairies converged before him.

He took a deep breath. There was no point in mincing words. "The Mark comes to challenge me at dawn," he told them quietly. "Will you stand with me against him?"

There was complete silence. Ben looked from one face to the next, then nodded. "Very well. Let me put it another way. Kallendbor, the Lords of the Greensward gave me their word that they would pledge to the throne if I rid them of the dragon Strabo. I have done so. He is banished from the Greensward and all of the settled parts of the valley. I ask you now for your pledge. If your word means anything, you will give it to me."

He waited. Kallendbor looked uncertain. "What guarantee have we that you have done as you say—that the dragon is gone for good?" demanded Strehan harshly.

He isn't gone for good, Ben was tempted to say. He's gone for as long as I'm King and not a moment more, so you ought to think seriously about helping me stay alive!

But he didn't say that. Instead, he ignored Strehan and kept his eyes on Kallendbor. "Once your pledge is given, I will command that the people of Greensward cease all violation of the waters that feed into and sustain the lake country. Your people will work with the people of the River Master to clean those waters and to keep them clean.

He turned. "You, River Master, will then fulfill your promise and give to me your pledge as well. And you will begin again to teach to the people of the Greensward the secrets of your healing magic. You will help them to understand."

He paused again, eyes fixed now on the chiseled face of the sprite. There was uncertainty in the River Master's face as well. No one said anything.

The wind brushed suddenly against his face, sharp and quick. From somewhere distant, there was a low rumble like thunder. Ben forced himself to remain outwardly calm. The dawn had begun to break against the skyline.

"No one," he said softly, "will be forced to stand with me against the Mark."

He felt Questor's hand clamp roughly on his arm, but he ignored it. The clearing had gone still but for the quickening of the wind and the growing sound of the thunder. Shadows faded into streaks of silver and rose. The people of the lake country slipped deeper into the forest gloom; the knights and their war horses began to grow restless.

"High Lord." Kallendbor came forward a step. His dark eyes were intense. "It matters nothing what promises passed between us. If the Mark has challenged you, you are a dead man. You would be so even if we chose to take your part in this. None of us—Lords or fairy people—can withstand the Mark. His is the strength that only the greatest magic can overcome. We lack such magic, all of us. Humans have never had it and the people of the lake country have long since lost it. Only the Paladin had such magic—and the Paladin is gone."

The River Master came foward as well. Those with him were glancing about apprehensively. The wind had risen to a low whistle and the thunder was beginning to reverberate through the forest earth. The clearing behind them was suddenly deserted, the rows of pads and rests like grave markers neatly placed.

"Fairy magic banished the demons centuries ago, High

Lord. Fairy magic had kept them from this land. The talisman of that fairy magic is the Paladin, and none here can withstand the Iron Mark without the Paladin to aid us. I am sorry, High Lord, but this battle must be yours."

He turned and walked from the dais, his family hastening to follow.

"Strength to you, play-King," Kallendbor muttered, and then he wheeled away as well. The other Lords trailed wordless after, armor clanking.

Ben stood alone at the forefront of the dais and stared after them for a moment. Then he shook his head hopelessly. He guessed he hadn't really expected them to help, anyway.

Thunder shook the dais to its foundation, rolling through the earth beneath in a long, sustained rumble of dissatisfaction. The dawn's faint silver light disappeared in a sudden press of shadows.

"High Lord—get back!" Questor was at his side, his gray robes whipping wildly in the wind. Willow appeared as well, and Abernathy and the kobolds. They surrounded him protectively, hands taking hold firmly. Bunion and Parsnip hissed ferociously.

The darkness thickened. "Stand away—all of you!" Ben shouted. "Stand down off the dais! Now!"

"No, High Lord!" Questor cried in response, his head shaking emphatically.

There was resistance from all, and he shrugged free of them. The wind began to howl furiously. "I said stand away, damn it! Get back away from me and do it now!"

Abernathy went. The kobolds bared their long teeth against the wind and darkness, and they hesitated still. Ben grasped Willow and shoved her into their hands, pushing all three aside. They went, a stricken Willow looking back frantically.

Questor Thews stood his ground. "I can help, High Lord! I have control over the magic now, and I . . . !"

Ben grasped his shoulders and swung him about, fighting the thrust of the wind as it broke free from the netherworld and stung with its force. "No, Questor! No one stands with me this time! Get off the dais at once!"

He propelled the wizard a good half-dozen feet with a single shove and motioned him to continue on. Questor looked back briefly, saw the determination in Ben's eyes, and went.

Ben stood alone. The Lords of the Greensward and their knights and the River Master and his fairies huddled in the shadows of the forest, shielding their faces against the darkness and wind. Questor and the others crouched down against the side of the dais. Flags snapped and rippled as the wind tore at them. Silver stanchions shuddered and bent. Thunder rolled in one continuous, frightening shudder.

Ben was shaking. Great special effects, he thought absurdly.

Shadows and mist swirled and joined at the far edge of the clearing, separating humans and fairies crouched within the trees. The thunder boomed sharply, as if exploding.

Then the demons appeared, a horde of dark, misshapen forms breaking from invisibility into being, spilling over from the black. Serpentine mounts snarled and pawed at the earth, and weapons and armor clanked and rattled like bones. The mass expanded and spread like a stain against the frail dawn light, pushing forward toward the dais, clogging the rows of kneeling pads and rests.

The thunder and the wind died away, and the sound of breathing and snarling filled the sudden stillness. The demons occupied almost the whole of the Heart. Ben Holiday and his small band of friends were an island in a sea of black forms.

A corridor opened at the army's center, and a massive, black, winged creature surged through the gap, half snake, half wolf, bearing on his back an armored nightmare. Ben took a deep breath and straightened resolutely.

The Iron Mark had come for him.

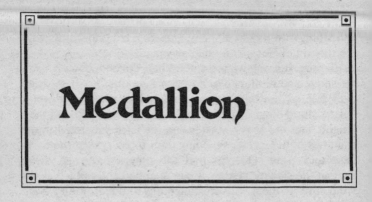

Medallion

It was the most terrifying moment of Ben Holiday's life.

The Iron Mark advanced the wolf-serpent through the ranks of the demons, slowly closing the distance that separated them. The black armor was scarred and battered, but it gleamed wickedly in the half-light. Weapons jutted from their sheaths and bindings—swords, battle axes, daggers, and a half-dozen more. Serrated spines ran the length of the Mark's limbs and back, bristling like a porcupine's quills. The helmet with the death's head had the visor closed down; but through iron slits, eyes glimmered a bright crimson.

Ben had never noticed before. The Mark was at least eight feet tall. The Mark was huge.

The wolf-serpent lifted its crusted head, its massive jaws parted and its teeth bared. It hissed, the sound like steam released under enormous pressure, and a snake's tongue licked at the morning air.

All about, the breathing of the demons was a harsh and eager reply.

Ben was suddenly paralyzed. He had been frightened before by the things he had encountered and the dangers he had faced during his brief time in Landover—but never like this. He had thought he would be equal to this confrontation, and he was not. The Mark was going to kill him, and he didn't know how to stop it from happening. He was captive to his fear, frozen in the manner of an animal who has been brought to bay at last by its most persistent enemy. He would have run in that instant if he could have made himself do so, but he could not. He could only stand there, watching the demon advance on him, waiting for his inevitable destruction.

It was with great effort that he managed to reach within his tunic and clasp tightly the medallion.

The carved surface pressed its outline of island castle, rising sun and mounted knight into the palm of his hand. The medallion was the only hope he had, and he clung to it with the desperation of a drowning man clinging to a lifeline.

Help me, he prayed!

There was a sharp hiss of anticipation from the demons. The Mark slowed his wolf-serpent and the helmet with the death's head lifted watchfully.

It isn't too late—I can still escape, Ben screamed out in the silence of his mind. I can still use the medallion to save myself!

Something tugged at his memory then—something indefinable. Fear has many disguises, the fairies had warned. You must learn to recognize them. The words were just a nudge, but it was enough to ease the iron grip of his fear and let him reason again. The floodgates opened. Bits and pieces of conversations and events surrounding the medallion recalled themselves in a frantic rush. They spun and swirled like debris in a stream's sudden eddy, and he grasped for them desperately.

Willow's calm voice whispered to him in the midst of his confusion: The answers you need are there.

But, damn it, he couldn't find them!

Then the fingers of his memory closed about a single, small admonishment that he had nearly forgotten in the chaos of the days and weeks now past, and he snatched it clear of the others. It had come from Meeks, of all people. It had been contained in the letter that had accompanied the medallion when it was first given to him.

No one can take the medallion from you, the letter had said.

He repeated the words, sensing something important hidden in them, not yet understanding what it was. The medallion was the key. He had always known that. He had sworn his oath of office upon it. It was the symbol of his rule. It was recognized by all as the mark of his Kingship. It was the key to passage in and out of Landover. It was the link between Landover's Kings and the Paladin.

The Mark dug iron spurs sharply into the scaled body of the wolf-serpent, and the beast heaved forward once more, hissing with rage. The demon army came with it.

He cannot take the medallion from me, Ben decided suddenly. The Mark must have the medallion, but he cannot take it from me. Somehow, I know it is so. He waits for me to use it so that I will be gone from Landover forever. That is what he expects me to do. That is what he really wants.

Meeks had wanted that as well. All of his enemies seemed to want that.

And that was reason enough not to allow it.

His hand lifted the medallion clear of his tunic, and he let it fall gently against his chest, free of his clothing where all could see it. He would not remove it. He would not use it to escape. He would not leave Landover when he had worked so hard to stay. This was where he belonged, alive or dead. This was his home.

This was his commitment.

He thought suddenly, once again, of the Paladin.

The Iron Mark closed on him, and a lance with spikes jutting from its tip lowered toward his chest. Ben waited. He no longer felt the fear. He no longer felt anything but a renewed stubbornness and determination.

It was enough.

Light flashed at the far edge of the clearing, brilliant and white against the shadows and gloom. The Mark wheeled about and there was a low hiss of recognition from among the ranks of the demons.

The Paladin appeared out of the light.

Ben shuddered. Something deep within drew him almost physically to the apparition—pulled him in the manner of an invisible magnet. It was as if the ghost were reaching for him.

The Paladin rode forward to the forest's edge and stopped. Behind him, the light died away. But the Paladin did not fade with the light as he had each time before. This time he remained.

Ben was twisting inside of himself, separating away from his being in a way he had not thought possible. He wanted to scream. What was happening? His mind spun. The demons seemed to have gone mad, crying out, shrieking, milling about as if they had lost all direction. The Mark spurred forward through their midst, his carrier grinding them underfoot as if they were blades of grass. Ben heard Questor cry out to him; he heard Willow cry out as well—and he heard the sound of his own voice calling back.

He recognized something grand and terrible then through his haze of confusion and physical distress. The Paladin was no longer a ghost. He was real!

He felt the medallion burn against his chest, a flare of silver light. He felt it turn to ice, then to fire and then to something that was neither. Then he watched it streak across the Heart to where the Paladin waited.

He watched himself be carried with it.

There was just enough time left for a single, stunning revelation. There was one question he had never asked—one that none of them had asked. Who was the Paladin? Now he knew.

He was.

All he had ever needed to do to discover that was to give himself over to this land of magic when it truly meant something. All he had ever needed to do to bring the Paladin back was to forgo the option of escape and to commit finally and irrevocably to a decision to remain.

He was astride the Paladin's charger. Silver armor closed about him, encasing him in an iron shell. Clasps and fasteners snapped shut, clamps and screws tightened, and the world became a rush of memories. He was submerged within those memories, a swimmer fighting to come up for air. He lost himself in their flow. He changed and was born anew. He was from a thousand other times and places, and he had lived a thousand other lives. The memories were now his. He was a warrior whose skill in battle and combat experience had never been equalled. He was a champion who had never lost.

Ben Holiday ceased to be. Ben Holiday became the Paladin.

He was aware momentarily of the present King of Landover standing statuelike on the dais at the center of the Heart. Time and motion seemed to slow to a standstill. Then he spurred his horse forward, and he forgot everything but the monstrous black challenger that rose to meet him.

They met in a frightening clash of armor and weapons. The spike-studded lance of the Mark and his own of white oak splintered and broke apart. Their mounts screamed and shuddered with the force of the impact, then raced past each other and wheeled recklessly about. Fingers of metal plating and chain mail gripped the hafts of battle axes and the curving blades lifted into the dawn air.

They came at each other again. The Mark was a black monstrosity that dwarfed the worn and battered figure of the silver knight. It was an obvious mismatch. They thundered toward each other and collided in a resounding crash. Axe blades bit deep, lodging in metal joints, slicing through armor. Both riders lost their balance and careened wildly astride their chargers. They wheeled and broke apart, axes hammering. The Paladin was yanked violently backward and pulled from his horse. He fell, clinging to the harness straps of the wolf-serpent.

It seemed the end of him. The wolf-serpent twisted violently, reaching back with its jaws to finish him. He was just out of reach. The Iron Mark wielded his battle axe with both hands. The axe hammered down, blow after blow, as the Mark sought to shatter his enemy's helmet.

The Paladin dangled from the harness straps, twisting to avoid the terrible blows. He could not release his grip. If he were to fall backward, the weight of his armor would not let him rise again and he would be trampled to death. He groped blindly for his assailant, finding at last the weapons harness the demon wore strapped about his waist.

His fingers closed on the handle of a four-edge dirk.

He wrenched the weapon free and buried it in the Mark's knee where the jointed metal armor gaped open. The Mark shuddered, and the battle axe dropped from his nerveless fingers. The Paladin grappled with the demon, trying to yank him off balance, seeking to pull him clear of the harness seat. The wolf-serpent wheeled wildly, hissing with rage as he felt his rider slipping. The Mark clung desperately to the reins and harness straps, kicking out at the Paladin. Kneeling pads and armrests shattered like deadwood as the combatants careened through the center of the Heart, and howls rose from the demons caught within.

Then abruptly the Paladin jerked the four-edged dirk from the Mark's armored knee and jammed it downward into the wolf-serpent's shoulder where it joined the scaled body. The monster reared and bolted, throwing both knight and demon to the ground in a crash of armor.

The Paladin landed on hands and knees, fighting to keep his balance. Dizziness washed through him. The Mark sprawled a dozen feet away, but he lurched unsteadily to his feet despite the massive weight of his armor. Both hands reached down to a giant broadsword sheathed at his waist.

The Paladin heaved himself upright then and freed his own broadsword just as the Mark reached him. Sword blades hammered into each other in a frightening clash of metal, the sound ringing out against the sudden stillness. The Paladin was thrust back by the heavier form of the Mark, yet kept his feet. Again they lunged and again the swords hammered down. Back and forth across the Heart the combatants staggered as the broadswords rose and fell in the half-light.

The Paladin experienced a sudden, unfamiliar sensation. He was losing this battle.

Then the Mark feinted and reversed the swing of his broadsword so that it cut downward in a sweeping motion toward the Paladin's feet. It was a glancing blow that careened off the tarnished armor, yet it caught the knight by surprise and knocked him sideways. He went down heavily and his weapon spun out of reach. The Mark was atop him at once. The demon's giant broadsword arced downward, and the blade caught and lodged in the Paladin's shoulder plates, wedged between the joints. Had the Mark released the sword, it would have been the end of the Paladin. But the demon clung fast to the weapon, struggling to free it, refusing to let go. It gave the Paladin one last chance. Desperately he groped his way up the demon's armored body, grappling for the weapons harness once more.

His fingers closed about the haft of the iron-headed mace.

The Paladin reared up, one hand clinging to the Mark's armored body, the other bringing up the mace. The ridged crown crashed into the helmeted death's head and the Mark shuddered. The Paladin swung the weapon upward a second time, the whole of his strength behind the blow. The metal visor split wide, and the face within was a nightmare of blood and twisted features. Silver light flared from the body of the Paladin. Once more the mace rose and fell, and the death's head disintegrated.

The Iron Mark tumbled to the earth, a shapeless mass of black metal. The Paladin rose slowly and stepped away.

A stillness shrouded the Heart, a mantle of hushed silence that was its own terrifying sound. Then the wind rose with a howl, the thunder reverberated through the forest earth, the air swirled black with shadows and gloom, and the gateway to Abaddon opened suddenly about the demons. Howling and crying, they disappeared back into the netherworld.

The clearing stood empty once more. Gloom and shadows dissipated. The dawn's new light fell across the Paladin as he climbed back astride his charger. The light gleamed on armor that was no longer tarnished or worn, but like new. The light flared, reflecting momentarily from the knight to the medallion worn by Landover's King as he stood alone at the forefront of the dais.

Then the light faded and the Paladin was gone.

Ben Holiday breathed the morning air and felt the warmth of the sunlight on his body. He felt momentarily weightless in the light clothing of Landover's King, free once more from the Paladin's armor. Time and motion thawed and quickened until all was as it had been.

He was himself again. The dream, the nightmare, whichever part of both he had survived, was over.

Shadowy figures stirred within the forest trees and emerged into the Heart, humans and fairies, Lords and knights of the Greensward, and the River Master with his people of the lake country, picking their way carefully through the debris. Ben's friends appeared from their shelter at the base of the dais, stunned looks on their faces. Willow was smiling.

"High Lord . . ." Questor began helplessly and trailed off. Then slowly he knelt before the dais. "High Lord," he whispered.

Willow, Abernathy, and the kobolds knelt with him. Fillip and Sot reappeared, as if by magic, and they, too, knelt. All across the clearing the men of the Greensward and the men of fairy dropped to one knee—the River Master, Kallendbor, Strehan, the Lords of the Greensward, all that had come.

"High Lord," they acknowledged.

"High Lord," he whispered back.

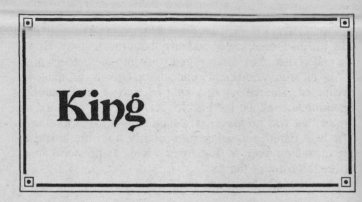

King

It was all pretty simple after that. Even a neophyte monarch like Ben didn't have much difficulty figuring out what to do with all those astonished subjects. He got them back on their feet and marched them directly to Sterling Silver for a victory feast. Things might have been tough up until this morning and they might be tough again by tomorrow; but for the remainder of this day, at least, it looked like smooth sailing.

He ferried his friends, the River Master and his immediate family, and the Lords of the Greensward and their retainers across in the lake skimmer and left soldiers and assorted entourage to camp along the shoreline. It took several trips to bring everyone invited across, and he made a mental note to construct a bridge before the next get-together.

"There *was* a bridge in the old days, High Lord," Questor whispered surreptitiously, as if reading his thoughts, "but when the old King died, the people ceased coming to the castle, the army drifted away, and traffic eventually stopped altogether. The bridge fell into a terrible state of disrepair, boards cracked and rotted, bindings frayed, nails rusted— just a large clog in the lake that reflected the sorry state of the entire kingdom. I tried to salvage it with magic, High

Lord, but things just didn't work out quite the way I had planned . . ." He stopped rambling and trailed off.

Ben's eyebrows lifted. "Things?"

Questor leaned closer. They were midway across the lake on their final trip. "I am afraid I sank the bridge, High Lord."

He peered reluctantly over the skimmer's bow. Ben peered with him. It was hard to keep from grinning, but he did.

He gathered his guests in the great hall and seated them about a series of tressel tables pulled together. He worried belatedly that Sterling Silver could not find the means to feed them all, but his fears were groundless. The castle reproduced provisions from her larder with newfound strength and determination—as if she could sense the victory that had been won—and there was food and drink enough for everyone, inside and out.

It was a marvelous feast—a celebration in which all shared. Food and drink were consumed with relish, toasts were exchanged and adventures recounted. There was a fellowship that transcended lingering skepticism; there was a strange sense of renewal. One by one those gathered rose to their feet, at Questor's urging, and pledged once more their loyalty and unconditional support to Landover's newest King.

"Long life, High Lord Ben Holiday," the River Master prayed. "May all your future successes match today's."

"May you keep the magic close and use it well," Kallendbor advised, the warning in his voice unmistakable.

"Strength and judgment, High Lord," wished Strehan, his brow clouded with a continuing mix of awe and doubt.

"Great High Lord!" Fillip cried.

"Mighty High Lord!" Sot echoed.

Ah, well—it was a mixed bag, but a welcome one. One after another, they gave him their pledges and good wishes, and Ben acknowledged each courteously. There was cause for optimism, no matter how difficult tomorrow might turn out to be. The Paladin was returned—brought back from a place in which no one would have thought to look, freed from the prison of Ben's own heart. The magic was returned to the valley, and Landover would begin its transformation back to the pastoral land it had once been. The changes would be slow, but they would come. The mist and gloom would clear and there would be sunlight again. The Tarnish would fade; Sterling Silver would be Castle Dracula no more. The blight that had stricken the Bonnie Blues would weaken and die. Forests, grasslands, and hills would heal. Lakes and rivers would come clean. Wildlife would flourish anew. Everything would be reborn.

And one day, a day far in the future, perhaps past the time that he would live, the golden vision of life in the valley that he had been shown by the fairies would come to pass.

It can happen, he told himself firmly. I need only believe. I need only remain true. I need only continue to work for it.

He rose when they had finished. "I am your servant, first and always—yours and the land's," he told them, his voice quiet. The noise died away and they turned to listen. "I am that to you and I ask that you be the same to each other. We have much to accomplish together. These things we shall do immediately. We shall cease polluting the waterways and ravaging the forestlands of our neighbors. We shall work with each other and teach each other what we can to protect and restore all the land. We shall devise commerce agreements that facilitate free trade between all our peoples. We shall institute public works programs for our roads and waterways. We shall revise our laws and establish courts to enforce them. We shall exchange ambassadors—here and with all of the peoples of the valley—and we shall convene regularly at Sterling Silver to air our grievances in a peaceful and constructive fashion."

He paused. "We shall find a way to be friends."

They toasted him, more for the thought than the feasibility of what he was proposing, he knew—but it was a start. There

were other ideas to be implemented as well: a workable taxing system, a uniform currency exchange, a census, and various reclamation projects. He had ideas he hadn't even begun
to think through thoroughly enough to propose yet. But the
time would come. He would find a way to put them all to
work.

He passed down the table, pausing by Kallendbor and the
River Master. He bent close. "I rely on you, most of all, to
stand by your promises. Each must help the other as you
have sworn you would. We are all allies, now."

There were solemn nods and murmured assurances. But
a veil of doubt remained in their eyes. Neither was certain
that Ben Holiday was the man to hold their enemies in check.
Neither was convinced that he was the King they needed.
His victory over the Mark was impressive; but it was only
a single victory. They would wait and see.

Ben accepted that. At least he had their pledge. He would
find a way to win their trust.

He thought back momentarily to the battle fought between
the Paladin and the Mark. He had told no one what he had
learned of the link between the knight-errant and himself.
He wasn't sure yet if he ever would. He wondered if he could
bring the Paladin back again if the knight were needed. He
thought that he could. But it chilled him to think about the
transformation he had undergone within that suit of iron—
the feelings and emotions he had shared with his champion,
the memories of battles and deaths over so many years. He
shook his head. There would have to be a very compelling
reason for him to call the Paladin back again . . .

Another toast was proposed by one of the Lords—his
good health. He acknowledged it and drank. Count on it, he
promised silently.

He switched subjects. He must begin work immediately
on restoration of the Heart. So much had been damaged during the battle with the Mark; the ground had been torn, the
white velvet kneeling pads and armrests had been destroyed,
and the staffs of the flags and the tall stanchions had been

shattered. The Heart must be put right again. It meant something special to them all, but to no one more than him.

"Ben." Willow left her seat and moved next to him. She lifted her wine glass. "Happiness, High Lord," she wished him, her voice soft against the background of noise.

He smiled. "I think I've found that happiness, Willow. You and the others have helped me find it."

"Is this true?" She looked at him carefully. "And does the pain of what you lost in your old life no longer haunt you, then?"

She spoke of Annie. A momentary image of his dead wife passed within his mind and then faded. His old life was over; he would not be going back to it. He felt he could accept that now. He could never forget Annie, but he could let her go.

"It no longer haunts me," he answered.

Her green eyes held his own. "Perhaps you will permit me to remain with you long enough to make certain, Ben Holiday?"

He nodded slowly. "I wouldn't want it any other way."

She bent close and kissed his forehead, his cheek and his mouth. The party continued unnoticed around them.

It was after midnight when the festivities ended and the guests began to retire to the rooms that had been prepared for them. Ben had finished saying good night to all who remained and was giving thought to the comforts of his own bed when Questor approached, looking a bit embarrassed.

"High Lord," he began and stopped. "High Lord, I regret troubling you with so small a problem at this hour, but it needs attending to, and I believe you best suited to deal with it." He cleared his throat. "It seems that one of the Lords brought a canine pet with him into Sterling Silver—quite a close member of the family, I am given to understand—and now it has disappeared."

Ben lifted his eyebrows. "A dog?"

Questor nodded. "I have said nothing to Abernathy . . ."

"I see." Ben glanced about. Fillip and Sot were nowhere in sight. "And you think . . . ?"

"Merely a possibility, High Lord."

Ben sighed. Tomorrow's troubles were already upon him. But then, of course, so was tomorrow. He grinned in spite of himself. "What do you say, Questor—let's go find out if the gnomes are planning a midnight snack."

High Lord Ben Holiday, King of Landover, began the new day rather earlier than expected.

About the Author

A writer since high school, **Terry Brooks** published his first novel, *The Sword of Shannara*, in 1977. It was a *New York Times* bestseller for more than five months. He has published seventeen consecutive bestsellers since, including *The Voyage of the Jerle Shannara: Ilse Witch* and the novel based upon the screenplay and story by George Lucas, *Star Wars*®: Episode I *The Phantom Menace*™. His novels *Running with the Demon* and *A Knight of the Word* were each selected by the *Rocky Mountain News* as one of the best science fiction/fantasy novels of the twentieth century.

The author was a practicing attorney for many years but now writes full-time. He lives with his wife, Judine, in the Pacific Northwest and Hawaii.

Visit us online at www.shannara.com and at www.terrybrooks.net.